the

GERMAN CHILD

BOOKS BY CATHERINE HOKIN

The Fortunate Ones

What Only We Know

The Lost Mother

The Secretary

HANNI WINTER SERIES

The Commandant's Daughter

The Pilot's Girl

The Girl in the Photo

Her Last Promise

the
GERMAN
CHILD

CATHERINE HOKIN

bookouture

Published by Bookouture in 2024

An imprint of Storyfire Ltd.
Carmelite House
50 Victoria Embankment
London EC4Y 0DZ

www.bookouture.com

ISBN: 978-1-83790-007-7
eBook ISBN: 978-1-83790-006-0

For Randi,
who knows how hard it is to go looking

PART ONE

CHAPTER 1

POLAND, SEPTEMBER 1941

The women came as they always came. Huddled, bleating. Clutching their children as if they still had a claim to them. Trapped like flies in sticky amber by a summons which had ground their small town to a halt.

> All children up to and including the age of twelve are to report to the Ogrodowa Street schoolyard on Sunday, 21 September at 2 p.m. Mothers only are to accompany them. Two weeks of residential care will be provided while parents are assessed for appropriate work placements. One small suitcase of clothing suitable for outdoor activities is required per child. Feeding equipment should be provided for infants.
>
> By order of Hans Frank
>
> Head of the General Government, Kraków
>
> 19 September 1941

No one reading the sign had dared to say what they

wanted to say: that nothing about its wording made sense. Nobody had dared to point out its obvious flaws. That *care* was an alien concept to the Nazis who ruled them with such a brutal hand. Or that, after two years of German occupation and hardship, there wasn't a child anywhere in Poland with enough decent clothes to fill up a suitcase. Or that life nowadays ran on orders and punishments and no one was assessed for anything. And none of the parents whose hearts stalled as they read and reread the black type were able to cling on to 'I'll fight back; I won't do what they want' for more than a fleeting moment.

Not that it matters if anyone does decide to play the fool and hide them. We have their names. We'll track them all down in the end.

Helene stood on the top step of the shabby schoolhouse which had been commandeered to act as a clearing station for the day, scanning the road, waiting for the moment when the town became hers. A moment which would start, as it always started, with the women. When they looked at her and were mesmerised. When they compared their lank dirty hair, which hadn't seen a decent bar of soap in months, to her elegant honey-coloured twist and their mouths fell open. Or compared their patched skirts and worn cardigans with the neat lines of her sapphire-blue dress. Whatever it was that hypnotised them, they would fall into line with one look.

'Because you are a vision of elegance and calm, my dear. You are a joy to behold. Whatever you ask of them, they'll obey as meekly as sheep.'

Those had been Himmler's exact words six months earlier, and Helene still treasured them. She had mesmerised him too. His mouth had dropped open just as comically as the women's would when he saw her standing on the steps of another school in another faceless town. Dressed in her jewel-blue dress, waiting to weave her web for the first time. The Reichsführer-

SS's smile was a notoriously rare thing, but Helene had conjured it.

And he's never once frowned at me since.

A sudden swirl of dust danced over the fence and caught at her throat, bringing Helene back from past triumphs to present ones. The families were approaching the schoolyard. They were pale, uninspiring specimens – the mothers had slipped from twenty to fifty in a fraction of the years that change should have taken; the children resembled a collection of twigs. First impressions didn't look hopeful, but they rarely did. Experience had taught her that it took time to find the viable stock, and Helene was in no hurry.

She flicked through the sheets pinned to her clipboard. The first page was a list of the children registered in the town, their names the starting point for the day's selections. The second – headed *Possibilities* – and the third – headed *Jewish* – were both blank.

Helene expected that the Jewish sheet would remain that way, although she wasn't complacent enough to take that for granted. All the town's Jews had already been removed, despatched to the ghettos at Warsaw and Lodz, or transported directly to the ovens at Auschwitz. The Jewish children had left on the first train because removing them quickly was the first rule of clearing, a rule which was – as far as Helene and every loyal party member was concerned – exactly as it should be. The Führer had assigned a value to everyone in the Reich and its conquered lands, and for Jewish offspring that value was zero. Jewish children – like the sick and the disabled and the mentally ill – had no worth; they had to be stamped out before they grew old enough to breed. Unfortunately, first rule or not, some of them always seemed to slip through.

Helene glanced up at the figures toiling towards her, wondering which if any of the women had been foolish enough to fall for a tearful mother's pleas and take a cuckoo into her nest. Life would go very hard for those who had. Helene could ferret out a hidden Jewish child in a heartbeat – all it took was a few pointed questions. They couldn't tell her what the inside of a church looked like. They couldn't pronounce their newly given Christian names correctly. They stumbled when she asked what they loved best about their mothers. The Jews never got past her if they came, no matter how well their fake parents had prepared them. And if they didn't come with the rest when a town's children were summoned? If there were names on the registers and no bodies to match them? Well, there was a list for that too. And dogs, and search parties.

'Stand back. Put your weapons down.'

Helene didn't have to look at them to know that the soldiers flanking the schoolhouse had started to shuffle forward. She could already sense their fingers growing itchy. She waited until the muttering stopped before she made eye contact.

'We don't need guns at the ready; we don't need to frighten our guests. Go back to the fence line and stay there. I won't explain that to you again.'

The soldiers hated her. They thought she was unwomanly. They hated that she had Himmler's ear and his trust, that she issued orders like a man. But they did as they were told – the Reichsführer had threatened them with court martial if they didn't – so Helene didn't care what they thought. She didn't need trigger-happy soldiers spoiling her work.

Experience had also taught her that the mothers walked a very fine line between compliance and panic, and panic wasn't a state that Helene permitted. The doctor in charge of her first training session had lost control of his selection detail, and the mothers had stormed the railway station where their children were being held, screaming for the little ones to run and fighting the guards with their bare hands. The result had been a blood-bath which had whipped up the partisans and infuriated Himmler. So there would be no panic today. Or the extra complication of transporting and then loading unwanted cargo onto trains. There would be efficiency and initiative, and a delighted and smiling boss at the end.

The soldiers retreated.

Helene turned to the troops she actually relied on. 'Why is it our job to manage the mothers who come to us, rather than a task for the soldiers?'

The women arranged on the steps below her turned round. The day's chief assistant answered. 'Because we can control their behaviour far better than men can. The mothers believe we will be kind to them and to their children, because we are women too. They think that creates a bond which guarantees their safety.'

'Exactly.'

Helene beamed at her audience, who had no more belief in the existence of a female bond than she did.

To the untrained eye, her assistants – or the Sisters, as Himmler insisted the women were called, although none of them had any medical training – were a nondescript bunch. Their drab brown dresses and pulled-back hair rendered them invisible, which was exactly what was intended. Until they smiled and their faces turned soft and welcoming and impossible to resist. All it took then was a pocketful of sweets and even the most hesitant blond-haired child would venture too close to the garden wall or the playground's edge. And all it took after that was a strong right arm. By the time anyone noticed that the children were gone, Helene and her Brown Sisters had long disappeared, leaving nothing behind but the fear.

Kidnapping, however, was a tactic best saved for isolated hamlets where no one was watching, and busy cities where notices to report took longer to work. Today was about sifting through a bigger pot for the cream.

The mothers were coming through the gates now, their children pressed close.

Helene dropped her voice and spoke quickly. 'Today follows the same pattern as all the rest. Unless they carry enough spare flesh on their bones to guarantee a few weeks of forced labour, most of these children will be of no use to us.' She nodded to the left side of the steps. 'If I send them your way, take them into the main hall and hold them there until the mothers have gone.'

The Sisters nodded. This was the routine part of their work – ridding Poland of the children who were no use to the Reich, in order to make space for the German babies who would require its land and resources. A low-value population cut off at its roots and cleared to make way for a high-value one whose numbers were already growing. It was a simple-enough equation. But it wasn't the sole aim of the day. They listened carefully as Helene got to the core.

'But some of them, as unpromising as they might seem on first sight, may merit a second look. Those children, the possibilities, will go to the right. Take them to the classroom where the sweets are waiting and keep them occupied.'

There was no need to explain further. The Sisters were as keen as Helene to capture the day's real prize: blood that had been stolen, that should belong to the Reich. The Polish children whose bodies still carried the memory of all the years of German rule before their country had dared demand independence after the world's first great war. Blue eyes, blond hair, strong cheekbones. A spark that said, 'I am worthy of more.' Children whose Aryan bloodlines formed a key part of the Führer's plan to spread German power across the world. Who would be rescued and placed with good German families, their Polish identities stripped away along with their names and their language. Who would become Germany's new stock.

Helene was as good at spotting those possibilities as she was at spotting the Jewish interlopers. And she was good at the next stage too: supervising the tests to determine if the bloodline had stayed strong and the candidates met all the physical and mental criteria for reassimilation. That was her reward, her chance to wield her hands-on medical skills, and her failures were rare. That ability was where Helene's real value lay.

Unlike the children chosen by the other selectors, the majority of those that Helene identified passed their Aryan inspections with flying colours. And if one or two didn't make the grade? If ears protruded a little too much, if lips were a little too thick or eyes weren't the exact shade that the profiling charts demanded? There was no harm done; everyone was permitted a few mistakes, and mistakes were quickly rectified. Auschwitz was expanding. There were new extermination camps planned at Majdanek and Chelmno. There was plenty of space in the ovens for small bodies.

The yard was full now, the air thick with strained expectation. Helene waited until the last murmurs died down and all the mothers were looking towards her. Then she descended the steps with her arms and her smile wide. The sigh as the women released their tight shoulders caressed her like a soft breeze.

This is what I was born for. To take charge. To hold power.

That power flowed white-hot through her body as she handed out picture postcards of a castle that the children would never actually see. It flowed through her fingertips as she tapped shoulders and despatched her charges left and right. It lit up her smile as she described the adventures that awaited them among the battlements and towers.

Life and death. That's what she wielded. That's what power meant.

One nod from her and a tiny girl began her journey towards a new German family. Another and a too skinny and not too bright boy began his to the van waiting in the clump of trees at the rear of the school. That was an innovation Helene was particularly proud of. Rather than leading dozens of unpredictable children from the school and onto a train and ferrying them to yet another clearing house before their inevitable last journey, two of Himmler's mobile gas vans were ready and waiting in the woods. The children who hadn't made the grade would be dead and buried before their mothers had time to miss them.

Helene's smile widened as the last few families were processed. It had been an excellent day's work. Resources well used. A handful of potential new German citizens identified. Almost a hundred children cleared. Almost a hundred spaces created for the new German lives whose progress she was charged with checking on next.

Life and death hers to dispense and both their needs well satisfied. And so many more villages still to come.

CHAPTER 2

WASHINGTON, DECEMBER 1979

I think I was born in Germany not in America, and I don't understand who I am.

There's secrets in my family, about my birth and about what my father really did in the war, and I don't know where to turn.

My child went missing in 1942. Please will somebody help me find him?

Open any one of the dozens of folders littering Evie's desk and the pain poured out. Over thirty years of it, as bright and as fresh as if the wounds were still open.

And every one of them deserving an investigation and a detailed response.

That was a laudable ambition. Investigating suspected crimes which had their origins in World War Two and dragging their perpetrators out into the light was her new department's remit. For Evie it was a crusade, a dream job. And a maze. She was already drowning under the weight of the submissions she had managed to open and scan through, and as for the ones she hadn't yet reached...

Every surface in Evie's office was submerged under the tidal wave of bulky yellow packets which arrived on a daily basis from the archives and hidden corners of the Department of Justice. The rest of her over-stretched colleagues could tell the same story. The Office of Special Investigations had only been in operation for six weeks, but its creation had apparently prompted a spring-cleaning throughout the rest of the building. The material already amassed and awaiting attention would take months to assess, never mind clear, and the flow of packages showed no signs of slowing. Which – or at least for her first week in the OSI – had sounded exactly like the challenge Evie had signed up for. And Marty Breitman – her immediate boss in the OSI, who was as new to the role as the rest of them – had sounded exactly like the man to lead it.

'It's going to be a little chaotic till we find our feet, which is inevitable. This is the first concerted effort to build a detailed picture of how many Nazi war criminals are currently living freely here in the US, never mind actively pursuing them. And, given all the agencies that have been dodging the question and burying their files and all the years that have passed since the war ended, there's bound to be a backlog. Which means that it's a big task, but it's not an impossible one. All we need to do is to set our priorities.'

His new recruits – who were an eclectic mix of lawyers and historians and criminal investigators – had applauded his welcome speech. They were as eager to get started as he was. And then the folders had started to arrive by the sack-load and Marty had quickly come to regret his choice of words.

'What's the problem? All you have to do is set your priorities' had become his team's increasingly ironic response to anyone who dared complain about their impossible workload, or question what had happened to their personal life. They had, however, all jumped in, including Evie, who was as wedded to the principles of good organisation as Marty. She had at least three lists headlined *Priorities* and a special filing cabinet all set up and waiting for the folders she intended to rank. It hadn't helped. The piles kept growing, and she still couldn't decide which of her cases needed dealing with first.

Except that's not true. You know exactly where your interests lie, even if Marty isn't convinced it's where you should be channelling your energies. You keep picking out the same sort of letters.

Evie stared at the open folders in front of her as her inner voice – which always sounded like a bossy older sister version of herself – kept pricking. There was a pattern to the cases which jumped out at her; she couldn't deny it. The one about the child who'd been missing for thirty-seven years was a perfect example of the thread she was increasingly itching to follow.

His name is Piotr. At least it was then. Who knows what they changed it to when they snatched him? He was barely five years old when he vanished. It was my fault, I know that; I live with that burden daily. I should never have left him alone in the garden, not with the rumours which were flying around our village that the Sisters had been sighted. The witches who came for our babies.

Evie read slowly through the tightly printed lines, trying to prise the facts from the guilt before she added it to the pile she'd mentally labelled 'the lost'. She couldn't leave that pile alone. The folders filling the left side of her desk formed a thickening stack of the disappeared, the children who had gone missing in Europe during the war. Whose mothers, despite having lived in America without them for decades, couldn't let go of the search.

Or they formed the other, and odder, side of the coin – the displaced and the fearful. The letters from German-Americans which fell into two camps. Those whose personal research had made them question whether they had actually been born in Germany at all, or whether their birthplace was instead one of the countries occupied in the war by the Reich. And those who suspected that their German heritage wasn't as simple as they believed and that their families were keeping secrets. Which-ever camp they were in, both groups were convinced that some-thing they couldn't explain in their background was wrong. That they had been stolen from lives they never knew, or intended for lives that horrified them. The heartbreak in each letter was palpable.

You don't get over it. The not knowing, the wondering. You never stop checking faces, even when you can barely remember the one that is gone.

Forty years on but the pain was undimmed.

Evie put the letter down and closed her eyes as an unex-pected rush of tears threatened.

The pattern she was picking at hadn't appeared from nowhere. It came from her own past, even if the connection was a thin one, and now a lost one, which was another reason for the sudden flood of emotion. The children whose histories filled up her desk had been hiding in a distant corner of her memory for almost ten years. Ever since Ethan's Polish grandmother, his – and then Evie's – beloved Babcia, had told her the legend which sat at the heart of her ex-husband's family. Of a blue-eyed little girl snatched from a street in an occupied village and never seen again. Of the Brown Sisters, the child catchers – the specially trained bands of Nazi women who swarmed across Poland's cities and countryside like a poisonous mist, hunting out chil-dren with Aryan traits.

It was a horrible story. It had also, on first hearing for Evie anyway, sounded unbelievable. Ethan's family – which was partly Polish and mostly Jewish – was full of stories of the war which Evie suspected, from the way the details ebbed and flowed, had thickened over time. But the tale of the little lost girl had never altered, no matter how many times the old lady told it. In the end, Evie's legally-trained mind had taken that consistency as proof it was true. She had applied to the OSI partly because of Babcia's story and the answers it needed.

Because I know what it feels like to live with a damaged family.

Evie's eyes snapped open. Now it was Ethan's not Babcia's voice filling her head, his default *Oh come on, are you serious?* response to anything that smacked of indulgence flushing the self-pity away. The folders in front of her contained real anguish, a desperate yearning for answers, for help to mend shattered lives. They contained stories of a misery that Evie had never lived through. What could she really say about her own experience? *I didn't get on with my parents. My father is distant and barely acknowledges my existence. My mother is cold, with a cruel streak a mile wide.* It wasn't a fairy tale, but it was hardly comparable.

Evie knew who her parents were; she knew who she was. Yes, she disliked the loneliness which had coloured her childhood. Yes, she had moments even now when she wished for a more loving family than the one life had given her. But that was an everyday type of longing and a far cry from a lifetime of pain. And she wouldn't help anybody if she started to see parallels where there weren't any, or got too emotionally entangled. Years of legal experience had taught her that.

So get a grip. Deal with your own problems so you can concentrate. Call her, like you're supposed to. She mothered you poorly, but at least she mothered you, so pick up the phone. Tell her that you're looking forward to coming home.

It sounded easy enough; it always did. The problem was, as ever, in the execution.

Evie glanced at the handset on her desk, all too aware that she was already at fault. She was supposed to have called her mother yesterday, to arrange the annual visit for her father's birthday, which – if truth be told, which it rarely was in the Ritter household – was a family celebration none of them particularly wanted to endure as a threesome. She reached out to dial the number, but her fingers hung in the air and wouldn't make the connection. It had been a long day, a long week. She didn't have the energy for her mother's indifference.

'Sorry to bother you, but it's almost six o'clock and you said not to let you be late this time.'

Evie could have cheered at her secretary's knock. It didn't matter if she wanted to call her mother or not – there wasn't time to do it. Not if she was going to do what she'd promised Marty faithfully she would and get to the Hilton at the start of the party, not run breathlessly in at the end. Especially when he was so uncharacteristically anxious about the night's event.

'It's taken every ounce of my not inconsiderable charm to secure the invitations to this reception, which makes attending it a non-negotiable.' He'd refused to take any notice of the groans. 'I'm serious. We need to make a friend of the West German ambassador; we're going to need his connections. And – surprise, surprise given our remit – he's not the OSI's biggest fan. This is our chance to prove what an excellent and civic-minded bunch we are, so put on your best outfits, bring your best smiles and don't let me down.'

Evie had no intention of doing that – she owed Marty far too much loyalty.

She didn't just admire her boss; she was deeply grateful that he'd agreed to be her boss at all. Evie had known when she applied to the new division that she had very little to offer the OSI. Yes, her pedigree as a trial attorney and a section head with the Justice Department was a strong one, but that was a baseline of expertise all the applicants shared. Her European heritage was tenuous at best: her parents were Swiss, but they'd lived in America for so long they rarely referenced that part of their lives. She had no background in Holocaust studies – not, admittedly, that many did; the discipline was a new one – or specialist knowledge of World War Two. And no one could understand why such a high-flying performer as Evie would want to get involved with tracking down Nazis when she could be doing what everyone else was obsessed with and rooting out communists. Except Evie.

Overwhelmed or not, this is what I trained for. This is where I'm meant to be.

Evie put the letter back into the folder and added it to the stack. Marty had seen her passion; she'd made sure of that. She'd taken every inch of it into the interview. Every civil rights march she'd been on as a teenager. Every vulnerable family whose welfare she'd fought for as a trainee lawyer cutting her teeth on pro bono work. Every speech she'd ever given about justice knowing no time limits or borders. She'd taken those and her awareness – shaped as she watched the Khmer Rouge tear through Cambodia – that genocide wasn't a horror solely owned by the Nazis, but a terror that could still rear its head.

She'd also taken her understanding – from the friends she'd lost physically and mentally to the Vietnam campaign – of war's long and agonising reach. And she'd taken Ethan's family stories to explain how her eyes had been opened to the pain behind the statistics that she had been taught to associate with World War Two. She'd talked too much and she'd talked for too long, but Marty had listened. And he'd appointed her to his section of the OSI on the spot. So Evie wasn't going to let Marty down tonight or any other night. She was going to sparkle for the department and pay back his faith in her.

.   .   .

The Capital Hilton on Sixteenth Street was a piece of Washington political history.

Presidents held court there. Hollywood royalty – and genuine British royalty – attended gossip-column-filling parties there. Martin Luther King Jr had stayed in one of its rooms after he made his legendary 'I Have a Dream' speech. Marty, however, was more concerned with peace-keeping than political grandstanding.

'No shop-talk, remember. We're here to make friends. I don't want to hear the words *Nazi* or *criminal* or *war* come out of anyone's mouth.'

Evie nodded as Marty fussed over the instructions he'd already issued when he herded his team in from the snow. She wasn't really listening. She was transfixed by the Hilton's transformation into a Bavarian Christmas grotto.

The door to the ballroom where the reception was already in full swing was flanked by two giant Christmas trees encrusted with crimson and emerald-green baubles. The room itself was swathed from floor to ceiling with red velvet drapes and thick with the scents of mulled wine and gingerbread. And as for the food... Evie had already been presented with a pair of baby-sized knitted booties stuffed with chocolate-coated marzipan to celebrate St Nicholas's Day. Now there was a waitress approaching, carrying a tray of tiny meatballs piled on top of crisped potato fritters. It was all she could do not to walk off with the whole platter.

It was easy after such a lavish welcome to avoid darker topics. The ambassador's team was as determined to be charming as the OSI's was. The evening turned itself very quickly into the success Marty had pinned his hopes on. And turned as quickly for Evie into the chance of something a little more special.

She wasn't sure who noticed who first. Maybe it was him picking out her. Her slim-cut black-and-white twisted halter-neck dress was a sharp contrast to the sea of frills and pastels filling the room and had drawn considerable attention. Or maybe it was her picking out him. He wasn't easy to overlook either. The loose drape of his suit was unfashionable perhaps, but it was as flattering and as elegant as if he had stepped out of a 1930s film set. He'd resisted the lure of the current fashion for drooping moustaches, and his dark blond hair was just tousled enough. He certainly merited a second – and a third – look. Evie didn't stare. He didn't stare either. But she was conscious of him, and she sensed that he was conscious of her, and that gave the night an unlooked-for dimension.

Evie Ritter wasn't a giddy woman. She was thirty-five, not twenty-five. She'd weathered a painful divorce and a number of relationships before that – and fleetingly since – which had taught her that weak-at-the-knees sparks could fizzle out as fast as they came. She was also very aware that she was standing in the middle of what could have been the set of a sentimental, and definitely over-sweetened, Christmas movie. Everything about the evening was screaming *this is meant to be romantic*, a set-up which normally had Evie running in the opposite direction. And yet... There was a crackle she couldn't deny when they finally stopped stealing glances and shook hands.

'Sebastian Taylor from the Smithsonian, meet Evie Ritter from Justice.'

The colleague who'd pushed them together wandered away as soon as the slightly slurred introductions were done. Luckily it wasn't difficult for Evie to run with the conversation after that, especially when Sebastian immediately whittled down the entirety of the Smithsonian to the more manageable dimensions of the American History Museum. Not only was that a five-minute walk from her office, it was Evie's favourite *I need thinking time* retreat. Once she divulged that information, his obvious love of his work spilled out. They happily lost half an hour to the exhibitions Sebastian had curated, before he apologised and switched to, 'And that's more than enough about my work. Tell me about yours.'

All Evie's chatter suddenly dried up, and silence fell for the first time since they'd begun talking. She didn't know how best to respond. The echo of Marty's pleas for tact ringing in her ears made her reluctant to bring the details of her job into the room, but there were other, closer, considerations too. Although she had nothing but intuition to base it on, she had the sense that – outside his work, which he could clearly discuss for hours – Sebastian was a private man, more suited to academic than personal quests. She wasn't sure how, 'I'm hunting down ex Nazis who've been living here for decades so they can be brought to justice,' would play into that. But the pause stretched past uncomfortable and she had to say something. She opted therefore for the vaguest explanation she could.

'I'm sorry, I didn't mean to appear so mysterious. I'm part of a new division inside the Justice Department, an add-on to immigration if you like.'

She had tried to make her job sound too dull to invite questions. Unfortunately – or from his frown anyway – it seemed that all her vagueness had done was invite more of them. She decided to head him off first.

'It's nothing earth-shattering. We're investigating the background of people who were perhaps granted citizenship in the past with more ease than they should have been.'

And that blandness would do. The rest could wait for the second meeting she hoped would follow this first one. She was about to turn the conversation back to museum collections when he stepped closer and dropped his voice.

'A new division that's investigating citizenship? Do you mean the Office of Special Investigations? The one that's doing the deep dive into people who were... let's say repositioned, and allowed entry into the States from Germany in the forties and fifties? I'd heard it was due to become operational soon, but I didn't realise there was a team already in place. Have you started on actual cases yet? Do you have specific targets or areas of investigation in your sights?'

The OSI's creation wasn't a secret; its remit had been widely reported. And Sebastian had been tactful – he'd checked the room as he spoke and been careful with his phrasing. But there was an urgency in his voice and an intensity in his eyes which struck Evie as odd.

He looks as if what I say next matters more than it should to a museum curator.

That wasn't a comfortable feeling and, even if Sebastian had valid concerns regarding the OSI's remit, the party wasn't the place to air them.

Evie chose her next words carefully. 'Not exactly, no. We've only been up and running for a few weeks. The work itself was authorised months ago, but it's taken an age to get the funding through. Red tape. It's the curse of the city, but I'm sure you're no stranger to that.'

She was rambling, conscious of the crowd milling around them and all the words she wasn't supposed to say. And of Sebastian's deepening frown.

Why does he look so uncomfortable? Maybe he really doesn't think we should exist. Maybe he prefers his history neatly packaged.

She didn't get a chance to find out. A fork clinked against crystal, and the ambassador began a speech of thanks. By the time Evie turned back to Sebastian, he was gone. She scanned the room, but there was no sign of him.

For a moment, she considered going out into the lobby in search of him, but she stopped herself. Sebastian had left. That was his choice, and she wasn't about to go chasing him. Instead, Evie let herself enjoy what had been a pleasant flirtation, for a moment, and she let herself feel the disappointment of an opportunity lost, for a moment. Sebastian was a good-looking and charming man, but so were a dozen others at the party, and neither her heart – which had taken a long time to heal after Ethan and still bore the scars – nor her work-focused head needed the distraction of handsome, charming men. So she went in search of another delicacy-bearing waitress instead.

CHAPTER 3

WASHINGTON, DECEMBER 1979

It's Saturday. Why are you this wide awake, this early, on a Saturday?

Evie groaned, rubbed her eyes and gave up pretending that sleep was a possibility. The bedside clock told her, far too brightly, that it was five thirty. Too late to be night, too early to be morning.

Ethan's favourite time.

She shook her head to dislodge the sudden memory of her ex-husband, but it was no use; the image was already there. The two of them half-waking, bodies turning to find each other, his skin meeting hers. Their bed the whole world.

Until we stopped turning towards each other. Until the bed became a minefield we couldn't cross.

She couldn't do this. She couldn't start another morning picking over the failure that was her marriage to Ethan.

Then get yourself out there properly again. Find somebody else you can bear for more than the length of a few drinks.

She dismissed that thought with more success than she'd dismissed thoughts of Ethan. It was hard enough to contemplate finding a partner on a date in the evening, never mind at five thirty in the morning. A run of dull but earnest men had made staying at home a much more interesting proposition.

Evie threw the covers back and got up, running through all the other things she knew she wasn't about to do as she padded to the kitchen to make coffee. Go out for breakfast. Buy a newspaper and lose the morning. Go to one of the gallery openings and lunches she'd half-promised her friends she would attend. They were all perfectly acceptable and perfectly nice ways to spend a Washington Saturday and frequently her favourite pursuits. Except this morning her brain had already switched into work and the outcome of the previous day's meetings.

'The children issue is an important one, Evie – I know that. Whether they've been stolen or lost or bred to order, there's real tragedies in it. If we can make some kind of connection with victims and perpetrators living here, the personal angle could capture the kind of public interest we need. So I've no problem with you doing some investigating. But as a priority? I'm not sure about that yet. If we're going to keep our funding coming in, we need to land a big fish. We need another Eichmann, which is why I asked you to follow up on the rocket lead. Please God this witness you've got coming in today turns up something good.'

Marty hadn't needed to add any further explanation about Eichmann, Evie had got it.

Adolf Eichmann had been one of the chief architects of the Third Reich's Final Solution, the plan developed in 1942 to annihilate all Europe's Jews. When it came to tracking down fugitive Nazis, his capture by the Israelis in 1960 had set the gold standard. Eichmann's discovery in, and extraction from, Argentina had swung the spotlight back onto the fate of those members of the Nazi High Command who had escaped justice in 1945. And the harrowing testimony from the survivors of death marches and concentration camps at his trial in Jerusalem had switched the attention – at least for a time – away from the

Russians who had replaced the Nazis at the end of the war as the enemies of freedom. Unfortunately, that success had never been repeated, despite all the rumours that Hitler and his henchmen were living lavish lifestyles deep inside South America and just waiting to be caught.

The truth – as Evie and the rest of the OSI knew – was far less dramatic. South America had allowed plenty of Nazis in, that was true, but Hitler wasn't one of them. He had taken his life in a bunker in 1945 before the Russians could get to him. No one but conspiracy theorists and die-hard believers took issue with the certainty of that. Goebbels had died alongside his leader and Himmler and Göring had also chosen suicide over execution. Martin Bormann – the Führer's private secretary, who had last been seen trying to flee Berlin as the Red Army advanced – had never made it out of the city. A skeleton unearthed in 1972 near Berlin's Lehrter Station was almost certainly his. And now there were very strong rumours coming out of Brazil that Josef Mengele – the doctor whose medical experiments at Auschwitz were the stuff of nightmares and the man at the top of Marty's hit list – had died of a stroke while swimming. The really big fish were gone.

But that doesn't mean all the monsters are caught. There's others still out there who need catching and Karol Perlmann could well be our bait.

Evie took her coffee and a plate of thickly buttered toast into the living room and sat down at the dining table. She was getting obsessed, she knew it. There would be phone calls making exactly that point when she didn't honour any of the day's social commitments. But Marty was right: the OSI needed funding, and if she could help land that, and funnel some of it towards the cases she really wanted to follow, wasn't a few hours of lost personal time worth the cost?

I'll have a quick check of my notes from yesterday, to see if I've missed anything. I don't need to go over everything in detail.

And once that's done, I'll stop thinking about work and get on with the day.

It was a good plan. It delivered the *balance* her friends kept nagging her about.

She was barely a page into her notebook before Karol was there in the room with her and she forgot that she'd made it.

'It was hell on earth. People use that phrase all the time, don't they? It trips off the tongue so easily. Except for people like me. Who've been there, who know what hell is. We can barely talk about it at all.'

There was the Mittelbau-Dora concentration camp in Germany where Karol had spent the last months of the war as a forced labourer. A label the Nazis had stuck on their prisoners which Evie had quickly realised was better translated as slave. And *hell on earth* was the mine where Karol had almost lost his life.

'I was sent to the mine from Buchenwald towards the end of 1944, thousands of us were. We weren't aware of it at the time, but the Dora project was the Third Reich's last great hope of victory. We were being used to build the "wonder weapon". The V2 rocket which would be so fast no air defences could stop it, and so silently lethal you couldn't hear it coming. It was going to wipe out the Allies and win the war.'

His voice had been soft and hypnotic. It carried a richness better suited to bedtime stories filled with magic and myth. Instead, he told her a tale plucked from terror and darkness, of a vast underground factory deep in the abandoned mines of the Kohnstein mountain, and an army of the walking dead.

'I was lucky I suppose, even though I hate to use that word. I went in young and strong, but even then the work and the conditions broke me. It's hard to imagine on such a bright day as this, but the hours we slaved in the mine turned daylight into a memory. The tunnels and the caverns with their cold and their damp and their bone-grinding noise was the centre of our existence; it was our entire world.'

He'd looked at his hands then, spreading them out as if they still bore the mine's traces.

'The dust clung to our skin. It coated our eyes and our throats like a crust. There was no fresh air, no ventilation. There was only enough water to drive us mad with the longing for more. We became shadows. We lost the capacity for thought and action beyond following orders and remaining whatever passed down there in the dark for alive.'

He'd talked as if he was a million miles away from Evie's office, and Evie knew better than to stop him.

'We had no value – that was the worst of it. Workers died all the time; they fell where they stood. From ammonia burns, from the terrible weight of the machinery which we were all too weak to bear; from malnutrition and disease or because the soldiers chose to shoot on a whim. And we were replaced with no more thought than a guard lighting a fresh cigarette. Wagons full of bodies were removed every night; new batches were marched in the next morning. And I don't only mean men, Miss Ritter: there were children enslaved down there too. Some of them were so tiny they barely lasted a day.'

He had finally paused then, and swallowed hard. It had taken Evie's gentle, 'Go on,' for him to continue.

'Inhuman isn't a big enough word for the creatures who put us into that place. And yes, Rudolph was there. He was one of the worst. Striding the tunnels like God. Ordering floggings and hangings and forcing the rest of us to stand below the dancing ropes and watch.'

He was one of the worst. Arthur Rudolph. It was the name Evie had wanted to hear; it was still a jolt when Karol finally said it.

Arthur Rudolph was a name that had been familiar to Evie

– and the rest of America – for years. He was an all-American hero, dubbed by the press as the father of the *Saturn V* rocket whose development had enabled American astronauts to make their historic moon landing. Every little and not so little boy with an eye to the stars knew who Arthur Rudolph was. Except that they didn't know him at all. Because – if Karol's accusations, and the rumours which had reached Marty and set him on the trail in the first place, were true – Arthur Rudolph was a Nazi.

'And he won't be the only one, not if even half the whispers are to be believed.'

Marty's excitement at the suggestion that Rudolph might not be the hero he seemed had lit up the whole office.

'I've done a bit of preliminary digging and apparently, there were plane-loads of weapon scientists whisked out of Germany and into America at the end of the war, primarily to keep them out of Russian hands. The battle over which side would grab control of their technical knowledge was the first real struggle of the Cold War. Your father might have some stories about that, Evie. He was involved in the early days of the atomic programme, wasn't he? He might know something about the technology race that fed into that. I know he's Swiss, but he might have some recollections or contacts from that time who we could tap into. Next time you speak to him, ask him if he's ever heard of Operation Paperclip.'

Marty had responded to Evie's raised eyebrow with a shrug. 'I know, what a name. But it's a classic bland choice, designed not to attract attention to what was really happening. In other words, a cover-up, which sums up the whole operation.'

He'd dismissed her frown at that as quickly as he'd dismissed her scepticism over the operation's name.

'Trust me, I'm already learning that questions about that enterprise don't lead to straight answers. The one thing I'm certain about though is that there must have been whitewashing on a grand scale to get the Nazis' elite rocket and atomic specialists into the country. And that the CIA must have been involved since then in preserving the anonymity of the ones who stayed, no matter how blank they're currently pretending to be. So – with the caveat that there'll likely be brick walls and denials everywhere we turn – I think that Rudolph, and whoever may have come in with him, is a lead we should definitely be following.'

Evie had spent the last few weeks doing exactly that. She hadn't contacted her father – telephoning him never produced more than an awkward silence, and she doubted he would have much to add if she did bring the operation up in person. But she'd sent out other feelers about Paperclip – carefully worded so that they wouldn't lead to a libel suit – to the survivor organisations and the synagogues who the OSI had begun to establish connections with. And then one of those feelers had born fruit yesterday, and Karol Perlmann had stepped up.

And delivered.

Evie put her notes down again and didn't bother to look at the clock. Rereading his testimony had only cemented what she'd already decided: Karol was a good witness, clear and compelling and factual. He also thought that he could gather other survivor accounts together, which was essential because weight of evidence mattered. And Rudolph was certainly a high-profile prize; he could even be classified as a big fish.

But it won't be easy to go after him. People will shy away from attaching the label war criminal to a man like that. Even the ones who don't think we're wasting our time.

There was a hint of a following wind behind the idea of holding the past up to scrutiny. There had to be – without at least a chance of public backing, the OSI would still be a paper idea. The events of World War Two were no longer largely consigned to a Hollywood version of history which pitted Allied heroes against Nazi devils and didn't dive deeper; they had come into ordinary people's homes in a far more personal way.

A year ago, millions of American viewers had wept over the *Holocaust* television series, and the terrible sufferings endured by the fictional Weiss family. The publication in the *New York Times* of the names of over three dozen suspected Nazis who were living comfortable lives in American suburbs had stirred up a scandal. But memories were short, and a following wind could quickly blow out. The wave of death threats and the physical attacks against outed Nazis which had followed the *Times* article had unsettled the neighbourhoods they were sheltering in, stirring up a sympathy for 'harmless old men' that the OSI didn't need. And the space-race-hero aspect was also a major problem.

Evie was very aware that, in the Cold War-overshadowed world they lived in, scientists were the new gods. They were the twentieth century's frontier pioneers, the guarantee that the Russians couldn't outwit America in the arms race. Even her father still sat on a number of advisory boards and was a regular after-dinner speaker, although he had been retired from his research work for years. And no one counted the cost of technological advances.

Evie had seen the V2 rocket on display in the new National Air and Space Museum for herself. The information panel below it was a tribute to the wonders of its design and capabilities. There wasn't a single word about the mines and the broken bodies that had gone into its making.

And none of those problems mean that we're on the wrong track. Who someone is now shouldn't protect them from who they were then.

Evie got up, refilled her coffee and turned to a new page in her notebook. She was ready to start formulating next steps; she was ready for a chase.

When the phone rang, she assumed it was one of her girlfriends calling to point out the error of her work-obsessed ways, and she answered it primed with excuses. Instead it was Marty on the other end of the line, and her half-formulated apology was instantly forgotten.

'Perlmann is absolutely perfect. I'll write up my notes for Monday morning, but I want you to sit down with him too. He's exactly the type of witness who would shine at a deportation hearing, if we can get things moving against Rudolph that far. And I also think we need to bring Rudolph in – for a starting conversation at least – to see what if anything he spills. I've already requested copies of the Nuremberg files on Mittelbau-Dora to see what they say about his involvement in the abuses there... What is it? Why aren't you saying anything? I thought you said this was an important line of enquiry?'

'I'm not saying anything because I can't get a word in edge-ways. Can you be quiet for a second?'

Marty's voice was so tight, Evie immediately subsided.

'What you've got so far sounds brilliant, and I'll pick it up first thing on Monday, but Rudolph's not your priority anymore. Something else has come in, something that... I don't know what it is, but I need you to come in and deal with it now, Saturday or not. That guy you were so enamoured with at the Hilton on Thursday night, the Robert Redford look-alike, is here in reception, and he wants to talk to you.'

'I wasn't enamoured with anyone!'

It took Evie a moment to realise who Marty meant, then his assumption about the depth of her interest in Sebastian scratched straight under her skin. She'd gone home from the party without wasting another thought on the museum curator, and she'd been far too wrapped up in her work to think about him since. Except now he was in her head again and, much to her irritation, her pulse had immediately started to flutter. Which meant that she focused on the annoyance, and the embarrassment of that, and not the importance of what Marty had said.

'And I've no interest in seeing him again today. I'm busy. Can't you tell him to come back next week? I'm flattered he's so keen to see me, but...'

Evie pulled herself up, conscious that she not only sounded ridiculous, but that she'd completely misunderstood the reason for Marty's call.

'It's not personal, is it? Not if it's more of a priority than Rudolph.'

Marty at least had the grace to laugh rather than tell her how arrogant she'd been.

'No, it's not, or at least not in the way you thought. You have to meet with him, Evie, and it won't wait. I don't know if he's delusional, or fanciful, or what. But he says that he's Himmler's godson.'

CHAPTER 4

KURMARK LEBENSBORN HOME, OCTOBER
1941

'We take you into our community as a limb of our body. You shall grow in our protection and bring honour to your name.'

The speeches were solemn. The setting was impressive. The officers forming a guard of honour around the dais looked splendid in their black uniforms.

And it's because of me. Out of all of the mothers and babies gathered here, me and my boy are the ones who matter the most. How can that be possible?

Annaliese stood in the middle of the home's reception room – which had been draped with flags and filled with flowers for the day – trying not to be overawed and counting her blessings. Knowing that they were many.

She had given birth to a son who was healthy. Who was the most beautiful baby she had ever seen. A son who was the most important child in the room. She had done her duty by her country and her Führer, and that in turn had made Bruno very proud. And – if today was anything to go by – she'd risen far higher in the world than a secretary from one of Berlin's smallest suburbs could ever have hoped. Everything was wonderful. Except inside her head. Everything was a muddle in there.

Too many things weren't quite right with the day. Bruno wasn't beside her like a proud father should be. No matter how hard Annaliese tried not to miss him, his absence hurt. And no matter how hard she tried to be grateful, the gap between what was happening around her and the sentimental way she'd pictured her first baby's christening was an impossibly wide one. It wasn't even a christening – that was far too religious and old-fashioned an idea for the Reichsführer-SS. It was something he called a naming ceremony, a term Annaliese couldn't get used to, never mind use.

Although you'd better try. If you call it a christening again, she'll have you doing the laundry every day like a servant and eating nothing but porridge for a week.

Annaliese glanced up at the dais where *she* was standing, glued to Reichsführer Heinrich Himmler's side as if he was a movie star rather than a paunchy little man with an oddly weak chin. Luckily, Doctor Tellman wasn't looking her way. She was focused on the officer reciting the blessing, her lips moving in time with his. That didn't make Annaliese feel any more comfortable. She'd learned – as all the girls at the Kurmark mother and baby home quickly learned – that Doctor Tellman didn't need to be looking to know when somebody's attention had wandered away from the Party's demands.

And she's not Doctor Tellman; she's Helene. She's our friend – we're supposed to call her by her first name. Why can't I remember that either?

Annaliese at least knew the answer to that. *Helene* and *friend* when taken together made no more sense to her than *naming ceremony* did. Himmler's favourite – because that's what the woman was, and she made sure that all the girls under her watchful eye knew it – was far too formidable to be addressed so casually. And as for being their friend? The only word Annaliese could think of to describe that idea was ridiculous.

It was true that, once upon a time, Helene would have been exactly the sort of person Annaliese would have loved to be seen with. She was as elegant as one of the French models who'd been the queens of the fashion magazines, before the war made admiring French models unpatriotic. Her jewel-coloured dresses were stunning, and as for the gleam that danced through her blond hair...

In a different life perhaps, before Annaliese had become a mother with far more important things to think about than pretty dresses, Helene would have seemed like the perfect shopping and coffee companion. Appearances, however – as Annaliese's mother never tired of telling her – could be deceptive, and in Helene's case that maxim was true. She might be lovely to look at, but here, in the home? Where she wrote the rules and then swooped in every few weeks and changed them on a whim? She was cold and distant and definitely not someone to cross.

'You are a very special girl, Frau Stengel; you are bearing a child for the Fatherland. And you're very lucky to be here at Kurmark, where your son or your daughter will be prized and not shunned for your lack of a wedding ring.'

Helene's greeting on the day Annaliese had arrived at the home in the small village of Klosterheide – which had felt like light years not an hour's drive away from Berlin – had been a very confusing kind of welcome. Annaliese had assumed that *prized and not shunned* had been intended to mean 'there is no judgement here'. Except when Helene said it, the greeting had sounded very much like a judgement.

Helene's handshake had been fleeting, her tone had been clipped and, although her mouth had formed into the right shape for a smile, there wasn't a speck of warmth in it. Annaliese had felt as small standing in front of Helene as she had when she'd been forced to tell her father that she was pregnant. He'd stared at her stomach and her bare ring finger and hadn't even tried to make the best of the situation. Her 'I'm having a baby for Hitler' hadn't cut any ice with him. If Bruno hadn't stepped in and found her a place at the home for girls who were expecting officers' babies, Annaliese would have been stuck in a very unhappy place. Instead, she'd spent the last five months being thoroughly spoiled.

Her delight in her new life had started with her first glimpse of the house. That had taken her breath away from the moment Bruno drove her through its ornate iron gates – it was a palace compared to the cramped flat she shared with her parents in the city. The driveway was as long as her street, and the neatly laid gardens were a far prettier prospect than the scruffy park she'd always hurried past in Köpenick. And the inside was equally as grand. The wallpaper was so thick she could trace the raised floral pattern with her fingertips, and the carpets buried her toes.

The food too was a revelation. Rationing had begun to bite in Berlin, and the meals her mother constructed around potatoes and bread had become increasingly boring. It was another sort of life entirely at Kurmark. Yes, there was porridge in the mornings and too many raw vegetables at dinnertime. But there was also – unless Helene had taken offence and someone was on plain rations – fresh fruit and real coffee every day and chocolate cake at the weekends. Annaliese hadn't felt so coddled since the early days of Bruno's courtship, when he'd showered her with French perfume and real silk stockings.

Life had become an easy, pampered thing. A far more comfortable existence than the horrors Annaliese had been warned by her parents and her pastor would be the fate of anyone immoral enough to become an unmarried mother. They didn't understand that those threats – which had been wielded as a weapon since childhood to keep her on the 'pure path' her mother and father insisted she stick to – no longer counted. Or not for girls who'd fallen pregnant by an SS officer anyway.

Instead of being ruined, Annaliese had risen up.

She'd made friends. She'd grown plump and content and had, mostly, stopped worrying about Bruno's failure to visit her and the promises he still hadn't fulfilled. She was treated with respect in the home; all the girls were. Nobody cared who did or didn't have a husband. All of them – including the nursing staff – were known as *Frau* and not *Fräulein*. They were treated as women who'd made good choices, not as girls who'd sinned and fallen from grace. Annaliese knew it was a far cry from the way she would have been forced to live had she stayed with her parents. She would have been treated as a leper there; she would have been locked away. Her father would have carried on calling her all those terrible names which Bruno had told her to ignore. Names that had hurt almost as much as his hand when she'd told him the news of her pregnancy and he'd slapped her. Bruno had saved her from that miserable existence. He'd promised her that she would be special at Kurmark, and she had been.

And now my beautiful boy is special too.

Luck had carried on shining. Not only had the pregnancy been straightforward and the birth quick, Sebastian had been born on the seventh of October, on Himmler's birthday. Even Helene had managed a proper smile at that. Babies born on October the seventh were guaranteed a special place in the Reichsführer's heart and a glittering future in the Thousand Year Reich.

Bruno had sent a message to the home telling her that he was the envy of his fellow SS officers, along with the most beautiful bunch of white winter roses. It was still a shame that he hadn't been able to attend the ceremony, or visit in person and see Sebastian for himself. As much as she adored her boy, having no one to come and admire him except the nurses had left Annaliese feeling a little lonely. But duty had called as duty so often did when lives belonged to the Party, and Bruno had been forced to bow to it. Luckily, the picture he'd painted of their life together, after she was discharged from the home and into a little house of their own – a picture she sketched daily for Sebastian – was some compensation.

A bell suddenly rang out across the chamber, jolting Annaliese from her daydreams.

Helene was glaring directly at her, *Don't you dare make a mess of this* stamped across her tight face. Annaliese took a deep breath and pulled her meandering thoughts back together. This was the important bit, the part she had practised the hardest for. The moment that marked Sebastian out as the first among the rest of the babies receiving their names. Getting it wrong was not a possibility.

She stepped forward, holding Sebastian close, focusing on Helene's careful instructions. She walked six paces towards the dais. She stopped. She held her baby out, and she waited for Himmler to give his command. She didn't dare look up at him.

'The child is chosen. The child is pure and precious to me, because he is my godson and he is as precious to the Reich he will serve. Proceed to admit him.'

Another set of words which meant nothing and Sebastian was whisked out of her arms and away.

Don't cry, sweetheart. She'll blame me if you do.

Annaliese needn't have worried. He didn't. Sebastian lay on the pillow which had been placed on top of the swastika-draped table, blinking his new-born eyes and waving his tiny fists. Gurgling away as if he'd known all along what was expected of him.

'Do not flinch, do you hear me? What happens next is a

great honour. It turns the child into the soldier he was born to be. It is not a time to be sentimental and weak.'

Annaliese knew what was expected of her too – Helene's voice was permanently lodged in her ear. And she knew that this section of the ceremony would be over in seconds. It was still hard to hold herself steady and not grab her son back. To keep her eyes open as the huge sword came to rest across her baby's tiny body. As the blade balanced so close to his skin.

Annaliese kept watching because she'd been ordered to do so, but she pulled herself mentally away. She swapped the image in front of her for a far less frightening one. She replaced the candlelit and flag-covered chamber with a flower-decked church. She replaced the blue cloth bearing SS flashes which had been placed over Sebastian with the lace christening gown she and generations of her family had worn. She swapped Helene and Himmler for her parents. And she placed Bruno at her side, resting his hand on her shoulder, the wedding ring on his finger a perfect match for the gold band gleaming on hers. With the wife it was apparently too early for him to leave vanished clean away.

Which she will be soon enough. Now that I've borne him a son too. Now that I've proved I can be just as good an SS wife as she is, as well as being younger and far prettier than her and sure to have plenty more boys. He's got no reason now not to make our dreams come true and marry me.

A second bell rang out as loud as the first.

Annaliese remained where she was as Himmler approached the table and surrounded Sebastian with the gifts that proved how valuable the boy was to him, to the Führer and to Germany. The other SS officers in attendance formed up behind their commander, taking it in turns to touch the baby's head as he had done and to offer their own personal welcome. It was a slow and solemn procession, performed in a silence that bellowed through Annaliese's head.

It's too soon. He's not theirs, not yet. I'm his mother; he's mine.

It was too much. The black figures, the slowly moving circle. The tiny baby caught in the middle. Annaliese's heart lurched. She needed to hold her son, to claim ownership of him. She shot forward, Helene's instructions driven clean out of her head. And she realised a moment too late that she'd mistimed her move: the photographer hadn't completed his shot of the sacred tableau.

'Get back. You have no place in this.'

Helene's hiss cut between Annaliese and her baby with the sharp slash of a knife.

You have no place.

Annaliese instantly dropped her hands and her eyes. She moved away from her baby, although every newly forged maternal instinct was screaming *move closer*. She waited until the men had left and taken Helene with them. She waited until she could finally pick up her boy and run to the warmth of her room in the nursery wing, where it would be just the two of them.

Sebastian didn't fuss as she gathered him up; he carried on gurgling. He didn't seem disturbed by the ceremony at all. But Annaliese no longer felt special, and she didn't like that feeling, or the ones which came with it. That it hadn't been about her at all today – that today being a mother didn't seem to count as important. That Sebastian was on loan, not hers to keep and maybe, as unthinkable as it seemed, there wouldn't be a place in his life for her once he started to grow up. And that – no matter how many times she told herself that it couldn't be – the fluttering sensation in the pit of her stomach, which tightened when the baby was taken from her arms and away to the night nursery, wasn't excitement at the future anymore. It was fear.

· · ·

That feeling, once it took root, proved very difficult to shake. Annaliese's pampered life – where even the smallest decision was taken for her – began to feel less coddled and rather more like a prison.

Every area of the Kurmark home ran on a set of tightly fixed rules, and the nursery wing was no exception. Babies were placed in a separate ward from their mothers at night. Bottles replaced the breast at three weeks. Mothers spent their afternoons resting in their rooms while their babies were marshalled into a neat line of prams watched over by the nurses. The rules never faltered; no one was above them. Annaliese found them harder and harder to keep. They all seemed designed to replace her.

She still had a healthy milk supply even if her three weeks feeding allowance was up. She slept better if Sebastian was close by, so she assumed that he must do the same. She could rock a pram better than any paid carer. The only person her baby needed was her, but nobody seemed to understand that.

Annaliese began to argue when Sebastian was taken away. She began to ask questions. About why there were more babies in the garden than mothers anxiously waiting to swoop them back into their arms. About why the girls had separate bedrooms now when they'd been all in together before the births, and why they didn't socialise as a group anymore. And about the screams she'd heard late one night which she wanted to accept as normal – because she'd been ordered not to make the same noise herself when it was her time – but had started to worry was something more than a 'silly girl in labour'. Within a week of the naming ceremony, Annaliese had stopped being special and had turned into a nuisance. Which put her on Helene's radar.

'Why have I had to come back here before my next inspection is due in order to deal with this? Why are you causing trouble?'

Helene arrived unannounced as Annaliese was finishing what the nurse had insisted was her last early morning feed. There was no 'How are you?' No 'How is Sebastian?' Helene barely glanced at the milk-sated baby as she sent him away. And she didn't wait for Annaliese to reply.

'I've read your notes. Baby is thriving, but you seem determined to make life as difficult as possible for everyone else. Why would you do that, Annaliese? Haven't we been good to you? Haven't we given you a better life in here than you would have endured outside?'

Helene walked across to the small chest of drawers in the corner of the room as she spoke. Annaliese had put the candlesticks and the cup Himmler had presented to Sebastian on display there. She dusted them every morning and patted the photograph propped up against them while she waited for her baby to reappear from the night nursery. Helene picked them up, turning each piece over, running a polished fingernail across the scrollwork and engraving. She didn't turn round when Annaliese replied. She cut through her 'Yes of course, but—' with a sharp sigh.

'There is no *but*. There is simply *thank you*. We have provided an excellent home and excellent care, and yet you argue and you refuse to follow the rules. It's not good enough.'

Helene paused then and she turned, her fingers still caressing the cup. It was all Annaliese could do not to shiver. The woman's face was flint.

'And you keep referring to the child as *mine*. Why do you do that?'

Annaliese stared at her, at a loss for an answer. The question was ridiculous – who else did Sebastian belong to if not her? She shook her head. She started to say, 'I do that because he is.' But the words wouldn't come.

'Ah, there we are. Maybe you do understand how things work after all.'

Helene's face re-ordered itself into a smile which made it look harder. When she came and sat down on the bed within touching distance, Annaliese's skin flinched.

'You're not an unintelligent girl, so you should have put the pieces together by now. You heard what was said at the naming ceremony. You saw what was done. Sebastian belongs to Germany; he belongs to us all. He has the Reichsführer for a godfather; in a few months, he will be presented to Hitler. He is a soldier for the Reich, a leader for the future. And yes, you have the care of him now, but he isn't yours. Life will go far easier for you when you grasp that.'

Annaliese heard the menace. She heard *soldier* and *leader*. But she didn't want to hear those things, so she focused instead on *you have the care of him* which was the one thing that mattered. And she played straight into Helene's waiting hands.

'I am his mother though, aren't I? Whoever he gets presented to, whatever he's meant to become in the future, I'll always be his mother?'

Annaliese couldn't read Helene's expression. The flicker at the corner of her mouth suggested that she was amused, but that made no sense. Annaliese's stomach started to twist again.

'That's right, isn't it? That won't ever change?'

Her voice fluttered and threatened to break. She pushed back the bedcovers, overwhelmed by the desire to run after her baby. The shift in Helene was instant. She took Annaliese's hand in hers. Her face and her voice slipped into a softness that was so soothing, Annaliese's pulse slowed.

'That's better, that's calmer. Of course you are his mother, my dear. That's the one thing no one can take away.'

One more squeeze, a pat on her cheek and Helene got up, smoothed her skirt and returned to efficiency.

'There, everything sorted and no more nonsense. Now why don't I take these?' She gestured to the silverware. 'They could do with a proper polish, and I'm sure there's a presentation box downstairs somewhere. We don't want them to spoil, do we?'

'Can I keep the picture with me while you do that?'

Annaliese didn't care about cups or candlesticks, but the photograph she'd been given of the ceremony mattered, even if she wasn't anywhere in it.

Helene shrugged an 'Of course' and then she was gone, with an order for Annaliese to rest, which she was more than happy to obey. *The one thing no one can take away.* The promise filled her ears like music, lulling her into a sleep she desperately needed. It was hours before she realised that she had, once again, heard the words but had been utterly fooled by their meaning.

It was a car that woke her, the scrape of tyres across gravel. It was an unusual sound outside the nursery wing, where quiet was the order of the day and there were very few visitors to disturb the closed doors.

Annaliese climbed out of bed. She was groggy from the deepest sleep she'd had in a week. She had no idea what time it was. She crossed to the window, her curiosity piqued, and pulled back the curtains.

'Bruno! You came!'

She couldn't believe it was finally him climbing out of the car. She also couldn't believe that he was apparently deaf to her joyous greeting. She shouted again and banged on the window, which was too heavy for her to open. Bruno still didn't hear her. He was fussing with the passenger door and helping someone else out.

'What's she doing here?'

Annaliese took an automatic step back. The woman climbing rather inelegantly out of the car was Maria, Bruno's wife. She was dressed in one of the too-tight wool suits she habitually wore, and her hat had turned her hair into a pancake. Nothing about that was surprising. Frau Schneider had been a frump on the mercifully few occasions she'd appeared in the office where Annaliese and Bruno worked. She was a frump today. But she was also holding on to her husband's hand and walking with him to where Helene had suddenly appeared in the small courtyard.

It's nothing to worry about. He's here to see me and our boy; he's here to take us home.

Annaliese could have wrapped herself up in that thought. If Maria hadn't come too. If she and Helene hadn't nodded to each other as if they'd already met.

She dressed faster than she'd ever dressed. She didn't brush her hair; she didn't reach for her lipstick. She refused to give in to the shivers working their way at lightning speed through her body. She managed to stay perfectly calm. Until she ran to the door and the door was locked.

Annaliese banged on the wood until her knuckles bled. She screamed until her throat was raw. Nobody answered. Nobody came. By the time the door finally opened, she was a collapsed mess on the floor and the car had driven away.

It was Helene standing there. It was Helene who supervised the nurses who dragged Annaliese back to her bed and tied her hands to its frame. It was Helene who supervised the tray and the swab. Who pushed the needle into her arm.

'Hauptsturmführer Schneider is gone. He has been relocated out of Berlin so don't waste your time looking for him. Sebastian is with his father now and with the Hauptsturmführer's wife, a woman who is far better suited to raising the child than a slut who sleeps with married men.'

Helene's voice swooped in and out as the anaesthetic took hold, but her words stuck.

They were all Annaliese could hear in her head when she came round, and wished that she hadn't. The words left with her as the home's door closed firmly behind her on the following day. They stuck and they stayed. They became the beat of her broken heart for all the years yet to come.

CHAPTER 5

WASHINGTON, DECEMBER 1979

She'd got her wish. Lost and stolen children were suddenly at the top of her priority stack – Marty had made that clear the moment Evie rushed into reception. But this – dealing with a man whose knotted hands and twisted mouth was a testament to his pain – was a very different proposition from sorting through letters. Evie had been an expert at her job for years; faced with Sebastian's unfolding story, she suddenly felt like a clumsy beginner.

'I am a Lebensborn child. Do you know what that word means?'

He was already waiting in her office. Those were his first words. The lack of a greeting could have felt rude, and yet it didn't.

He needs to know from the start that I won't falter – or judge him.

Evie sat down and nodded, although she'd never felt less sure of her ground.

'In general terms, a little. I know that that Lebensborn broadly means fountain of life. I'm aware that it was some kind of... breeding programme based on creating a master race that Heinrich Himmler developed during the Third Reich.'

Evie managed not to stumble over *breeding programme*. Sebastian managed not to flinch. When he answered her, he barely drew breath.

'That's one way to describe it; that's the common way I suppose, but what it means for me is more personal. It means that I was born to be a soldier for Hitler, a leader of the Reich. And whatever else I've done or will do with my life, that's where it began. Not born to a mother and a father who wanted me as part of a loving family, but intended instead as a cog in a killing machine.'

He blinked, regrouped. 'I've been living under that shadow for years, and the weight is a hard one to carry. I need answers. I need to know who my father really was and why my mother disappeared from my life. I need your help, Evie – that's why I'm here. And that's why I've brought this with me, as proof that what I'm saying is true.'

The proof, which Sebastian set on the desk between them, was a silver christening cup. It was an innocent-looking thing. Apart from the tarnish which had built up over the years, she could have picked up its twin at half a dozen local stores. When Evie said as much, Sebastian almost smiled.

'Pick it up. Turn it around, read what it says. Then tell me how ordinary you think it is.'

It was anything but.

Sebastian

7.10.1941

Vom Patenonkel

H. Himmler

The inscription was cut into the silver in a series of jagged runic letters, the signature added with a flourish that must have tested the engraver's skill. Evie put it down and instinctively rubbed her hands. She had to force herself to look at him and not at it.

'That's my name and my date of birth cut into it. And *Patenonkel* means godfather.' He shook his head, although Evie hadn't spoken. 'You can't see the cup as commonplace now, can you? You can only see it as evil. Please God you don't see me the same way.'

He waved her instant and horrified protest aside with an 'I'm sorry, I didn't mean it' that they both knew wasn't entirely true.

'How long have you known?'

Evie had so many questions, yet this one seemed the only one that mattered. Sebastian took a proper breath now, closed his eyes and aged. When he opened them again, his face was stripped bare.

'I'm not entirely sure. Perhaps some of it for over twenty years. About this' – he nodded to the cup – 'for a lot less, but it feels like it's been in my life forever, casting a shadow I could feel but not see. I've tried to find answers, to understand what it means, but all I've hit is dead ends, and then I met you and...' He shrugged. 'I left the Hilton because I was too full of my own story to stay. I wanted to tell you it all then, which would have been crazy, and I want to tell you it all now, but I don't know where to start.' He stopped, his shoulders sinking.

The urge to get up, to go to him and take him in her arms was overwhelming – and a shock. It wasn't as if she hadn't heard difficult stories before.

But this is nothing like them. This is a life blighted before it barely began.

Evie squeezed her hands together under the desk until the impulse to hold him was under control. He needed professional guidance, not a woman who had suddenly forgotten her boundaries. She sat up straighter and picked up her pen, and gently led him into his story.

That poured from him without any sense that he had planned how to tell it. Evie guessed that he was still piecing what he knew together and had never shared his findings so fully before. What was clear was that Sebastian was already a long way down a road which had grown harder with every step. He didn't try to play that turmoil down. He didn't pretend that it had been easy to confront his past. To have to fashion a new version of his father; to have no sense at all of his birth mother. He said *drowning* and *swallowed up* more than once. And some of the memories, the ones resurfacing from his childhood, contained more pain than even he seemed to know.

'I knew I was German – I have some memories of living there, and I was ridiculed at school until I learned to lose my accent. But I didn't think about what being German might mean beyond a handful of tired insults. And I always thought my father was one of the good ones. I held on to that, until it was snatched from me.'

That recollection had needed a moment before he was able to flesh out his family.

'She wasn't my birth mother. She told me that the day he died. Part of me was glad: Maria was never kind; she was nothing like the mother I constructed inside my head. But I could live with that, until she told me that I was my father's Lebensborn bastard and I lost any sense of him, or my real mother, or myself.'

Evie had to keep her head down and keep writing so as not to let him see how sad she felt for the lost little boy he'd once been. Or how hopeless. The account he'd presented her with was heartfelt and compelling, but it was also a muddle of confusion and facts which would take a long time to unravel into a case.

If there's even a case to be made.

Evie wanted there to be one. She knew better than to stop
Sebastian's recounting and promise it. How could she tell him
that even if he had come to her with names and dates and
specific allegations of a provable crime against an actual American citizen, she couldn't promise him a case, never mind a
winnable one? The OSI had a budget and a dedicated team and
an unshakeable determination to see justice done, but it still had
far more bark than it had bite. This wasn't the time to tell him
the truth; that was hard enough to admit to herself. But it didn't
change the facts, no matter how heartbreaking the story.

The truth was that most of the cases the OSI were called on
to investigate simply didn't stack up. Too much of the documen-
tary proof had been destroyed in Allied bombing raids or in a
deliberate purge of the evidence by the Nazis. Too many of the
witnesses were dead, or were alive but had memories that were
muddled. That was all bad enough.

What was impossible to work around, however, was that all
the crimes likely to come under the OSI microscope had been
committed thousands of miles and dozens of years away, and
none of them had been committed on American soil. Unless the
law changed – and every member of the department fervently
wished that it would – the OSI had no power to file criminal
charges. All they could do was dig under the layers built by
respectable lives. Act as a spotlight and a lobbyist – pushing for
deportations through the civil courts, trying to persuade
Germany to take back their criminals and deal with them. And
even achieving that much wasn't a simple task: the Germans
were reluctant to reopen old wounds; the Americanised Nazis
would cling tight to their citizenship. Every stage of a case had
to be watertight. And Sebastian hadn't brought Evie watertight;
he'd brought her his pain.

*And that isn't enough on its own to move forward, no matter
how deep the damage runs.*

She let him finish. She let him tell her about the fights

which had torn his world apart and the hopeless trail to discover
the truth he'd been stuck on ever since. All of it was tragic, but
nothing Sebastian told her could be construed as a crime.

'Don't tell me that. Listen to the rest before you refuse me.'

Evie had given Sebastian a chance to gather himself when
he finally stopped talking. Then she eased as gently as she could
into the reality of 'I'm so very sorry, and I wish things were
different, but our remit is a narrow one, and I don't think there's
enough in this to bring—'

But he raised his hands like a stop sign and cut her off mid-
sentence.

'I know this is personal. I know that me uncovering my
family history isn't the OSI's responsibility. And I know that
what happened to me is nothing compared to the horrors of the
camps and the genocide the Nazis inflicted. But here's the
thing, Evie: I'm not the only one who could come in here telling
you that Himmler was their godfather, or that they were born to
be a soldier for Hitler.' He nodded as she frowned. 'It's true, I
promise. The scale of the Lebensborn programme, and what it
really intended, is just starting to leak out. There could be thousands of people like me, living here and in Germany and in all
the countries the Nazis occupied. People whose lives have been
built on a lie. Doesn't that put a different slant on things?'

Evie didn't know if it did or it didn't, but she offered him a
perhaps and she let him continue without interruption. To keep
cutting him down was too cruel.

'I can count on one hand the people I've found who understand what Lebensborn really was. Most people who've heard
the name – and they are few and far between – are less tactful
than you when they describe it. They think it was some kind of
satanic sex programme that matched chiselled-chinned Nazis
with blond nymphomaniacs.'

The sound he made as he said that was half snort and half
laugh and all bitterness.

'That's not true; that's the stuff of B-movies. The few experts who exist – who all said it was too early to call them that – tell it differently. They described Lebensborn to me as Himmler's personal project. They called it an integral part of the Third Reich's "racial purity crusade", and they defined the Nazi obsession with Aryan children as the key to it. What mattered was who had children. The "pure", to use their word, were encouraged to have large numbers of perfect offspring who would repopulate the world, who were destined to be shared out between "good" families. But that isn't the whole picture.'

He stopped for a second, as if the weight of the coming words was too heavy. Evie stayed silent, let him find his own way.

'The "impure" were discouraged, or sterilised, or killed, and those two parts of the programme – the births and the deaths – went hand in hand. There's got to be crimes in that, surely? There's murder for one. And there's so many lives potentially affected. There could be hundreds, maybe thousands, of children who, like me, were products of that madness living here in America, with no idea how they started. And the ones who designed it, who ran it and decided who lived and died, they could be here too.'

That was something. Evie didn't want to give him false hope, but if the architects of the murders were living free in the States? That could be something.

'What do you mean? Who might be living here?'

She tried to keep her tone neutral, but he heard hope anyway.

'I don't have proof, or names; I wish I did. But something happened when my stepmother was dying. I can't really explain it, but can I tell you the story anyway?'

He slowed down a little as she nodded. It was clear from the way he kept pausing that it wasn't an episode he'd recounted before.

'It was when Maria was in hospital and very frail, a few days from the end. She was in her own world and often confused, but I stayed with her. Most of the time we watched television, which at least filled up the silence. She didn't take much notice, but then this news bulletin came on... I don't remember all the details, but it was something to do with a women's health clinic, an interview with a woman who worked there, or ran it... It was nothing out of the ordinary at all, a human-interest piece I suppose.'

He paused, visibly searching his memory for any detail that would build his case, his face clenched in frustration as he failed. 'Anyway, the point is that, whether it was a face or a name, something broke through, and the effect on Maria was electric. She stared at the screen, properly focused on it, which was surprising enough, but it was what she said that floored me. "So Himmler's little pet talked herself in here too. That must have been quite the reinvention, but she always was a clever one. Well God help any of those mothers she gets near; she won't let the wrong ones survive."'

He nodded as Evie gasped. 'I know, it's bizarre, but they were her exact words, I promise. I've never forgotten them. And, of course, she lapsed back into silence or confusion after that, and I never did get an explanation out of her. But it can't be a coincidence, can it? What she said must matter?' He was racing again now, his hopes picking up. 'A woman living here who was *Himmler's pet*, who had some role involving mothers. And what about *wrong ones*? What did that mean? That she could still be a threat to the women she works with? That could suggest a Lebensborn connection, couldn't it? That has to be enough to start an investigation?'

It could be. If his interpretation is right, which is a big if, it could be.

He read her face too easily and sat forward, his expression

brightening. Evie forced herself to shake her head, to lower his expectations, even though her heart was suddenly racing.

'I don't know – that's the truth. If I'm honest, there's a lot in this that's speculation and hearsay, and far too little that's fact.'

'But aren't all your cases like that, at the start anyway? Aren't they all going to be hard to substantiate?'

Evie nodded, both because Sebastian was right and because she couldn't bear to say no again. And because her instincts were itching, telling her to take her time, to let this story breathe and take on air. To strip his story back to the real horror buried inside it: that the increase in the Aryan population was to be matched by the destruction of the groups who didn't fit the Reich's twisted race criteria. That was surely the very definition of a war crime, which put it under the OSI's remit. And if the woman in the bulletin was real and had the kind of background that Sebastian had implied...

This could lead anywhere. It could link the cases on my desk. It could lead to a big fish.

He was watching her again, scanning her face as if he could see beneath it. And he'd trusted her with his story, which surely deserved some reward.

He needs hope. He deserves hope.

Now it was Evie sitting forward, staring back at him.

'I'll take it to Marty, but that's about all I can do at this stage. I can't promise that he'll move forward – we're pursuing other suspects, and he might think this is too personal. I'd struggle to argue with him about that. But I'll take it, and I'll give it my best shot, and I'll call you when a decision's been made. Is that okay?'

His sudden smile told her that it was more than okay. The lightness in his face told her she'd done the right thing. He left her office looking like the man she'd met at the party, not a broken version of him.

Evie let Sebastian go with more reluctance and a longer

handshake than she knew was strictly professional. She didn't let herself notice when he turned at the outer door and looked back at her. She focused on the notes she'd made during the meeting instead, and how she could best turn those into a persuasive report. And then she caught sight of the clock. It was late and her morning flight to Alabama was an early one – she couldn't afford to do what she'd done earlier in the day and get buried.

Evie sighed, closed her notebook and got up from her desk. She wanted to stay; she wanted to get his story right. But as keen as she was to get started, the search which might lead to Sebastian's mother would have to wait while she dealt with her own.

CHAPTER 6

ALABAMA, DECEMBER 1979

Evie drove into the parking lot of the Beech Brook country club and handed the keys of her rental car to the waiting valet. Her clammy fingers had turned the metal unpleasantly damp, but he was too well trained to flinch. Evie wished she shared his resilience, but Alabama's almost permanent humidity was one of a long list of things she didn't miss about the state.

In the seventeen years since she'd swapped the South for the North, Evie had adjusted more than her accent. She was acclimatised to cooler weather now; she'd developed a delight for snow. At sixty-five degrees, the temperature in Birmingham was almost twice what it had been in Washington and her skin was in rebellion. The irony of an uncomfortable return to her home town wasn't lost on her.

Birmingham, Alabama – the place where Evie had spent her childhood – was widely known as America's 'magic city'. She had only the vaguest memory of seeing the giant metal sign which had spelled out that legend before it was demolished, but the nickname – which actually owed its origins to the city's prosperous steel industry and not the fairy tales of Evie's imagination – had stuck. Like the humidity, the name did not, however, resonate so easily with her. It had been a long time since she'd looked at Birmingham and seen magic. That spell had snapped when she was ten and had overheard one of the rotating group of maids her mother employed muttering, 'It's magical maybe if you're white.'

Mae had refused to explain what she meant when a shocked Evie had asked her. She'd also been clearly terrified of the trouble she'd get into if Evie repeated her words. Evie hadn't repeated anything. Her parents treated their maids and their cook as if they had no feelings, and Evie had no intention of making Mae's life worse. But she'd kept her eyes and her ears open from that day on.

She began to look properly at all the signs that hadn't been demolished. The ones that her parents and her teachers were apparently too unmoved by or too uninterested in to explain. The 'Whites Only' notice above the water fountain on 19th Street. The 'Coloreds Entrance' directing one part of the audience away from the gold-stencilled front door and into the dingy alleyway at the side of the cinema. The separate restrooms and lunch counter in the Kress Department Store where her mother preferred to shop. The signs that proved that Birmingham was two very different cities and that the *magic* – which Evie grew to understand meant money and freedom and respect – was only ever sprinkled across one side.

Evie looked and – when it became clear that nobody she could ask had any interest in answering her questions – she listened.

She learned the value of quiet; she collected up stories. Especially the ones about the mysterious organisation, the Klan, the KKK. A group which was never spoken about except in whispers. Whose members wore white hoods and terrorised black families with flaming crosses and raised fists. Who were apparently – or according to the hushed gossip that drifted around the country club and her parents' parties – drawn from

Birmingham's great and good. Who weren't despised by those gossips the way they should have been.

Evie filed all that information away until a day in September 1963 when she returned home for a visit from the University of Pennsylvania, a place where she shouted her anger at injustice from the middle of protest marches rather than swallowing it down. A day when Evie heard a sound whose ripples never left her. An explosion. A bomb placed in the basement of a Baptist Church where children were collecting their robes to go and sing in the choir. A bomb which killed four little black girls.

A murder it took fourteen years to solve, even though everyone in Birmingham knew from day one which Klan members were behind it.

Evie climbed the club's highly polished front steps with the dull thud of that long-ago explosion ringing in her ears. In some ways, she was thankful for her home town – its injustices and inequalities had set her on a career path that she'd never regretted. But she'd never felt comfortable in it, or in the Beech Brook country club, which was her parents' favourite place in the city to hold court.

It's no wonder Ethan hated it here. It's all gilt on the outside and rotten underneath.

The club, with its verandas and columns and overeager staff, was the picture of elegance. But a picture was all it was. Evie had always imagined that, if she prodded one of its lemon-washed walls with enough force, the building would collapse in on itself like a piece of mouldy fruit. Nothing about its style or its attitudes had changed since it was built in the 1920s. Integration not segregation might be the order of the day now in Birmingham, but that concept hadn't reached Beech Brook. Its members were uniformly wealthy and uniformly white, and very definitely not black or Jewish.

'I swear the manager's skin retracted when you introduced

me as Ethan Kaplan. If I'd come on my own, I would never have made it through the front door.'

The staff had been politely disdainful to Ethan that day. Her parents had been no better. They hadn't exactly been rude; they were too well bred for that. But they'd sniffed at his surname and asked what that meant about *his people*. And Ethan hadn't exactly called them patronising or elitist and right-wing after that first awkward meeting...

But either charge would have fit, then or when they were always unavailable to meet him or his family, or even attend our wedding. And he looked at me with new eyes that day, wondering how much of their snobbery had been dripped into me, although he swore that he didn't.

Evie walked into the club's hushed foyer, well aware that the lunch would be difficult enough without trailing resentment behind her. It was still hard to push away the memories of Ethan's father walking with her into city hall on her wedding day because hers was claiming ill health for the first time in his life. Or the way her parents had dismissed her ex-husband as being beneath their attention, in the same way they dismissed anyone who didn't fit their narrow world view. Or the memory of the one time when – fired up from her training and her first legal cases – she'd ripped off the plaster and called her parents' prejudices out. That confrontation had been an utter waste of time.

'How can you describe people who are struggling to hold their families together – whether that's because of a lack of money or power over their own lives, or for whatever reason that's broken them – as worthless? How can you even think such a thing? What gives you the right to judge them?'

Evie's anger had been met with blank stares. With a 'Why do you have to tilt at hopeless causes?' from her father. And a 'Have you ever considered that, given their circumstances, it would be better if these people had thought twice about having children in the first place?' from her mother which caused Evie to march out of the house. She'd had to accept from that day that she and her parents occupied very different spaces in the world. And that the space between them was widening.

And brooding on that now will ruin the celebration exactly as they expect me to ruin it, and lead to more lingering sighs and badly veiled disappointment.

So Evie didn't brood. She stuck on a smile instead. She kissed her parents' cool cheeks and shook hands with their friends whose views she also despised, as she'd done on countless occasions before. And she steered her way with all the skill of a captain aware of a hazardous undertow through the rocky waters of her father's birthday lunch.

She was nothing like the mother I constructed inside my head.

Evie sat alone at the kitchen table, wondering how soon she could decently leave and picking over Sebastian's words. She'd been mulling over everything he'd told her since she'd boarded the plane to Alabama. Most of her thoughts had centred around his troubled background and how she could help him.

This morning it was his comments about creating an ideal mother to replace the one he'd been dealt that wouldn't leave her. She could so easily have said them herself. How many times had she played that same game? How many times had she built her own imaginary mother out of the holes that made up the real one? Evie could see her construct now, as vividly as she'd conjured the woman up all those years ago. Standing by the kitchen window, warm and smiling. Proud of her daughter and eager to show it. At home for bedtime stories and birthdays. Endlessly loving.

Stop it. This isn't what you do anymore. This is a reaction to hearing about Sebastian's life; it's what being back in this house does. You're unsettled, and you're slipping into a self-pity that's really not pleasant.

She got up. She was restless, in need of distraction. She'd made it through the strained lunch and the mercifully short evening with her parents which followed – where the three of them had buried themselves in their books and then opted for an early night – by switching her brain off. Now it had woken up and couldn't find calm. It was under siege from both her mother and from Sebastian.

Two people who couldn't be more different if they tried.

That thought wasn't the comfort it should have been.

Evie liked Sebastian. She'd been drawn to him from the moment they shook hands at the party and, whatever she had pretended to Marty, she'd been pleased to see him again. Nothing she'd learned since then had changed that initial feeling. But she wasn't certain that the budding attraction between them – which still felt mutual despite his disappearing act at the party – was a good thing. Evie might be adrift from her past and her parents, but Sebastian was totally unmoored. Taking on his case from a professional standpoint was one thing, but letting a personal attraction develop? That was an entirely different matter. Never mind the dangers of getting too close to a case, she wasn't certain either of them was solid enough to take a risk on the other.

Or that I should be thinking about that aspect of our meeting at all, no matter how connected we seem to be.

Those connections were certainly there; the touchpoints they shared were strong enough to be red flags. Or green ones. No matter how many times she picked over that, Evie still wasn't sure which colour was right.

She wandered over to the sink, turning over their conversations again, ticking off the list building in her head. They both carried shadows that stemmed back to their mothers – that was a definite. Sebastian had also done his own share of reinventing.

He'd uprooted himself, swapped cities and states. Buried himself in a career that was everything and not quite enough. And he'd alluded to a marriage which had failed because he hadn't invested enough of himself in it. Ethan would say the same thing about her. He had done, every time she'd put off discussing having a family, even though she adored the nieces and nephews that marriage had brought her. Every time he'd heard her express the fear that she would turn into her mother and do a terrible job and decided that it was really a rejection of him.

There's a hollow place inside Sebastian that's the same shape as mine.

This time her internal *stop it* had a sharper edge.

Evie filled a glass with water and put it down again untasted. Yes, there were touchpoints, but Sebastian's past was far darker than hers and not to be measured in the same way. And yes, there was a bond developing between them – he'd said, 'I need your help, Evie,' not, 'I need the OSI.' But it was her professional expertise that he'd asked for, and he hadn't strayed beyond that. All this second-guessing of what they might somehow become to each other was because she'd walked into her old house and lost sight of herself.

Because a few hours with my parents – with my mother – makes me desperate to find someone who cares.

The pattern never varied. She didn't like the pattern.

So change it.

Evie knew what she actually needed, and it wasn't another relationship misstep. She wanted the same sort of grounding Sebastian was searching for. A deeper sense of her history, a way to cement who she was and where she belonged. A solid foundation to go forward from. The problem was that – in a house where family wasn't a subject for discussion or display – she didn't know how to find it.

'Everything's been lost. Everyone who mattered is long gone. Can that please be an end to it?'

Those weren't her mother's exact words, but they were an accurate summary. That account had never changed either. According to her mother – and her father, because he was always his wife's echo – there were no photographs on show in the house because they had been left behind in her parents' move from Switzerland to America. And there were no memories to stand in their place and pore over, because they had lost touch with both sets of families in the chaotic days after the war and remembering their dead was too painful. That had been the narrative of Evie's childhood and one she wasn't meant to disturb. The only time she'd tried in any real way to push through the silence – because her school history lessons had begun to make elements of her family background seem a little confused – it had gone very badly.

Her mother had treated Evie's 'I don't understand why everyone didn't leave Switzerland when you did, or why you couldn't find them again after the war' as if it was an insult. Her answering 'Do you think we abandoned them? Do you think we are liars and have something to hide?' had left Evie floundering. And her father hadn't come to her rescue, not that he ever did. He was his wife's defender, never his daughter's. He'd wrapped his arms around her stiff frame as if she was some fragile creature Evie had never met. He'd accused Evie of being the cold one, the unkind one. Evie had watched an embrace whose warmth she'd never felt and stopped asking questions on the spot. But those questions hadn't gone anywhere; she was still full of them.

So now it's time to calm the noise and go digging.

She left the kitchen and went into the hallway, pausing at the foot of the stairs to listen for voices or footsteps from the floor above.

There wasn't a sound. She knew without checking that her

parents' bedroom door would be firmly shut. That room was their private domain – Evie had no memory of ever being in it, even as a small child. If she'd knocked on the door, the response had always been *wait*. It had never been *come in*. The comment she'd overheard long ago from the cook – 'Why did those people have a child if they had no intention of paying her a minute's attention?' – had been upsetting, but Evie could hardly fault the logic. She'd spent most of her childhood longing for her parents to include her in their two-person world, rather than leaving her to the care of school or staff. Now she was glad of the quiet.

There was no loft in the house, but there was a garage which doubled as her father's workshop, where boxes were stored on a high shelf. If there was anything to find – because surely there had to be one family photograph somewhere – Evie was convinced it would be there.

She slipped out of the house. She located a stepladder and – carefully avoiding her father's neatly stacked tool boxes whose contents had always been firmly out of bounds – she began working her way methodically along the shelf, starting at the left and hoping that the boxes ran in date order. She took half a dozen of them down; she didn't get further than opening the first one.

'What are you doing?'

Evie jumped and the box – which had nothing in it except a pair of old curtains – slipped from her hands to the floor.

'Why are you in here snooping through our things?'

Her mother was standing in the doorway, her hands behind her back in the imperious way Evie associated with childhood scoldings.

She didn't mean 'our' to include me.

That word choice was as deliberate as *snooping*. Evie was being treated as a nosey and unwelcome stranger, not as a family member who had lived in the house for years and still had possessions there. Once upon a time, the implied *you have no place here* would have plunged Evie into an apology. Not today. She wasn't in the mood any more to indulge her family's secrets.

'I'm looking for us.' She shook her head as her mother rolled her eyes. 'I mean it. I'm looking for pictures of you and Father, or of the three of us together. For something that says there was a life with a couple and then a family in it. Are you honestly going to keep telling me that there's nothing, that there's not even one picture of my childhood, or your courtship?'

'Not the photographs again.' The sigh stretched through the words. 'Honestly, Evie, why can't you accept what I told you about the war? Why can't you simply be happy that we escaped that and came to America? Given that life has turned out much better for you here than staying put would have done, can't you be grateful? Rather than going poking about in the past when you know it upsets me.'

It was a familiar trick – blocking a question with a whole lot more. Both her parents were masters at that art. But something about this sounded odd.

What did she mean by my life being different if they'd stayed put? I was born after they came here.

Evie frowned. She was about to ask what her mother meant, but she stopped herself, assuming it had been a slip of the tongue and determined not to be led off track.

'I'm not trying to upset you. And how my life is now doesn't mean that I'm not interested in where I come from. Knowing so little about that is causing me problems, if I'm honest.'

She paused at *honest* then decided to pursue where that word wanted to take her.

'And, if I'm being that, I might as well tell you that I've never understood why leaving Switzerland meant you couldn't bring your personal belongings. I know you left before the war ended, while there was still fighting going on across Europe, but

Switzerland was a neutral country. You were hardly fleeing the advancing hordes.'

It was a calculated push, although it had turned more barbed than she'd intended.

Her mother's mouth thinned and set. 'And you can say that why? Because you have so much experience of living through a war?'

She's a brick wall. There's not a chink in her. Whatever problems I might be struggling with mean nothing to her.

Evie kept going anyway. 'No, I don't have that experience, or not directly. How could I? But maybe I've some more idea of its hardships than you think. I have a new job...'

She left her mother a pause to say 'Well done' or 'What is it?' She didn't.

Evie ploughed on. 'And what I'm doing now has given me a little insight into what it means to be displaced by the war, to have lost family and home. To still be struggling with that loss almost forty years later. The people I meet with have wallets crammed full of photos of their children and their grandchildren. It tethers them. It gives them a future that at least partly balances out the ruined half of their lives. And yet you...' She shook her head as the differences sharpened. 'You say you lost everyone, but you won't talk about who *everyone* was. And you don't have pictures of the family you've made since then on display. There's no wedding or engagement portrait of you and Father anywhere. There's nothing of me apart from a standard graduation shot which could have come from a catalogue. It makes no sense. So I thought that, instead of asking you and wasting my time again, I'd go looking and at least try to find some, I don't know, baby pictures perhaps.'

Evie ran out of steam and stopped, assuming that her mother would latch on to the last sentence and turn the argument into the one about Evie's ridiculous sentimentality or neediness, which was her usual default. But now it seemed that she had been listening after all.

'What is it – your new role? What has it got to do with the war?'

The unexpected interest made Evie a child again, eager for praise.

'I was going to tell you about it yesterday, but there never seemed to be the right moment. It's really quite exciting. I've moved from the Justice Department to a new initiative called the Office of Special Investigations. We've a remit to track down Nazi war criminals, and I'm looking into a Lebensborn case – the programme set up by Himmler to breed the next generation of Nazis. And another that involves the scientist, Arthur Rudolph. Actually, I wanted to ask Father about him—'

'You will do no such thing.' Her mother's face was suddenly carved into angles. 'You won't bother him with that nonsense. Arthur Rudolph has got nothing to do with your father.'

The interest had gone, if it had ever been there. Her mother was all brisk efficiency again.

'There'll been none of that, and there'll be no more digging. It's time you left, Evie. It's time you stopped bothering us with another of your ridiculous crusades.' She waved a dismissive hand as Evie started to argue. 'I'm sorry if you don't like me calling it that, and I'm sure you think this latest mission is all terribly worthwhile. I can't help it if it sounds like another complete waste of time.'

And there it was, her whole professional life dismissed in *ridiculous* and *another complete waste.*

Evie didn't even try to dampen her anger. 'Wow. Say what you mean and don't hold back, why don't you? Well I'm sorry too but, whatever you think, catching these criminals matters. People have to know that time doesn't run out when it comes to justice, no matter how many years have gone by since the crimes themselves were committed.'

She shouldn't have argued back. She should have known better. She shouldn't have gone on the attack. A light had come into her mother's eyes that Evie recognised all too well. It was the one that said, *I'm going to win this argument whatever the cost and however much it hurts you.* The all too familiar light from her childhood and teenage years. Evie took a step back, but she couldn't move out of range of her mother's tongue.

'Do they now? Well, we'll see. But if this job is so important, why are you standing here talking to me about it? Hadn't you better do as I said and get straight back to it? Heaven forbid that your *war criminals* get to live free a moment longer.'

Evie couldn't help herself. No matter how old she was, a part of her still craved her mother's approval. She started trying to apologise, to make everything right, but her mother was already done with her and turning away. Preparing to fling a last barb over her shoulder.

'There's nothing in here, Evie. I've told you that time and again. There aren't any albums filled with photographs of you as a child. We didn't take any. We remember all too well what a burden it was to raise you. We certainly don't need reminders.'

And there it was, the cruelty that lay beneath the elegant surface. The cruelty nobody else but Evie seemed to see...

Evie walked without speaking out of the garage, grabbed her bag and went straight to her car. Her legal, logical brain knew that her mother's attack was a deflection. That something in Evie's words, about her new job or about Rudolph perhaps, had hit a nerve she hadn't expected to hit. Knowing that didn't help.

'She's so kind. She can't do enough for her patients.'

The memory of that gushing endorsement almost made her stall the car. Evie hadn't met many of her mother's colleagues, but they'd all repeated the same line. The women her mother treated at her clinic had done the same.

They must have been brainwashed or bullied to talk about her like that.

No one who really knew her mother could tell such an outright lie. Not when the truth was the complete opposite.

That she might be a wonderful doctor, but she wasn't a wonderful mother. That she wasn't a saint, or generous, or kind-hearted.

That, when it came to her own flesh and blood, she was a monster.

CHAPTER 7

WASHINGTON, DECEMBER 1979

'I'm – I mean we are – taking your case on. Marty's green-lit it. The plan is to try and track down what information we can about where you were born and then, hopefully, about your mother. It's really good news.'

Evie's call had come yesterday; Sebastian was still flushed with the hope in her voice. And now she was on her way to meet him.

Sebastian stared at the menu whose choices were still a blur. He wasn't sure if his invitation to have dinner with him had sounded like an invitation to a date. It hadn't been. He'd suggested coffee or a meeting in the office as alternatives when Evie hesitated. But dinner it was and – he realised as he glanced up – dinner in a restaurant where the lights had dimmed on the dot of seven, candles had appeared on all the tables and couples had started to stare into each other's eyes. He was surprised to find himself envying that.

'You hold yourself back all the time – have you any idea how hurtful that is? I'm your wife. Whatever it is that's upset you, I'm meant to share it. I'm meant to help you get through it.

How can we – or you – ever be happy if you can't understand that?'

Lainey had tried so hard to fill in his gaps. He'd still let her down in the worst possible way. She had been kind and patient. She had opened him up to a degree he hadn't thought possible. And he'd valued her for it. He'd managed to tell her a great deal about his life, more than he had told any previous girlfriend. That was part of the reason why he'd married her. That and her noisy and equally warm family.

He'd laid his early days in America bare for her, and had admitted how lost he'd felt until he'd chipped away his German edges. He'd told her about the father who had seemed to genuinely care for him but had died when Sebastian was twelve, leaving him with no protection against the mother who'd turned out not to be his mother. Who had never wanted the *nasty little cuckoo* that Bruno Taylor had dropped into her home.

He'd told Lainey about the hole in his heart where his real mother belonged. He'd even told her about the day in 1964 when his half-brother Peter had been killed in Vietnam and Maria's thin veneer of civility towards him had completely shredded. When she'd screamed and sobbed and shouted in his face that the body in the coffin should have been his and not her real son's. Sebastian had confided everything in Lainey.

Except what really haunts me.

He ordered another Old Fashioned to stop the waiter hovering. He'd opened his soul to Evie who was virtually a stranger. He had never offered that much intimacy to his wife.

Sebastian closed his eyes as the past swept over him. Nearly six years had gone by and yet the events which had started him down the path that had led him to the OSI were so vivid they could have happened this morning. They could have happened an hour ago. He hated reliving them. He hated the way that day had turned him into a man who was so caught up in himself, he had destroyed his wife's trust when she needed him the most. But the past was coming, and there was nothing he could do to stop it.

The house was a shrine.

It was 1973 when he walked into it; it could have been 1964. Peter had been dead for nine years, but Maria had clung on to every last scrap of him.

Sebastian hovered in the doorway of the cramped living room, feeling like the intruder he essentially was. The Pittsburgh house had never been his home. Maria and Peter had moved there in the immediate aftermath of Bruno's death, leaving Sebastian behind in the Chicago academy to which – luckily for both of them – he'd won a full boarding scholarship. His visits to her had been few and far between after that, and there was never more than a begrudged couch waiting for him when he did arrive. In the end, he did what Maria clearly wanted and gave up going. So he arrived at the house after her funeral prepared to feel like a stranger. What he hadn't been prepared to encounter, however, was such a temple to grief.

Every surface of the living room was crammed with photographs chronicling Peter's life, from beaming baby to sports-mad teenager to overeager soldier on his way to war. The table by the window was a thicket of basketball trophies, and as for his bedroom...

Sebastian took one step inside that and had to stop – the depth of Maria's despair soaked through every inch of it. She had left the room completely untouched. Bridget Bardot smouldered down, all tumbled hair and bare shoulders, from the walls. There was a dog-eared copy of *Mad* magazine on the chest by the bed, a dust-covered Beatles album still on the turntable. Everything had stopped when Peter did.

I shouldn't be here. It's not my place to be doing this.

If there had been anyone else to call on to come and sort out the house, Sebastian would have been straight on the phone. Unfortunately, the relatives who'd persuaded Maria to leave Chicago for Pittsburgh in 1953 were all gone themselves. There had been nobody but himself and a couple of neighbours at the funeral. There had been no one, including Sebastian, to grieve. He'd been sad when Peter died – their relationship might not have been a close one, but it was such a waste of a life. He'd been sad for Maria too: although he had done his duty at her hospital bedside, her death was a lonely one. He had mourned them, but he hadn't really cried. Now, faced with the evidence of two stalled lives? He stood in his half-brother's room and the tears came pouring.

It took him two hours to bag Peter's life up. After that, Maria's bedroom felt almost bare. Sebastian still hated being inside it. Sorting through the belongings of a woman who'd loathed him – who had told him that his arrival had ruined her marriage and ruined her life – felt far too familiar.

This time he worked fast and didn't let anything interrupt him. He emptied drawers into bags without touching their contents, he barely looked at her more personal possessions. By the time he pulled the last box out from under her bed, he was in control again, his earlier upset banished. And half an hour later, he was broken.

Geburtskunde
Bruno Johann Schneider
ist am 25. Mai
in Moabit, Berlin

The birthdate and the birthplace and the name Bruno were correct, but the surname wasn't one Sebastian recognised. He sat on the floor, trying to remember his life before the family's emigration to America in 1949, trying to remember who he had been. The memories were hazy, a set of images he'd pushed so far away, they didn't feel like his life. Maybe Bruno had once been a Schneider; maybe he had too. Now he thought about it, Taylor was hardly a German name. He'd never seen his own birth certificate so he couldn't be certain; that had apparently been lost during the war along with the rest of his family's papers.

But I was always Taylor, from my first day in school. I'm sure I was.

He stared at the certificate, scouring his head for the German words he'd pushed out of it when he'd longed to be nothing but a straightforward American. *Schneid* and *cutting* he thought could be a match. *Taylor* wasn't so far from that. There had been a *Fischer* at his school who'd quickly dropped the letter C and plenty of others – or so he'd gleaned from the older neighbours who wished themselves returned to the 'old country' and returned to themselves – had chopped the *dorf* or the *berg* from their surnames. Reinvention was a necessary way of surviving in a country where Germans were too often the bogeymen, so perhaps that was what Bruno had done. Sebastian folded the birth certificate into his pocket and decided not to set too much store by it.

He went back to the box, determined to get his morbid task finished and leave.

The second item he pulled out of it was, at first sight, no more of a challenge than the altered name. The leather case was worn and cracked, but its contents – a blue cloth containing a pair of silver candlesticks which still gleamed where the air hadn't got to them – had weathered the years without significant damage. Sebastian instinctively began to craft an explanation for them as smoothly as he'd made room in his head for his father's changed identity. They were probably a wedding gift, although he wondered why he had no memory of ever seeing something so grand on display.

He stopped wondering that a moment later. When he unrolled the cloth and saw the lightning flashes embroidered onto it. And the sunlight fell on the candlesticks and spotlit the swastikas carved into their sides.

'What the hell!'

The sticks fell from his hands; the cloth went fluttering after them. Sebastian's fingers stayed rigid, the tips stretched away from him as if they were contaminated. He stared at his hands, half-expecting to see burn marks appear, to see them shrivel. Wondering now what reinvention really meant, and chasing a more complex version of his father around his head. Unable to marry up the man he remembered as being protective and kind with this box of poisoned memorabilia.

Sebastian's throat constricted. His eyes snapped open. He forced himself to let go of Pittsburgh as the restaurant swam back into view. The memory of discovering the christening cup – the next thing he'd pulled out of the box and recoiled from – always came the same way. On a wave of the nausea which had gripped him when he first read the cup's chilling inscription.

When I became somebody else. Somebody I never asked to be.

The Sebastian who had existed before that day and the Sebastian who existed after it were two distinct entities in his head and he had never been able to shake off the division. The first one was a man wary of shadows and suspicious of the past who'd been unable, despite a couple of clumsy efforts, to add any flesh to Maria's grief-crazed allegations. After the first flurry of insults, she had refused to speak about his birth again and Sebastian hadn't dared to push her. But that Sebastian had, broadly speaking, been in one piece. The second man couldn't claim to be that solid anymore, because the second man was the Sebastian who knew.

From your Godfather, Heinrich Himmler

Nothing had been the same from the day he pulled out the cup and read that inscription. Except for his certainty that he was tainted. That evil had seeped into him before he was old enough to know what evil meant.

Before I was gifted a curse that I could never pass on to a child of my own.

Now it wasn't the hope he'd felt when Evie called which flooded through him; it was shame. That he hadn't confided the truth about his discoveries in his wife. That he hadn't explained to Lainey why her husband had become a husk of a man, lost in books and long phone calls to historians and academics which demanded locked doors and no discussion, and brought him no peace. And why, a few weeks after his trip to Pittsburgh, when her hope of a pregnancy she thought they both wanted had come to nothing, his first – and unforgivably obvious – reaction was relief. Their marriage had ended that day, although its death throes had dragged out far longer.

How can you ever be happy?

It had been a fair question. After everything fell apart, Sebastian had assumed that he wouldn't be – or not fully. His life had become if not miserable – he loved his work far too much for that – certainly a subdued place. A place where everything was flattened by a search for answers he wasn't convinced would ever come. And then he'd met Evie, who was filled with *it will* not *it won't*. Who had listened and hadn't judged, who he felt a connection to that he couldn't explain, and a light had flickered back on inside him.

'I'm late, I'm sorry. It's work – it's always work – which I know is a terrible excuse.' She noticed his drink and grinned at the waiter. 'Oh, that looks so good – can I get one too? With an extra stick of cherries on the side?'

Evie was there, as suddenly as if his thoughts had conjured

her up. Smiling at the waiter, smiling at him. Confident, poised. Beautiful. Sebastian got to his feet as Evie slipped into the booth, making her smile again at his chivalry.

'So, there's a lot I can do and a lot that I can't but that I might be able to find a way around. And I might have to travel to Germany to find some of the answers, and you can come too, if you want to, I mean...'

His 'Of course' was automatic. He didn't know if he wanted to or not. He'd considered going to Germany and digging into his past, but the thought of what he might – or might not – find had always stopped him before. And now here was Evie, saying, 'Come with me,' as if it was the simplest thing in the world.

Maybe it would be, with her.

That was another unexpected thought. Sebastian sat back and let Evie talk, giving himself time to adjust to this new possibility, as she began explaining how his case and the next few weeks might come together. She was brimming with ideas but also not afraid to point out the pitfalls, which helped. Sebastian needed enthusiasm, but he also needed to know that Evie understood how difficult the search could be for him. And that she wouldn't be thrown if he was overwhelmed, or disappointed, or saddened. By the time he decided to share that, and Evie answered, 'I won't be,' he knew he really did want to go.

Snow was falling as they made their way outside at the end of the evening, which was a shock after the warm cocoon of the restaurant and made the night far too cold for lingering. Besides, they were colleagues, nothing more; it had most definitely not been a date. But then Evie smiled at Sebastian with such warmth that his heart suddenly danced. And she leaned into him as if the wind was blowing too hard to stand up straight when he smiled back. And she said 'Yes' at once when he plunged in with another invitation to meet.

That *yes* sang like music. It gave him the courage to behave completely out of character and press his lips lightly to her cheek when he said goodbye. To hold her hand for a second or two longer than a colleague should hold it. And, for that moment – as the two of them stood in the quiet of the falling snow – it gave him the courage to hope that *happy* might not be such an impossible word.

CHAPTER 8

BERLIN, JANUARY 1980

They'd been travelling for what felt like an eternity.

It had taken eight hours to fly from Washington into Frankfurt Airport, where they'd picked up their connecting flight. There had been a lot of waiting around at odd hours and a time difference which meant that Evie was beginning to lose her grip on what day, never mind what hour it was. She was overtired and hungry for the wrong meal, and her bones felt like they'd solidified. She turned to Sebastian, about to share a grumble about the miseries of modern travel compared to the glory days – as she imagined them anyway – of the great ocean liners. She stopped before she got further than, 'How can anyone enjoy...' He was rigid in his seat, staring out of the window as if his gaze was a searchlight.

He's been on this journey for years.

Complaining about confusing breakfast with dinner and having a cramped neck suddenly seemed very petty. She rested her hand lightly on his arm instead and waited for him to come back to her. It took him a few moments.

'I've never seen Berlin from the air before. When I was a child, the city seemed huge, endless. Now it looks as if I could reach out and gather it up in my hands. Maybe it's the Wall, not just my age and the plane, that's distorted everything. I didn't expect the place to look so... sliced.'

Evie leaned round him to get a better view. It was an odd choice of words, but it was an accurate one. Evie had thought she knew everything there was to know about the Berlin Wall. It had been a symbol of communist repression throughout her youth. She'd seen it captured in a dozen photographs featuring sobbing and separated neighbours held back by blank-faced and gun-waving soldiers, whose actions were guided by Moscow. She'd always imagined the Wall itself as a clean cut bisecting the city. Instead it had slashed East Berlin from West in a series of jagged angles, as if it had been created by a bolt of forked lightning and not a military planner's pen. It was also rising up to meet them at an alarming speed.

'Oh wow, we're so close to it. It feels like we're about to land on the top.'

Evie hadn't been prepared for the Wall's random brutality. She also hadn't been prepared for what the reality of flying over Berlin at ten thousand feet – the height imposed by the German Democratic Republic who controlled the whole city's air space – rather than a standard approach at thirty thousand actually meant. Marty, and the pilot, had warned her that the drop to the city's regulated flying height would be sudden. That the landing would be low and fast and turbulent. They'd both been right. But what they'd failed to mention was that the experience was also incredibly thrilling. Evie craned as near as she could to the window as the city zoomed up through the clouds.

'Does anything scare you?'

Sebastian had stopped looking at Berlin. He was watching her with the smile that made her skin glow. A smile that had been absent for most of the journey.

'Letting people in and then paying too high a price for it.'

The answer came out of her mouth before she had time to

consider it. Given that her hand was still on his arm and how intently he was now staring at her, it also felt far too pointed. Evie was suddenly glad that she wasn't a woman who easily blushed. And she was equally glad that he managed a smile when she blamed her too personal answer on the plane's too rapid descent.

This is your job; he is your colleague. You need to get a grip.

Up in the air and sitting so close, and in pursuit of a quest that blurred lines, it wasn't quite so easy to remember that.

It had taken four weeks from the time the OSI had agreed to take on Sebastian's case to arrange diplomatic visas for entry into the GDR, which was a fraction of the time it would have taken to organise civilian ones. She and Sebastian hadn't been strangers during the waiting. They'd met a couple of times for coffee, once more for dinner and once for a debrief about the trip's etiquette in Marty's office. The reason given was always the case, and that was always the main topic of conversation, but they'd also begun to stray into less definable areas.

Although we're still dancing around each other and not entirely sure of the boundaries. As I've just proved.

Evie sat firmly back in her seat and locked her hands in her lap the second that realisation hit her. There was a closeness growing between them, but there was a distance too. Sebastian was holding himself back; so was she. Part of that was deliberate, on her side at least. Evie was trying very hard to focus on the task at hand and to set out clear expectations for their fact-finding mission to Berlin where, despite the D stamped on his visa, Sebastian would have no official status. Proving to Marty that nothing personal would muddy the waters of what was potentially a diplomatically delicate trip mattered.

This was the first OSI departmental visit to the American Embassy in East Berlin. It put them all on show, and Marty – or someone at the same level if not higher – should have been running it. Unlike the embassy in the west of the city, whose origins went back to the late eighteenth century, the office in the east had only been running for five years, its set-up impossible until America finally extended diplomatic recognition to the GDR in the mid 1970s. As Marty had explained, the team based there were still in the early stages of building trust and forging relationships. More importantly, they were still learning how to operate effectively under the eagle eye of the Stasi – the GDR's secret police, whose notorious reputation for all-seeing surveillance and control was a worrying one.

'But, Stasi or not, you'll still likely get more mileage out of a meeting in East Berlin than you would if you tried to go over the road here to speak to the CIA. Or, God forbid, if you tried to gate-crash your way into the FBI's hideaway at Langley.'

Marty had met with both the CIA and the FBI to discuss his concerns over the implications of Operation Paperclip and the ripples potentially spreading out from the Lebensborn programme. Both organisations had treated him as if he was making up fairy tales. Their blank refusal to accept that the OSI might be working on the same side as they were – and could make a valuable contribution to American homeland security – had snapped his normally steady temper. And wiped away any doubts he'd harboured about financing the Berlin trip.

Authorising Evie rather than himself to lead it – and allowing a civilian with close personal ties to the investigation to accompany her – was a huge show of trust. The connections she established there could be vitally important to the OSI. The evidence she hoped to uncover regarding Nazis who had rinsed their backgrounds clean enough to earn American citizenship – whether they were scientists or the doctors whose twisted experiments had apparently been forgotten because of the medical knowledge they'd gained – could be invaluable to a number of investigations. Evie was therefore very conscious of her professional position, and she knew Sebastian was conscious of it too. That accounted for a lot of her reticence, but as for the rest...

He would have kissed me by now if I'd given him the slightest encouragement – I can sense it. And I don't think I'd have pushed him away if he'd tried.

She glanced at him again. He was staring out of the window and she couldn't see his expression. But as the plane began to rush towards the runway, his hand suddenly settled over hers. The contact was unexpected, but it felt comforting and natural.

Because we keep doing it, as if to test out the waters.

They'd fallen into a pattern of kissing hello and goodbye in a most un-American way. Of touching an arm or a hand when 'Look at that' or 'It'll be fine' would have easily done the job. And they'd started to slowly unfurl their lives.

Sebastian had shared the bones of his marriage with Evie; Evie had shared the bones of hers with him. He'd described Lainey as generous and kind; she'd said the same about Ethan. They'd set out their mutual failings – their tendency to withdraw from conflicted situations; their attraction to the pull of a close loving family which had made the pull of their partner stronger than it perhaps really was. They'd admitted the sadness that those failings had caused to good people. The life story Sebastian had laid bare in her office in December had acted as a bridge. It had carried them into the kind of deep friendship which Evie had always thought took years not weeks to build. That was special and precious. But she was no longer certain that friendship was enough.

What if I want more? What if he does too? Would either of us have the courage to say it? To act?

Evie didn't know the answer to that, but she felt his hand on her elbow as they stepped off the plane, and she didn't shake it away. She let it stay there as they made their way through the crowds in Tegel Airport. Not because she was letting him take charge, but as if it made more sense to stay in contact, to acknowledge that they were on this quest together, than to stand apart.

Evie could hear German around her in the babble of voices, and English and French but no American accents except theirs. The air was bitterly cold, but the January sky was a crisper blue than the one Washington currently shivered under.

We could be as different with each other here as this city is to home, if we chose to be.

They'd come to Berlin burdened by old shadows. But they were also about to leave the West and enter a country where neither of them had been before, a country that was finding new ways of living. Evie leaned into Sebastian's side; when she glanced up, he was smiling.

We could rewrite the script here if we wanted; we could be new.

The past was what had brought them to Berlin, the past needed solving and putting to rest. But maybe there was a future here too.

'Well we're certainly not in Kansas anymore, Toto. Can you imagine the raised eyebrows back home in the office if they could see this display? It's a shame we're not allowed to take photographs.'

Evie's tone was deliberately light. And a long way from how she actually felt.

West Berlin had been a blink-and-miss-it experience. A diplomatic car had taken them on the twenty-minute drive from the airport to the border crossing point at Bornholmer Straβe. And that drive had taken them out of their reference frames and their comfort zones. The West's busy sidewalks had vanished into a graffitied No Man's Land as they turned into the streets the Wall had bisected. Along with any attempt at conversation beyond Evie's slightly strangled, 'Do you feel as small as I do right now?' as they drove alongside its length. And Sebastian's equally shocked, 'Yes, I don't see how you'd ever get used to the height of it.' Even actions as familiar after their long journey as a passport check seemed suddenly alien.

The checkpoint where their first driver dropped them to wait for their second was a silent place, shrouded in shutters and clipped voices. The GDR border guards checking and re-checking their paperwork addressed them in German and couldn't or wouldn't switch into English, despite Evie's apologetic inability to engage with the language and Sebastian's butchered attempts to try. That two of the soldiers who kept coming and staring at them started speaking Russian to each other, plus the fact that the drab waiting room was decorated with stern-faced portraits of Lenin and Marx, only added to the sense that they were very far from home. For Evie, whose childhood had been coloured by the warning to be on the alert for reds hiding under the bed, it was an eye-opening situation, even if she was long past listening to such nonsense. But its strangeness didn't make her flinch the way Sebastian flinched.

'It's the Russian. Hearing the soldiers speak it. That language was everywhere at the end of the war, and nothing good ever came with it. I'd forgotten about that. I've clearly forgotten a great deal. I think there may be more demons waiting here than I anticipated.'

A flurry of activity at the door stopped Evie from replying.

'Evie? Sebastian? You've arrived in one piece – well that's an excellent start. Welcome to the GDR. I'm Todd from the East Berlin Embassy. The car's waiting outside – shall we get to it?'

Their host's appearance, and his energy, not only woke up the room, it lightened the atmosphere. Their papers reappeared fully stamped. They were wished a pleasant stay in perfectly clear English. Todd nodded and waved and barrelled past the soldiers as if their guns were invisible, which made Sebastian's shoulders relax. They were inside a second diplomatic car – which was black like the other one but felt as solid as a tank – within five minutes of Todd's arrival. And all without him apparently drawing breath.

He's keeping us moving; he's trying to distract us.

It was a good effort, but it didn't work. The eastern side of the Wall was nothing like the western version and no amount of chattering could hide that. It wasn't covered in graffiti; it was flanked instead by dog runs and guard towers and trip wires, and a second wall running in parallel to the first. And there was no doubt on this side about its purpose: this was a construction intended to keep the population of East Berlin in, not to keep western attackers out. The sense of being locked away from the world she felt safe in was so overwhelming, Evie had to force herself to concentrate on what Todd was saying. She still struggled to keep pace with him.

'Apologies for the first names and the informality. Acting as if we're all old friends tends to quicken up clearance through the checkpoint for some reason, probably because the East Germans never know quite what to do with Americans. They assume that we're all spies, but they need the validation our embassy brings with it, so they have to treat us politely. And they like to do everything in obsessive detail to prove how in control they are. Which I like to counter by ignoring the red tape and going at full speed while I do it.'

He noticed Sebastian reaching to wind the window down and pressed a button that overrode the back seats' controls without missing a beat.

'Sometimes that approach works and sometimes it doesn't, which is when the apparatus clamps down – it's a balancing act like everything in the GDR. You'll get the hang of how the place works and you'll be fine here, as long as you remember the cardinal rule and trust no one.'

Being dropped into a city which people couldn't easily get

out of had already unnerved Evie so much, she immediately kicked back. 'Trust no one? Isn't that a little dramatic?'

Todd reacted to Evie's raised eyebrows with a frown that reminded her of a disappointed school teacher. 'No, it's not.'

He turned round properly so they could both see his face. He wasn't smiling anymore.

'The GDR is a fascinating place, but it's also a dictatorship and that makes it very different to anywhere you're used to. I know you're here to find answers, but there's ways things have to be done. And the most important one, the one where trust nobody comes in, is that you can't go off-plan and start talking to people outside the embassy unless I authorise it first. You could put them in danger that way, never mind yourself.'

He shook his head as Evie's frown deepened. 'Nobody ever likes that bit. Everyone always thinks I'm exaggerating. I'm not. You saw the fortifications we drove through. They should tell you that the GDR runs to its own rules, rules that the Stasi are here to police. And I'm sure you've been briefed about that lot, but what you won't and can't appreciate, because you don't live here, is how embedded and invisible their operatives are. I bet you don't know, for example, about their informants, the ordinary citizens who work for them? About the vast numbers of people that network involves?'

Evie – who was feeling thoroughly chastened by what definitely felt like a telling-off – had to admit that she probably didn't.

Todd didn't appear to be surprised. 'You should, because they're more of a problem than the official employees. The informants are the ones who do all the real looking and listening, and their number runs into tens if not hundreds of thousands. And I'm not exaggerating when I say they are everywhere, not that you'd be able to spot them. Take the embassy, for example. The German staff we employ there as secretaries and cleaners are chosen to work for us at application stage by the Stasi. We know that, they know that we know that and, despite all the misinformation we feed our supposedly loyal employees, the good stuff still gets through, and we can never sufficiently stop up the leaks.'

He paused and nodded this time when Evie made no attempt to contradict him. 'Nothing is out of the Stasi's reach and – although our diplomatic credentials give us some immunity – that includes us. Be on your guard. Assume you are being watched, assume your hotel room is bugged. And don't give them any reason to pull you in for questioning.'

'Would they do that?'

This time it was Sebastian who asked.

Todd shrugged. 'It's possible, and you would be the likely target if they did want to go digging around into the reason for your visit here. You're German by birth and you're not a diplomat, so they'd have less hesitation about pulling visas or blocking our investigations, especially if they know about the question marks over your family. The old guard here were Nazi hunters themselves back in the day and they cling hard to old hatreds. That might work in your favour, or it might not. Like I said, everything here is a balance.'

It was hardly a reassuring response, but neither Sebastian nor Evie had time to question it. The car was slowing down, pulling up outside a long row of featureless buildings whose peeling and pock-marked facades had seen better days. As soon as it stopped, Todd got out, making a discreet sweep of the street as he did so before he waved at the two of them to follow. They did so far more warily than they would have done without his warnings.

'This is the Edel Hotel. It's one of Berlin's oldest and – although it's lost its gloss badly nowadays – it apparently used to be one of the loveliest in the city.'

Evie hadn't noticed the entrance to the hotel until she was standing directly outside it. The Edel sat neatly in the centre of its taller neighbours, the curve of its arched doorway and windows separating the two nearest buildings out as if they were wings. The short flight of steps up to its recessed entrance gave the place the appearance of a secret hideaway.

Todd was still talking and moving at what seemed to be his usual fast pace. Ushering them on, keeping up a stream of conversation that Evie suspected was intended to stop them from lingering.

'It was also the first hotel here where every bedroom had an en-suite bathroom and an interlinked telephone system. Which is probably why the Stasi have approved it for westerners to use. I imagine it's been very easy to bug.'

They followed him up to the wooden and glass-panelled door, their noses wrinkling at a sour smell in the air which Todd blamed on the cheap brown coal used to heat East Berlin's buildings. It was clear he was a man who missed nothing, not even the smallest change in expression. Evie chose to be reassured by that.

The foyer he led them into was built on a grander scale than the modest entrance suggested it would be. It was also chilly and soulless and decorated in a drab assortment of shades that barely shifted their palette beyond beige and dark brown. The sour smell that had pricked at Evie's eyes outside was replaced here by a sharp chemical scent that reminded her of hospital corridors and was equally unpleasant. Elegance was the last word she would have pinned to the hotel and yet...

When Evie stopped grimacing and properly looked, there were faint traces of past glories still visible. A sweeping double staircase. A run of brocaded wallpaper in a side hallway which had managed to escape burial under the cheap panelling which was the lobby's main feature. A flash of black-and-white tiles in a corner where the linoleum was peeling. A line of elegantly arched windows patterned with pink and green lozenges.

Branching light fittings in the walls and the ceilings which had no doubt once dripped with crystals.

It's been stripped of its dignity, its memories discarded. Turned into an old lady who nobody wants.

She turned to Sebastian, wondering if he felt the same sense of sadness for lost days which had suddenly gripped her. But Sebastian was staring at something she couldn't see and had turned as rigid as he had when he saw the Wall from the plane.

'What's the matter? Do you remember the hotel? Have you been here before?'

Once again it took him a moment or two to reply and, even then, his answer was as hesitant as if he was diving deep into his past and wasn't sure of the way.

'Not the Edel, no. I don't think I've ever been inside it. But the area itself seems familiar, especially that last much wider street we drove down. It's changed a lot, and I wasn't much older than seven when I left – the images are coming back so fragmented, I'm not certain of anything. But I have an idea that this whole sector of the city, never mind just the hotel, was once far grander. That it wasn't in its current half-derelict state.' He paused, still searching. 'And a dim memory of standing at the foot of a giant flight of steps, looking up at huge columns – of being dwarfed by them – that's so strong it must have come from somewhere besides my imagination.'

'Perhaps that's because the wide street you're referring to is Wilhelmstraße. Once upon a time, before it was bombed to pieces in the war and then mostly demolished in the 1950s, every building lining that street was an imperial palace, built in the exact grand pillared style you described. People who remember it say it was spectacular.'

Todd had returned from the reception desk and was now hovering as if he wanted to whisk them back out to the car again. For the first time since he'd begun talking, he dropped his voice.

'Under Hitler, all the major ministries which formed the Third Reich's governing machinery were situated along Wilhelmstraβe in those palaces – including the Reich Chancellery which housed his bunker. There's only one of them left standing now, but, from the pictures I've seen, the street was an imposing sight, all columns and gigantic flags. Perhaps that's what you're remembering. Perhaps you visited one of those offices as a small child with your father.'

He stopped as Sebastian turned white.

'I'm so sorry. That was clumsy, and it sounded like I was being judgemental, which I promise you I wasn't.'

He battled on as Sebastian and Evie stared at him, both at a loss as to what to say, although Evie knew that Sebastian had heard the allusion to his father's workplace as clearly as she had and must be brimming over with questions. For the first time since he'd whirled into the checkpoint, Todd no longer sounded as if he was delivering a lecture when he continued.

'Look, your rooms are ready but – trust me – you won't want to spend any more time in them than you have to. Never mind the listening devices, the standard of comfort they offer is a basic one compared to what you're used to.' He glanced at his watch and appeared to make a decision. 'Obviously, we could go straight to the office. My team has pulled together what information they could about your father and your birth mother, and it's all there waiting for you to review. But I wondered – if your jetlag is manageable and you're not too exhausted – if you would rather go about this in a more personal way than digging through folders.'

Todd paused and looked at Sebastian, waiting until Sebastian pulled himself together and said, 'Go on,' before he continued.

'Okay then. It's still early; we've got time. So I wondered if you might want to drive out to Klosterheide. To the Lebensborn home where we think it's very likely you were born.'

CHAPTER 9

KURMARK LEBENSBORN HOME, JANUARY
1980

'Having your father's German name was a major help in trying to track down the possible candidates who could be your mother. I'll show you the paper trail when we're back in the office – and it isn't perfect by any means; the records are very patchy – but we think she was a girl called Annaliese Stengel. Annaliese was your father's secretary from the middle of 1940, and her name appears on the admissions list for the Kurmark home in April 1941, which would tie in with your September birth date. I'm not saying it's definitively her, but I think it's a very high probability.'

Silence settled on the car as Todd stopped talking and the driver pulled out of the parking space in front of the Edel. Sebastian's face was unreadable, but his fingers wrapped around Evie's when she stretched out her hand towards his. She held on as he took a deep breath and briefly closed his eyes.

'How old was my... was Annaliese when she had me, do you know?'

'Young. Around twenty, we think.'

Evie watched Sebastian absorb Todd's information and

hoped he could focus on *secretary* and *young* and the lack of choices those words might contain. It wasn't the time to ask, and it wasn't her place to direct him.

'And what about my father – what information do you have about him? You implied earlier that he was a Nazi and you clearly know where he was working if you have his secretary's details.' Sebastian paused and then he rallied himself. 'What did he do? How bad is it?'

Todd – who was sitting in the front passenger seat – answered Sebastian's question without turning round, in the same way he'd answered the first one. His posture could have suggested indifference, but Evie guessed – from the intent way Todd was watching Sebastian through the rear-view mirror – that the privacy afforded by his turned-away gaze was intended as a deliberate kindness. Nothing he had to say was going to be easy to hear.

'Probably not as bad as you are imagining. He was an early Party member, there's no doubt about that or that he was in the SS, so we can assume he was a committed supporter. But there's no record of him at a camp. And there's no trace of war crimes attached to his name.'

Todd paused briefly to let that sink in.

'He appears to have been an excellent soldier – he made his military reputation, which was apparently a glowing one, during the invasion of Poland. He was promoted to Hauptsturmführer after that and seconded to the OKW, the Upper Command of the Armed Forces, where he seems to have been an advisor on the invasion of France. We think that's when he met Annaliese.'

A Nazi then which was bad but a soldier, not the brute stalking round Dachau and stoking the ovens the way he's been imagining.

Evie glanced across at Sebastian, hoping he'd been able to

draw some comfort from that. It was impossible to tell. His eyes were tightly closed this time, and he was clearly in no mood to talk.

They continued the journey out of Berlin in a renewed silence that was a long way from comfortable. Sebastian had retreated into a private world. Evie – who longed to help him navigate that but had too much compassion to intrude in the public space of a car – had to content herself with staring out of the window.

The view did nothing to lighten her mood. East Berlin was a sickly-looking place. The newer buildings were a uniformly washed-out grey. The older ones were chipped and flaking, held together by spindly webs of brittle vines and as crumbling as dry cake. There were no brightly lit advertising boards or busy window displays to divert her. The one hoarding she could see was a grim invitation to 'Travel with the Soviet Railway System' which did not look enticing. There were queues at every street corner but nothing in the shops to merit a second glance.

She was weary of the city long before they left its last concrete-box suburb, and tempted to give in to the jetlag pounding at her temples and close her eyes too. Except that Todd was too visibly alert. He wasn't watching Sebastian anymore, but he was still staring as intently through the rear mirror.

'What are you looking at? Your eyes have been on stalks since we left the Edel.'

Todd started to say *nothing*, until Evie told him not to.

'I'm checking that our tail is a routine tail and nothing more to worry about.'

Evie instantly turned round: nothing in the word *tail* sounded like nothing to worry about. Sebastian opened his eyes and turned with her. There was a car directly behind theirs. It was keeping pace and following the same route as they were, but it was a perfectly ordinary black Opel Kapitän, a twin to the one they were sitting in, except for the lack of diplomatic plates. Evie started to say as much, but Todd shook his head.

'It's not ordinary, which I assume is what you were about to say. Ordinary here is a Trabant. Everyone – including the police – drives a Trabi here; it's the only kind of car you can get if you earn a normal wage. If it's a more expensive model like an Opel and it's not one of ours, then it's the Stasi. And they want us to know that they're here.'

He shook his head again as Evie asked, in a smaller voice than she intended to, if that meant they were in danger.

'You can never be sure, but I don't think so. They have run diplomatic vehicles off the road before if they suspect a spying mission, but it's still light and there's other cars about, and those aren't their preferred conditions for an ambush. I imagine this is a "we've got our eyes on you so don't get clever" kind of situation. And if for some reason it's not...' He shrugged. 'Well this car's reinforced and bulletproof – that's why it's so heavy.'

There wasn't any kind of conversation to be had after that.

'This is it. This is Kurmark, the Lebensborn home which was closest to Berlin.'

Closest didn't seem like quite the right word. Berlin was an hour's drive and a world away from their stopping point. The village of Klosterheide where the home was located was set among forests and farms, within reach of a large sleepy lake. It was the kind of place which barely changed from one century to the next.

And it is far too peaceful to be the place where Nazis came to populate the future.

Evie climbed out of the car after Sebastian as the black Opel which had followed them the whole way accelerated and sped past. He didn't appear to see it go. He was standing in front of a pair of heavy iron gates, tracing their pattern with his fingertips, and scanning the large house which commanded the sweeping driveway on the other side.

'It's elegant. I didn't expect that. In my mind, the place was square and dark and more like a prison.'

His words were an echo of Evie's thoughts. She stared through the black ironwork at the arched wings flanking the building's main entrance, taking in the ochre walls and the green cupola floating on delicate pillars which crowned the top of the red tiled roof. The house was dilapidated – the plasterwork needed repair, and cracks ran like frost across many of the upstairs windows – but it had retained far more of its beauty than the Edel had managed. There was still an air of comfort about it, a suggestion that the girls who'd come to it would have found care inside its walls, not judgement or blame. Evie tried to say as much, hoping Sebastian would find some peace in the house's grandeur. Her words bounced off him.

'Maybe they did; what does it matter? It's all a deception. Look.'

Sebastian was pointing at the gates, his fingers curled into a fist. Evie followed his finger and stopped believing in warm firesides and laughing babies.

'Their symbols are still here, marking their territory.'

Evie stepped closer. The iron was twisted into a pattern that mixed oak leaves with repeated SS flashes and spiky runic symbols, including what looked like an angular three-branched tree. All thoughts of comfort and care disappeared.

'There were swastikas originally set into them as well. The Russians had those removed in '45 when they turned the house into a hospital for their wounded.'

Todd was beside them, pushing the gate open, beckoning them through.

'They should have torn the whole monstrosity down, never mind ripped out a few emblems.'

Sebastian kicked the gate shut behind them with a clang and started furiously down the drive. He only stopped because Todd yelled at him to wait and calm down.

'Maybe they should, but, by that token – that anywhere linked to the Nazis doesn't deserve to stand – there wouldn't be a building left. Germany didn't have the same war as America, which sounds obvious, but it's easy to forget. Most of the cities were bombed beyond recognition; the whole country was broken. The Russians, like everyone else, needed somewhere safe to shelter and tend to their injured. You can't blame them for that.'

Sebastian was still growling about some places being too tainted to save, but Todd refused to listen.

'That's all very noble, but it's not how things worked. People were homeless and hungry and desperate. They didn't care what a place had been used for as long as it had a roof and solid walls. And they wanted to forget – and quickly.' He gestured to the houses nestled in a dip behind them. 'If you were to ask the older residents in that village now what happened in this house during the war, they'd most likely say it was a sanitorium for sick children then, whether they believe that was true or not. Memories are short; people do what they can.'

They'd reached the front door, but he waited for a moment before he rang the bell.

'And yes, I'm very aware that I've been delivering a lecture again. But – as hard as coming to this place might be for you – we're here as guests of the clinic's director, and we won't be here long if you go crashing in flinging blame and disgust around. I told you: they pride themselves in the East as being far more anti-Nazi than the West ever was, so let's go along with that. Or' – Todd paused and his tone softened – 'we don't have to go in at all. If you've changed your mind, that's okay. That's understandable.'

'I'm fine. I won't ruffle any feathers. I want to see where I started.'

Sebastian was pale, but he'd regained control of himself. Todd nodded and stayed silent this time until the door opened. There was paperwork to check, which came as no surprise. There was tea and a history of the house up to 1939 which neither Evie nor Sebastian listened to. Half an hour of bitten lips passed by until finally the director – whose English was fluent and clearly, or to his liking, under-used – pulled an envelope out of a drawer and pushed it across his desk.

'These came to light during some recent restoration work. I kept them, rather than passing them straight on the way we did with the patient records because more people like you, Herr Taylor, are turning to us for answers, and I believe we have a duty to help.' He coughed and glanced round as if other ears than theirs might be listening. 'I am considering mounting an exhibition, or perhaps a memorial; a place to come and remember. If that is permitted of course. I'm not sure what shape it will take, but if you ever wish to have a say in how Kurmark's part in the war is told here, I would be happy to hear your thoughts.'

He got up and moved to the window, where Todd joined him. Evie stayed where she was while Sebastian took a deep breath and tipped out the envelope's contents.

The first thing to appear was a set of photographs. Black-and-white shots of the home and its staff and routines. A line of prams covered in flower-sprigged material and lace-trimmed hoods, sitting in a garden under the shadow of a swastika flag. A group of white-capped nurses holding bottles and fat bundles. Toddlers playing with buckets of water in the sunshine. There was also one picture of an SS officer standing beside a portrait of Hitler and a large vase of flowers, but his back was turned to the camera and it wasn't clear what he was doing. There were no photographs of the mothers. Sebastian turned each picture over without comment before passing them to Evie. Apart from the flag and the uniforms, the scenes were so normal there was nothing to say.

After those, there was a document which Evie recognised but Sebastian didn't. When she explained that it was a racial testing chart, listing the physical characteristics against which children were graded as Aryan or other, he shoved it away. It was the last item – a brochure with the same three-branched tree on its cover as they'd seen on the gates – which made them both gasp and brought the director back over.

'Ah yes, finding that was quite a surprise. That tree-like thing on the front is the runic symbol for the Lebensborn programme. It appears to be a publicity brochure, encouraging pregnant women of the right type to come to one of the Lebensborn homes to give birth. It explains the programme and lists many of the houses, and countries, which were involved. It's rare to discover a document as damning as this and in such a well-preserved condition – the Nazis were usually very efficient about removing any kind of evidence.'

He stopped and gathered himself as Sebastian drew a sharp breath.

'There were also some letters with it, but they were too blurred from water damage to read. This was pushed further inside the brickwork where the rain didn't reach it. Take your time with it, Herr Taylor. Perhaps it might fill in some of the blanks in your mother's background, given that she was accepted as a suitable candidate. Obviously I can't let you take it, but please photograph anything that you want.'

He moved away again. Evie pulled out the slim Kodak pocket camera which lived in her handbag as Sebastian slowly turned over the pages and read their descriptions aloud.

Who will be Accepted, a Profile of Suitable Candidates.

Questionnaire (Child's Mother)

Questionnaire (Child's Father)

Proof of Aryan Descent

Proof of Genetic Health

There were thirty-three headings which, when taken as a whole, provided a picture of the ideal maternal candidate and the experience she could expect if she chose to give birth in a Lebensborn home. Evie captured a record of each key category. And of the document's final rallying call, a message written by Himmler himself.

All our struggle, the political fight of the last fifteen years, the build-up of the Wehrmacht for the protection of our borders, would be in vain if the victory of the German spirit is not followed by the victory of the German child.

'And there it is, the proof of what we were intended to be.' Sebastian pushed the brochure back into the envelope with the photographs. '*The victory of the German child*: in other words, there'd be more of us than our enemies would ever be allowed to have. We were an army, dedicated to victory. This was our first barracks.'

He got up, brushing away Evie's 'Are you all right?' with a nod which belied his twisted lip.

'Can I see it? The nursery where I was born? The garden where I lay in my pram?'

'Of course – or what remains of them anyway.'

The director tidied the envelope away and led his visitors out of the office and along a wood-panelled corridor.

'From what I can establish, the house was divided into two

parts. One wing was for the pregnant women; the other was for the mothers and babies and the older children who stayed here, presumably while they were waiting to be allocated to suitable families. That also seems to have been part of the programme's remit here, although we don't know how many babies stayed with their mothers and how many didn't, or what the criteria for that decision might have been. The rooms have been gutted, but, according to the plan and the notes left by the Soviet commander whose troops discovered the building, this room was a nursery.'

He opened a heavy door and led them into a long narrow room whose high windows were still covered by wooden shutters.

'According to his testimony, thirty infants could be accommodated in here, in two rows of fifteen cots facing each other. That doorway in the corner leads to another set on the floor above which were once bedrooms. And this one, as I'll show you, runs out into the garden.'

They followed him outside. The sky had turned leaden, the air was sharp with the promise of snow. Evie shivered and realised that Sebastian was shuddering too. She placed her hand on his elbow and breathed a little easier when he steadied.

'It's the spot in the photograph where the prams were lined up. Look.' He pointed to a piece of wood sticking out from under the low roof. 'That's where the flag was fixed, the swastika that hung over our prams. We must have been positioned so that we could look up at it.'

He moved away from her and began to pace, sweeping his fingers across the leafless bushes, trailing them over the benches set against the wall.

'I must have been here; maybe my mother sat here with me. I want to feel something; I've been aching to feel her with me for years. There's nothing.' He stopped, his hands still outstretched as if he was groping for a pram – or a person. 'What's that? What's that statue over there?'

The director followed his gaze and coughed. 'Something we don't know what to do with if I'm honest. Something that feels like a parody of everything that happened here.'

Evie stepped forward so that she could get a better look. The statue Sebastian was pointing at was a carefully carved depiction of a mother breast-feeding her baby. It had been skilfully done – the mother looking down and the baby looking up from the cradle of her arms completed a perfectly linked circle. It was beautiful. And, in this place, it was obscene.

My child went missing... please will somebody help find him.

Sebastian's hand was suddenly in hers. And when he spoke, she knew their thoughts once again were running in parallel.

'For every baby born here, there was a mirror image in the world outside. A child who wasn't Aryan, who wasn't the ideal. Whose life was taken to make room for ours.'

Nobody spoke. It was the truth. There wasn't any comfort to offer.

Sebastian pulled himself away from Evie and from the statue and turned to the director. His body was stiff, as if it required a conscious effort to hold himself in place.

'What happened when the war was lost? What happened to the children who were still here then?'

They waited, the three of them, Todd included, staring at the director. Evie knew what they were all hoping to hear. A simple, 'There were none left to worry about.' Or, 'They were taken to safety and well cared for.' The director didn't offer either of those possibilities. He looked away across the winter-bleak garden instead.

'We don't know. I'd like to tell you that they were found homes, that the locals stepped in and offered help and shelter. But there were bodies found here by the Soviets in one of the rooms, mostly small ones. They're buried now in unmarked graves. We would like to remember them too.'

Evie blinked as 1980 flickered away into a collage of frightened faces. As the wind filled up with sobs. As Sebastian gasped. When she lifted her eyes to find his, his hard-won control had finally shattered. His face was haggard and he, like she, was silently weeping.

CHAPTER 10

EAST BERLIN, JANUARY 1980

They'd returned to the Edel late in the evening and gone their separate ways. That decision had not been a certainty. There had been a moment in the lobby when they'd both wavered. When Sebastian almost said, 'I don't want to be alone, but I have to be.' When Evie almost said, 'I can stay with you as long as you need me to stay.' Both of them had hovered, unsure how to say goodnight, unsure if they wanted to. They'd both said it anyway.

Evie was glad of the pause. Part of her had wanted to follow her heart not her head and go to his room. But her head knew that the intimacy of talking could have too easily led to the intimacy of his bed, and neither of them was ready for that.

Some barrier had been crossed between them, but Evie didn't yet know what it was. Sebastian had clung to her hand in the car on the way back from Klosterheide like a drowning man. She'd clung to his in the same exhausted way, her head ringing with the cries of all the children whose lives had been ruined or lost. She could see from the hollows pitting his face that his head was as crowded with grief as hers. Finding solace in each other's arms would have been an understandable impulse after that; it would have been one way to hide from the sadness.

But we would both have regretted it. It would have been an impulse born from a place of pain, and I don't think either of us really wants that.

Evie hadn't let herself think about what she might actually want. She'd crawled beneath her thin quilt expecting sleep to run from her; instead, jetlag had felled her within seconds. She'd got up resolving to pretend that neither of them had even got near to a line and gone down to breakfast expecting to find Sebastian still haunted and holding himself separate.

He wasn't. He was waiting for her with a pot of coffee that the young waitress promised was the genuine article and not the GDR's dreadful pea flour and chicory substitute. And a plate heaped with crisp golden slices that the girl told Evie was a local speciality called *arme ritter* and turned out to be the most delicious French toast. And he was waiting for her with a smile.

'If all the Stasi's informants are as cheerful as she is, I don't think I'll have much of a problem being spied on. And if the rest of the food is half as good as this, I'm going to need wider waistbands. I've already eaten most of a plateful.'

Evie copied him, piling plum jam onto her toast and taking a huge mouthful.

'You do look better this morning. You look far less strained.'

Sebastian took another bite and gave a sigh of pleasure which made Evie laugh.

'That's because I am. Yesterday was a shock in so many ways, but it was also a wonderful day. I have a mother, Evie.' He shook his head in obvious delight as he said it. 'I have a name for her. That got past me somehow while we were at the home. I have a mother, and that feels like the start of something, which is a miracle after so many dead ends. And, yes, my father wasn't the man my memories want him to be, but he also wasn't the monster who'd taken up residence in my head. This morning it feels like there are reasons to be grateful, and I'm going to hold tight to those.'

We remember all too well what a burden it was... We certainly don't need reminders.

Her mother's spiteful words came crashing in from nowhere. Evie put the toast down.

'What is it? Have I said something wrong?'

The concern flooding his face was instant and heart-warming. Evie knew that he would have listened to anything she was able to share. That didn't mean she wanted to bring her mother into the room. But his gaze was warm and his honesty deserved no less in return, so she took a deep breath and offered it.

'No, of course not. I'm so happy that you've started to find answers, that you can pull the good from the bad. I'm happy to see you so much brighter. That's exactly what I hoped would happen here.' She paused, then continued in a rush before she changed her mind. 'But it's just that my mother and I aren't close at all; we're quite the opposite. I don't know if she's ever loved me to be honest, although I've never admitted that to anyone before, and – like you – I once played at constructing a more perfect version of her. And just now, your face lit up at the possibility that you might finally find the mother you need and...' She stared down at her plate, suddenly embarrassed. 'This doesn't sound great, I know, given what it's cost you to get here and how many steps it could still take to find Annaliese, but for a moment there, I think I was jealous.'

'Which is okay, Evie, I promise.'

Evie looked up as his hand cupped hers, in a gesture that was more intimate than the previous night's wavering.

'The ideal family. Isn't that what we're all searching for? If we can't find it with our parents, we go looking for it with our partners. Trying to find enough love to fill up the holes where the love has gone missing.' His fingers laced through hers, anchoring them together. 'And I don't have a clue if this will work out for me, Evie. If Annaliese doesn't turn out to be the ideal I imagined, if I even find her at all, things might not go well. She gave me away after all; maybe she's never given me a second thought since. I can't control any of that. But I don't care if you're jealous. I understand it. You don't feel loved by your mother – that's hard, that's horrible. How can I blame you for wanting more, for wanting to find the same happiness that I'm searching for?'

The restaurant's chatter slipped away. Evie stopped worrying about the importance of maintaining their professional relationship at the expense of anything closer. She stopped worrying whether anyone was watching or listening or taking notes. Nothing mattered except the brown eyes fixed steadily on hers.

'Do you think anyone ever does? Find it, I mean. Do you think anyone who hasn't had the childhood they craved can ever feel completely whole?'

His smile was sunshine on a grey morning. Evie felt it warm through her body as his fingers held hers.

'I don't know, Evie. But it has to be worth the search, don't you think? It has to be worth having hope.'

Evie liked to think she was a practical woman. Her head wasn't easily turned. She didn't see glamour if there was no glamour to be seen. She was also very aware of East Berlin's shortcomings – the air tainted with brown coal and brick dust, the drab and too often decrepit buildings and the ever-present full-stop of the Wall. And yet, this morning, bathed in the glow of Sebastian's smile, in the knowledge that his quest was her quest too because he wanted her to share it...

The sky was blue and cloudless. The wind hadn't filled with sour smoke yet and whipped the freshness out of the streets. And their driver nodded when Evie asked if there was time to take them on a short tour before they had to be at the embassy.

He chose his whistle-stop route well. From the back of a warm car, the Brandenburg Gate was majestic. The Unter den Linden was as wide an avenue as any that Paris could provide, and the column-fronted buildings lining Museum Island could have stepped straight out of Ancient Greece. Even the Spree was sparkling. By the time the car completed its short loop and arrived at the American Embassy on Neustädtische Kirchstraße – which was an elegant fresco-adorned building and not the faceless concrete box Evie had expected it to be – she was quite prepared to find East Berlin a fascinating place. And she was ready to approach the files waiting in Todd's office in the same optimistic way that Sebastian had greeted the morning.

'It's not well organised, I'm afraid, or not yet. It's all a bit ad hoc. We've scoured our archives – which also aren't particularly impressive – and put out a call to some of the friendlier contacts we've made, including the historians at the Humboldt University for anything they hold on Lebensborn. And we had these, which is how we identified Annaliese.'

Todd pushed two slim folders across the table. One was headed *Kurmark Registration Forms*, the other *Ministry Staff*. Both covers were stamped with a bright red *Incomplete*.

'As I'm sure you're both aware, there's nobody we can call on as a Lebensborn expert. The reality behind what that programme did is a picture that we – and the academics – are only starting to piece together and I'd be lying if I said it's anywhere near done. We have better data on Kurmark than most other places because it's on our doorstep. But the information from there is as limited as everywhere else to the bits and pieces which the Nazis didn't destroy. There are no staff lists and no record of what happened to the children who were born or possibly kidnapped and taken there.'

He fell silent. It took them all a moment to move on from the echo of Kurmark's unmarked graves.

'And as for the trial, that was another toothless exercise.'

'What trial?'

Sebastian asked the question at the same time as Evie.

Todd went to his desk and located a single sheet of notes. 'The Race and Settlement one.'

He passed the paper to Evie when she shook her head at the name.

'I'm not sure how well researched that's been yet. It came under the Nuremberg umbrella, although the verdicts weren't delivered until 1948, and it was wide-ranging, which was probably part of the problem. The prosecutors lumped all the Reich's racial crimes in together, including Lebensborn, the kidnapping of children for Aryanisation and the extermination policies. And even then only fourteen defendants out of the thousands who were involved were actually arraigned.'

He nodded as Sebastian swore. 'I know, and it gets worse. Out of the few who were prosecuted, only one – Ulrich Greifelt, who was Himmler's deputy and Chief of Staff for the department responsible for what the Nazis called "The Consolidation of German Nationhood" – got a life sentence. Five of them were completely acquitted.'

This time it was Evie who cursed.

'I told you it got worse. Anyway, I've sent for the trial papers and supporting documents in case you're able to match up any names in them to the testimony you've collected in the States, but it's going to be a challenge. So many people have made new lives for themselves since then, it will likely be needles and haystacks.'

'And what about my mother? Is she a lost needle too?'

Sebastian had opened the Kurmark folder and located Annaliese's name. There were no details recorded beside it except the date of her admission, her age – which was too smudged to clearly make out – and the single word *approved*.

Todd – in what Evie had come to realise was his usual fashion – didn't waste time on platitudes.

'At the moment she is, yes.' He nodded to a pile of folders stacked as high on his desk as Evie's cases were. 'But she's on the top of my list; she's a priority. There's no trace of her so far after 1941, which could mean a lot of things, including – as you've no doubt already considered – that she didn't survive the war. But we're looking and we've spread the net wide. We're calling in emigration records up until the mid-fifties as a starting point, and we've considered the possibility that she changed her name, although we're really hoping she didn't.' He paused and his voice suddenly softened. 'I have people here who love solving puzzles. We'll do our best not to keep you waiting too long for some sort of an answer.'

Sebastian blinked and coughed and looked away. Evie mouthed her thanks to Todd, who immediately began bustling around and ordering up supplies of notebooks and coffee.

Once everyone was back to themselves again, Todd gestured to the collection of boxes laid out on the table.

'The three on the left are everything we've gathered together so far about Lebensborn and stolen children, including information on the homes and also any leads on the kidnapping issue. Letters are starting to come to us about that from America, and also from Norway and France and Poland. They're all the same desperate pleas that I'm sure you've seen, Evie – begging for help to plug holes in broken lives. They don't make easy reading, but I imagine you know that too.'

He stared at the boxes for a moment then shook himself back. 'We're setting up an archive and employing a dedicated researcher who will be a key point of contact going forward for you. Make notes and take photographs, but obviously don't take actual pieces away. And if you do want copies of anything, let me know and I'll compile a list to be sent on in the diplomatic pouch. The Stasi could very easily search your rooms, or your bags at the airport, and finding information on German citizens in them could really stretch our immunity. And if they don't try it, the— Anyway, them's the rules so don't go breaking 'em.'

He'd visibly pulled himself up short and then tried to cover his stumble with a flippancy that jarred. It didn't fool Evie for a second.

'And if the Stasi don't check, the CIA might. Either here, or when we change planes in Frankfurt. Don't worry, you haven't said anything I didn't expect. They've hardly been a model of co-operation so far.'

Todd pulled a face and waved his hand at the second stack of boxes. 'It's not missing or dead children that's the issue. The Agency's shown no interest in that, although I assume they know we've begun an investigation – they monitor what we do as diligently as the Stasi. It's Operation Paperclip that's got them jumping about. I made one call to our team in the West referencing that initiative after you mentioned it and it's apparently set off alarm bells.'

Sebastian had already started opening the first Lebensborn box. Evie was happy enough to leave those to him. He understood the parameters of the project as clearly as she did, and his curator's eye was more than capable of sifting through evidence, especially now that he wouldn't be distracted by, or searching for, personal information.

She pulled the second stack towards her. 'So I presume these are all relevant to Paperclip then?'

Todd nodded. 'Yes, and it's another partial and badly organised collection – I cannot wait for the day I don't have to apologise for that, although it may be longer coming with this lot. The Lebensborn programme was hidden, but Paperclip is completely shrouded in secrecy. Getting information on any aspect of it – in the East or the West – is like breaking into a vault. The Russians won't admit that the operation even existed. As far as they are concerned, there was never a talent race between them and us, and they've never had a Nazi scientist working for them. All their geniuses are born and bred Soviets.'

He managed a grim smile at Evie's '*Really?*'

'Oh yes, that's the line, but there's no point in arguing against it. What we have done, and what we're still doing, is to collect whatever we could find on the rocket programmes and the key players involved. Bear in mind though that a lot of it is guesswork and gossip – quite a few names vanish from one document to another, or the information about them is too redacted to make sense of.'

He left them then. Sebastian was completely engrossed, his notebook open, his pencil already flying across the first page. Evie began opening her boxes, lifting out sheaves of paper that, on first sight, looked completely unconnected. Incomplete and heavily redacted trial reports, Ministry staff lists, newspaper articles and photographs of rockets in various stages of production. She recognised the V2, although it looked far more threatening when primed and fixed to a launch platform than it had in the museum. The name Mittelbau-Dora came up on more than one document, along with what appeared to be a second key location at somewhere called Peenemünde. And there was a photograph of a pile of stick-thin bodies which made her stomach twist, and another of a group of liberated slave workers who looked barely more alive than the dead.

The records were, as Todd had said, full of gaps and out of order, but they began to gradually take on a shape and reveal links as she worked her way through them. And it was a relief to be back doing this kind of forensic analysis after the emotional turmoil of the previous day.

By the end of their second hour's collating, Evie had three piles of information organised into categories and one box left to go which felt like a very positive result. She stood up and stretched, wincing as her shoulders creaked in protest. Her *ouch* brought Sebastian's head up for the first time since they'd begun working.

'Breakfast is beginning to feel like an age ago. Shall I go and see if I can rustle up some suitably American snacks?'

His half of the table was as well organised as hers, and his notebook was neatly ruled into headings. Evie had to force herself not to grin at him in a completely unprofessional manner. An absorbed and methodical approach to research might not be the stuff of storybook heroes, but it worked wonders for her. As did the promise of snacks.

'That would be wonderful, thank you.'

His hand brushed against hers when he got up to leave. Evie sat down again, telling herself that her skin couldn't possibly be tingling and thrilled that it was.

She grabbed the box to bury a sudden rush of distracting thoughts and untucked the flaps. The first thing she drew out was a plan of a set of barracks and workshops that she now recognised as Mittelbau-Dora. Below that was a report from the mine's liberators which would require more detailed reading than she had time for now. And below that...

The world does not stand still. It does not stop. Neither do hearts unless they have reached their final beat. Breath cannot freeze or forget to come. Evie knew all that. And yet all of that happened.

VÖLKISCHER BEOBACHTER Berlin, Samstag, 20
Februar 1943

Evie spread the newspaper out. She carefully smoothed the cover. She ran a finger across the swastika displayed in the centre of the title banner. She turned to the pages whose numbers were listed under the photograph which dominated the front one and promised to continue the story. There they all were, history's monstrosities: Hitler, Goebbels, Himmler and Göring. Wearing flowers in their buttonholes, smiling like proud uncles at the happy couple at the centre of the shot.

Evie didn't react. She carried on moving in slow motion, refusing to let her eyes connect with her brain. The photographs inside the newspaper ran to three pages. There were posed ones at the service and on the steps of what the caption said was Berlin Cathedral. There were more natural pictures at the wedding reception, where the names of the guests were recorded, but she couldn't make out the location. Evie took in every detail of who was sitting next to who and who was raising a toast, then she turned once again to the front cover.

The photograph which had frozen her and frozen time was a flatteringly lit close-up studio portrait which took up half the page. The couple beaming out of it were perfectly matched. The groom was in uniform and dashingly handsome. The bride, wreathed in white roses and lace, was a beauty. They could have been film stars; they were clearly some kind of celebrity, at least in the eyes of the Nazi party grandees who were guests of honour at their wedding. Evie read the caption under the picture again, but the words kept sliding away from her.

Die Hochzeit von Helene Tellman und Ulrich Reitter, ein perfektes Paar

She had no idea what the German meant, except for the one word – *perfektes* – which was surely wrong. And she had no idea who those people had been in 1943, but she knew who they were now.

Not Helene Tellman and Ulrich Reitter. Not anymore.

Helen and Alex Ritter.

Her parents.

PART TWO

CHAPTER 11

BERLIN, FEBRUARY 1943

'I was so worried when you said you would be having a winter wedding. Finding the right dress to wear and any decent flowers at all in this cold weather is hard enough, and now we have to worry about rationing on top of everything else. I've been quite beside myself, and yet you don't seem to have struggled at all. Everything looks wonderful.'

Helene sat in the back of the car, wishing that her mother would give her a moment's peace to enjoy the ride. The woman's knack for stating the obvious was never-ending. She didn't reply – she had no intention of spoiling one minute of her day with another of the pointless conversations her mother excelled in. Of course everything was wonderful – it was her wedding, what else would it be? And why would she struggle to find the right dress or suitable flowers? What did rationing have to do with her?

Helene had tried to explain to her mother that the circles she moved in didn't concern themselves with restrictions and shortages. That had been too big a concept for Britta to grasp. Everything about Helene's life was too big for Britta to grasp. She lived hers according to the Party's dictate that women should be silent second-class citizens, and she wished – far too often – that her daughter would stop stepping out of her station, as she put it, and do the same. Not that it mattered to Helene what Britta thought or didn't understand about her life or her circle. Mother of the bride or not, Helene hadn't allowed her within a mile of the wedding planning. If Britta had been in charge, Helene would be dressed in a sensible suit and presiding over a reception whose highlight was an array of cold meats, not riding in a Daimler and dressed like a queen.

The Party's great and good had all stepped up to make Helene's day special, Minister Goebbels had made certain of that. The flowers in her bouquet – a fragrant fall of white roses and camelias dotted with edelweiss and tied with trailing silver ribbons – had come from the hothouses at Carinhall, Reichs-marschall Göring's beloved country estate. The tiara holding her veil – a circle of diamond-encrusted leaves set with emerald berries which was worth more than her parents' house – belonged to his wife Emmy. The bias-cut cream satin dress which clung to Helene's body like a second skin had come from the house of Hilda Romatzki, the designer who dressed Eva Braun. And the floor-length white fur cape which would keep her warm on the cathedral steps was a gift from Propaganda Minister Goebbels himself. The last person to wear it had been the screen icon, Laura Solari.

'Who doesn't possess a tenth of your elegance, my dear. The photographers will go into a frenzy.'

And that was precisely the point, and another concept that Britta would never have grasped. Helene's wedding wasn't simply a family occasion; it was hardly that at all. It was a public affair, and – like every other public affair in the Reich – it was a highly orchestrated one.

'This is about you and Ulrich, of course it is. It's your day and it's a love story, like any happy marriage should be. But it's also about us, about the new Germany and the new world we are building and every element of it must be carefully designed.'

Design was Goebbels' favourite word. Nothing about the Reich's public face – from the cut of its uniforms and the shape of its processions, to the statues it built and the fonts used on its proclamations – could ever be left to chance. The Propaganda Minister's attention to detail was legendary, and Helene was more than happy to have his forensic spotlight turned her way. She'd given him the running of everything, and everything had been perfectly done.

Himmler, not her mild-mannered and all too ordinary father, would be the one walking her down the aisle. Every moment of the day – from her first appearance at the cathedral to the last moments of the reception at the Edel Hotel – would be captured by a battalion of press photographers. Goebbels had organised the guest list and circulated it to every gossip-hungry journalist, with precise timings of when the Führer, and the bride, would arrive. And he'd whipped up so much interest in the wedding, and the golden couple at its centre, that the event was all anyone in Berlin was talking about. Apart from his latest speech.

'Because they are part of the same package, my dear. The war is dragging; Germany needs a push to get through the tougher times that are coming. I will, of course, do what I do best – I will make the hard truths palatable and provide the rallying cry – but you will provide the sweetener.'

His smile at that had been so predatory, Helene had wondered if there was a clumsy seduction attempt coming. Luckily he'd known better than to embarrass himself.

'You and Ulrich are more than just the loyal and hard-working faces of the Thousand Year Reich: you are its movie-screen version. The spectacle and the glamour. Helene Tellman and Ulrich Reitter, what a story you are – the beautiful young doctor helping our next generation of children to thrive and her handsome rocket-scientist husband, the hero working on the weapon that will bring us to victory. The ideal couple on their ideal wedding day.'

His smile had softened then, so Helene had returned it.

'And that will be far more thrilling than a bunch of politicians telling them that life is about to get a great deal worse before it gets better. People will listen to me, and they will take notice, of course they will. But they will see you, and that image will stay with them far longer.'

Helene had told Goebbels that his prediction was nonsense because he had expected her to. They both knew that he was right, that the timing of the ideal wedding day was deliberate.

Goebbels' speech at the packed Sportpalast, which he had delivered two days earlier, had been one of the most important he'd ever made. It had been impeccably choreographed and suitably dramatic. He had acknowledged to his packed audience – and the thousands more listening to him on their radios – that the German victory was coming slower than expected and that it would require hard sacrifices to secure it. He had called for a total war, a complete civil and military mobilisation of the country. He had railed against the two-pronged threat from 'Jewish evil' and 'Soviet devilry' which he insisted was the cause of Germany's temporary setback. He had promised his listeners a glorious future and roused the packed benches in the auditorium to a well-planned fever pitch.

It had been reported as a roaring, passionate and perfectly judged performance, in the same way all Goebbels' performances were reported. But Berlin's citizens were used to passionate speeches, and they were increasingly cynical of them. They were also starved of luxury. Which was why they'd been filing into the frost-tipped Lustgarten at the foot of the city's cathedral since long before Helene had sat down at her dressing table and let the beauticians begin their work.

'Oh my goodness, I didn't expect the wedding to be on such

a lavish scale. Why didn't you tell me it was at the cathedral? Why didn't you warn me there would be so many people here? I should have worn something grander than this plain coat. I'm going to let you down.'

The car had reached its destination and Britta was working herself into one of her states. Helene wanted to ignore her mother. She wanted to focus all her energies on being the star of the day. She could see cordons and policemen flanking the cathedral steps, and crowds already jockeying for a better position. She could hear the hum even through the car's closed windows. The excitement was everything that she, and Goebbels, had hoped it would be, but Britta's doughy face was a perfect circle of horror, and her breath was coming in short gasps. It was clear she was seconds away from refusing to get out of the Daimler, and Helene didn't have time to indulge that.

She clamped down on her irritation and patted her mother's gloved hand instead – in a gesture which clearly came as a surprise – then she tutted as if Britta was a silly child. 'Stop it now. You're nervous, that's all. I knew you would be – that's why I didn't tell you all the details beforehand. This is a big day for everyone, and you won't let me down. You look perfect.'

Britta looked very far from perfect, or at least in the way the anxious woman would have defined the word. The dark green wool coat which Helene had encouraged her to buy for the ceremony was cut too high in the neck and had turned her body square. Her low-heeled black shoes were heavy and prim. Her one good sapphire brooch could have been made of paste when compared to the diamonds crowning her daughter. But she was perfect for the part Goebbels had cast her in, the part Britta didn't know she was playing. The humble German *Hausfrau* whose pedigree ran solidly down through the decades. The stocky and loyal backbone of the Reich, happy to march behind her dazzling leaders wherever she was ordered to go. Britta was as much a part of the story Goebbels was telling as Helene and Ulrich.

He should have put her in a dirndl and a headscarf – that certainly would have been quite the vision.

The chauffeur was standing to attention beside the car door. Helene fluffed out her bouquet and arranged her veil so that the lace-trimmed tulle would cascade over her cape. She stepped elegantly out and was immediately rewarded by a loud gasp as the sunlight caught her tiara and turned the diamonds to flame.

'Don't speak to Himmler. And don't forget to stay in the car for a moment or two now like I told you to do, so you're well behind me on the walk up.'

Don't speak and *don't forget* didn't really need saying. Neither Himmler nor the rest of the VIP guests would notice her mother, who would be far too intimidated to address them, and the flight of steps was a steep one for a woman as roundly built as Britta. Helene would probably be inside the cathedral at Ulrich's side before her mother wheezed her way to the top. But *doesn't need saying* didn't exist in Helene's book, not when every element had to be done exactly right.

Take your time, take a breath. This is your day. They will wait for you.

Himmler had positioned himself on the second tier of steps, high enough above the crowd to make sure that he was seen. He was smiling down at Helene as widely as if he was about to marry her himself. As widely as he'd smiled at her in that first Polish schoolyard.

'If only I had a thousand of you to go forth and do my work, the East would be ripe and ready for planting before the year's done.'

Helene had refrained from pointing out to him then that one of her was all he needed. He'd learned the lesson quickly enough.

He can't remake Germany's future without me.

There was nobody to match her. Nobody questioned her authority in the Lebensborn homes. Nobody escaped her eye in the field. She had supervised the birth and placement of dozens of Aryan children; she had cleared dozens of Polish towns and villages. She had never once put a foot wrong. No one else could claim such an outstanding track record.

I deserve every last one of his smiles.

Helene moved slowly forward, holding her dress a fraction above the ground so that it appeared as if she was gliding. The crowds started to cheer. When she leaned forward to kiss Himmler's cheek, the cheers grew louder. And by the time she turned to face her well-wishers – framed inside the cathedral's vast vaulted doorway and oblivious to the panting woman scuttling below her – the voices were roaring loud enough to lift the roof clear off the Sportpalast.

'He couldn't have been a more perfect fit for you if I'd chosen him myself. Which I did think at one point I might have to.'

Helene smiled at her new husband as if he had her full attention when he rose to lead the wedding toasts. She was actually watching her guests. Himmler's response to their engagement had contained as much relief as delight – Helene's lack of a husband had started to weigh on her boss as an unsuitable state, and he'd spent the year before she met Ulrich suggesting acceptable partners. His concern had always been couched in kindness, but it had still rankled. It suggested that she might be on the wrong path, and Helene had spent too long finding her way down the right one to allow a misstep like that.

She glanced around the tables filled with Party dignitaries, all raising their glasses in homage to her. Every carefully weighed decision she'd made since she was nineteen years old had brought her to this. Choosing medicine as a career, because it offered her a life a million miles away from her mother's.

Joining the National Socialist Party in 1931 when it became obvious which way the political wind was blowing. Switching her student specialism to women's health two years later when Hitler took power and the purge against female doctors began. Pushing her way onto every programme that advanced the cause of population engineering in line with the Führer's thinking – eugenics, euthanasia, racial science – and pushing herself to the top of every class. And denouncing the professor at Berlin's Charité hospital who told her that she should be ashamed of hitching her star to a regime which classified people according to hatred and lies.

Helene had laughed at that, before she marched into her local Party office to ruin his life and accelerate her own. She had always known what she wanted her world to look like and it wasn't the Germany that had blighted her childhood. That country was broken and poor and struggling under the burden of the Great War's defeat. A burden Helene believed was a cruel and unjust one. And as for the men who were in charge in those days? She despised them; they'd lost any sense of pride. They had allowed the country to be taken over by degenerates and thieves. They had destroyed standards and destroyed savings and decimated the economy, leaving six million people without work. They had turned decent hard-working people into beggars, and Helene was disgusted by that.

Until you brought our heads up again.

Helene turned to Hitler and raised her glass towards him as the rest of the room toasted her.

She'd wanted a new beginning in 1931 and, from the first moment she'd heard Hitler promise to defend her country from the forces who would drag it deeper into the mud, she'd known he was the man to deliver it. Hitler was hope. Helene had no doubt about that. She'd cheered him at every opportunity from the start. She'd loathed the people who loathed him, the communists and traitors who'd written hysterical articles insisting that the only thing the Führer was building for Germany was a funeral pyre. Helene had never let anyone speak to her about him like that; she had walked away – or worse – from anyone who talked about shame.

Hitler wanted Germany to be strong and proud again, purged of its antisocial elements and a commander on the world stage. Helene wanted the same thing. And Helene had always wanted more. She'd wanted to play a part in building the future; she'd wanted power of her own. She'd never seen any shame in that either, although it had been a trickier path to tread.

I wonder if you know how much easier you made it. Perhaps I should thank you one day.

Helene caught the eye of the woman commanding the table next to the bridal party's and nodded. Magda Goebbels, the wife of the Reich's Propaganda Minister and the Führer's 'dearest friend'. The exception she'd based herself on. The Führer had always been very clear where women fitted into his vision of a flourishing society and it wasn't in government. Women would be home-makers and mothers. They would be idealised and placed on pedestals and deprived of a voice. That rule was as fixed as the one which said that Jewish children were a plague which needed exterminating. But as Helene had quickly – and thankfully – learned, there were fixed rules and then there was Magda.

She was always at Hitler's side, in elegant hats and pearls perhaps rather than a uniform, but always there. The amount of time Hitler spent consulting with Magda Goebbels would have raised eyebrows, if anyone had dared admit that they'd noticed. But the inner, and the outer, circles all watched the odd couple, and Helene had watched closest of all.

Magda was a masterclass in how to wield power and influence from the sidelines. She deferred to her husband at National Socialist rallies and receptions as if he was a fountain of wisdom. She didn't draw attention to herself by stamping around and issuing proclamations like the men did. She rarely spoke in public at all. Instead, Magda whispered in Hitler's ear, as she no doubt whispered into her husband's. She nodded at this minister and that, and bent the Führer to her favourites, while she smiled and she flattered and pretended that her ideas were his. She was the Reich's First Lady in all but name, and she certainly had a voice. And a very attentive pupil.

Helene had studied Magda's tactics in detail and learned from them. She'd copied her understated approach the first time she managed to manoeuvre herself in front of Himmler. Praising his determination to build a race of Germans who would lead a new Reich. Calling his plan to manipulate the population's make-up a masterful one. Flattering and showing off just enough knowledge to intrigue but not threaten; binding his attention to her with honey. It had worked. She had stepped from the edges to the centre.

And now this marriage will keep me there.

Himmler had been right. Ulrich was perfect for Helene in every way. He was a devoted Party member, an Untersturm-führer in Himmler's beloved SS and one of the leading lights of the Reich's rocket-science programme. He was also as hand-somely Aryan as if he'd been made to order, and he was as clever and ruthless and ambitious as she was.

And we chose each other, which makes us unbreakable.

Helene was in love with Ulrich Reitter – although she would have married him even if she hadn't been – and Ulrich was in love with her. That she had fallen so deeply for him was still something of a surprise. Helene had been avoiding marriage and the control she feared tying herself to a husband would bring since she was nineteen years old, despite the pressure she had increasingly come under as a good German woman to end her single state. She had been reluctantly coming round to the idea of letting Himmler find her the right man and be done with it.

But then, a year ago almost to the day, her work had taken her to a bitterly cold village clinging on to the edge of the Baltic Sea and – as her new husband was now acknowledging to great applause in his speech – a rocket of a more romantic kind than he normally designed had burst into life. That memory had been reshaped now by Goebbels into an anecdote which praised Hitler and the Reich as much as it honoured the first flush of love. It was still a day worth remembering...

'They don't look like much, but they have quick feet and very nimble fingers.'

Helene nodded at the shivering children lined up against the wall whose ages ranged, as far as she knew, from six years old to ten.

'And they are free, which is a bonus. Himmler thinks that your facility could make good use of them.'

The facility at Peenemünde was – according to the briefing sheet Helene had memorised on her way to it – the world's largest armament research centre. A four-hundred-kilometre testing range dedicated to developing the rockets which would not only win the war for Germany but would open up the new frontier offered by space travel. It was also, at least to Helene's eyes, a very bleak proposition. The wind whistling around the giant red buildings and wide-open launch pads was vicious. But it was a place which needed workers who could assemble tiny components and climb into small spaces, and Helene had an endless supply of those. And it was her choice to be shivering on the north coast rather than tucked up in a warm office in Berlin.

She hadn't needed to make the journey accompanying the children herself – she had plenty of deputies who could have done that. She'd offered to take the first batch anyway, and Himmler had been so impressed by her devotion to the war effort – which had been her intention – he'd offered her the use of his personal train. And arranged for a cattle car to be fitted to the back of it for the children. All in all, freezing winds or not, acting as a chaperone had been an excellent move on her part. A sentiment the handsome officer who'd welcomed her to the base seemed to share, even if he was less than enthusiastic about the condition of the delivery which she'd brought him.

'They're not the healthiest specimens. What happens when we wear them out?'

'No one will come looking for them if that's what you mean. You don't need to account for losses. And as soon as you need replacements, let me know – child workers are one thing we're not short of.'

Untersturmführer Reitter's admiration of her had visibly flared at that answer and he'd immediately invited Helene to go with him and watch the test firing of what he called a vengeance weapon. A rocket so powerful it could apparently turn a city as far away as London into a heap of rubble and mangled bodies. That had been far too good an opportunity to miss, so Helene hadn't wasted any more time with the children. She escorted them to their barracks, deaf to their complaints that they were hungry or to their shock at the cramped bunks and the thin blue-and-white uniforms which would be as much use as tissue paper against the wind. They would get used to their situation quickly enough, or they wouldn't. It didn't really matter which.

She locked the door on their sobs and made her way back to a site that was suddenly bustling, filled with field cars heading towards the vantage point on top of one of the furthest-away workshops. Helene jumped in beside her new admirer and held on tight to his arm as they raced past row after row of low hangars which were linked by the train lines that brought in machinery and parts. The view from the top of the building he led her to was breathtaking – Helene could see the whole sweep of the site and the grey curve of the coast. And when the black-and-white rocket broke free from its launch pad and hurled itself up into the sky...

That was when I knew.

Helene joined in the applause as Ulrich sat down beside her at the flower-laden head table and Hitler shook his hand. That had been the moment – when the rocket flew out over the water in a graceful arc and Ulrich's face lit up at the wonder of what it could do – that Helene knew that marriage to him wouldn't be a burden or a barrier. That it would be another step forward.

I have Himmler's trust, and now I've married one of his brethren and bound myself further into the inner circle. By any measure, I've surely climbed to the top of the tree.

She turned to her husband with a kiss as the waitresses bustled around the lively room, bearing trays of sparkling apple juice and platters of eggs in mustard sauce.

The ballroom was beautifully decorated – each place setting had a silk wreath of edelweiss wrapped round the cutlery which was a nice touch and in keeping with the hotel's restrained elegance. It was all very lovely, but if the choice of venue had been left to Helene, she wouldn't have chosen the Edel. She would have picked the much larger and far showier Adlon around the corner, with its balconies where she could have held court. She also wouldn't have served her guests a teetotal and vegetarian meal, no matter how creative the hotel's chefs could be without meat and alcohol. But the hotel was one Hitler adored – it was one of the few places he could tolerate in Berlin, which was his least favourite German city – and the meal was composed of his favourite foods. And the efforts she'd gone to to please him had left the Führer – as he kept saying – delighted with the whole day.

Which is another job well done.

Helene sipped at her drink. Not only had the organisation of the wedding been a triumph, she was a respectable wife now, not a single working woman of thirty-one. She had removed the one question mark which had hung over her.

Except that's not true. There's still one more hurdle to climb.

She fixed her smile into place and gestured to the waitress to fill up the glasses ready for the next toast, although it wasn't one she was happy to drink to. Himmler was going to give it. As he'd pointed out when her father tentatively suggested that perhaps that role might go to him, who was more qualified than the leader of the Reich's race programmes to talk about the importance of delivering the next generation?

Helene raised her glass ready as Himmler stood up to offer a toast that was essentially a blessing on their marriage: a hope of children to come for the happy couple and for their Führer. She couldn't see anything happy about it. Helene didn't want children; she never had. As far as she could see, all children did was slow a woman down, and the idea that she should bear four of them – which was the number Himmler believed was the minimum requirement for a healthy SS couple – was appalling. But even she wasn't brave enough to admit that, not with the Führer and the rest of the guests beaming in her direction.

So I'll do my duty and I'll have one and no more. Then I'll get on with my life, and I'll pay other people to be what I won't be to it.

It was far easier to smile and drink and act delighted at that thought than at the house full of unwanted brats everyone else had in mind for her future.

CHAPTER 12

MITTELBAU-DORA CONCENTRATION CAMP,
OCTOBER 1944

It was a girl. She'd given birth to a useless girl in a world which only valued men. Seeing Evie for the first time was the closest Helene had ever come to feeling like a failure, and the fury that caused her remained a tangible thing. The child was supposed to have been a boy. Helene was supposed to have given Ulrich a son, a soldier for the Führer, and turned her perfect unit into a perfect family. She could have loved a boy; she was certain of it. Instead, she'd wasted nine months of her life on a project that was pointless.

At least Ulrich doesn't expect me to go through the whole sordid business again. No matter what he pretended to the doctor.

Her marriage was the one thing which truly felt as if it was going the way it ought to be going. Ulrich understood that one baby was her limit; it was his limit as well. He paid lip-service to his sworn duty as a faithful SS man to pass on his Aryan heritage to the Reich's future generations, but he had no more interest in having children than she did. And he certainly hadn't expected her to turn into a *Hausfrau* – he'd been as eager as she was to hire a nanny the moment the child was born, so that the two of them could get back to their lives. They were still as completely aligned in their commitment to each other and nobody else as they had been on the day of their wedding. Unfortunately the rest of the promises which had surrounded that day hadn't stood the test. The pledges made in Goebbels' total war speech that Germany must and would succeed in winning the war, that the country would rise up and break loose a storm of violence and defeat over their enemies, had hardly come to fruition.

Helene leaned her head against the train carriage's window and gave herself up to a rare moment of doubt. Her loyalty to the Party was unswerving – nothing would ever change that, nor her desire for a swift and decisive German win. And she was still Himmler's favourite – that he had once again lent her his private train and given her latest mission his blessing was proof of his ongoing faith in her. But they both knew that she was far less valuable to him than she had been a year ago.

That was partly because pregnancy had been exactly the brake on her life that Helene had expected it would be. She'd managed inspection trips to Kurmark, and some of the other Lebensborn homes that were easily reachable from Berlin, almost up until her final month. But the clearances in Poland had become increasingly difficult to manage, and that wasn't only because of her physical condition. Helene had acquired a reputation which had begun to arrive in her hunting grounds before she did.

Anioł Śmierci. The Angel of Death.

The name had begun to weave its way through Poland's cities and countryside not long after a particularly vocal set of mothers who she'd relieved of their children had realised that their sons and daughters weren't coming back.

Warnings to be wary had started to circulate. Someone had caught sight of Helene in a village a little further down the road from her last clearance and the children living in that one had instantly vanished. It had taken a week not a day to track them all down, and Himmler had not been best pleased. Then Helene's photograph had appeared on a widely circulated poster which stuck a picture of her face on top of an angel's body. It also named her as a *Cel,* one of the few targets that the resistance had drummed up a reward for.

Being on the partisans' hit list hadn't worried Helene, but it had made Himmler nervous. He was concerned that her notoriety would compromise his efforts to build the new master race. When she'd announced her pregnancy, he'd instantly used that as an excuse to put limits on her work. Not that their work – like the war – had been going particularly well before the prospect of a resistance ambush or Evie's imminent birth had confined her to Berlin.

Far more German soldiers were dying than women were having babies to replace them. The disastrous Stalingrad campaign, which had ended in a brutal defeat for Germany in February 1943, had taken the lives of half a million men. The Allied landings in Normandy – whose success had torn through Germany's confidence a few months earlier – had ripped away three hundred thousand more, the lost troops either dead or wounded or captured. There weren't enough Aryan children waiting to be rediscovered in Europe to compensate for that many holes – although none of the searchers had slowed down their efforts – and German girls had fallen short in their duty.

Instead of the four or five offspring which was the Party goal for every woman of child-bearing age to deliver, most of them were still only producing one or two. The six hundred battalions of Lebensborn babies which the programme had promised the Reich – Himmler's magic number for success – was so far out of reach that he no longer allowed anyone to mention it. The new generation that would lead the Thousand Year Reich had started to take on a mythical quality which wasn't the one Hitler had intended.

At least I've been able to help deal with the surplus of useless ones. That's a plan I can take credit for.

As the need for children to fill in the gaps left by the dead increased, some of the searchers who were less ruthless than Helene had grown sloppy. As a result, Germany's orphanages and holding centres were in danger of being overrun by completely inadequate stock. That was a drain on resources which nobody needed. The ovens were obviously an option, and they were well used, but Helene had come up with a far better idea. Her suggestion that she replicate the child-worker scheme from Peenemünde to the new and far larger rocket base at Mittelbau-Dora, thereby saving the facility a considerable amount of money, had won a great deal of favour. And gone a long way to re-establishing her reputation as a positive asset.

That was a memory to cherish; it was one to push doubt away. Unfortunately she didn't get a moment to enjoy it.

The train brakes suddenly shrieked and the engine shuddered, banging Helene's head against the window. For a moment, she couldn't think where she was; she was too busy waiting for the signs of an explosion and trying not to scream.

She jumped to her feet and pressed herself against the glass, but there was no smoke and no swooping planes. The train continued on its way as if nothing had happened.

Helene sat down again and closed her eyes as its rhythm resettled. Then she counted to ten and repeated the mantra she'd been repeating to herself for over a year.

Don't think about it. It is over; you survived. There's nothing to dwell on but that.

It was sound advice, but – now that she was once again on a similar journey to the one she'd made delivering children to Peenemünde in 1942 – it was harder to listen to. And it was harder still to let go of the sense of shock which inevitably came with the memories.

Helene had barely been touched by the war. She hadn't

suffered from the shortages; she hadn't experienced any of the bombing raids which had hit Berlin. And despite the amount of travelling she'd done through eastern Europe, she had never been near a battle zone. Which meant that nothing had prepared her for the onslaught which pounded the base at Peenemünde in the August of 1943 when she was there on a private visit to Ulrich.

The carnage came at night when there wasn't a sound but the wind whispering over the water. Hundreds and hundreds of RAF bombers in a wave that was so dense, it was as if the sky had doubled in thickness. For a moment or two, Helene – who never slept well in the summertime – had stood at the window unable to move, mesmerised by the sight of the sky rippling like a piece of tossed fabric. Ulrich had had to drag her into a bunker, and then he'd had to force her to stay there.

Helene wasn't good at being confined; she'd never been held at the mercy of others before. The thud of the bombs hitting the ground and tearing through the workshops was relentless, a physical pain which raged through her body from her feet to her head. There was no light in the bunker – the electricity failed within minutes, and no one dared waste oxygen on candles. Helene had curled herself into a ball, convinced she was destined to be buried alive. It was the first time she'd tasted fear and – like failure – she hated the helplessness of it.

But the bombardment ended and they survived. And they survived again the next day when the planes returned long before nightfall and pounded Peenemünde again. Another raid was coming, or so the patchy, and late, intelligence reports said. Neither Helene or Ulrich had been prepared to test their luck a third time. They'd escaped on a goods train crammed with the site's best scientists. And – on Helene's orders as Himmler's mouthpiece and as the hours ticked away and the desperate passengers threatened to overwhelm the few serviceable carriages – they'd left the slave workers, including the children she'd brought there, behind.

Which, given how many of them were killed, could be a decision that comes back to haunt me if things continue to keep going wrong.

Helene's eyes snapped open as a fear which was far worse than the memory of falling bombs gripped her. Things were going very badly wrong for Germany indeed. Paris was free. The Allies were advancing from France along the Rhine. The possibility of a liberated Europe was starting to take root. Nobody in the German High Command, whatever they might say in public, was certain anymore that Germany would win. Goebbels could keep promising that they were only one successful battle away from victory as long as he liked, but his rhetoric hadn't been any better than the army at delivering those successes.

And nerves are starting to fray and I've been refusing to see it.

Odd phrases and furtive expressions suddenly jumped from the back to the front of Helene's head. She'd seen files being shredded, but nobody would explain the reason. She'd overheard Himmler on the telephone talking about damage limitation. She'd assumed he was asking Goebbels to control the newspapers, or dealing with nervous officers. Both of those were reasonable assumptions, but now there was a new voice in Helene's head and it was intent on whispering *what if...*

What if we actually lose? What if the Allies order investigations into some of our programmes, the ones they would no doubt refuse to understand? What if he's preparing for that?

Suddenly Himmler's eager acceptance of her offer to accompany the first batch of slave children to Mittelbau-Dora – which she'd made, as she'd done the last time, with the sole purpose of currying favour – took on a more sinister hue. He hadn't made a single objection to her going, despite the fact that the levels of care in some of the Lebensborn homes were starting to break down and they urgently needed overseeing. He hadn't even pointed out that it was barely a month since Evie's birth.

Why? Why did he jump at my suggestion that I could lead this project?

And then another phrase leaped into Helene's head and her blood ran cold. War crimes. What if the High Command was expecting allegations of war crimes if the war really did go the wrong way? Helene had seen that term crop up more and more in Allied propaganda, alongside demands for justice. And there was precedent: there had been trials based on that charge in Germany after the first war.

And the things that have been done in this one – that I have played an active role in – will damn us in the eyes of those who won't understand the beauty of what we were trying to build.

The *what if* voice in her head stopped niggling and started to roar.

What if I'm being taken for a fool? What if I'm being turned into a scapegoat?

It wasn't beyond the bounds of possibility. The train she was riding in was pulling a wagon-load of all too human evidence. She was certain that the delivery records for this shipment, as well as the paperwork from the Lebensborn homes and the clearances, would be stamped all over with her name. She couldn't remember Himmler putting his signature on any of the documents that had crossed his desk for a very long time.

'We're fifteen minutes out from our destination, madame. The porter will be along shortly for your bags.'

Helene nodded as the guard appeared in the doorway. Ulrich would be waiting for her at Dora, which was one piece of comfort. He would listen to her fears and he wouldn't dismiss them – he was far too in tune with her to do that.

She got out her compact and checked her appearance.

There was no sign on the surface that she was anything other than her usual unflappable self. She smoothed her hair and applied a fresh coat of pink lipstick in a shade that was subtle enough for those who wore it to pretend that their faces were up to Party standard and make-up free. Appearances were vital now. Ever since the summer's failed bomb plot against Hitler by a group of disaffected officers, the Party was paranoid about traitors. Even a hair out of place on a normally immaculate woman could start rumours.

And I am thinking like a traitor now, so I can't afford a single slip.

Helene took no pride in that word; it sickened her to be associated with it. She hated traitors. She had no intention of losing her faith in the Party or her belief that Germany was the war's only morally acceptable winner. But she had to be practical. She had to be as alert to other possibilities as she suspected the men in charge of her country's destiny would be. Which meant that, if there was danger coming, if there was damage limitation to be done, Helene was going to deal with it exactly as she'd dealt with every other challenge in her life. She was going to work out the solution with the best possible outcome and – whatever that might be and whatever achieving it might cost – she was going to get to that solution first.

The concentration camp at Mittelbau-Dora was enormous. Helene had visualised a base on a similar scale to Peenemünde. Instead, Dora was a vast complex which stretched out beyond the Kohnstein mountain and its mines to include dozens of sub-camps and thousands of slaves. There was no sign of the wonder weapons Ulrich was obsessed with; there were no visible launch pads. Unlike Peenemünde, however, which had contained acres of empty space, every inch of this site swarmed with shouting soldiers and barking dogs and prisoners hurrying to obey the latest volley of orders. It was impossible to imagine a moment when it was silent or still.

Helene climbed out of the car which had brought her to the base from Nordhausen station and handed over the keys to the locked truck containing the children. And then, before Ulrich could come and claim her, she took a moment to stand still and watch the place which she instinctively knew would be the one to either break or to save them.

'We've done it. We've made the V2 rocket work. We've killed thousands of civilians in Antwerp and London, and we can kill thousands more.'

Ulrich was so overexcited when he jumped from his field car, he appeared to be seconds away from grabbing her hands and swirling her around. Helene stood perfectly still and hoped that he wouldn't do anything so foolish. He was far too enamoured with his beloved technology and its success to notice her reticence.

'And it's not just the deaths that matter, although they send a huge message – the fear we've created in their wake is as powerful as the explosions. The British are terrified. They're blaming the devastation on gas leaks rather than admitting the truth – that their air defences can't hear our rockets coming and can't stop them. And now that we're into full production? We can turn out three hundred missiles a week; we can launch them from virtually anywhere. It's a triumph, Helene, an absolute triumph. And now that we've achieved this, there's no reason why we can't go on to greater things and conquer space travel or win the nuclear race. The Americans and the Soviets will never catch up with us.'

As soon as Helene realised that, as excited as he was, he wasn't about to behave in an undignified way and draw unwanted attention, she relaxed and let him run on. She listened and smiled and poured praise on him. And she didn't do what Himmler had told her to do. She didn't ask about the failures which had left her boss cursing the useless scientists who kept letting Germany down. The launch pad and in-flight explosions. The issues with accuracy which meant that too many rockets fell short of their targets and were picked up, and then pulled apart, by the British. Or the reports of sabotage by foreign slave labourers which slowed down production and had to be dealt with by executions. Which slowed production down further. She hung on instead to *the Americans and the Soviets will never catch up with us.*

That certainty was why Ulrich didn't need to know that the High Command wasn't as thrilled with his baby as he was. That certainty was Helene's winning hand.

Ulrich believed in his work. He believed that he was the scientist who'd made the V2's success possible. He was so eloquent, Helene almost believed that the rocket was perfect too.

And if he can sound as convincing as this to the Americans, then they'll believe that he's the master of the most successful weapon ever invented and my plan will work.

So Helene didn't make any move to dampen Ulrich's enthusiasm or swamp it with her fears. Instead, she followed him into the camp's roll-call square with her smile firmly in place, picking her way carefully across stones that could snap an unwary ankle as he pointed out the site's features.

'None of this existed when we moved our operations here from Peenemünde.'

He gestured to the compound packed with single-storey barracks which stretched out behind them.

'The workers were mostly kept underground in those days while the tunnels were blasted out. But now that we're up to over twelve thousand of them on site, our main problem is overcrowding. We're going to have to expand the facilities again to include more sleeping quarters and a bigger hospital if we're going to keep the death rates down.'

He smiled at Helene's raised eyebrow. 'Don't look at me as if I've gone soft. It's a question of resource management, that's all. It's a nuisance if too many of them die at once. That causes production delays and means time wasted on training. It's in our best interests to keep a reasonable proportion of them alive, but alive is all that's needed. I'm talking about more sheds with more bunks jammed into them, not an extension of the Ritz.'

Helene hadn't been looking at Ulrich in the judgemental way he'd imagined. She'd been filing away thoughts of a hospital extension and better accommodation as another tool she could use. It wasn't, however, the right time to share that, not with so many untrustworthy ears about.

She stepped to one side as a long line of prisoners began to form up ready to move out of the gate towards the mine's main entrance. The column was endless; the workers were cowed. They moved forward in a shuffle not a march. They looked as if they didn't have a breath left between them. It was hard to believe Ulrich's estimation that even the weakest-looking ones could still provide a fortnight or so's labour if they were correctly deployed. Helene had to force herself not to hold her nose as the blue-and-grey-clad figures came closer. The smell rising from their emaciated bodies was atrocious.

'It's a terrible stink, isn't it? You never get used to it. And it's worse down there. I keep out of it as much as I can.'

Ulrich nodded to the mine out of which another, albeit filthier, column was steadily emerging in the same silent, shuffling way.

'It's incredible what we've built inside the mountain – some of the halls are high enough to hold a complete missile in the upright position.'

He paused as more workers filed out with their heads turned away from the sun and their arms bent over their faces.

'And I know you said that you wanted to visit it, which is fine, but I won't pretend that would be a pleasant experience. The tunnels extend for fourteen miles now, which means there's always accidents it's not worth trying to get to, and we don't remove the bodies we do collect until the end of the day. Add to that the dust which can tear your lungs out and you'll need to wear a breathing mask the whole time we're inside.'

Before she arrived at the camp, Helene had very much wanted to see the mine in operation. Sharing the fine details of their work was an important part of her and Ulrich's relationship, and she was hardly a squeamish woman. But now, with her senses on full alert, entering the maze of tunnels like a tourist suddenly seemed to be a far less attractive idea.

If I don't see what happens in there, then I don't know. And if I don't know, there'll be no point in anyone questioning me later.

The thought felt cowardly, an impulse to be ashamed of. But it also felt like self-preservation, and that was an impulse Helene was quickly learning to live with.

'Could we go and talk somewhere instead, Ulrich? Somewhere private?'

He knew her too well, and trusted her too much, to question her change of plan. He dismissed the driver waiting to ferry them underground and steered her towards his office inside the far more spacious and comfortable barracks which the SS occupied.

'What is it? Is Himmler trying to curtail your duties again?'

'No, it's the opposite. I think he'd rather I took on more responsibility for the day-to-day running of the race programmes than he does, and this time that's what's set red flags flying.'

Helene sank into the chair opposite Ulrich's desk and lit what was for her a rare cigarette. 'What you've achieved here is magnificent; you're right to be proud of it. But tell me honestly

– given the defeats piling up on the western and the eastern fronts and all the men that we've lost, do you think the V2 really is a wonder weapon? That it's enough to ensure that Germany wins the war?'

He didn't answer straight away. When he did, Helene was shocked at how utterly exhausted he sounded.

'If we'd perfected the technology a year ago, I would have said yes without hesitation. With that kind of time, we could have destroyed London; we could have broken the British. Perhaps we could have even wiped New York from the map. But now? We'll inflict terrible damage on our enemies, I've no doubt about that. But it's too late to pretend that we can achieve any more, whatever all the promises coming down from the top say. The Allies have the scent of victory in their nostrils now, and not even the world's greatest rocket can pull that back.'

'So do you think we're going to lose?'

Helene hated asking the question – its treachery ripped at her throat. She hated the hollow look in Ulrich's eyes when he nodded even more.

'I think we already have. It's a waiting game now.'

He stopped and stared down at his hands. Helene let the silence sit for a moment, then she got up and walked to his side of the desk. She wrapped her arms around his slumped shoulders and kissed the top of his head when he let it fall back against her body. The end was coming. She knew it; so did he. One day they would mourn that, but not now. Now they had to look to the future before any chance of a next act beyond a prison cell or a bullet was snatched away from them. She kissed him again, then she moved round to face him.

'We're not going down with this ship, Ulrich. I love my country, but I'm not going to get caught up in its death throes, and neither are you. We've got to protect ourselves from the revenge that's surely coming.'

She checked the door. It was firmly shut. There was no one loitering outside the window; there was no one within earshot.

'There's going to be a hunt for scalps when this is done, and there's going to be a scramble to stay alive. People like us, who've been at the heart of things, will get one chance to rewrite ourselves as objects of value, not as targets, and the window to get that version in place will start closing the second Germany falls. Which means we need to start thinking now about what story we want to tell, and what story will be told about us. And we need to do that before everyone else with your kind of knowledge, and mine, starts doing the same thing.'

She had his full attention. He was pale, but he was nodding.

We are unbreakable. We are everything.

Whatever else happened, there would always be the two of them together. For the first time in what felt like a very shaky day, Helene was filled with hope that their lives would continue beyond the Reich's. She took a deep breath, pushed the word *traitor* out of her head and began to spill the first seeds of her fledgling plan.

CHAPTER 13

BERLIN, FEBRUARY 1945

There were three elements which needed to come together for Helene's plan to succeed.

The first was a sweep of the evidence surrounding her and Ulrich's activities, some of which had to be collected and saved and some of which had to be wiped away. The second required finding a safe place to wait out the last days of the war, in a location which meant that the Americans, not the Soviets, would be the first troops to find them. And the third, and by far the trickiest, was deciding when to make their final move and shed their old selves.

That was the part which gave Helene the most sleepless nights.

Make it too early and get caught and the Party would turn them into examples of treachery. Make it too late and they ran the risk of being lost among all the other desperate men and women trying to wipe out their pasts and make deals with a conquering army.

By the middle of February 1945, Helene was as much in control as she could be of parts one and two. Part three remained balanced – like Germany's future – on a knife-edge.

Despite the losses suffered on all fronts, Germany was not only still fighting, but total war now truly meant total.

Anyone who could be classed as a man – from twelve-year-old boys in their Hitler Youth uniforms to sixty-year-old grandfathers who thought that their fighting days were long gone – had been forced into military service. The army had gone on the offensive in Alsace and the Ardennes. V2 rockets were raining down on a terrified London on a daily basis. The Führer insisted that victory was still within Germany's grasp and he wouldn't give in. But everybody else knew that the end was coming, no matter how many times he roared that it wasn't. That none of the efforts and sacrifices he demanded meant Germany could possibly beat the Allied armies. And everybody else was right.

As 1944 limped into 1945, all the war-changing offensives had stalled or been pushed back. By the middle of January, Warsaw belonged to the Soviets, the rest of Poland was about to follow and the German army was in retreat all over Europe. And by the end of the month, Hitler had seen the writing on the wall and retreated down into his bunker, and the Red Army was less than fifty miles from Berlin. The end was coming, but, for anyone trying to pick their moment to break free, it was still impossible to determine exactly when it would arrive. It was still a tense waiting game.

'Things are becoming seriously unstable here. I think we may have reached the tipping point.'

Ulrich's voice was so hushed, Helene had to press her ear hard against the telephone receiver.

'There's a plausible rumour that we'll be ordered to suspend rocket launches by the middle of March, and everyone's getting jumpy about Allied bombing raids targeting the mine before that. Or about being assigned to a military unit and sent to the front line as foot soldiers.'

He stopped suddenly as a door opened and closed somewhere behind him. Helene had to force herself to breathe calmly through the waiting.

'It's fine; it's nothing. Everyone's on edge, watching everyone else. Rudolph and some of the others are paranoid about being caught by the Soviets and shipped off to Moscow. They're whispering about decamping to the Bavarian Alps and doing what you said they would do – taking as many secrets as they can to bargain themselves a passage to America or London. I'm playing along with them, and I don't think they'll dare do it yet, not for the next few weeks while we're still launching attacks anyway. But it won't be long before the exodus happens, and I could be in serious danger if I backtrack on joining that. It's time to slot the last pieces into place, Helene. It's time to get ready to go.'

The last pieces. Those were hers to account for. And this time it wasn't about collecting evidence but removing it.

Ulrich had played his part to perfection. He'd made sure not to sign his name to any new order at the mine since October, with the exception of the request for the hospital extension. And when it came to gathering documents, he was a dozen steps ahead of Rudolph. Getting access to the specifications and blueprints relating to the V2's development – and the implications of that technology for the nuclear and space programmes which he also needed proof of – wasn't a straightforward task, even for an officer of Ulrich's standing. The papers were stored in a safe in the office belonging to the camp commandant, Otto Förschner, and he was under strict instructions not to give them to anybody but Rudolph himself. Luckily, Ulrich was as skilled as Helene when it came to persuasion.

Förschner – whose weak command of the base had enabled resistance activities to flourish among the mine's forced workers – was deeply unpopular. Most of the other SS officers at Dora loathed him and were campaigning to have him removed. The man was lonely and bitter and afraid for his future. So Ulrich befriended him. He sat up with him night after night, watching the commandant drink brandy and pretending to do the same, letting the man moan to his heart's content. And when Förschner got drunk enough to start snoring, as he did every time, Ulrich took his keys and opened the safe and drew another careful copy of another blueprint. By the end of February – when Förschner was finally dismissed – Ulrich had the full set. That part of the evidence – the technical records which proved that Ulrich was a highly valuable asset to the Allies – was therefore safely secured. Helene's challenge, however, was a rather more delicate one.

She'd taken the first steps to erase any trace of her name, although – given that travel beyond Germany's borders to the east was now an impossibility except for the military – the places she could search for mention of it were limited.

Her first call had been to the Race and Settlement Office in Prinz Albrecht Straβe, where all the central files relating to the Reich's racial engineering programmes – including Lebensborn, Aryanisation and clearance – were stored. She arrived there expecting to have to offer a raft of excuses for accessing her personal information at such a paranoid time. The Ministry, however, was almost deserted.

According to the one harassed secretary still trying to maintain some kind of order, most of the staff had begun leaching away once Himmler had left it. He'd been relocated by the Führer to Schneidemühl in north-western Poland to build a defensive wall against the approaching Soviets and his once immaculately run offices were now in a state of chaos. The filing cabinets had been smashed open and ransacked; the floors were littered with half-shredded documents. There was nobody around except people like Helene, who didn't want to discuss what they were doing. It was a mess, and it was perfect.

Helene made one brief search of the Lebensborn office which produced no results and, when that was done, she walked calmly away. There was nothing to fear there, even if her name was all over a dozen incriminating documents. No invading army would waste its time digging through such mayhem, no matter how desperate for revenge they were. Kurmark, however, was a different proposition. That was a place potentially full of very dangerous loose ends.

It was on one of those bitterly cold February days when the sky never shifts from a leaden shade of grey that Helene made the drive out to the Lebensborn home. In the six months since she'd last visited it, the building had badly deteriorated. The front lawns were a sea of mud; the front steps were slick with moss. No one answered when she rang the bell. She walked round to the back and knocked heavily there. She was greeted once again with silence. When she pushed the unlocked door open and went inside, there was no temperature change: she could still see her breath.

The hall carried the sour scent of neglect. There was no sense of comfort anymore; there was no sign of life. The ground rooms were deserted and sprinkled with dust. From the splintered state of the furniture, it appeared that the last people to live in the house had run out of firewood and coal. From the empty shelves in the kitchen, they also appeared to have run out of food.

Helene wasn't particularly surprised by that: Berlin was a city of the starving and the frozen now, and nobody got special privileges anymore. And she wasn't surprised, although she was grateful, that the house was empty. Himmler's interest in breeding the next master race had got lost somewhere in the middle of all the army's lost battles. He'd stopped asking about the homes long before he was redeployed.

After that, and with her own future of far more concern to her than the Reich's, Helene had stopped inspecting the ones under her remit and so, she assumed, had her deputies. Looking around her now, she imagined that the nursing staff had disappeared from Kurmark as eagerly as the accountants and administrators had run from the Ministry. As for the mothers and the children... Helene moved on to the main office where the filing cabinets were kept without looking for traces of them. Pregnant women and the babies nobody would want any more were no longer her concern.

The cabinets were locked, but Helene had brought a full set of keys as well as a full box of matches. She worked her way systematically through the files they contained, and this time she was rewarded. The grate was soon blazing with dozens of documents which she'd signed or which mentioned her by name.

She did not, however, destroy everything she found. A folder containing letters which had been authorised not by her but by Himmler and a copy of a recruiting brochure which carried his personal message made her pause. For a moment, Helene considered taking those documents with her, to use as her own form of collateral if the rest of her plan ran aground. Until she considered the explanations that producing a set of papers which could fix her firmly in the Reich's inner circle might entail, and she realised that the risks far outweighed the benefits.

I won't take them, but I'll leave them where they can be found. And where I can point to their presence if I need to.

She pushed the paperwork into a crevice in the wall and blew out the last sparks in the fireplace.

I am no longer anywhere here.

Relief rushed through her. It wasn't a watertight solution. There could be posters decrying her activities still circulating in Poland. There could be mothers or nurses who remembered her, who might be willing to trade her in to keep themselves safe. But with the upheaval and the savagery the end of the war would likely visit on Germany, and on Eastern Europe, those threats were nothing. Those were scraps in the wind. Helene closed her eyes for a moment and allowed herself to feel a real hope that the end was going to be navigable.

What was that?

The thin cry startled her. For a few seconds she forgot where she was and thought it was Evie. She waited for the nanny's soothing voice to restore order. But then the cry came again. And it was followed by a scuffle of boots against wood from the ceiling above her and a strangled *hush* that was very definitely not Evie's brisk and businesslike nurse.

'Who's there?'

Helene ran into the hallway. Nobody answered. She walked slowly up the stairs; she didn't call out again. It was clear from the silence that whoever was up there didn't want to be found, which meant that Helene was determined to find them. She had to fling open three bedroom doors before she did so.

'What are you doing hiding up here?'

A frightened jumble of women in grubby uniforms and a tangle of equally unkempt children were huddled on the floor. It was the last sight Helene wanted to see, no matter how overjoyed they were to see her.

'We thought you were a Russian soldier, come to kill us or worse.'

Helene vaguely recognised the girl scrabbling to her feet. Anya, that was it. A country girl and – like the other women gazing slack-jawed at her – not one of the brightest the home had recruited. Too inclined to be kind to be of any real use. Helene ignored what struck her as a very silly statement given that she'd knocked and rung the bell, which was hardly what a murderer would do, and focused instead on counting heads as the group separated out. A dozen children between the ages of two and three, four babies under one and four nurses.

All of them filthy and shockingly thin and one of the infants so blue, Helene doubted it was alive. That they were still in residence without food or warmth made no sense and she said so.

'We'd managed to stretch the supplies out until a few days ago, although God knows when any of us last had a decent meal. I did try to go in search of more food, but the locals here hate us. They threw stones and called me dreadful names and said that the Russians were coming to deal with women like me. Everyone with somewhere to go has gone, but we're stuck. We can't leave all these children; they wouldn't survive a day on their own.'

Helene couldn't argue with Anya's tearful assessment. She also couldn't see why the nurses were so worried about the children's welfare when nobody else would be.

Don't they understand that these are Nazi babies? That the Soviets will kill them all the moment they discover what went on here?

From the way the girls were fussing over the little ones, it appeared they didn't understand very much at all. And Anya couldn't stop talking.

'You will help us, won't you, Doctor Reitter? You'll get us some food and some firewood? And maybe find us all a better place to stay? You'll tell us what to do?'

It was the use of her name which sealed Anya's fate – and the fate of her companions. Up to that point, Helene hadn't decided what to do with them, but that mistake turned the children and the nurses into evidence and that, in Helene's mind, was that. She didn't betray herself. She nodded and patted Anya's arm, being careful not to touch the grubby skin. All that mattered now was keeping the group calm until she could get away.

'Of course I will. I'll head back to Berlin right away and send somebody from head office straight out to you. There will be food and fuel here by nightfall, I promise. But in the meantime, I think you should stay safely in here, don't you?'

She gave Anya a second to nod, to accept the idea as her own. 'Good girl. The Soviets haven't reached the city yet, but they are very close, and goodness knows how brutal they'll be, especially if the villagers send them this way. You did the right thing by hiding up here and staying together. You kept your charges safe, and I'm proud of you for remembering how much these little ones matter. So let's carry on being sensible, shall we? And let me help you get more comfortable before I go.'

It took no time at all for Helene to run downstairs and gather up the discarded folders from the office, or to rip the heavy curtains down. When she returned bearing those and a jug full of water that was browner than she would drink, she was smiling as if what was coming next would be a huge adventure.

'Here we go. I have a couple of matches too, so you can build a fire from this old paper and then everyone can snuggle under these drapes and get warm. And I know that water won't fill hungry tummies, but it will help until the food arrives. And you are all clever girls, aren't you? You're resourceful the way that I've trained you to be? You can manage for a little while longer?'

Anya and her fellow nurses agreed that they could.

As Helene turned to leave, they were bundling the children up in the velvet and trying to encourage voices that had reached their last notes to join in a cheerful song.

I am done. It's time to move on.

Helene went downstairs again and opened all the highest windows, pulling her coat tight against the freezing wind which blew straight into every room as she made the rounds. Then she left the house and locked the back door behind her. She did the same with the front door and with the iron gates at the end of the drive.

Nobody in the village would come near. She wasn't going to alert anyone in Berlin. The fire would burn for a few hours, if that. The curtains they were curled under were damp. The water wasn't fit to drink. By the time soldiers of any description arrived, the children and the nurses would be as much use to them as the ashes in the grate. And Helene Reitter would not only be wiped from the house; Helene Reitter would no longer exist.

CHAPTER 14

SCHLOSS KRANSBERG, APRIL 1945

'We've been through this. We can do this. It's a repositioning of who we are, that's all.'

Helene wasn't sure if she was talking for her benefit or for Ulrich's, but as this could be their last moment together and she needed to feel at one with him, she kept talking anyway.

'You worked at a V2 rocket complex in the Harz Mountains. We don't have to give the exact name. And if they've already discovered Dora, we stick to the line that you were a scientist there and not a camp guard and that you had no say in how the facility was run. You are a valuable asset, not a Nazi, and so am I. I've worked throughout the war as a children's doctor, trying to do my best for my charges in impossible circumstances. We don't know what they know, Ulrich, but we've got a good idea of what they want. Now all we have to do is to give it to them.'

How many times had they repeated those words to each other over the last four weeks as Germany fell apart around them?

Helene shifted Evie's weight more comfortably onto her hip as the line of jeeps with their stars and stripes advanced along the driveway. This was it; this was the test. They'd perfected their stories; they'd perfected their English. The documents which Ulrich had brought with him were safely buried in the castle grounds, ready to be produced once the Americans had taken the bait. They were prepared; they were ready.

And this could still all end in a bullet.

Helene shifted the baby more prominently across her body as the convoy slowed. They'd worked too hard for this chance for any part of it to go wrong now. They were within touching distance of a new life.

'And it will work, my love, don't doubt that for a moment. We'll both play our parts exactly as we've practised, exactly as you wrote the script. We are an unbreakable team – don't ever forget that.'

Ulrich had sensed her hesitation. His hand was on her shoulder; his lips were on her hair. Her breathing eased as his words wrapped round her and the jeeps stopped. Helene could see the soldiers crammed into the back of them clearly now. They were young and far healthier looking than anyone in Germany, but their faces and bodies were battle-hard. Evie – startled by the unfamiliar noise of roaring engines – gave a sniff that threatened to turn into a cry. None of the men showed the slightest flicker of sympathy as her little face crumpled.

What if all they are seeing when they look at her is another little Nazi in the making? What if holding her is making things worse?

There was nothing Helene could do. If she hadn't severed all ties with her parents once she and Ulrich had taken the decision to get out of Germany, she would have left Evie behind with them in Berlin. And Ulrich's family was in Munich and completely out of touch. She'd brought Evie in the end because she thought Americans were soft-hearted over children. She could hardly drop the child now.

I have to be the one who speaks first, not them. I have to take control. That was the first part of the plan.

Unfortunately, that part didn't seem quite as easy now as it had when they'd practised on their own in the castle. Not with rifles and hostile faces trained their way. Helene could feel her confidence draining, and that wasn't something she was used to.

And then a man jumped out of the front vehicle and, unlike all the others, he wasn't pointing a gun at her. Helene knew nothing about American uniforms – especially when they were battle-stained and the epaulettes and other markings which could have offered her some clues to his rank were missing – but she knew an officer when she saw one. This one walked slowly towards the steps, taking in their carefully posed family group. There was an unhurried air about him which Helene could work with. He looked like a man who might make time to listen.

'*Guten Tag. Ich heiße...*'

He started to speak, his accent mangling the words. Helene didn't let him continue. She stepped forward instead and addressed him in an English that was as crisp as his German was clumsy.

'Good day to you too, and welcome to Castle Kransberg. My name is Doctor Helene Reitter, and this is my husband, Ulrich. He is a rocket scientist, one of Germany's best. We want to speak to somebody from military intelligence regarding that, if you could arrange it please. I'm quite certain that they will want to speak with us too.'

'This is quite the home you have here. Working for Hitler must have paid very well, or is this an old family treasure?'

Their gamble had worked. The American major had requisitioned the castle – and allowed his men to ransack it – but he'd also placed a call on his unit's field radio and requested intelligence support. Helene had guessed correctly: German scientists were in such high demand that nothing else about Ulrich's background beyond his training and experience would matter. The major hadn't wasted time any time questioning either of them about what they'd done or been in the war, and neither did the man on the other end of the line. From what Helene had managed to overhear of the call, both the Americans and the Russians had agents scouring the country for Germans with weapon and technical knowledge, and the search had turned into a race.

And they don't know whether to loathe or admire the men that they find.

The American intelligence officer sitting opposite them – who'd told them to call him colonel but hadn't offered his name – was definitely caught in that camp. And letting him think that they owned a castle wouldn't do the perception of their worth any harm, so Helene ignored his question. The Americans would find out the truth soon enough.

That Kransberg, where she and Ulrich had gone into hiding at the start of March, had a far more complex pedigree than as a simple family home. That the ancient citadel had been renovated and redesigned by the Party's chief architect, Albert Speer, so that it could be used as one of the Führer's military headquarters. That it had also been one of Göring's favourite retreats. The parties he'd thrown there in the early days of the war – which Helene had attended as Himmler's guest – had lasted for days.

Luckily, Helene, who'd kept her ear firmly tuned to Party gossip since the war had turned in the wrong direction, had discovered at the start of the new year that Kransberg was to be abandoned because it lay directly in the path of the advancing American army. Which was precisely why she'd chosen it as their safe place.

The drive from Berlin to the castle, which sat on a steep rock an hour or so outside Frankfurt, had been a fraught one. The roads were littered with potholes that could snap an axle. They'd seen more than one body hanging from a tree, bearing a sign that labelled its wearer as a traitor. They'd expected to be challenged at every road block. But Ulrich's SS uniform – which he'd burned the moment they were safe inside the castle – had waved them straight through, and the journey had been worth all the risks. Kransberg had been in a state of uproar when they'd arrived; nobody cared who they were or why they'd come. And within days of their arrival, the last German officers and administrators had fled and left Helene with her perfect stage.

She sat back now as Ulrich took over the meeting. She watched the colonel's eyes light up as her husband, with his usual eloquence, explained his pivotal role in developing the V2 and started to outline all the applications he would share about the technology in return for a set of plane tickets and a new home. The colonel was hooked within minutes.

He doesn't know anything about the conditions at Dora or, if he does, he doesn't care. And he doesn't care that Ulrich has to have been an officer in the SS to have risen as high in weaponry as he did. All that matters to them now is winning the peace. Coming first in the nuclear race, conquering space. Pushing the Russians firmly into second place. They're so greedy, we can literally design our own lives.

So Helene waited until Ulrich had thoroughly reeled the colonel in, then she did exactly that.

'We don't want to go where the other scientists you're collecting are going.'

She let the colonel have his raised eyebrow and his 'That's not for you to dictate'. She could see *I've won the prize with this one* written all over his face; she knew where the power lay. She carried on as if he hadn't spoken.

'Ulrich is the best resource you will find, but we're not stupid enough to think that you'll stop with him. I imagine that you will soon have a shopping list of the scientists you want to... let's call it recruit and take back to America. That's fine, but we want a completely new start, not a half-life. We could easily get that from the Russians, and I'm sure we could do a deal with the British which will match whatever you offer us.'

She watched his face tighten at *Russians* and then *British* and knew that she had him.

'So what we don't want is to be put into some kind of German ghetto in an American town where the locals will hate us and we'll be made to live like second-class citizens. We want a base away from the rest, where we can make a life that doesn't come trailing... unfortunate misconceptions. You can do that for us, can't you? In return for all the knowledge Ulrich is offering – and the names he can give you, which will speed up your search. You could make us Austrian or Swiss perhaps? Whatever is needed to make our move work.'

It was another gamble, but Helene was certain now that she was holding a winning hand. And she was also aware that, given who they were and what their country had spent the last five years doing, it was a dangerous move to mention ghettoes and second-class citizens. The colonel could easily have reacted to her demands with disgust, or ordered their arrest and made a mockery out of her doing deals with the Russians or the British. She knew he wouldn't do any of those things. That he would do instead whatever was required to land his big fish.

We've done it. We've won. The future might not be the one we've been dreaming of for the last twelve years, but it's still ours to direct. And maybe, if we can find the right place to settle, there'll still be good work to be done.

She slipped her hand inside Ulrich's as the colonel got up to make the necessary calls. The plan had worked. There wouldn't be a trial; there wouldn't be a cell or a bullet or an executioner's rope. There wouldn't be any price to pay at all.

'You did it.'

She shook her head as Ulrich brought her face up to his. She turned *you* to *we* as his lips found hers and the future bloomed once again in their kiss.

PART THREE

CHAPTER 15

EAST BERLIN, JANUARY 1980

Evie ran.

She didn't wait for Sebastian to return. She didn't leave a message with the startled secretary in the outer office. She stuffed the newspaper into her bag and she ran out of the embassy with her mind in freefall.

A cathedral. They got married in Berlin Cathedral. Hitler was a guest of honour at their wedding. Who in God's name were they? And how did I not know?

Her feet moved without her involvement, operating on instinct, carrying her back down the Unter den Linden towards Museum Island and the dome she'd briefly glimpsed from the back of the car. She ran blind. She barely registered the pedestrians who were forced to dodge out of her way. She took no notice of the one man who was brave or angry enough to ask her what she thought she was doing. Somewhere between scooping up the newspaper and hurling herself down the street, she started to cry. Evie could taste the salt in her mouth. She could feel the wind scouring the tracks patterning her cheeks. She couldn't stop the tears from falling.

But you must. You have to calm down. This is the wrong place, and the wrong time, to attract attention.

It took a moment or two for her sensible self to shout loudly enough to be heard. It took another shocked body jumping out of her way to properly wake her. But the warning lights flashing through her muddled brain finally flashed brightly enough and Evie slowed down. She dragged her sleeve across her face and realised she hadn't brought her coat. That she was shivering with cold as well as with shock. And that people were now crossing the road to avoid her.

The old guard here were Nazi hunters back in the day and they cling hard to old hatreds.

Todd's words burst over her like a bucket of iced water. Her rational self instantly retreated.

My parents were Nazis. They must have been prominent Nazis to be featured in the paper like that. To have had such a spectacular wedding. What if they're still remembered? What if someone sees my mother's features in mine? What if I would count as a prize here?

Paranoia gripped her. It was an alien, horrible sensation, but she couldn't shake it. She needed to get off the street; she needed to be invisible. Before a car filled with Stasi officers drew up beside her, before an informant's hand grabbed hers.

Evie stared frantically around for a place to hide, her eyes watering as the wind barrelled around her. Without the protection of a car, the street no longer reminded her of Paris. It wasn't beautiful; it was too wide, its thoroughfares separated by a sickly and straggling line of trees which offered no cover. Its buildings were huge, closed and forbidding, or bitten into by rubble-strewn spaces which resembled the aftermath of a poorly cleared earthquake. There were no shops to duck into; there wasn't a single open door that might offer her sanctuary.

And suddenly there it was. *Sanctuary.* The magic word which would save her.

Evie quickened her pace, images of hunted men banging on church doors pushing her on. Whatever else it might be or have witnessed, the cathedral she was running towards would be a safe place. It would be somewhere quiet in which to regroup; it might even offer some comfort. She was at the foot of its steps before she realised that no comfort or quiet was coming.

Evie stared up at the squat building, trying to equate its blackened and broken front with the elegant domes and spires which the newspaper had promised. Trying to match the cracked and weed-sprouting steps to the ones her mother had waved from as if she was queen of the city. There was no more elegance left here than there was at the Edel. The cathedral's towers were stumps; its main dome was a lump of rusting metal. As Evie peered closer, she could see crevices and craters in the walls that had to be bullet or shell holes. And the huge doorway which had framed her mother like a precious work of art was wrapped round with chains and padlocked.

Why can't this city rebuild itself? Why can't it let the war go? I should never have come here. I should never have seen the newspaper.

Evie turned round, frantically searching for a more welcoming corner to curl into. The patch of ground behind her was a concrete wasteland with no defences against the bitter wind whipping in from the Spree. There wasn't a seat to fall onto; there wasn't a shrub to soften it. The square whose photographs had promised fountains and flowers was as desolate as the cathedral.

This is where the crowds stood to cheer and wave back at her.

The thought that her parents had been Nazis was too terrible to contemplate. The thought that her mother could once have been well known enough to summon crowds of excited well-wishers was absurd. But the one that followed was no better. A memory from a history textbook, an image of a square that wasn't empty and grey but filled instead with red-

and-black flags and columns of soldiers marching in crisp formation.

Evie suddenly knew where she was. She was in the Lustgarten; she was in their heartland. This was the Nazis' parade ground, their victory square, where they'd come to pay homage and celebrate the Reich's unbeatable strength.

Where they came to worship my mother.

For the first time in Evie's life, her knees buckled. She sank down onto the frozen steps, no longer caring who was watching or who might be coming for her. Trying to stay steady as the world bucked and kicked.

'Evie?'

Her mind was so caught up in the past, the voice came to her from years away. And her own voice was gone.

'Evie, look at me. What's wrong? What's happened? Why are you sitting on the ground?'

His questions buzzed round her as impossible to catch hold of as flies.

She blinked, forcing herself to focus until she could at least identify who was talking to her. Not a Stasi officer, not a Nazi soldier. It was Sebastian, sitting down beside her, wrapping her warm coat round her shoulders, offering the comfort the cathedral couldn't. Evie slowly began to resurface.

'That's better. I've been so worried. Todd's secretary said you ran out of the building as if a pack of dogs was after you. You didn't take your coat; you didn't explain what you were doing. When there was no sign of you outside, I came looking. What on earth spooked you like that?'

'How did you know I'd come here?'

It was easier to ask rather than answer a question. She needed more time to gather herself first.

Sebastian shrugged. 'I didn't. But I remembered what you said about going to the Smithsonian when you needed thinking time, so Museum Island seemed like the logical place to start. I saw you standing here as if you were lost, then you sort of toppled and...'

He ran out of words, but Evie couldn't fill the silence. She opened her bag; she pulled out the newspaper and dropped it into his hands. She didn't explain why; she didn't know how to. She left him to stare at the cover and turn over the pages. She could see from his frown that he'd made a connection between some of the photographs and where they were sitting. It was unfair to expect him to do any more than that without help.

'That couple on the front, and in the pictures inside, are my parents.'

Saying the words out loud broke the spell. The fear of being recognised as a Nazi's daughter disappeared. The numbness that had gripped her since she'd drawn the paper out of the evidence box faded away. And fury and disgust rushed in.

'I'm serious. That perfect couple celebrating their wedding with every monster the Third Reich spawned are my parents. Helen and Alex Ritter.'

She ignored his startled, 'What did you say?' If she stopped talking, she'd never start again.

'You heard me right. I'm such a fool. All these years I thought they were a fairly average, if unlikeable, doctor and scientist, pillars of their community. Refugees from the war who were forced to flee from their quiet lives in Switzerland and make new lives in America, with all their possessions and family lost. But oh no, it turns out that was a lie. It was the soundtrack of my whole life, and it was a lie. They weren't Mr and Mrs Average at all. They weren't Swiss. They were high-ranking Nazis, some kind of sick celebrity couple. They've been in hiding from their past their whole lives. They've been in hiding from me.'

She was grateful that Sebastian didn't recoil or ask if she was sure. That he didn't move from her side when she suddenly laughed.

'You see what this makes us, don't you? We're both the children of Nazis. What are the odds of that?'

And she was grateful too that he held her tight when her laugh collapsed into a sob and a rush of horrified words that took no account of all the hurt he'd been through.

'I was born in America, but what if things had been different? What if I'd been born here to be a child for the Führer, like you were? What if I was also meant as a cog in the killing machine?' She felt him flinch then and a rush of guilt made her stop. 'I'm sorry. That was heartless. But how do you live with that knowledge? How will I?'

Sebastian pressed his lips to her hair. 'With difficulty, until you find people who care enough to help and ways to make the fear of it smaller. But that's my life, Evie; it's not yours. You're not some offering for Hitler, so don't throw yourself down that road.'

He paused and then he continued as her breathing slowed. 'And I'm sorry too, but I have to ask... All of this, not being Swiss, not being refugees. You called yourself a fool... You never suspected a thing?'

The question was gently put, but it ran through Evie with a jolt. Her immediate reaction was to say, no, of course not. But pieces of the past were raining down like the confetti that had once covered the cathedral's steps and no wasn't the right answer.

'I'm not sure.'

She wriggled out of Sebastian's tight embrace, although she kept hold of his hand. It helped to see the compassion in his face.

'It's not true to say that I had no suspicions. There've always been odd things in the story they told me that I couldn't square. And the last time I saw my mother, they got odder.' She glanced down at the newspaper and shivered. 'I knew something wasn't right in the account that they fed me, but I never questioned it too deeply. And I never imagined this.'

'Nobody could, no matter how odd things might have seemed.' He paused then continued in the same gentle way. 'What were those odd things, Evie? What didn't feel right? Would it help to talk about them now?'

She didn't know if anything would help, but his voice was as soothing as his touch, and the weight she was now carrying was threatening to bury her. Evie swallowed hard. There were so many blind spots and inconsistencies filling her head, maybe it was time to try and give a shape to them.

And if not with Sebastian, then with who? Who else could possibly understand this?

She gripped his hand tighter as she began feeling her way through the maze in her head.

'My parents have never been kind people; they're not what you would call good. They put everyone in categories, and they treat the ones they don't respect – which is basically anyone who isn't white and well-off and conservative – either with indifference or disdain. When I was growing up, I thought that was down to their age or their politics, or my father's semi-military background, given his work for the space programme. I hated it. I rebelled against everything they believed and I ignored them. But then I met Ethan...'

She stumbled as her marriage fell around her again. All the hope it had started with, and all the misery at its end.

'Ethan was Jewish, which I knew was a problem for them. Not because of his religion particularly.' She stopped, her stomach suddenly twisting. 'Well maybe actually that was the whole problem, given what I know about them now. Anyway, I didn't challenge it at the time, which I should have done. But they never voiced their disapproval out loud. They were never overtly hostile. They were simply cold to him, and to us. They didn't even come to our wedding. And I'm not blaming them for my marriage failing, but it didn't help. My parents didn't like him, and he grew to dislike them. And it didn't matter how much I railed against their uptight political views too, or how illogical Ethan knew he was being, but, when things started to fall apart, he started to question how I'd been brought up and how much of their attitudes I'd swallowed.'

She shook her head as Sebastian tried to tell her that Ethan's mistrust wasn't her fault.

'I know that, and so did Ethan. My parents' values, or lack of them, became something we hid all our other failings behind. But he made a comment once – after the first rumblings about what some of the scientists involved in the moon landings might have done in the war – that's been stuck in the back of my mind for years. About how it was very convenient for my father that he studied to be a rocket scientist in neutral Switzerland and not some far more dangerous country, and how he'd never realised that the Swiss had been such a technically advanced military machine.' She grimaced at her blindness as his words came back. 'I could see Ethan's point – having to flee from Switzerland, which never played any role in the conflict and was never attacked, hadn't made much sense to me for years either. But we were in the dying days of our marriage then, and the gloves were well and truly off. I didn't have the courage to dig below his sarcasm.'

She closed her eyes briefly and waited for Ethan to melt away.

'There's other things too. There isn't one family photograph on display in my parents' house, and they never discuss the past. They could have arrived on the planet as a fully formed married couple. And as for my mother...' She stopped, blinked and shook herself again. 'My father is distant and uninvolved, and I've never had much of a relationship with him – maybe if I'd been a boy, things would have been different. But my mother...

she's different. She's the coldest woman I've ever met. I told you that I don't think she loved me, but it's more than that...'

The words were getting harder to find, but Evie was glad that Sebastian stayed quiet and didn't try to find them for her. She'd never discussed her mother so openly before, and she needed to get the telling right.

'She's a closed book to anyone except my father. She's never talked about or shared anything that's remotely personal with me. I'm a nuisance to him, but she resents my existence, and I know that sounds dramatic, but there's no other way to explain the way she acts towards me. And she won't be questioned – or challenged. On the few occasions I've tried, she goes on the attack. When I went to see them a few weeks ago, when I mentioned talking to my father about Arthur Rudolph...'

Evie paused for a moment as her mother's cruel dismissal of her flared back. 'Well, she was badly thrown, I knew that. But I didn't get a chance to ask why she flinched at his name; she went for my throat too fast. And I didn't ask why about that either. I never do. It's as if I've always known on some level that there was a chasm a step away and one wrong word from me would tip us all into it.' Evie stopped again and nodded at the paper. 'But I swear, whatever I suspected, I never knew a thing about this.'

She finally fell silent, and then the tears came again, in a quiet river now not a storm but painful nonetheless. She gave in to her misery and let Sebastian hold her and whisper the 'I know' and 'How could you?' that she needed to hear. She stayed in his arms despite the bitter cold and the hard stone. Until he suddenly stiffened, dropped his arms from her shoulders and picked the newspaper up off the steps.

'Have you looked properly at these?' He was pointing to the pictures of the wedding reception. 'I mean at the place they were taken, rather than at the people?'

Evie hadn't but she did now, rubbing her aching eyes and frowning as he continued.

'It's the Edel, I'm certain of it. Look past the flowers and the chandeliers and you'll see.'

It took Evie a moment to do as he said and strip the trappings away. There was no mistaking the hotel's discreet front entrance or the buildings flanking it when she did.

'We have to go back there, right now. They could have archives, records of events that were held there. We have to find out what they know.'

Sebastian scrambled to his feet a handful of seconds after Evie did, grabbing frantically at her arm.

'You can't do that, Evie. You know what Todd said – we mustn't go around speaking to anyone who hasn't been authorised, and that definitely includes the staff at the Edel. This is delicate. We need to go back to the embassy, show him what you've found and work out a plan from there.'

But he was flinging his words into the wind. Evie was running again. She was already halfway down the street.

'I do not know how they do things in the United States, and I do not care to. But here we treat people with respect. We do not raise our voices and fling accusations and demand that they hand over information which they could not possible have.'

Evie didn't reply. The irony of being reprimanded by a Stasi officer about the way she'd managed, or not managed, her attempted interview with the Edel's manager wasn't lost on her. But neither was the seriousness of the situation she was in. She'd behaved like an idiot. She'd ignored her training; she'd ignored Todd's instructions. She'd forgotten basic common sense. And she'd put herself and goodness knows how many others potentially in danger. She was mortified and sorry and, faced with the reality of the Stasi, she was more than a little afraid.

The room in the basement had no windows, but it had a map of Berlin with enough red dots and arrows on it to make her uneasy and enough folders on show in the tall cupboard to suggest that she wasn't the first person to be interviewed inside its airless walls. And the officer sitting opposite her hadn't smiled once. He also wasn't wearing a uniform. He was dressed in a cheap-looking and wide-lapelled brown suit whose cut and colour was a parody of Western fashions. Her Washington colleagues would have laughed if any of their colleagues had appeared wearing such an unfortunate outfit. There was nothing funny about him here. His English was impeccable. In line with his own rules, he didn't raise his voice or make threats. But he exuded a menace that Evie knew could easily thicken.

'And we do not accuse hard-working hotel managers of running an establishment that caters to Nazis. I assume even an American understands how deeply insulting that is?'

That question at least gave her a way in.

Evie immediately nodded. 'I do, and I'm very sorry. I'd had a terrible shock, and I was trying to find out if the hotel could help me make sense of it. But that's not an excuse. I conducted myself very badly, and I deeply regret it.'

Evie meant it. The way she'd shouted at the poor manager was unforgivable in any circumstances. Demanding that he give her access to his office and to all the Edel's historical files. Yelling that his hotel's air of respectability was a tissue of lies. Flinging *Nazi* and *disgrace* and *secrets* at him like missiles and waving the newspaper so close to his face, she'd accidentally caught him hard across the cheek with it. It was no wonder the reception staff had summoned help. Her apology was heartfelt, and she was prepared to repeat it to everyone who needed to hear it.

That made no impression on the officer. He glanced down

at the paper spread across the table which separated them and his lip curled. 'I gather this is the shock you alluded to. That these people pictured here are your parents. And that, or so the evidence in these photographs would indicate, they were members of Adolf Hitler's inner circle.'

He waved away her 'Yes, but...'

'There are no buts when it comes to fascists. We purged the Nazis out of the East in 1945. Unlike the West, we did not tolerate them then, and we certainly do not tolerate them now. And neither do we tolerate their descendants behaving in the same high-handed and arrogant way that they did, no matter how many diplomatic credentials they carry.'

He folded the newspaper and pushed it back towards her with the tips of his fingers, uncovering one of the black folders whose twins lined the shelves as he did so. He made sure Evie could see that it was her name stamped on the cover. She didn't know how or if to respond to it, or to him. The sight of the file plus the implication that she'd behaved like a member of the Third Reich had taken her breath away. But the officer wasn't finished with her.

'I have kept copies of the photographs which I will hold in your file. And now that we're done, it's time you left the GDR. Immediately.'

Evie's first reaction was to say, *No, that's not fair.* She stopped herself. If there was ever a time for the diplomacy she'd forgotten earlier, it was now.

'I understand why you think that's appropriate, but could I ask you, please, to reconsider? Whatever you think of my behaviour today, or my parents, I'm not a Nazi. The investigation I'm working on could help a lot of people. I would be so grateful if I was allowed to stay and complete it.'

Her diplomatic skills didn't matter; she'd still answered back.

The officer leaned forward, and Evie suddenly saw the bulk that the suit camouflaged. Nothing she'd said mattered to him.

'Why do you think that you have a voice in this? You are leaving because this is our country and we don't want you here. There is no discussion. Your embassies in both the west and the east of the city have been contacted. They both agree that you have outstayed your welcome, so you have two hours to gather your things and present yourself at the crossing point. Or you can choose not to comply with this instruction and I will have you sent to a prison where you can consider how sensible that choice is. A prison which, as far as anyone outside its walls is concerned, does not exist.'

He closed the folder with a snap and flexed his fingers in a gesture that made Evie's neck crawl.

'Your people will, of course, eventually extract you from there. But that will take time. It could take months if there are issues with the paperwork, and there will be issues. It could take longer if you prove to be a difficult guest, which I have no doubt that you will. And do not be under any illusions that you will receive special treatment because you're an American. However long you remain there, whether it is a day or a year, you will not come out the same woman.' He folded his hands on top of the folder. 'So, do we have an understanding? Will you leave without a fuss?'

If I say one word he can twist into a refusal, I'll be lost inside that prison before Sebastian knows I've left the hotel.

Evie knew it wasn't a bluff. He was watching her, tapping his fingernail against his watch face as he did so. It was the smallest movement but – as with everything about him – it was terrifying. Evie nodded. She got up when he told her to and followed him out of the room into a stairwell that suddenly felt horribly dark. He didn't speak to her again. He didn't acknowledge either Todd or Sebastian when they reached the busy foyer. He disappeared into the bustle without looking back.

'How long did he give you to get out?'

Todd wouldn't meet her eye when he asked; he didn't suggest that anything could be done to reverse the decision. As soon as Evie told him that she had two hours, he muttered something about ticking clocks and hurried off to organise a car.

Evie turned to Sebastian, her tightly held body starting to shake. 'I'm so sorry. I know you wanted to spend time in the West. I know this has messed up the search and that I've caused you nothing but trouble. Maybe they'll let you stay and—'

She didn't get a chance to finish the sentence. Sebastian's arms were around her; her face was buried in his chest. And all she could hear was, 'None of that matters now; all that matters is that you're safe. I'm coming back with you.'

The hotel staff had already packed their bags by the time they returned to their rooms. Todd hustled them into the car with a hurried promise to follow up on everything and a very brief goodbye.

The trip back through East and West Berlin to the airport was a silent one. So was the flight home. Their hands stayed locked for hours, but neither of them commented on that, and neither of them had the strength for a conversation that went beyond basic practicalities.

Evie's head was filled with the nightmare that her parents had become. She assumed that Sebastian's was filled with Annaliese and the abrupt end to his search for her. She was no longer thinking about the happy future she'd hoped that the trip would provide. There was no space anymore for that. Instead of coming closer, they were both caught in the past, exhausted from Berlin's revelations. And buried beneath a new layer of secrets.

CHAPTER 16

WASHINGTON, FEBRUARY 1980

*ANOTHER BEVY OF BEAUTIES ARRIVES ON
AMERICAN SOIL*
It's time to get yourselves down to the harbour, boys!

The newspaper article Evie had discovered in a New York archive told a more welcome story than the last one she'd found. She told Sebastian that as she passed it over the desk to him, but he still hesitated. He didn't speak. He spent what felt like an eternity poring over the photograph and the list of names, which included Annaliese's. And then he sat back, pushed the photocopy away and said nothing.

I thought he'd be happier than this.

Sebastian's face was blank. His hands were tucked under his thighs. It wasn't until he drew a sharp breath that Evie realised he wasn't unhappy; he was overwhelmed.

'How did Todd find this? It can't have come from Berlin.'

His voice was clipped, his face colourless.

Because this is another lead, but it isn't the complete answer. It's a bit of hope that could easily be dashed.

She couldn't say that; she couldn't even ask him how he felt.

They were treating each other like strangers again, circling round the gap that had opened up between them since their return from Berlin.

Two weeks and no contact will do that.

Evie couldn't comment on that either. She knew her reasons for staying silent, but she could only guess at his.

Evie had been walking around inside a protective bubble since their trip, refusing to engage with the revelations about her parents until corroboration arrived. She hadn't called Sebastian; he hadn't called her. When the phone didn't ring, she assumed he was locked inside the same waiting game as she was, and had no more desire than she did to engage in meetings filled with pointless speculation about his mother or hers. And – because Ethan had crept back into her head again – Evie had also assumed that her parents being revealed as Nazis, and potentially high-ranking ones, had made him wary of being anything closer to her than colleagues. That line of thinking had made sense when they were apart. But now that he was in front of her again? Looking at her in that intense way he had? Being strangers to each other made no sense at all.

I should have gone to his bed in Berlin.

Evie snapped that thought shut. From not speaking for two weeks to regretting not sleeping with him was far too big a leap. She reached for the documents Todd had sent instead. This meeting was about Sebastian's needs, not hers, and that demanded her professional face, not her personal one.

'No it didn't come from there. Todd got a hit on the emigration records and that's what led me to this. Annaliese hadn't changed her last name, and she showed up on a Hamburg America Line passenger manifest for August 1951, sailing from Cuxhaven to New York. When that information came in, I set up a search there and the researcher found this picture. It's from the *New York Daily News*.' Evie glanced at the cluster of women gathered on the gangplank in their bell-shaped summer dresses. 'It's a lovely photo. When it first arrived, I thought it was part of a fashion shoot.'

She hesitated. She'd ringed Annaliese's face based on the order given in the caption below. The picture was black and white and grainy, and she didn't want to spin too much from it, but the resemblance between the young woman and Sebastian was striking, and she said so. The tension clinging around him loosened a little, and he picked the paper back up. This time he let himself linger on it. The longing imprinted on his face was so intense, Evie momentarily forgot her own story. All that mattered was helping him to unravel his.

'It's good news, Sebastian. She wasn't one of the women interviewed for the article, which was a shame, but we have a starting point for her now. She didn't get lost in post-war Germany; she came to America. It's likely that she stayed. And given that she was calling herself Stengel in 1951, I think it's also safe to assume that didn't change for a while, if at all.'

His lips had reappeared; he no longer looked hollow. It was hard not to reach across the table and take his hand. Evie contented herself with a smile.

'The wheels to track her down are in motion, Sebastian. I'm hopeful that there'll be something else soon.'

Sebastian nodded and rubbed his face as though he expected to find tears there. 'Thank you. I don't think I honestly believed we'd get this far, and now here she is. Literally, here she is. I can't thank you enough.'

And then he smiled, and his smile brought back all the colour which Berlin had taken away. The connections which ran so deeply between them, and the hope she'd held for a different kind of future, were there in its warmth.

Now Evie sat forward, stretching out her hands to meet his. 'I should have phoned you before this. I don't know why—'

But Sebastian spoke at the same time she did, and his question turned the world back to grey.

'What else did Todd send over? Was he able to find out any more information about your parents?'

Evie sat back again; she pulled her hands away from the desk. She didn't want to have this conversation. She couldn't push the certainty of *if I don't discuss it, then it won't be real* out of her head. And she couldn't admit to Sebastian how irrational she was being. She could barely admit that to herself.

She hadn't just been living in a bubble; she'd been living in a state of denial ever since she'd pulled the wedding pictures out of the evidence box. Telling herself that the photographs were staged, that they were some kind of propaganda piece. That her parents had been forced into a charade that they were now deeply ashamed of, and it was that shame which had dictated all the lies that had followed.

She'd clung tight to that fiction. She hadn't rung them to ask what was real and what wasn't. And she hadn't told Marty the whole truth when he asked her what on earth had happened in Berlin. She'd blamed their early exit on a mistimed conversation and an overeager informant, and Marty had accepted that version, although he hadn't tried to hide his disappointment. Evie had apologised to him. She'd convinced herself that her parents weren't Nazis but dupes. She'd got through the days. And then the bag had arrived from the embassy and proved that they were anything but.

When she didn't answer him, Sebastian put the photograph of Annaliese down. 'What else came, Evie? I can see in your eyes that there was something. What is it that you can't or don't want to face? Tell me – let me help.'

If there had been an ounce of judgement in his voice, Evie would have cut his question off. But this was Sebastian, and there was never judgement of her with him.

Or not until now anyway.

She couldn't hide behind the fear of that, and neither of them needed more secrets. Evie reached for the folder which she'd stuffed into her desk in the hope that it would disappear and forced herself to start talking.

'The truth. That my parents are exactly who the paper portrayed them to be. Todd managed to find more detailed records for them than he did for your father, which I suppose tells a tale in itself.'

She pushed the folder towards him; he didn't open it. He kept his eyes on her face and let her carry on talking.

'It's all in here, and it's horrible. Both their names were on the National Socialist Party membership list, and they'd joined it long before joining could be explained away as a necessary evil. My father was a Sturmbannführer in the SS, and he and my mother were also on a list of potential witnesses – or defendants, it wasn't clear which – who were to be called, or investigated, at Nuremberg. And both of them were recorded a few months after that as being no longer of interest due to what was listed as *special circumstances*.'

She paused for a moment, hating everything that term implied. 'There's no explanation in the file for that, but Todd said that specific wording usually meant that the individuals concerned had cut some kind of a deal with the Allies, one that whitewashed their past in exchange for their knowledge. Which would make sense for my father, given that he was in fact a rocket scientist, although he worked for the Nazis not the Swiss.'

She stopped, relieved to have at least part of what she had to tell him over and done with.

Sebastian nodded as if he wasn't surprised. 'That would explain why your mother reacted so badly when you mentioned Rudolph's name to her – it sounds like your father came here as part of the Paperclip round-ups too. Which trial was he originally going to be called at? The Mittelbau-Dora one?'

Evie pulled the file back and flipped it open at the trials page. 'Yes. The records show that he was based at the mine, although there wasn't a date given for when he first went there.' Evie checked herself before it sounded as if she was about to defend him. 'But he must have known about the inhumane way the workers were treated, even if he didn't write the orders setting up the conditions there himself.'

I could leave it there. This is bad enough. I could bury the rest.

Evie knew that she couldn't. Even if Sebastian didn't ask why Helen had also been listed on a trial sheet, she had to tell him. Some things couldn't stay hidden, even if the telling might turn out to be the one hurdle he couldn't get across. And the only way to do that was quickly.

She pushed the folder back towards him. 'And my mother's name is here, look. On the Race and Settlement trial list.'

This time he did what she asked and looked. The effect was immediate. Evie could have bitten out her tongue as he turned white. She stopped looking at him and stared down instead at the page she already knew by heart.

'I don't know why she's mentioned here, and I don't know where she worked or why she was being called to the trial. The records for her didn't include that level of detail. But she was a doctor, so whatever she did can't have been good. Maybe she was at a camp like Mengele, carrying out experiments. Or maybe she...'

Evie stopped; she couldn't say the next words.

But Sebastian could.

'Was carrying out selections, or kidnappings, or running a Lebensborn home.'

When Evie managed to scrape up enough courage to look at him again, he was staring over at the picture of Annaliese, not at her. She had to bite her lip hard to hold back the tears which were filled with *I've lost him.* But then he looked up too, and he rallied.

'Or maybe she was going to be called as a witness and she wasn't responsible for any actual crimes.'

He took a deep breath at Evie's, 'I don't believe that and neither do you.'

'No, I don't suppose that I do. I think in all likelihood, given the circles she moved in, her story will be a dark one and it may overlap with mine in ways that neither of us want. And I'm not going to pretend that's anything other than dreadful.'

He stopped, reached out and closed the folder so that neither of them could see its cruel words.

'But listen to me, Evie, please. Whatever she was doing, it's not your fault. Are you hearing me? It's got nothing to do with who you are, in exactly the same way that my father's role in the SS, or the reason why he and Annaliese had a child, has got nothing to do with me. The shadow only clings as hard as we let it. I'm still learning that, and it's hard to accept it, but you may need to learn it too. You said that you didn't see evil in me when I sat here holding my christening cup – do you remember?'

He smiled when she managed a yes, and his smile was a lifeline.

'You didn't hesitate, even though you didn't know me at all, Evie, and that made me believe I could hold my head up. How could I ever see evil in you after that?'

And that was it. That was the moment when Evie stopped running from her feelings and accepted that she was falling in love with him. She didn't say it – if there ever would be a right time to admit that her feelings were running so deeply, this certainly wasn't it. She said a simple *thank you* instead and knew from the way Sebastian held her gaze that he heard the hint of more.

Which can't come until the harder conversations are done, if it ever comes at all.

Evie picked the folder up – tidying it away into her desk drawer gave her a moment to gather herself.

'I hid all this when we came back, from Marty as well as myself. I've told him the truth now, and he's agreed that my parents need to come under the scope of the OSI investigation. And I told him that I want to run that myself.' She shook her head as Sebastian started to protest. 'He didn't like it much either, but I have to. The same way you'll need to take the lead in the search for Annaliese if we make any more progress. There's some things that can't be left to other people – you know that. And I'm not going to waste any more time avoiding what has to be done.'

'What do you mean, *what has to be done*? What are you planning?'

This time Evie made sure not to look at him. She'd only made her decision earlier that morning; she hadn't run it past Marty, and she didn't intend to. He would advocate caution and so would Sebastian, and the last thing she needed was anybody trying to talk her round. *One mistake and she'll have the skin off my back* had been lodged in her head since dawn. She was going to do what was needed anyway.

'I'm going to telephone my mother. I'm going to tell her that we've found some photographs from 1943, in the course of another investigation, which raise questions about her and my father's background. I'm going to give her a chance to explain them if she can. And I'm going to do it tonight.'

'What is this about, Evie? What point are you trying to make? Are you so disappointed in us as parents that you have to cast your father and me as *villains*? Really? Are you still playing the aggrieved child at your age? Don't you think it's time to finally grow up?'

Evie had to hand it to her mother – the woman's ability to maintain an ice-cold composure whatever the situation was remarkable.

Helen had lost interest as soon as she picked up the call and realised it was Evie on the other end. She'd sighed when Evie led straight into her discovery of 'questionable photographs' dating from the war. And then, when Evie asked if she could provide an explanation for why she and Alex had featured in those, Helen had not only dismissed the idea that she should explain anything, she'd implied Evie was needy and a nuisance and not to be taken seriously. Helen had, in fact, done everything that Evie had expected her to do, short of immediately putting the phone down.

Which will also be an answer, if that's the next tactic she tries.

Evie gave her mother a moment to assume she would apologise or fold. Then she continued.

'*Villains* is an interesting word choice, and not one I would argue with. Let me be clearer. The photographs I'm talking about were taken in Berlin, in 1943. Does that ring any bells? They weren't holiday snaps; they were your wedding photographs. A whole newspaper filled with them, and a caption calling you and my father a perfect couple, which – given the context – was a disturbing choice of words.'

Evie paused. She didn't expect a response, not yet. She presumed her mother would be waiting to find out what else Evie knew. But her voice had started to rise, and she wasn't prepared to offer her mother the slightest hint of weakness.

It seemed, however, that this time she'd broken through the ice. Helen's immediate and unexpected, 'What on earth are you on about?' had menace running through it, but it also had shock. Evie forced herself not to seize on that but to remain factual instead and to use her lawyer's calm voice.

'I'm talking about the coverage of your wedding at Berlin Cathedral on the twentieth of February 1943, which was featured in a newspaper called the *Völkischer Beobachter,* a publication I now know to be the Nazi Party's mouthpiece.

There was a studio portrait of you and Father on the front cover and a dozen more pictures inside. You were shown posing on the cathedral steps and waving at the crowd, and standing outside its main doors with your arm linked through Heinrich Himmler's. And there was a series taken at the reception too, of you and my father laughing and smiling with—'

The names were too much. Evie's voice broke. She forced herself to continue anyway.

'With Hitler and Goebbels and Göring. It looked as if you were all the greatest of friends. Which explains the lack of photos in our house perhaps but is an odd situation, don't you think, for a couple who'd supposedly been living a quiet life in Switzerland before they fled to America? To have the full cast of the Third Reich at your wedding?'

She stopped to catch her breath and to regain control. She could hear Marty in her head, worrying that she wouldn't be able to act as a lawyer when she was a daughter reeling in shock. She could hear Ethan too, asking her why she was surprised that her elitist and right-leaning parents had turned out to be actual Nazis. And her younger self, asking why anyone had had to run from a neutral country like Switzerland and being dismissed. There were so many questions burning through her, it was hard to pull them into a coherent shape. And she waited too long to try. Helen broke the silence first and came back fighting.

'What do you want from me? An apology because we chose to keep a part of our lives private? Or some tear-filled admission of guilt?'

The 'Guilt for what? What did you do?' which burst out of Evie's mouth was too desperate, too angry. It took any vestige of control she had away. She couldn't tell if the noise her mother made in response was a sigh or a laugh.

'Here you go again. Homing in on every word as if we're in court. For nothing, Evie. There is no guilt, no remorse for past wrongs if that's what you're looking for. There is no great revelation coming. There is nothing I intend to discuss with you or with anyone else.'

The ice was back, the menace was thicker.

I could tell her about the trial lists. I could tell her that this conversation doesn't end here, whatever she thinks. That she isn't the one running the show.

But Evie's self-protection instincts kicked in and she didn't say any of that. Her mother heard it in the silence anyway.

'This stops, Evie. Whatever you think you've uncovered, whatever your overheated imagination is conjuring up, it stops. Don't think we are a case. Don't take this any further. You will be very sorry indeed if you do.'

It wasn't advice; it was a warning. And it wasn't a mother talking to a daughter; it was a declaration of war. Evie refused to react. She didn't reply. She chose to be the one who put the phone down. But she stood beside the replaced receiver for a long time. And she felt Helen's malevolent presence curling through her apartment for a lot longer than that.

CHAPTER 17

BIRMINGHAM, FEBRUARY 1980

She's found more than a handful of photographs. She's holding something back.

Helen Ritter had very little in common with her daughter, but they shared one trait: they'd both learned the value of self-preservation. Where they differed was that Evie's need to take refuge in that state only ever surfaced around her mother. Helen's applied to every facet of her life. She put the receiver down a second after Evie cut the call off, but she didn't stand beside the telephone table picking over the conversation. She didn't waste her time wondering what Evie was doing. She focused on herself and her fury.

We should have left her behind in Berlin.

That wasn't a new thought. It was a certainty which Helen had nurtured over the years, breathing new life into it every time the child tried to insert herself and her exhausting demands into her and Ulrich's lives. She'd never felt guilty about thinking it; she'd never tried to suppress the emotion. She would have gladly shared the sentiment with Evie on multiple occasions, except that the story they'd always told her was that she'd been born in America, and the story was everything.

Unless she does what she seems to be intent on doing and tears our lives down. Then I'll tell her exactly how I feel.

Helen walked from the hallway into the living room, poured herself a brandy and sat down on the couch. The sun had set but the sky was rich and clear, and the fairy lights which Ulrich – because he would always be Ulrich not Alex in her head – had twisted round the trees were twinkling through the branches like trapped stars. Helen sipped her drink and watched the show. She loved this house. Its shingled roof and shuttered windows and the arched portico which framed the front door reminded her of the stately villas which sat beside the lake in Wannsee, Berlin's most sought-after borough. The ones her mother had sighed over as if they were palaces on summer day trips out of the city.

This is where I belong. This is my reward. I'm not going to lose it or any other part of our life, not after I've worked so hard to get us here.

Helen shook herself. That wasn't right. Achieving a new life hadn't been her doing alone. It had never been *I* with them; it had always been *we* and *us*. She and Ulrich had worked as one since they first met, and nothing about that had changed with the war's end. Their bond was unbreakable; it was where they drew their strength from. And they had never shied away from doing whatever was needed to protect the only thing which mattered: each other. That was as true now as it had been in 1945, when they'd laid down the roots for all that came next...

'The scientists the Americans are rounding up are going to be sent to a research facility called Huntsville in Alabama. I've heard the soldiers talking about a special area being set up to accommodate them there, which the men have already christened Sauerkraut Hill. I won't be part of that. Wherever they send us, it won't be there.'

While Ulrich enticed the Americans with the breadth of his technical knowledge, Helene turned herself into a spy. She crept round the castle, flattening herself behind open doorways, hiding in the corridor where the field radio was kept. If there was a conversation she missed, it was a rare one. And she used Evie to open the doors that otherwise might have stayed closed to her. Once the men had finished raiding the castle and slept, they were far more amenable to a baby's smiles. And they were far more talkative than they should have been when Evie was around to distract them.

The colonel who came to collect them acted as if his intelligence mission was top secret; it was clearly anything but. All the men knew about the push to gather up German scientists faster than the Russians could, and – although they might hate the possibility of Nazis working in America – they couldn't stop talking about the scheme. Helene squirreled away every nugget of information she gleaned and, once she heard the quickly hushed, 'As long as they keep the Krauts out of the nuclear base at Los Alamos, maybe it won't be so bad,' the final piece of her plan fell into place.

The colonel was furious that she knew about the facility's existence when she told him where she wanted her family to live. The young soldier who liked to show off his insider knowledge was whisked away under threat of court martial. But Ulrich had done his homework well and could discuss the technology which would drive the nuclear arms race with as much confidence as he could discuss the space programme. Their move to Los Alamos was never in doubt.

Helen, as she then became, had achieved what she wanted – a base where no one cared where anybody came from – but she hated it there. She hated every minute of the three years they spent in New Mexico, although it brought the whole family American citizenship and her an approved medical licence. She loathed the wide open and too empty spaces, the extreme heat and the extreme cold. She loathed the long, enforced separations from Ulrich. Los Alamos was an isolated place where the scientists worked punishing hours and Santa Fe – where Helen demanded to be housed when she saw the rough family quarters on offer at the base – was as graceless in her eyes as a frontier town. Three years in and Helen had begun to think she'd made a terrible mistake, and then salvation came, in the unlikely shape of Alabama and Huntsville.

Alabama, where Ulrich was finally transferred to in 1948 when Los Alamos closed, was a very different place to New Mexico. And Birmingham – the closest city to the base – with its strict racial divisions and its belief in white superiority, was a very welcome one. By the time the Ritters reached it, they'd become Swiss – and American. They kept their distance from the scientists who'd been working at the Huntsville facility since 1945; not that they needed to worry. There was no one left from the original German cohort there who knew Ulrich. Or, if there was, they were also too busy reinventing themselves to be concerned with the appearance of a colleague who preferred to place his past in a more neutral country. And Helen knew better than to accept a house in Sauerkraut Hill. She found a prettier neighbourhood, and she chose well. There were plenty of people in her part of the city who privately – and sometimes publicly – considered that the Nazis' programmes around population control weren't so misplaced.

Helene and Ulrich weren't foolish enough to reveal their true backgrounds even to their closest friends, but they quickly found themselves in a like-minded community. And when they encountered a problem? When a snooping cleaner found a photograph of Hitler – before Helene stripped away every trace of their past lives – and the woman was convinced that the man at his side looked like Ulrich? Or when a young Jewish boy called Helen 'a nasty piece of work' because she refused to have someone called Goldstein cut her lawn? Or when a black man

wasn't quick enough to step off the pavement when she passed
by? Nothing overt ever had to be done; everything could be
managed. Some prejudices easily transcended country borders;
vulnerable people could always be persuaded to leave or to be
quiet if the threats were strong enough. All it needed was the
right word in the right ear at the club and all their problems
were solved. That was a lesson Helen quickly learned to make
very good use of.

*And now I'm the one repaying the favours and making the future
better for us all.*

Helen got up and walked to the picture window which
looked out over the spotless garden. The house was beautiful.
Their life in Birmingham's elegant suburb of Mountain Brook
was a comfortable and privileged one. On the rare occasions,
like now, when she was forced to consider what their fates could
have been, her blood ran cold.

The checklist that lived in Helen's head was one of the few
things that could bring her to tears. For the Party's leaders
who'd been lost to the bullet or to poison. Who – in her eyes –
had chosen a more dignified ending than the Allies would have
given them. And for all the men and women who had, like her
and Ulrich, been trying to create a better world and were
pursued through the courts and imprisoned for that. Or were
treated like outcasts by the same people who'd cheered them in
happier days, then instantly pretended that they hadn't.

*We've built a good life here, but it could never be the one we
truly wanted.*

That was another memory it was hard to dwell on, although
Birmingham had staunched it a little.

Helen and Ulrich's dreams of a new world had died along
with Nazi Germany's hopes in 1945, and they both carried that
failure like a wound. It had been a relief to find a city where the

social ideals they'd lived by there still flourished. 'Birmingham's a right-thinking place' was the Beech Brook country club's unofficial motto, and she and Ulrich had espoused that along with everything else that the club had to offer. The connections they'd made there, and the *right kind of thinking* which ruled in the city, had allowed the Ritters to live the segregated life that they – if not their ungrateful daughter – desired. A life free from unwanted contact with the type of people who'd been so successfully purged from the Reich.

A legacy which lives on even if the misguided lawmakers insist that we're all equals now. A legacy which allows me to continue my work.

Helen put down her empty glass. She didn't refill it: she was too fond of a clear head to ever have more than one drink. Her work was what mattered. Ulrich knew that: he supported her as he'd always done and always would. But Evie would never understand it, and Evie was, once again, becoming a nuisance. Money had solved that problem when she was younger and could be left to schools and staff. Money wouldn't work now, but there were other ways. Helen was under no illusions about her daughter. Evie was dogged to a fault and never knew when to stop pursuing one of her ridiculous causes.

So now it's time to make sure that she learns.

Helen pulled down the blinds and went back into the hall. She had two telephone calls to make. The second one would be to Ulrich, who was away overnight at a conference in Atlanta, to warn him what Evie had discovered. She doubted the girl would be stupid enough to ring him and try to divide and conquer her parents, but she wasn't about to leave anything to chance. The first would activate a contact she hadn't needed since their relocation in 1948.

Helen opened her purse and took out a business card from a concealed inner pocket. It wasn't the original one she'd been given; the phone number and the name of the agent had changed over the years. But the instruction which had accompanied that first card – 'If there's ever the slightest hint that anyone is sniffing around, call us at once and we'll deal with it' – was the same. And now here was Evie doing far more than sniffing, and there were more people than the Ritters with their reputations at stake. The CIA's message to her had been a simple one; Helen's to them would be the same.

'Deal with my daughter, however you need to, before her interfering gets any worse.'

She picked up the receiver and dialled.

CHAPTER 18

WASHINGTON, FEBRUARY 1980

'We need better security. This package was harmless, but it might have been a very different story. There's already been two attempted bomb attacks against Nazis from the *New York Times* list who we're investigating. This could be retaliation. I wouldn't underestimate anything those bastards are capable of, not given their histories.'

No one had disagreed with Marty's assessment that improved security would be a good investment. Evie had got as big a fright as anyone else when the bulky packet arrived. It was covered in *Fragile* stickers and too many stamps and had Marty's name misspelled on the label, all the tells they'd been warned to look out for that could signify a parcel bomb. Everyone had agreed that more checks and a guard on the office door would be a good idea. Unfortunately, they'd left the meeting and immediately got buried back in their burgeoning caseloads, so actually instigating the changes had fallen to the bottom of the office's endless priority list. Faced now with the man filling her door – who hadn't been announced because it was late and Evie was the only one still working – Evie wished they'd all possessed better memories.

Not that her visitor was a bomber or an arsonist – Evie was certain of that. She knew exactly who he was before he stopped looming and introduced himself. Agent Miller's outfit singled him out as effectively as his title: it was plain even by conservative Washington standards. Most departments had embraced the livelier approach to men's fashion that the last decade had brought in. Plaid suits and patterned shirts, wider ties and even the odd sports coat no longer raised eyebrows. Miller, however, was a model of restraint.

His suit was plain navy blue, his shirt was white and his tie was nondescript and tightly knotted. He looked to Evie like the kind of man who kept dark sunglasses on his nightstand. What he did for a living was as obvious as if he'd been wearing a badge. She assumed that the effect was deliberate: that he wanted her to know from the start exactly who he was. But if he was hoping to wrong-foot her, he'd wasted his time. Evie had been expecting someone like Miller to appear since she'd put the phone down on her mother.

The CIA hadn't been the driving force behind Operation Paperclip – the Agency wasn't formed until 1948 – but, as everyone in the OSI knew even if they couldn't prove it, they were the ones who had inherited and were now protecting the military's dubious wartime assets. And protecting was the right verb, as an increasingly furious Marty had learned.

He hadn't been able to uncover even half of what he'd wanted to about the mechanics of the Paperclip programme, despite weeks of effort. What he had discovered – from the handful of intelligence files he'd been able to secure before the memo not to let him get near them was circulated – was that rounding up German scientists before the Soviets could get to them had been a key military goal. And that being a Nazi wasn't perceived as a barrier to employment in America but as a 'troublesome detail'.

He'd also discovered that the intelligence services' determi-

nation to conceal the scale of the operation, especially from a
public who might have been deeply disturbed by it, ran deep.
According to his sources, thousands of files containing the
details of Paperclip participants had been destroyed in the
1960s for security reasons that nobody could or would explain.
The meeting in which he announced that finding had been one
of the most dispiriting team briefings Evie had ever sat through.
She could hear the despair which had clouded Marty's voice
echoing through her head as Agent Miller made himself
comfortable.

'They let in a tidal wave of murderers and Hitler-lovers no
one should have given houseroom to. Nobody asked who those
men, and possibly women, really were in '45 because nobody
wanted to know. And now that some of us do, well...' Even the
normally upbeat Marty hadn't been able to strike a positive note
as he issued the team's instructions. 'It's not going to be easy. I
told you to expect brick walls and denials. I think it would be
more accurate to say, expect downright lies and resistance. The
truth about our targets will be stowed away very deep.'

Evie waited for Miller to speak with Marty's warning loud
in her ear, knowing that he hadn't come to be helpful. And
knowing that whatever he had to say would also have a very
personal dimension. But as prepared for him as she was, his
sudden appearance in her office was still deeply unpleasant.

Miller carried the same cold air of authority, and the same
belief that his orders wouldn't be challenged, as the nameless
Stasi officer had worn in Berlin. And like him, Miller didn't
waste time on greetings or on explaining why he'd come. Or on
outlining what he hoped the meeting might lead to. He simply
stated his position.

'Your parents are off limits. Whatever investigation you're
running continues – or preferably doesn't – without their
involvement.'

The voice was quiet, the hands were relaxed; there was no

overt threat. The modus operandi was the same as the one the East German official had followed in Berlin, but what worked there didn't work here. Evie wasn't the same person the Stasi had frightened. She wasn't in a foreign country where she didn't know the rules or the language; she held a position of authority herself. And she wasn't going to be treated as if she was a criminal or a fool.

She matched Miller's calm gaze and his soft tone with her own and shook her head. 'They aren't and it doesn't. We don't consider anybody off limits, no matter who they are. And my parents are exactly the kind of people who fall under the OSI's remit.'

She expected Miller to leap in and rebuff her. When he remained silent, she continued, warming to her theme.

'As I'm sure you're aware, we believe that they were eminent Nazis, part of Hitler's inner circle. From the records we've already obtained, it would also appear that my father was brought into this country under the umbrella of Operation Paperclip.'

She waited for a flicker of recognition. When none came, her hackles started to flare.

'That programme appears to have been the subject of a very well-orchestrated cover-up, by your agency among others, but we can come back to that. We do know that my father was stationed at the Mittelbau-Dora mine and may have crimes to answer for there, not that anyone seems to have investigated that possibility then – or since. We suspect that my mother's crimes may run wider. And the fact that you're here, using the language you've just used, only adds weight to that suspicion. If they have nothing to hide, why would they need your protection?'

Evie stopped to let him answer. She was surprised – although she refused to show it – that he'd allowed her to continue for so long without interruption, particularly when she'd referred to a cover-up. From the way Miller was sitting – with his head slightly cocked and his fingers steepled – he appeared to have been giving careful consideration to what she'd said. And then he began to speak, and Evie realised that what he'd actually been doing was letting her run off steam. That he had absolutely no interest in her opinions about the CIA's behaviour or anything else. And no intention of answering her question.

'I find this obsession your department has with conspiracies to suppress evidence, and with a programme whose existence is based solely on conjecture, deeply disappointing.'

Miller waved a dismissive hand and carried on talking as Evie tried to protest at *conjecture*.

'And I find it equally disappointing that a public servant, which is what you are in case you need reminding, would attempt to interfere with national security. Oh don't look so aggrieved, Miss Ritter. What else are you trying to achieve by painting the intelligence services in such a negative light except to discredit us? Aren't you a little old to be playing the subversive? Or are you perhaps a communist who doesn't deserve to hold any form of legal position in this country at all?'

His arrogance was as breathtaking as his patronising manner, and Evie had no patience to indulge either.

'Is that really your best shot? That you are the guardian of America's well-being, and I'm the problem?'

His lack of any response set her blood boiling. She went on the attack and couldn't stop.

'So it is, wow. Okay, then what's next? If Paperclip is a figment of my imagination, what else am I wrong about? Are you going to pretend that the intelligence services didn't run protection for the hundreds of murderers who got away scot-free at the end of the war? What about Klaus Barbie? Is he a figment of my imagination too? Or was it perfectly acceptable to spirit Barbie – a man who was personally responsible for the

torture and killing of thousands of innocent civilians in France
– away to Bolivia and safety, because America wanted him as
an anti-communist agent? Or Eichmann – what about him? The
CIA ignored the lead that pointed to Eichmann's hiding place
in Buenos Aires years before the Israelis were able to track him
down; was that okay too? And, while we're at it, let's revisit
Paperclip, why don't we? Let's unpick the evidence on that one
a little. Or are you going to just deny that it existed, or that it
welcomed more Nazis into America than the Jewish refugees
whose lives they'd destroyed?'

Her chest was heaving; she'd run out of breath if not anger.
And she'd made a terrible mistake. Losing her temper so
completely and launching into a tirade had been a very ill-
judged move. The accusations she'd flung at Miller were true,
but this wasn't the time or the place to be flinging them.

*I should apologise or try and backtrack somehow for
Marty's sake,* flashed through her head, but she couldn't do it.
And she couldn't read Miller. Unlike her, he wasn't betraying
any trace of emotion. His hands had stayed folded and his
facial expression had stayed neutral throughout her onslaught.
His continued composure no matter the provocation
reminded Evie of her mother, and it was equally as
unnerving.

'That was quite a performance, Miss Ritter. It told me a
great deal about you, and also about the attitudes which I
assume prevail throughout your department. The one thing I
remain unclear about, however, is whether this current witch-
hunt that you're bent on pursuing is OSI-sanctioned or a
personal crusade. Why don't you help me with that? What
exactly do you want to happen to your parents, do you know?
Do you want to see them in jail, or deported, or is being publicly
humiliated by false accusations enough for you?'

Evie didn't have an answer for him. She didn't yet know the
extent of what they'd done, or what they deserved. Or what she

was capable of unleashing against them. She couldn't tell Miller that, but he saw her hesitation and he pounced.

'Do I need to remind you how delicate OSI funding is? Do I need to spell out how many people in high places are uncertain whether your investigations are a proper use of resources? Or are concerned that chasing after old men and women to accuse them of crimes they may or may not have committed in another land and another time might be an embarrassment?'

His voice dropped, but the menace didn't.

'Do you want America to look foolish, or cruel, on the world stage? Maybe that doesn't matter to you, although it should. Maybe I need to point out instead what digging about in the past has already led to. Threatening letters. Citizens afraid to step outside their homes. Arson attacks in peaceful suburbs, against respectable neighbours who have lived good, quiet lives. Or is that what you want for your country, Miss Ritter? Does a place ruled by vigilantes and mobs sound acceptable to you?'

There was so much at fault in what he'd said, but Miller didn't give Evie a chance to counter any of it. He got up, brushing his jacket down as if the air in her office was contaminated.

'I won't be coming back. I won't be having this conversation with you a second time. I hope that's clear.' He turned to her as he reached the doorway. 'And let's not either of us pretend that this was a friendly chat. It's a warning. Ignore it and nothing good will result.'

He was gone before Evie recovered her voice. Before she could shout back at him that he had no authority over her and no right to issue warnings or threats. Before she could demand that he explain what *nothing good* meant. She knew that he was serious, that she was meant to be afraid. She wasn't. She'd been standing up to bullies throughout her whole legal career, so she wasn't frightened; she was furious. And more determined than ever to dig as deep as she had to for the truth.

.   .   .

'Which is all well and good, but we need some idea of where this might be going, before we go into full battle mode. And you have to be certain that what's coming – an uncovering of the past which is likely to be painful and destructive – is something that you can honestly handle. None of the reservations I had about you being so closely involved have been helped by James Bond turning up.'

Marty might still have concerns, but the night Evie had spent pacing her apartment and waiting to speak to him had done nothing to weaken her resolve.

'I told you: I can do this.'

Marty opened his mouth to argue, but she wouldn't let him speak. 'My parents have kept secrets and told lies to me my whole life. They've told lies to everyone and built a very comfortable existence which I doubt they deserve out of that. And maybe they won't turn out to be as bad as the images that currently live in my head – if *as bad* is even a term that applies here. But I have to know. I have to follow the evidence through to its conclusion. And I can't do the rest of my job effectively if I walk away from this one.'

Marty studied her for a moment, then he sighed. 'Fine, fine, I'm clearly not going to win. But we proceed with far more caution from this point, okay?'

He waited until she managed a nod before he went on.

'Right, this is how it's going to go. I'm not going to be intimidated by the spooks flexing their muscles any more than you are, but I'm not going to pretend I'm happy with it either. So there's to be no more phone calls that could put either you or the department at risk. In fact, it would be best if you had no more contact with your family at all, at least in the short term.'

His jaw relaxed a little when Evie agreed. 'Right, well we approach this case in the same way we approach all the others, as an information-gathering exercise first. Speak to Todd. Get him to comb through the archives again and focus on your mother. Pull Karol Perlmann back in and show him the wedding photographs – let him take them away if he wants. Maybe they'll jog his or somebody else's memory and help us get a fix on exactly where the two of them were before 1945, and what exactly they were doing.'

All of that sounded perfectly reasonable. Evie was half out of her chair, ready to set both tasks in motion, until Marty's next suggestion made her forget what she was leaving to do.

'It might also be possible to go down the immigration route and question the basis on which American citizenship was granted. Your parents told you – and presumably everyone they met once they left Germany – that they were Swiss. If they put that nationality on their application form when they were actually Germans, then there may be grounds to have their citizenship revoked.'

That sounded reasonable, and Evie said so. Especially as questioning the basis for citizenship was always the first stage that had to be completed before there could be any move towards a deportation order. It was what he said next that tipped everything off balance.

'That's a long shot, of course. Especially as the intelligence services will be the ones who managed the entry process, and I think we can safely assume that there'll be no help from them. It could also take years and countless appeals to resolve, which could be a huge strain on you, never mind the additional complication that you'd be part of the investigation.'

He stopped as Evie frowned.

'What do you mean? Why would a citizenship trawl affect me?'

The compassion that swept over his face made her skin freeze. As did his 'Oh God, you don't know'. She hadn't until that moment. But Marty's shocked expression brought her mother's oddly phrased *life has turned out much better for you* rushing back. And then she did.

'I wasn't born here, was I? I was born in Germany. I came to America with them.'

She barely registered Marty's brief *yes*. The world had started shifting around her, spinning her back to Berlin Cathedral's ice-cold steps and the anchor formed there by Sebastian's arms. And the lie that his *that's my life, Evie; it's not yours* had now turned into.

'Evie, are you all right?'

'I don't know.'

It was the truth – she was numb. And then she wasn't, and that was worse.

'I'm German; I'm not American, or at least not by birth. All those files I've been reading, that are full of people whose lives were so different from what they'd been led to believe. Who were born to order or stolen to feed the Nazis' races theories. I'm one of them.'

Marty tried to interrupt, but Evie wouldn't let him. 'It's true. If you met my mother, you'd see in an instant that she didn't have me because she was longing for a baby. There isn't a woman in the world less suited to being a mother than her. I imagine I was born out of duty, as a child for the Führer, not because she was swept away on a tide of maternal hormones.'

She shook her head. She might not be numb anymore, but she didn't know whether she wanted to cheer or to weep.

'That would certainly explain a lot. About my life and my relationship with my parents, especially with her. Maybe it wasn't my fault that I never felt loved; maybe it really was theirs. It makes sense. Once the hope of a Thousand Year Reich was shattered, what possible use could my parents have for me? What else could I be to my mother but a mistake?'

Everything she was saying was terrible; she could see that in

Marty's stunned face. But there was a clarity in it too, and that was what Evie chose to grab on to.

I was a cog in the machine, the same as Sebastian. And when the machine broke, there was no further need for me.

That realisation should have dropped on her like a weight, but it did the complete opposite. Her shoulders lifted and lightened.

Now I know where I stand, and where she does too.

The phone call to her mother and the subsequent appearance of Agent Miller had proved one thing beyond all doubt. Helen had drawn up her battle lines and, irrespective of the fact that it was her daughter standing on the other side, she would be ruthless in her determination to win.

Which isn't new. This is the path we've all been on for years; this is the collision course my parents' lies built. And now it's done, and their lies and their past will get no more control over me.

She'd never felt stronger than she did in that moment, but Marty was staring at her as if he needed to call for help. As if he was regretting that he'd ever agreed this case could be her show. Which was the exact opposite of what Evie had intended.

'It's all right – I'm okay. You don't have to look at me like that. I've never been clearer about anything. When I applied to the OSI, I was worried I wouldn't get the job because I didn't have the right background. It's ironic now, don't you think, that I'm apparently the best qualified person to work here. Who better to be a Nazi hunter than one of their own?'

She thought she'd sounded perfectly logical, but all she'd done was activate Marty's already buzzing alarm bells.

'Evie, for God's sake, that's enough. You're not making any sense – you're not your mother or your father, and you're certainly not a Nazi. This is all too much for you. I'm going to get one of the team to take it over. I should have done that from the start; I should have known better than to give in.'

Evie knew he meant well, but he'd misunderstood. She wasn't in pieces. She didn't need to be protected or soothed. She stopped smiling – having rather belatedly realised that acting as if she was delighted she was about to go hunting after her Nazi parents made her look less not more in control – and stood her ground.

'No, please don't. That might feel like the right thing to do, but it's not.'

She took a deep breath, smoothed her hair. Did her very best to look trustworthy and calm and professional.

'I appreciate your concern, Marty, I really do. And I can understand why you think I may have lost some perspective here. But I'm fine and I'm keeping this case. I'm going after them – I have to. Wherever it leads, whatever it costs. You have to understand that, and you have to trust me. My involvement means that I'm the best person for the job, not the worst – don't you see? I know them; I know what kind of people they are. And I promise that this will be good for me, not bad.'

He was still frowning, but he was also still listening, and that was enough to spur Evie on.

'We've been given a remit to prove that no person and no crime is above the law. Bringing my parents to justice, if that is what they deserve, is the right thing to do for the sake of that principle. But it's also the right thing for me. Dragging their past into the light will be what sets me free of them. I need that, Marty; I want it. I'll do a better job because of it.'

They stared at each other across the table. Evie knew that Marty could refuse and that she would have to give in with good grace if he did. Or walk away from a job that she loved. And that he was right – she was far too close. But he hadn't said no right away. And he didn't say it when she added a heartfelt, 'Please, I won't let you down, I swear.'

He sighed and rubbed his face, but he nodded, and that was all Evie needed to see.

CHAPTER 19

FLORIDA, FEBRUARY 1980

She won't want me grew stronger with every mile, spinning in tandem in his head alongside *She rejected me once and now she'll do it again.*

All the stories that Sebastian had told himself to make his abandonment bearable – that Annaliese had been young and powerless and under the control of a regime which viewed children as commodities – had fallen away along the journey from Washington to Florida. And the hope which Evie had tried to pour into him, on the day she telephoned to say that the search had been a success, had fallen away too.

'We've found her.'

The words had taken his breath. They'd taken the floor. He'd had to get Evie to repeat them.

'We've found Annaliese. She married after she came to America, but she never changed her name, so tracking her down turned out to be very straightforward. And I'm not trying to tell you how to feel, Sebastian, but I think that there's a lot to hold on to in that. Most women change their names when they marry, especially if the wedding was in the fifties or sixties, but she didn't. Maybe she hoped that you'd come looking for her one day.'

He had so wanted to believe that. He'd almost succeeded. And then the doubts had come creeping back in.

In the time it had taken since Evie's call to clear his work schedule and make the travel arrangements, Sebastian had somersaulted between joy and despair and a dozen emotions in between.

His mother was alive and apparently well and living in Jacksonville on the northern stretch of the Florida coast. Sebastian had barely heard of the place. He knew nothing about it beyond the information recorded as an aside on two information boards in the History Museum. That the city had changed hands several times between the Union and Confederate armies in the Civil War and that it had been the unwilling host of a huge fire in 1901, which was still noted as one of the worst disasters in Florida's history. But now Sebastian could never view Jacksonville as a footnote again. His mother lived there, which made it the most significant place in America.

And the city in which I'll either be welcomed with open arms or finally turned away for good.

Sebastian's hands clutched the steering wheel. He was exhausted, which didn't help. He was starting to regret the decision to drive rather than taking a plane and saving himself such a rigorous journey. It was barely a two-hour flight from Washington to Jacksonville – it would have made much more sense to fly rather than spreading his trip out over two days. Two hours, however, had felt too abrupt, too short a time span to prepare for such a seismic change in his life. Two days alone in a car and a night in a faceless hotel had seemed, by contrast, the right amount, the breathing space he needed to damp down his demons.

Unfortunately, the calculation had misfired: his demons were as vivid as ever. Their voices – their *she didn't want you then and she won't want you now* – were as endless as the miles. And they'd made him ignore the phone number Evie had given him, the one he was supposed to use to make initial contact with Annaliese and test the waters.

Because I didn't want to tempt fate; I didn't want to give her a chance to say no. The element of surprise was supposed to help me.

That certainty had also fallen away as the journey neared its conclusion. This close, he couldn't envisage a happy outcome. He couldn't imagine the joyful embrace he'd longed for happening anywhere outside his head.

I wish Evie was with me. I wish I'd been honest with her, and myself, and admitted that this was too much to face on my own.

That regret was the drive's second rhythm, although changing it was also long past his control. The truth was, everything was simply harder without her.

It had been on the tip of Sebastian's tongue to ask Evie to go with him to Jacksonville, but when the moment to suggest it arose, he couldn't ask and she hadn't offered to come. That had hurt. Evie had referred to the search for Annaliese so often as *ours*, Sebastian had come to see it that way too – until he realised he was being unfair.

Evie had said *our search* and meant it, but she wasn't the kind of woman who pushed and directed, who tried to overlay her feelings onto his. She left space for him to listen to his own heart. That was one of the reasons, he suddenly realised, *that I'm falling in love with her.*

He jerked the car so badly he almost plunged off the road.

And now I'm leaving without her, even though I'm certain that something is wrong.

Evie had retreated again. She'd refused to meet up before he left, and there was clearly something more to that than the, 'I want you to have the time to focus on Annaliese,' that she'd offered him. He suspected it was her mother at the root of the problem. The timing was too much of a coincidence. The phone call to Helen, which she wouldn't discuss, had pushed Evie back into the box she'd taken refuge in when they'd come home from Berlin. The one heavy with secrets.

His first thought when he'd recognised that had been, *I'm losing her.* His first instinct had been to push at her and force her to talk. But he'd known better than to follow that first instinct with Evie.

Because I have to let her solve her situation in her own way and at her own speed. I have to show her the respect she shows me.

That had been the right decision, but it was easier said than done.

Sebastian slowed the car down as he approached the end of the Talmadge Bridge which straddled the Savannah River. The harbour bustled below the bridge as cargo ships made their stately way in and out of the port. Savannah's lights twinkled like a star-strewn carpet before him. Sebastian barely registered his surroundings beyond the directions his map had told him to follow to find his hotel. He was in the wrong place and the wrong time.

He didn't want to be driving towards a long-lost mother, without knowing whether she would welcome or turn him away. He didn't want to be that open to pain. And he didn't want to be waiting for Evie either, hoping she would love him once she'd fought her battles alone. He wanted to be at her side. He wanted to be wearing armour, riding on horseback over a moat. Charging through a forest-filled land to rescue the woman he loved from the monsters who were besieging her castle. He wanted to be the hero in her story.

The way she's been the hero in mine.

.   .   .

Avondale, the riverside borough where Annaliese lived, was a charming enclave of pretty houses, manicured lawns and solid oak trees. Sebastian drew up outside the pristine white house on Almira Street and got out of the car. He was glad he'd completed the bulk of the eleven-hour drive from Washington on the previous day and taken refuge overnight in a hotel – he might still be a barrel of nerves, but at least his linen suit was freshly pressed and his appearance was less chaotic.

He hovered on the sidewalk, scanning the neat garden and the latticed porch, trying to catch a glimpse into the front window as the short pathway to the front door stretched into miles. There was no one around, which didn't help his nerves and wasn't what he'd expected. Annaliese was sixty or more. Sebastian had assumed she would be retired, that Monday morning would find her at home. He didn't have a plan for the house being empty.

I don't have a plan at all, whether she's here or not. All I have is assumptions.

That realisation had hit him too late to be useful and offered no reassurance. Sebastian was a planner by nature. He was methodical, he considered the facts before coming to a well-supported conclusion; those skills were what made him good at his job. He hadn't employed a single one of them here.

He hadn't considered any aspect of Annaliese beyond her being the point of his quest. He hadn't put her into a workplace. He hadn't thought about the family she'd built in America and how his arrival might impact them. He didn't know if his birth had been discussed or was a secret. Or whether a husband – or her children, which was another element he hadn't factored in – might be angry, or saddened, or shocked to find an adult child turning up on their doorstep. He hadn't followed up on a single thing beyond the fact of her existence.

I should have telephoned first. That would have been the

safest strategy for everyone. I shouldn't have cast myself as the only person who mattered and blundered in.

Every decision he'd made suddenly felt wrong.

Sebastian turned, ready to drive away and look for a phone booth and redo his whole approach. The front door opened before he got a chance.

'Can I help you with something?'

The woman standing on the porch was squinting into the sun and had her hand raised to her eyes, but there was no mistaking who she was. Annaliese had stepped out of the photograph in the newspaper and become flesh and blood. She could have been the woman on the gangplank. Her hair was the same dark blond; her peach skirt swung out like a bell.

'I'm...'

His voice was a whisper. It was too thin to cover the short distance between them. Sebastian tried again. This time he managed to get as far as *I'm looking for* before he stalled.

'If it's my husband Tony you want, I'm afraid he's not here at the moment.'

She dropped her hand and moved a step or two closer. Sebastian could see the years now. Time had blurred her features and woven silver strands through the blond. He would still have known her anywhere.

And she knows me.

It was a ridiculous thought. If Maria was to be believed, Annaliese hadn't seen him since he was a tiny baby. She could hardly connect a new-born with a six-foot-tall, thirty-nine-year-old man. But she had. The evidence was there in her white face and open mouth. In the hand that was impossibly, perfectly, stretched out towards his.

'Sebastian?'

How could one word be poetry? He managed a nod. She pressed her hands to her mouth. The gesture didn't feel like a denial.

'Sebastian.'

She said his name again, and this time there was music in it.

'Oh dear God, it's really you. I've waited for this for so long, I'd almost given up hope. I followed you to America, to find you, and I couldn't. And with every year that passed, I lost a little more belief that you'd ever find me.'

She stopped. She stared at him. Suddenly the woman who was half his weight, whose head barely reached his chest, had him locked in an embrace that was so tight and so fierce, she carried the power of a grizzly bear. And all Sebastian could think as she clung on to him was, *I've come home.*

Their hands were still entwined when Annaliese led Sebastian past an immaculate kitchen which she described as 'my Tony's pride and joy' and into a sun-filled living room. Sebastian had more questions than he had words for and an inability to begin asking any of them. Tony, thankfully, was a way in.

'Does your husband know about me? Will it cause you problems that I'm here?'

The hesitation before she answered was slight, but it was there. Sebastian had to tell himself to ignore her bitten lip, that it was too soon to pry. He let her resume talking as they settled themselves onto a thickly padded couch. It had to be enough, for now, to know that she'd been longing for him as much as he'd been longing for her. It was surely too early to start delving into the shadows.

'He knows I have a son who disappeared in the war, who I haven't seen since he was a baby, who I've missed every moment since. When he proposed, he knew you were the reason I could never change my name.' Annaliese's voice strengthened: it was clear that Tony was her certainty. 'And he'll be happy that you're here because I am, and that's all that matters to him. He's a good man, and I want you to meet him. He owns a restaurant in town, and Monday is always a busy day – orders and menu-setting and all kinds of decisions that tie him up for hours. But that's not a problem, is it? You're going to be here a while? I'll have you for more than today?'

Part of Sebastian relished the hunger in her eyes. It told him that he was as welcome and wanted as she said. But her words – especially *disappeared* – were hard to hear. They suggested that Tony had been given carefully curated highlights of her life. He didn't get a chance, however, to probe further – Annaliese's questions were still tumbling.

'Have you been happy? Was your father kind to you? Has your life here been good?'

There was hunger in her questions too. A desperate need to hear him say, 'You did the right thing; there's nothing to blame you for.' He couldn't say it. He knew even if she didn't that there was anger to come, and pain on both sides to address and far more information needed than the vague hints about what had happened to him than he could glean from, *Was your father kind?* He didn't want to give Annaliese an answer that time would reveal as a lie.

The stakes have got higher.

It was a shock to recognise that. To know that his heart was still braced for a withdrawal on her part. Or for a terrible revelation and a rejection that would hurt so much more because he'd felt the depth of the love in her. Sebastian needed the ground between them to settle before he started marching across it. So he didn't answer her directly. He gave her a quick recap of his life instead, one which omitted Maria's cruelty and his discovery of the truth about his birth, and left out his painful divorce.

When he finished, Annaliese did the same. She offered him a version of herself which included a kind husband who was part of a generous and loving extended family, and her children, a half-brother and half-sister who lived several states away and would want to get to know him too.

Once they'd traded reports, however, an uncomfortable silence fell between them. A silence Sebastian knew would thicken and become their pattern if he let it take root. He summoned up his courage instead, and he broke it.

'When was the last time you saw me? My stepmother Maria said I was two or three weeks old – is that true?'

He offered her that question as a pathway into the past. He used Maria's name and his age when she left him as a hint to Annaliese that he was aware of at least some of his background. He steeled himself for the first mention of Kurmark, of Lebensborn. They didn't come.

'No. But I understand why she said it was. That was the last time I was supposed to have had any contact with you. That's when you were taken from me. But no, it wasn't the last time I actually saw you.'

All of a sudden, Annaliese closed her eyes and began to speak in a softer voice which instantly made Sebastian imagine all the missed bedtime stories. Thirty-nine or not, its cadence made him want to weep.

'That was in 1948, when you were six going on seven. You were so beautiful, so precious, and he wouldn't let me near you. It's not a day I could ever forget...'

Annaliese emerged from the war hollowed out. Like everyone else whose lives had been ruined, she existed, she got by, but she didn't feel truly alive.

She had no home of her own anymore. She found a room in a shattered building with other survivors who were as faceless as she was. She found a job as a secretary in a factory that was trying to get back up off its knees. She walked and she talked and she moved through the world doing what it required of her.

But underneath her thin coat and patched dress, she was a shell.

Her parents had been killed in 1943, in an air raid which had destroyed their apartment block and left her without bodies to bury. Once the Soviets drew close to Berlin in 1945, she'd fled Köpenick's broken streets for the western side of the city where there was at least some hope that less terrifying armies would eventually arrive. By the time she saw Sebastian again, Annaliese was utterly alone, unable to form anything other than the most transient relationships. She didn't question that state. Her heart had been torn from her body when her baby was taken, and that emptiness had become all she was.

The one thing which had remained constant throughout the years was her search for her son. That was the only thing that had kept her going, although – until a late spring afternoon three years after the war ended and almost seven since she'd lost him – the search had only ever drawn blanks. So when Bruno and Maria finally appeared, walking along the quiet shores of Krumme Lanke, each of them holding the hand of a small blond boy, Annaliese assumed she'd conjured them up.

That wasn't unusual: she saw Sebastian everywhere; she was used to apologising to startled mothers. If Bruno hadn't looked up and caught sight of her, if he hadn't immediately bundled the smaller of the two boys behind him, Annaliese would have gone on her way. But this Bruno was real enough to panic. Which meant that this Sebastian was real too.

'Sebastian! Sebastian! It's me; it's your mother!'

Her frantic call lifted the boy's head. It also alerted Maria, who immediately grabbed the child from Bruno and clutched him to her side. And it brought Bruno running to where Annaliese was standing before she was able to call out a second time. If the lake had been busy, she would have stood a chance, but there was rain in the air and the other walkers had vanished. Her arm was pinned behind her back before she could draw breath. She was in a shady copse, her head slammed against a tree trunk before she could fight him off.

'Leave us alone. Stay away.'

He hissed the warning, his mouth too wet, too close to her face. He kept his hand across her throat to cut off her reply.

'He isn't yours. Come after us and I'll see to it that you disappear.'

Bruno hit her across the temple then and knocked her dizzy. By the time Annaliese emerged from the trees and back onto the shore, the family and her boy had vanished.

'I lost you twice, but I never gave up, especially after that second chance woke me from the daze I'd been living in. I used what money I had to pay for a private detective, which is how I knew you'd gone to America. And it took a long time to save up, but I got here in the end too. Except the trail was cold by then. So I waited and I hoped, and now here you are – you came.'

There was violence in the room and another new Bruno for Sebastian to absorb. And for all that Annaliese had managed to tell him, there were still secrets and omissions too. Sebastian had no memory of that afternoon, and he was a step behind what she was saying. Trying to shake off the image of his father beating his mother. Of a desperate woman standing alone by a rain-spotted lake, mourning her snatched child for the second time.

Annaliese was exhausted. Sebastian could see that, but he no longer cared about safe ground and careful steps. She'd opened the gate to the whole story and he had to lead her through to the rest.

'I know where I was born.'

Her hands clenched; her body started to tremble. Sebastian had to look away. She had to have considered this possibility, and if she hadn't, if she was so filled with denial? He pushed the thought down before the anger which was bubbling through him started to take hold. He couldn't be a footnote anymore. He stared out of the window and kept going.

'I know that my father was in the SS. I know that I was born in a Lebensborn home. Maria, who hated you and therefore hated me too, told me that much years ago.'

Annaliese's groan tore at his skin, but all the pent-up years were pushing at him and, now that he'd started letting them go, he couldn't stop.

'And I know that Heinrich Himmler was my godfather – I found a christening cup in my stepmother's things with my name and his engraved on it, and a swastika-embossed cloth and a set of candlesticks. And I also know that I was born on Himmler's birthday, which meant that I was special, that I was supposed to be groomed as a leader of the Thousand Year Reich.'

The words were pouring out now. He couldn't look at her; he could barely draw breath.

'Can you understand how that knowledge has crippled me? How it's been a stain on my life? You have to help me make sense of it – no one else can. I have to know why I was born and why you left me, for my own sake and for ours. If we have any chance of building a future beyond this moment, beyond today, you have to tell me the whole truth.'

His voice broke. When he finally stopped and looked up at Annaliese, she was so small and so lost, part of him wanted to take his words back. To apologise. To say, 'None of this matters; we've found each other and that's enough.' But, for all he'd tried to convince himself earlier that that sentiment was true, it wasn't. And everything was now in Annaliese's hands. If she refused, or lied, he would have to leave. His body sagged with relief when she gathered herself up and met his eye.

'I am sorrier than I can say that you found those dreadful things. And for the burden you've carried. I can't change that, but I can promise you one thing: that you were wanted and that you were loved, Sebastian, by me for yourself. Yes, Himmler and the others wanted you for the Reich, for their great glittering future, but that meant nothing to me. You were my son and I cherished you, and I thought you were the start of the happy family Bruno had promised me would be ours...'

She shook her head as Sebastian reacted to the tears pouring down her cheeks and tried to get her to take a moment to breathe.

'No. I have to keep going – I'm not going to fail you again. You have a right to know the truth, and I have a duty to tell it.'

Annaliese dried her eyes and sat up straighter. Then she took him back to 1941 and the Kurmark home, and she told him it all.

'And that's the whole story, I promise. I don't think I was a Nazi, but maybe I was by default. I was certainly one of the sheep – I was happy to take advantage of the system when it worked for me. I went into the home because I believed what they said about my pregnancy making me special. I never thought for a moment that I was disposable. And I'm not proud of how I acted, but I've paid for it: I've never felt complete since they took you away, and to know that you've suffered too is unbearable.'

She stopped and swallowed hard. When she started speaking again, her desperation stabbed through him.

'But now you finally know it all, so perhaps there's a chance that we can heal together.'

Sebastian was worn thin, wrung dry. He couldn't speak. The image of Annaliese clawing at the door had burned a scar into his soul. He didn't know how to tell her that.

When she said, 'Tony knows none of this and, although I've no right to ask any favours of you, I'd like to keep it that way,' all he could do was nod.

Annaliese got up and went out of the room. A moment or

two later, the scent of coffee filtered through. It was the normality of that – his mother in the kitchen making him something to drink – which finally broke him.

When she came back, balancing a tray loaded with cups and a cake that was definitely home-made, Sebastian was the one reduced to tears. There was a catharsis in that, and in the tenderness with which she found him a tissue and held his hands and forced him to eat. There was a sense of belonging which – once he'd dried his eyes and eaten more cake than he'd eaten in years – sparked an urge for more.

'Did you keep anything of mine with you once they took me away and you left the home? Did they allow that?'

He had no idea what he hoped for – a toy or a piece of clothing perhaps. What he didn't expect was her frown.

'I'm sorry if that sounded like an odd question. But, given the cup and the other things I've seen, it would help if there was something more normal to wipe their legacy away.'

It was awful how fast her face fell. It was a shock how quickly she jumped away. And her 'Nothing I've got would do that; it would only make things worse' hit Sebastian in the pit of his stomach and turned him desperate again.

'What do you mean? Don't shake your head. You can't say that and nothing else. There can't be any more secrets.'

From the way she was looking at him, Sebastian thought Annaliese was going to argue. Instead, she closed her eyes briefly, and then she left the room again. This time she was gone for so long, Sebastian wondered if he should go in search of her. When she eventually came back, she was holding a small envelope with the tips of her fingers as if it was toxic.

'I have this, but it's a dreadful thing, Sebastian, as bad as the cup and the rest of it. It was never meant for you. I should have destroyed it years ago and not kept it hidden, but it was all I had to remember that you were real.'

He suddenly didn't want to see whatever the dreadful thing

was, but his hand was already out waiting. Annaliese acted as if she hadn't seen it. She opened the envelope herself and put the photograph it contained on the coffee table slightly out of reach.

'It's from your... not christening – that's too good a word for it. They called it a naming ceremony then.'

Sebastian stared at the picture. He understood why Annaliese had recoiled from it; he didn't want to touch it either.

'That's Himmler, isn't it? Standing beside...'

He looked at the baby lying on the cushion and couldn't say *me*. He knew that if he did, he'd be sick.

Annaliese's hand found its way back into his. 'Maybe it's a good thing that you've seen this; maybe it will help you finally understand. Yes, it's Himmler, and it's you. But you didn't choose to have him there; you didn't choose to be part of their ceremonies or their plans. Don't look at him; look at yourself and perhaps then you will really see that none of this was any of your doing. You weren't a soldier, Sebastian; you were a tiny baby. You were, and you are, completely innocent. They were the ones filled with evil and hate, but that never flowed into you. How could it?'

'What is that? Why do you have it?'

Both of them had lost track of time; neither of them had heard Tony come in.

Annaliese leaped to her feet, but she wasn't quick enough to stop her husband snatching the photograph. She couldn't find an answer beyond a tearful, 'I'm so sorry,' when he asked what a picture of Nazi scum was doing in his house. And Sebastian couldn't help her at all. The photograph was torn up and in pieces within seconds of Tony grabbing it, but he could still see the shot in its entirety. And it wasn't Himmler's face that was seared on Sebastian's soul. It was the face of the woman standing beside him. The one looking down at the baby – at him – as if he was prey. It was the same woman who had smiled out from the wedding photographs Evie had found in Berlin.

Helene.

Now it finally resonated. The name he hadn't registered when Annaliese had described the doctor who had dragged him away. Helene. She was the villain in his story, the thief who had stolen him. The woman who had tossed aside his life and Annaliese's for the sake of the Fatherland. Sebastian stared at the floor, at the shredded face which was Helene's but carried too much that was Evie in its cheekbones and eyes.

How could I ever see evil in you?

He'd meant it then. He'd been able to separate Evie from her mother then. But now? Looking at the woman who had ruined his past and now threatened his future? He didn't want to. He knew it was wrong. He knew that seeing poison where there wasn't poison was what had destroyed Evie and Ethan. He knew the price to be paid.

It still didn't matter.

How could I ever see evil in you? wasn't a question he could ask anymore.

Evil was all Sebastian could see.

CHAPTER 20

WASHINGTON, FEBRUARY 1980

The Angel of Death.

Every time Evie pictured the words, flames danced in a halo around them.

'Only one of my contacts had heard, or rather seen, that description before. Józef recognised it from a poster in Poland; he'd stuck some of them up himself in his early days as a partisan, and the image – of a woman's face stuck on top of a drawing of St Michael holding his sword – stayed with him. When I showed him the wedding pictures, he matched that memory to Helene Tellman in seconds. But he didn't know the details of what she'd done, and I couldn't find anyone who could corroborate his story. And the others I spoke to recognised her as Ulrich Reitter's wife, but that was all.'

Evie had stopped herself from pushing Karol to go back to his fellow survivors and dig deeper. He was starting to look tired and ill and had lost weight since their first meeting. It was obvious that collecting testimonies and reliving his past had taken too great a toll. When Evie had suggested it was time for him to start focusing on the present and the happier parts of his life again, he didn't argue.

Only two or three of the survivors of Mittelbau-Dora who Karol had approached remembered seeing her mother there, but they all identified Ulrich Reitter as being a permanent fixture at the base. None of them, however, could remember allegations of cruelty being specifically attached to him, and they all confirmed that he'd spent most of his time in the research laboratories and the workshops and very little actually underground in the mine. Evie – who hadn't mentioned her relationship with the Reitters to Karol, for fear of the judgement she might see in his eyes – had breathed a little easier at that. The monsters she carried in her head started to shrink. Until Karol told her about Józef's angel and they leaped back even bigger.

What could she have done to deserve such a terrible name?

There were no good answers to that. The paths that thought led to were littered with broken bodies and a woman in a white coat wielding a needle. With shrunken faces and pleading, terrified eyes. Those paths led to a murderer.

And I'm not ready to face that possibility yet.

Evie jumped up. She couldn't get on with her work as if everything was normal. She couldn't turn Karol's interview into an objective report. She had to find a moment's peace or go mad with the images looping through her head. She grabbed her coat and bag and headed out of the office, her destination already decided. It was a February Friday; the schools were in session. The American History Museum would be quiet and would provide – as it always did – the refuge she needed.

And maybe somebody there will know Sebastian's movements or have an idea when he might be coming back.

Evie hadn't heard from Sebastian since he'd left the previous weekend to make the long drive down to Florida and Annaliese. She'd barely stopped thinking about him. And – as much as she was trying to pretend that it didn't and that it was her fault for holding him at arm's length again – his continued silence hurt.

You should have gone with him kept replaying through her head, which didn't help either. Letting him go to his mother alone, giving him the privacy that their first meeting needed, had seemed like the right thing to do at the time. Evie had pretended not to notice the pause he'd left when he announced his decision to go to Jacksonville, a pause he'd clearly hoped she would fill with, 'Let me come too.' Now, without any word from him about how the reunion had gone, coupled with the sinking feeling that his prolonged retreat from her meant bad news, that attempt at kindness felt cold.

More worthy of my mother than me.

Helen and her flames roared instantly back.

Evie hurried into the museum and headed straight for the familiarity of her favourite object, a doll's house whose charms extended across four intricately imagined floors. Evie loved the plaything's incredible attention to detail – the beautifully rendered and organised miniatures it contained could always be relied on to calm even her most jumbled thoughts. Except this time the magic didn't work. This time the love its onetime owner had poured into creating a world filled with comfort for the little Doll family didn't mesmerise Evie; it had her blinking back tears instead.

The house was too perfect. The smiles on the tiny painted faces were too fixed. The father should have been ignoring his children, not sitting reading with one perched on his knee. The mother standing in the bedroom door to check on her babies was a parody of her own. Evie found herself peering into the corners, searching for skeletons and secrets, until she couldn't look at the house for a minute more. She stumbled to her feet and rushed out of the darkened gallery, moving so quickly she immediately bumped into a man who was walking at a more museum-friendly pace towards her and absorbed in a clipboard.

'Evie?'

It took her a moment to make the leap out of her own head,

to realise that the man she'd stumbled into was Sebastian. It took another to understand that he hadn't reached out to steady her, that there was no trace of warmth or welcome on his face.

Annaliese rejected him. She's broken his heart all over again. I should have been with him; it's too cruel that he had to face this alone.

His silence turned from a snub into the pain Evie had dreaded. Her hand flew instantly onto his arm.

'It didn't go well, did it? Oh, Sebastian, I'm so sorry. I wish I'd gone with...'

The sentence broke apart; she wasn't able to finish it. His face had hardened; he pushed her hand away. He became in an instant a man she didn't know.

Which isn't possible. He must still be reeling from the shock, that's all it is. I can ease him back to me again.

But she couldn't. He wouldn't let her get further than, 'Did Annaliese—'

'Don't, Evie. Don't put this mess on her. None of it was her doing from the start. She loved me; she wanted to keep me. She was as innocent in all of this as I was.'

His words came out in a torrent and – although Sebastian clearly believed them – as far as Evie was concerned, the last part didn't ring true. Annaliese may have been naïve and she may have been duped by an older man, but she'd accepted a place in a Nazi mother and baby home, and she must have understood the implications of that. *Innocent* felt like a far too easy cover-all. But Sebastian's haunted expression told her how badly he was suffering, so Evie held her tongue.

'I was stolen from her – that's the truth of it. She had no say in what happened and no choice, and that nearly killed her.'

Why is he looking at me as if what she suffered was my fault?

Evie managed to hold her tongue for a second time. She told herself that this was the fallout from a fraught reconciliation and the result of anger that Sebastian couldn't find a place for.

That he was so vulnerable, he would have lashed out at anyone who asked him the wrong question. She tried again.

'But how did such an awful thing happen? Was it your father who was responsible? Did he take you away from her without Annaliese's consent?'

'Stop saying her name! You don't have any right to it.'

The explosion came from nowhere. Sebastian's shout turned heads. Evie stared at him in horror and ran out of things to tell herself.

'You don't mean that.'

But he did. He took a step away as Evie took a step closer. When he raised his hands as if to ward her off, her hard-won control broke.

'What did I do? Why are you behaving like this? As if what happened to you both is my fault, when all I ever wanted for you was a happy reunion?'

'Because all I can see when I look at you is her.'

Saying it drained the fight from him. His hands dropped to his sides; his face sagged. It drained the life from Evie. She froze. All she could hear was *her*. There could be no doubt who he meant: Helen slotted like a wall in between them. When Sebastian started talking again, the past wrapped round him like a shell.

'Your mother broke mine. She was there at the home; she was the one giving orders.'

He shook his head as Evie managed to find enough strength to say, 'No, that can't be true.'

'Don't bother – I saw the proof. There's a photograph of her at my naming ceremony, standing next to Himmler as if they were the best of friends. Staring at me as if I was a prize. She was heartless; she was a thief. She told Annaliese she wasn't worthy to have me. She stole me away while my mother banged her fists into pulp against a locked door and screamed herself sick. And the better part of me knows that Helen's sins aren't yours, but I don't seem to be able to find that better part anymore.'

He delivered that line as if he'd stopped looking. There was no 'But you could help me' clinging to his words, although Evie tried her best to hear them.

Her mouth ran dry. She wanted to say, 'This is the worst, but we can get through it.' She couldn't: there were no words which could atone for her mother's cruelty. She wanted to say, 'I'm so sorry,' and, 'I love you; I won't let this break us.'

She managed the first; the second was impossible.

When Sebastian didn't respond to her apology, Evie turned to leave because there was no other option. She wasn't a woman who begged, but she could have done it, for him. If his face hadn't set so rigid, if his voice hadn't dripped with contempt. She had to go before she broke into all the pieces her body had become, but there was still one question she had to stop and ask.

'Was your mother glad to see you?'

For a moment, her Sebastian was there. His eyes lit up and his face turned familiar as he nodded. Evie's joy was genuine, but her 'Oh thank God, at least there's one happy outcome from this' crashed down the shutters again.

'No, there isn't. Because your mother has ruined that too.'

His voice was shards, every one of them cutting through her.

'Annaliese's husband knew about me, but he didn't know about the Lebensborn part of my birth and now he does. Now he thinks she was a Nazi and he's threatening to leave her. There's nothing happy here – how could there be? It doesn't stop; it never will. What your mother did – and has done to God knows how many others – ripples on and on and causes nothing but misery.'

The Angel of Death.

Evie knew there was more to Helen's war, that there was worse still to come. She didn't reply when Sebastian said he was the one who had to go, that he couldn't bear to talk to her any longer. She watched him walk away. She had no idea if this was their ending, and she couldn't dwell on that. If she let herself believe that she and Sebastian were done, she would fall apart, and Helen's power to cause pain would continue. Helen would win.

And that cannot happen.

It was the only certainty Evie had left. She pulled the words around herself, breathed their strength in.

That cannot happen.

By the time she got back to her office – public smile in place, head high, plan forming – they were fuel.

'I know this seems like an odd thing to ring out of the blue and ask you for, but I need you to speak to Babcia. I need to know if this name means anything to her.'

Ringing Ethan had been awkward – they hadn't even pretended to part on friendly terms – but awkward was nothing to Evie now. Not when his grandmother might be a witness to the crimes Helen had surely committed. She didn't give her ex-husband the whole picture; she didn't mention her mother. She talked in general terms that wouldn't bring his pity or his condemnation down on her head. She held herself tightly together, even when he called her back.

'You were right – that name did mean something. She knew it at once.'

There was a pause on the other end of the line which Evie allowed to play out. If the conversation had been as difficult as Ethan's hesitancy suggested, there had to be meat in it.

'I wish I'd taken more care when I asked her about it to be honest. The whole *Angel of Death* thing sounded so overdramatic to me, but it didn't to Babcia. She reacted as if I'd slapped her.'

Evie forced herself to stay silent as Ethan stumbled again. Babcia's account had to come without her shaping it. It took him a moment but he eventually restarted.

'And I didn't really understand how close the past is to her, how much she still lives with it. She tells her stories about the war all the time, you know that – you were her best listener, and her favourite...'

Evie drew a sharp breath that instantly stopped Ethan. The intimacy of a shared memory had warmed his voice so much, it was too painful to hear. She was grateful when he coughed and reverted to a brisker tone.

'Anyway, they've become so much part of the furniture, I'm not sure she listens to them herself anymore. But this Angel of Death anecdote clearly hadn't softened with time. It hit home; it unnerved her. Your hunch was a good one: the name came from the area where she'd lived in Poland after the occupation; it was given to the child catcher who was apparently the worst of them. The one who ordered the village clearances and decided which children were to live and which ones were to die. From what Babcia said, the woman's reputation was terrifying. Which presumably came from the fact that—'

He paused again, but this time the hesitation wasn't Evie's doing. 'God, this is horrible. This angel of yours was apparently a close ally of Himmler's and, according to Babcia, when she selected which children were to die, she carried the killings out herself there and then. She brought mobile gas ovens with her.'

Ethan's voice tailed away. When Evie thanked him for his help and said that nothing else would be needed, he was more than happy to go. She put the phone carefully down. She went to the bathroom and was sick until she was empty. Then she went back to her office and collected her things.

Marty had counselled caution and no contact with her parents. He'd told her to follow the plan which he'd devised carefully, completing each stage thoroughly before she moved on to the next. He'd warned her to stay objective and not to go diving in flinging accusations. Evie had agreed to all that. She was so relieved that he'd let her continue managing the case, she would have agreed to anything. But she hadn't known then about the way Annaliese had lost Sebastian. Or about Helen's role in that and in the Lebensborn home. Or the depth of her mother's relationship with Himmler. She hadn't known about angels and ovens and the power of life and death. And now that she did? Now that she knew exactly what kind of a monster Helen was?

That changed everything.

CHAPTER 21

BIRMINGHAM, FEBRUARY 1980

Sebastian hated himself. He hated himself even more when Marty confirmed what he'd started to fear in the early hours of the morning: that Evie wasn't just ignoring his calls, she had vanished.

'She left the office without a word yesterday afternoon. She hasn't come in this morning, and she's not answering her phone. Nobody has any idea where she is, and nothing about that sits right. Evie's far too conscientious to go AWOL like this.'

She hadn't answered her phone the previous evening either, when Sebastian had called to try and make amends for his terrible behaviour at the museum.

Sebastian's head had still been in Florida when he bumped into Evie. He'd left Annaliese behind in a dreadful state, not knowing whether her marriage would survive. He'd left forgetting about heroes and rescues and love triumphing. He'd returned his rental car and flown back to Washington nursing a grudge, needing someone to blame for all the lost years and the shadows hanging over the ones still to come. Still reeling from the naming-ceremony photograph and brooding on his anger, unable – and unwilling – to separate mother from daughter.

He'd felt justified in not letting Evie know he was back. He'd felt justified in unleashing his fury across her. Until he returned to his office, replayed their exchange and bitterly regretted every word of it.

The horror in Evie's eyes as he made her the scapegoat for Helen's crimes shamed him. Sebastian had no idea anymore how he could have overlaid one face with the other. There wasn't an inch of Evie that belonged to Helen, and there wasn't an inch of him that was worthy of Evie. That was the garbled message he'd left the first, and the second, time he'd called her home number. He'd left the same plea for forgiveness again in the early morning, when the call he'd been waiting all night to place had also rung out with no answer. He'd gone straight to Evie's office after that, afraid that she wouldn't be there, convinced that his cruelty had pushed her into a very bad decision. He'd had just enough pride left not to admit the full extent of his desperation, and his guilt, to Marty. Who had still, rightly, guessed that whatever had caused Evie's erratic behaviour, Sebastian had played a significant part in it.

'Can you shed any light on where she might be? Can you assure me that she's not gone chasing after her parents?'

Sebastian wasn't a prudish man by any measure, but even he flinched at the volley of curses Marty let rip as he stumbled over his reply. 'I think I can' in answer to the first question was one thing, but his 'No, I'm sorry but I can't' to the second was definitely the wrong answer.

'What is she playing at? I told her to stay away from Birmingham after she rang her mother and the CIA immediately came muscling in. She promised me she'd do what I asked. What's changed in the last twenty-four hours?'

'What do you mean, *the CIA came muscling in?*'

Marty had caught Sebastian completely off guard. His hurried description of Evie's call to Helen and Agent Miller's subsequent visit to the office – coupled with Sebastian's shock that she hadn't told him about the latter – didn't improve Marty's mood or the room's atmosphere.

'Something else has come to light, I know it. She had an interview yesterday with one of the Dora survivors who's been looking for people who could place Ulrich Reitter at the mine. But I can't find a report or her notes, so I've no idea how that went. And she also apparently placed a call to her ex-husband, which is odd given their history, although he's from a Jewish family with links to Poland so maybe there's a connection in that. But, once again, she's left no record of what was discussed, so I'm scrabbling about in the dark. I've never known her to behave like this and I don't like it.'

It was obvious from his pacing that what Marty actually meant was, 'I'm seriously worried.'

And now I'm going to make that worry worse.

There was no point in stalling. Sebastian ran as quickly as he could through what he'd discovered about Helen's Lebensborn connections and her role in his separation from Annaliese, and what he'd said to Evie as a result. He was desperate to offer a solution before Marty could explode again.

'I made an absolute mess of it, so yes, I think it's highly likely that she's gone to Alabama to have the whole thing out with her mother. Which is why I'm heading straight down there now.'

'Over my dead body you are. You've caused enough trouble. This is a departmental matter, and it doesn't need you playing the knight in shining armour.' Marty picked up his briefcase and began sweeping folders haphazardly into it. 'From everything Evie's said about Helen Ritter – and from the way that woman instantly set the CIA on her own daughter – Evie could be walking into danger. Which means it's my job to go after her, not yours. It's my responsibility. I was the one who let her stay on the case when I shouldn't have done. I'm the one who put her in this position.'

The jibe about *playing the knight* cut, but Sebastian wasn't about to let Marty's anger derail him.

'No, you're not, Marty. Or not alone anyway. We're both responsible for this. And so is she.'

Marty looked up. His hands curled into fists; his shoulders set into a square. Sebastian carried on talking, not entirely sure if Marty would actually take a swing at him but determined to be heard anyway.

'Hear me out please. You know Evie as well as I do; you probably know her better. You know that she doesn't back down when she's found a crusade, and that – for better or worse – she's not afraid of a thing. She leaves the fear of what might happen to her to us and our greying hairs.'

Sebastian didn't know if it was the pride or the love or the worry in his voice, but Marty's fingers relaxed, his lip uncurled. And his grudging 'That's true enough' gave Sebastian a chink to push into.

'So let me be the one to go. I'll stay in close touch, I promise. I'll make her report in to you tonight if I can find her and persuade her to do it. But let me fix my part in this. Don't let me lose her.'

Evie had told Sebastian enough about Marty for him to know that honesty and passion were the keys to the man. And Sebastian couldn't speak about Evie with anything less.

It worked – Marty agreed, although he carried on giving Sebastian instructions until the moment he left the office. About all the telephone numbers he could be reached on. About how he could jump on a plane in an instant and magic up arrest warrants to bring with him if he had to. About how Sebastian was to tell Evie that, if she wanted to keep her job, she had to come straight back to Washington and start following the rules. Most of it was bluster. Except the 'Be careful; keep her safe' which accompanied the piece of paper Marty had scribbled the Ritters' home address on. That part was heartfelt. Sebastian held that instruction close all the way to Birmingham.

The brakes are fine. The car's not pulling. You're not used to this model, that's all.

The journey was the kind of short hop Evie normally relished – a two-hour plane ride, a drive that took far less time than it had to hire the car to take her from the airport into town. She'd spent every moment of it standing on a ledge. All the single male travellers on the airplane had transformed into CIA agents. The hire car company's representative was so slow, and was called away to the phone so often, he was clearly in the Agency's pay. The car itself shuddered as if it had faulty brakes and suspect steering. Evie was gripped by a paranoia she couldn't shake, and she hated the stomach-churning feel of it.

Nobody is following me. Nobody has tampered with the car. Neither my parents nor the CIA have a clue that I'm coming.

By the time she reached Mountain Brook, she was repeating that mantra out loud.

Evie had driven along the roads which led to her childhood home with gritted teeth. None of the sights she'd grown up with felt real or charming to her anymore. The English Village with its quirky tower and canopied restaurants looked like a cheap film-maker's version of Europe. The clapperboard houses with their wrap-around porches offered a southern welcome that Evie no longer trusted, and the closely planted trees which gave Mountain Brook its countryside feel hung dense and oppressive. Compared to the classic lines of Washington's wide avenues and solid stone buildings, the gabled architecture and thick leafy canopy felt alien and threatening.

And that's all in my imagination too.

Evie parked the car opposite her parents' home in Rockridge Road and rolled down the window, determined to stop seeing demons everywhere. The weather, unfortunately, didn't help her scraped nerves: the air was hot and wet, a humid heatwave crawling across her skin. The silence was no help either. There wasn't a soul to be seen, not that Evie had expected the street to be busy.

The area – or at least for the people of her parents' age and class who were its main residents – had always run to its own genteel rhythm. Front lawns were for show; porches were for the evening. Outside the demands of the highly paid careers the men – and much less often, the women – enjoyed, daytime was for golf and canasta and light lunches at the club. In the evenings, couples moved in a stately procession between a handful of carefully selected restaurants and suitable homes, drifting from the cocktail hour through a dessert-free evening which politely concluded by ten o'clock. That pattern had existed for as long as Evie could remember.

Home had always been a hollow word to her. Both her parents had been absent figures, wrapped up with work and each other. She had few memories of family evenings spent together. She'd never known Helen to cook, even on the few days a month when the clinic didn't demand all her attention. Her parents mostly ate out, unless they were entertaining and extra staff were on call. Whichever option they chose, dinnertimes rarely included Evie. Her meals had been taken in the kitchen, or at the school in Atlanta where she was one of a handful of boarders who were equally unloved. Or – as she grew older – in the homes of friends who she had gravitated towards because their families were warm and welcoming, and always had a seat ready for her at their noisy tables.

And my childhood isn't relevant to what has to be done here. It's not going to make me small again.

She shot the window back into place and checked her watch. If she had her timings right, she would be just in time to catch her mother and father as they left for Beech Brook and their inevitable steamed fish and chopped salads. If she had it wrong and one or both of them had work or social obligations, she could wait.

She got out of the car, closing the door behind her with a slam. Let the neighbours jump, let them be rocked out of their complacency. If she'd had a trumpet to announce her arrival, Evie would have blown it hard. What she didn't have was a key – that had been surrendered to her mother's outstretched hand long ago – and the moment of surprise that would have brought with it. She knocked loud enough on the front door to set hearts racing instead. And when Helen opened it, Evie said the only thing she could say:

'Why did they call you the Angel of Death?'

Evie hadn't planned to open with that, but the words spilled before she could stop them. The second they did, she steeled herself for an immediate 'What on earth are you talking about?' denial. Or, if not that, fury and an attack. Evie was prepared to deal with either of those scenarios. But she wasn't prepared for Helen.

'Because they were afraid of me, which they had every reason to be. I held such incredible power over their lives.'

There was pride in the answer and an accompanying smile that was chilling.

She's still revelling in what she did. She's still that woman.

Evie's stomach heaved. She swallowed hard and struggled to gather her scattered thoughts back together while Helen – who now looked visibly bored – waited, tapping her fingers against the doorframe and looking pointedly at her watch.

'Is that it? Is that your only question, or have you got some nonsense about rockets to discuss with your father?' She stepped back as Evie stared blankly at her. 'No? Good, then I'll be going. We do have a life to get on with.'

The shock of the dismissal and the prospect of a closing door snapped Evie back.

'Of course it's not my only question. What is wrong with you? How can you dismiss that name or the rocket programme so easily, or the photographs that placed you in Hitler's inner circle? How can you expect me to? Don't you understand how serious this is?'

Helen stared at Evie's restraining hand on the door as if she was contemplating slapping it away and shrugged.

'Is it though, Evie? Serious for us, I mean? Honestly, I'm surprised, and a little disappointed, how little *you* understand. I thought Miller would explain things very carefully to you – his kind don't usually leave room for doubt. But now I wonder.'

She looked Evie up and down as if she was a particularly puzzling specimen. 'Surely you don't still believe it's the bleeding hearts at the OSI who matter, do you? Or whoever has waved *angel* in your face and filled you with their sad recollections of days long gone by? Oh you do, I can see it in your eyes. Well it's not. Your father and I are the valuable ones – we always have been. We are the ones the authorities will protect. Not you, not your department; not the ones who won't let the war go. Do you really need another visit from our mutual friend to spell that out?'

Evie could feel the strap of her bag cutting into her shoulder. It was loaded down with case studies. With the files full of lost and stolen children whose ruined lives she'd been intending to fling at her mother in an attempt to shock her by their sheer number. To demand if not guilt or remorse, then at least answers. And all the evidence she'd brought with her was pointless.

Because she knows the numbers already and she'd wear them with pride if I gave them to her.

Evie's voice finally came back. The shock of her mother's complacency made it too high and too desperate. It was a loss of control that simply passed the upper hand to Helen. Evie heard that at once, but she couldn't rein herself in.

'Don't any of the children you had such *incredible power* over matter to you? The ones who were stolen from their villages and raised in false lives? The ones who were sent to the ovens? The ones you tore from their mothers' arms in the Lebensborn homes?'

The questions were as pointless as the folders. All they produced was one of Helen's deep sighs.

'You are so quick to judge, but you don't have the slightest idea what you're talking about.'

Her voice switched to the patient, measured tone a teacher might use to correct a confused pupil.

'Of course the children mattered – they all did. We were working to create a better future and what is the future if not children? It's very simple. The ones whose parents carried the correct lineage and the ones we nurtured, who we placed in more suitable homes than the ones they were born for, were vital to the Party's success. And the ones who lacked the correct pedigree, who we removed from their useless existence, weren't. Why would you have a problem with that? How does any society benefit when the wrong kind of people are allowed to raise more children than the right ones? Who on earth is the winner in that scenario?'

She's talking about more than the past. She's working to create that same future now. She's not remembering the power; she still has it.

Evie didn't know where that thought had come from, but its certainty made her step back. There was a light in Helen's eyes which had taken years from her face, a level of belief in the validity of her twisted creed that flared bright and fresh. Evie knew that if she carried on looking at her mother for a moment longer, she would start to see flames.

'I can't do this now.'

That was an admission of failure, but Evie didn't care. She needed to leave and regroup. She needed to work out if paranoia had gripped her again or if there was some new missing piece. She took another step back, vaguely aware of a cab pulling up and almost immediately driving away again.

Helen laughed. 'You can't do it at all, isn't that closer to the truth? None of the names or the rumours you think will damage me or your father count for anything. You can stop wasting my time with them right now, and you can tell your colleague that we are done and there's no need for him to come wading in.'

My colleague? Has Marty come too? Was that him arriving?

Evie turned round, ready to warn her boss that this wasn't a fight they could win today. That there were holes she didn't yet understand and needed time to consider. Except it wasn't Marty standing behind her; it was Sebastian. And he wasn't looking at her – he was staring at Helen, his face rigid with shock.

Evie's first thought was that he'd come to avenge Annaliese. She waited to hear *broken* and *heartless* and *thief* – all the words he'd flung at her in the museum. But they weren't the ones that came. The words Sebastian actually used were Maria's. The ones she'd thrown at a news bulletin from her hospital bed, and this time they hit their target with all the precision of a perfectly balanced arrow.

'You're the one from the clinic who won't let the wrong ones survive.'

Now it was Helen who stepped back. Whose face turned to chalk. Who – for the brief moment between Sebastian's accusation and the sharp slam of the front door – looked suddenly, deathly afraid.

CHAPTER 22

Evie managed to drive one block away from Rockridge Road
before her shaking hands forced her to pull the car over. The
last few minutes had run by so quickly, she'd barely had time to
breathe. Now the need to get away from Helen had been
replaced by the need to understand exactly what Sebastian had
meant by his outburst.

She turned to him, intending to ask, 'Are you sure it was her
that Maria saw on the news?' But he was staring out of the
window as if he wasn't clear where he was. And he'd said
nothing since she'd dragged him off the front lawn and into the
car. He hadn't explained what had brought him chasing after
her to Birmingham. He hadn't explained how he knew where
she'd gone. So the question which actually came out was, 'What
are you doing here?'

Sebastian reacted as if she'd clapped him out of a trance.
When he whipped round to face her, his hunger was raw.

'I thought I'd lost you. I know I deserve to. But whether
that's true or not, I couldn't let you confront that woman alone.'

There was so much love in his eyes. There had been so
much love in his countless phone calls. All the hurt and resent-

ment Evie had been carrying since their encounter in the museum dissolved. She suddenly understood that some things were far bigger than pride.

'I know you called me. I listened to your messages.'

She shook her head as he tried to explain why he'd left them.

'It's all right, I understand. I didn't reply or pick up not because I was punishing or ignoring you, but because there are things that I've discovered about my mother that you don't know, that are terrible. I had to confront her on my own, and I knew you'd try to talk me out of that. I didn't want to give you the chance.'

'And the rest? The things I said at the museum?'

There was relief in his voice, but there was fear too, and she never wanted to hear that again.

She took his hands in hers before she answered. 'You hurt me, Sebastian. I'm not going to pretend that you didn't. But you were in pain, and you lashed out, and I can get past that. As long as you promise that you will never look at me again and see her, as long as we are always honest with each other. I can get past anything if you'll do that.'

Seconds later, she was in his arms, falling into a kiss that was a whole conversation. That wiped away the need for apologies and promises because everything Evie needed to hear was there in his lips.

It took them both a little while to surface, to disentangle. To remember they were no longer teenagers and there were better places for bodies to say 'I love you' and 'I want you' than in a parked car. And to remember the reason why they were both in Birmingham.

Filling in those gaps took a little while too. Evie told Sebastian what she'd learned from Karol and Ethan. Sebastian – once he'd absorbed the weight of Helen's wartime epithet – repeated everything Marty had told him to say and elicited a promise from Evie that she would contact her boss, especially now that they had more information to give him.

'Are you sure that Helen was the same woman from the news bulletin? It was a long time ago, and you said yourself that you barely caught a glimpse of her.'

Sebastian's face had confirmed that it was Helen when he'd seen her on the doorstep, but Evie needed to hear him say yes.

He nodded. 'I'm certain of it. I don't know why I didn't make the connection sooner – maybe because she's fixed in my head as the younger version from the wedding photographs. But, yes, it was definitely her. And look at the way she reacted when I repeated what Maria said – that's a woman who's still got something to hide.'

It was a relief to hear him say that; Evie had begun to wonder if her imagination had started running away with her. But when Sebastian asked her what she knew about the work Helen did now, Evie didn't have a clear answer.

'Not a lot now I think about it. I've been too busy focusing on what she did in the war. I know that she's always specialised in women's health and that she's a director of a women's clinic, although I don't know how actively involved she is now. I only visited it once or twice as a child – it was always her domain, and she didn't like me having any part of it.'

'And that clinic is here, in Birmingham? In Mountain Brook?'

Evie shook her head. 'It's in Birmingham, yes, but not around here. It's on the other side of the city, out past Kelly Ingram Park, in a much less polished area than this. Which I always thought was an odd part of town for her to be working in, if I'm honest.'

Evie paused. It wasn't easy to find the correct words to explain what she meant, without sounding as if she was passing judgement on the treatment which Helen's patients deserved.

'Everyone my mother mixes with in the rest of her life –

everyone that she's always mixed with – is as privileged as she is. A lot of the women in the community where the clinic is situated aren't, or they weren't in those days. Things may have changed for the better now, but from what I saw then and from what I knew about Birmingham, the women who lived there were poorer, more at the mercy of financial hardship and prejudice than anybody living here. And more desperate for help, obviously, which is why I assumed Helen was working among them. Except that doesn't make sense.'

She stopped again. That assumption was another inconsistency, another contradiction in her mother's life which Evie had managed to square as a child but now came with flashing warning lights.

And it's where we're going to find the missing piece – I can feel it. My mother would never do anything from kindness.

She turned to Sebastian, her investigative instincts kicking in and pushing to join up the dots.

'Before you arrived, I asked whether she cared about the children she'd hurt in the war or not and her answer was terrible – it's been pricking at me ever since. She said that I didn't understand. That the decisions over which children lived and which ones died were essential to building a *better future*. The thing is, the way she said it... Oh God, this makes no sense either, but it's like what you said about her having something to hide. I got the weirdest feeling that she wasn't talking about work that had stopped.'

She won't let the wrong ones survive.

Maria's words were inescapable. They'd leaped back into Sebastian's head with the same sickening speed they'd jumped into Evie's. She could see it in the tight lines round his mouth.

'We have to go to the clinic now. We have to see the place for ourselves.'

Evie was already pulling back onto the road as he said it.

. . .

Fountain Heights occupied a different city to Mountain Brook, even though the two neighbourhoods were barely a twenty-minute drive apart. The residents of the Heights had been the standard-bearers for the civil rights movement in the 1960s, and the recipients of some of the worst of the treatment which had led to that push for change. They'd spearheaded the fight for a fairer Birmingham and a fairer country, but the area they were proud to come from had paid a high price. Families had moved away as the streets became a battleground, and the money which was needed for a district to flourish had leached away with them. Now the Heights was a complicated mix of construction sites and hastily put-up new builds and too many homes that had once been the picture of elegance but were now abandoned and derelict. The area had got worse, not better, and Evie had been right: it wasn't the most obvious setting for Helen.

The Fountain Women's Medical Centre was located in an area of scrubby and badly cleared land at the furthest end of 12th Street, an address which had grown scruffier and more run-down over the years. The building didn't fit its surroundings. The clinic was housed in one of the few remaining Victorian villas which continued to survive the area's economic difficulties and the sprawling chaos of the nearby interstate. It was a solid and comfortable-looking place, a nineteenth-century red-brick square topped with squat chimneys and brightened by rows of well-polished windows. Evie wouldn't have been surprised to see lines of nurses in long aprons and lace-edged caps flanking its spotless front steps. It reminded her, uncomfortably, of the Kurmark home and the false welcome offered there. But she didn't make the connection with the clinic's name or the stylised three-branched red tree at the centre of its signboard until Sebastian swore.

'The Fountain clinic. Of course that's what she called it. Look at the sign. That tree is the Lebensborn symbol, the same one that was on the cover of the brochure at Kurmark.' Sebastian blew out his breath as if he didn't know whether to laugh or start swearing again. 'She's advertising her beliefs and her background in plain sight, in the full knowledge that nobody will be able to read it. That's a twisted sort of a joke. And it proves that we're right to be suspicious about this place and what she's doing here.'

It wasn't just the building and the clinic's branding which now reminded Evie of Kurmark. Sebastian was wearing the same furious expression Todd had told him to lose at the home, before his anger stopped them from being admitted.

She caught his arm as he began a march on the front door. 'I can see it now and, trust me, I feel as sick as you do. And yes, we have to take the sign and the name as a warning, which means we have to be doubly careful how we present ourselves when we go in.'

He'd stopped marching, which was something, although his expression was grim. Evie kept a tight hold on him anyway.

'I don't like this place any more than you do, Sebastian, but I also don't want to be back outside here in minutes, or have them alert my mother, because we're the ones raising suspicions. We need to pretend the sign means nothing. We need to go inside calmly, and you need to leave the talking to me. Okay?'

She breathed easier when he nodded. Whatever else Helen was, she was clever, and – if her circle at the club was anything to go by – she knew how to surround herself with like-minded people. Evie had no more intention of trusting the clinic's staff than she trusted her mother. She led Sebastian up the steps in a deliberately leisurely manner, refusing to react when he muttered that they were about to walk into a carbon copy of Kurmark. Luckily, the reality could not have been more different.

'It's as modern as a top-tier hospital.'

The outside of the clinic might be red-brick Victorian, but

the inside was a vision of white and chrome, a dazzling display of highly polished surfaces. And it was staffed not by stern matrons and scuttling and regularly scolded nurses, but by efficient-looking women in lab coats and neatly fitting scrubs.

'It's quite a surprise, isn't it? You step between centuries as you walk through the door.'

The smiling receptionist in her pretty pink blouse had captured the transition perfectly. Evie assumed she trotted the same line out to every startled first-time visitor. That didn't make the welcome any less warm, so Evie made sure that her smile was as equally delighted.

'It's wonderful; it's a perfect balance of the old and the new. Although I don't remember the contrast being so startling when I was last here, which, admittedly, has to be more than twenty years ago. You must have the most generous benefactors in the state.'

The receptionist agreed that they did, that they were very lucky to be so well supported. She didn't divulge any further information than that. If she thought that Evie mentioning benefactors was a strange observation, she didn't comment. She carried on smiling.

'You came here when you were young – how interesting. Do you have a connection to the clinic?'

And here it was, the first part of the gamble. Neither Evie nor Sebastian knew if it would pay off, but they hadn't been able to come up with a better way to get themselves inside the building than an edited version of the truth.

'Actually, I do. I'm Evie Ritter, Helen Ritter's daughter. I've just arrived from Washington for a visit after far too long away, and I thought I would drive here from the airport and surprise her, if she still works here every day that is.'

The receptionist's smile faded a little. 'As if she would normally do anything else. But what a shame. I'm afraid Doctor

Ritter isn't with us today, which is a rarity – I'm sure I don't need to tell you how hard your mother works.'

She did need to tell Evie exactly that, and what specifically Helen was working on. But the woman was reaching out for the phone and offering to call Helen at home, and Evie's main priority was to stop her.

'That's fine, don't worry. I'm glad she's taking a day off, if I'm honest. I do worry that, given her age, she's in danger of overdoing it.'

That fishing expedition was dismissed with a laugh and a comment about how everyone in the hospital wished they had a half of the doctor's incredible energy. Then the receptionist gestured to the notes piled on her desk and began to say, 'Well I should really get back to this if that's all...' in a way which was clearly meant as a goodbye.

Evie didn't let her finish. She jumped in with the second part of the gamble instead. 'I don't suppose we could have a quick look around anyway, could we? I'd love to be able to properly tell my mother how proud I am of everything she's built here.'

If the receptionist had been older and remembered Evie, or if she knew Helen personally at all, she would have seen Evie's excuse for the nonsense it was. But she was young and – beyond the discretion about the clinic's workings which had been drummed into her – she was inexperienced, and unsure how to handle her formidable director's daughter. So she hesitated when she should have said a polite no.

'I'm not sure about that. I think I should ask first and get somebody to accompany you.'

When – to Evie's relief – she didn't immediately do that, Evie grabbed Sebastian's hand. She hurried them both away from the desk with a, 'Don't worry, we'll obey all the No Entry signs,' which she hoped would buy them some time to explore.

It bought them less than five minutes.

'Miss Ritter, what a pleasure. I always hoped I would meet you one day. Do let me take you around our facility. I would hate you to walk into the wrong exam room.'

The receptionist wasn't quite as green or slow to act as she seemed. And the deputy director who collected Evie and Sebastian as they tried to peer through the frosted glass which masked all the downstairs rooms wasn't green at all. She swept them round the few public spaces which were apparently available for viewing at a breakneck speed. The tour was a bland one, filled with *success* and *community* and *giving back.* It showed them precisely nothing. And despite Evie's best efforts to avoid that exact scenario, she and Sebastian were back outside on the steps being wished a pleasant goodbye in no time at all, and without a single opportunity for questions.

'Wow, that was a whistle-stop. Anyone really would think they had something to hide.' Sebastian loosened his tie as the sun hit him. 'All the staff are white; did you notice that? Didn't you think it was odd given how diverse the population – and presumably therefore most of the people who come here – is in this part of town?'

Evie nodded. She had noticed, and she had thought it was odd. But it told her nothing of use, except that the city's education system had more than likely remained a very unequal one.

'Miss Ritter, can I have a word with you?'

The voice came in a whisper from the side of the building.

'Please, it's important, but I can't risk being seen.'

That was enough to get Evie and Sebastian moving. When they ducked into the shadowy recess, they were greeted by a nurse dressed in scrubs bearing the clinic's red logo. She was young, little more than twenty and, from the way she was fidgeting from foot to foot, she was very nervous.

She addressed Sebastian first, in the same whisper she'd used to summon them, before nodding at Evie. 'I was out here having a cigarette when you arrived, and I followed you in. I heard what you said about being suspicious. Did you both mean that, even though you're the director's daughter? Was that why you were trying to look round the clinic on your own?'

'Yes, we both meant it.'

Evie dropped her voice as the girl frowned. She was poised on her toes, ready to run. This wasn't the time to either be over-cautious or to ask questions that might scare her, so Evie kept her explanation short and didn't ask anything.

'My mother is the subject of what could be a serious crim-inal investigation and we're concerned that her work at the clinic might be involved. That's why we're here – without her knowing – and why we really need any information you can give us about the place – or about her. I assume doing that is why you approached us.'

Her honesty worked. The nurse studied Evie's face, and Sebastian's, for a moment, then she began talking so quickly, Evie had to work hard to keep up.

'The other nurses all act as if Doctor Ritter is a saint who's doing great work, but I don't like it here at all. Something feels very wrong. They're all racists for a start, the staff and the management. They don't employ black people. I overheard that the day I came for my interview, but I needed the job so I pretended I didn't. And as for the girls who come here for medical care, for the help that nobody else round here is willing to give most of them…'

She twisted around again, checking the closed windows above and the narrow passageway behind her. Her fingers were wrapped up in knots as she started speaking again.

'It's not only who they do or don't hire that's a problem; they don't treat the patients the same way. We don't get many white girls coming in, but I've done enough aftercare to know that they never get their tubes tied after they've given birth like the others do. And if they give their babies up for adoption, they meet the families first. The other girls don't.'

The girl glanced round again and began talking even faster. 'They get talked into adoption whether they want that or not, and their babies get taken away without any warning. They get told that they're too young or too poor to raise a proper family. It's not unkindly done – or at least it doesn't sound that way – and maybe that kind of advice is common practice when mothers are struggling, but it's not what I saw in my training and it doesn't feel right. And I can't keep turning my back on that.'

Evie's head was spinning. She'd heard Sebastian's sharp intake of breath at *taken away*. She didn't need to look at him to know that he'd heard Maria's *wrong ones* ringing out as loudly as she had. She forced herself to focus on the nurse and not to disappear down that rabbit hole.

'Have you told anyone else about your concerns? Have you tried to gather any proof?'

The nurse shook her head. 'No, not really, which I'm not proud of, but I didn't know what to do. I'm leaving the minute I get a new job. I need a reference, not trouble. But I'm not lying – what reason would I have to do that? You do believe me, don't you? And you are going to do something? Somebody has to.'

Her pale face regained a little colour when Sebastian and Evie immediately said yes.

'Then take this – it's the one thing I do have.' She thrust a piece of paper into Evie's hand. 'Call her. She was different; she was the one who made me think twice about what I'm doing here. She was angry. She came back asking about her baby because she'd changed her mind about having him adopted and she shouted the place down when no one would tell her where he'd gone. Then she went after the filing cabinets in the office. The way they spoke to her when she did that, the way they threatened her...' The nurse shook her head. 'After I saw that, I knew I couldn't stay.'

Evie tried to take hold of the girl's hand along with the paper, but the nurse stepped back before she could.

'We'll talk to her, I promise, and anybody else we can find. But can we talk to you again too?'

She was too slow; the nurse had already fled.

'She won't be back, and we can't stay here.' Sebastian looked winded. He was slumped against the wall; his breathing was jagged. 'What is going on in this place? Why are some adoptions done with the mother's involvement and some aren't? Why are the white patients treated differently from the rest?'

Evie couldn't answer him; she wasn't sure he expected her to. The options in her head were too dark, too impossible. It was 1980; it was America. It wasn't 1940; it wasn't Nazi Germany. They didn't live in a world which based its twisted and ferocious belief system on *we live because we're worthy and you die because you're not.*

We don't think like that, but Helen does.

Evie glanced at the paper with the phone number and a name, Kersiah, scribbled beside it. Sebastian was right: they couldn't stay where they were – the nurse had taken a huge risk talking to them; hanging around any longer would have been foolish. Evie's instinct was to drive back to her mother's house and start screaming for the truth, but only a fool would do that. The sensible thing to do would be to go back to the motel and make a plan. To ask if they had a private phone so Evie could call Kersiah and Marty who – whatever this was or wasn't – she really couldn't keep in the dark anymore. And this time, the sensible thing was what had to be done.

'You're right – we should go. There's no more answers to be found here, not today anyway.'

She linked her arm through Sebastian's for support, and they made their way back across the parking lot in silence.

They were both so lost in thought, neither of them noticed the car sitting underneath a clump of trees on the opposite side of the road. They were both so caught up in the nurse's story and all the warnings running through it, neither of them gave any thought to whether the deputy director had placed a call to her boss. Or to the fact that Helen could have driven from Mountain Brook to the clinic as quickly as they had. And they were so lost in thought neither of them noticed that the sun had shifted its position while they were standing with the nurse. And that the vantage point Helen had chosen to watch them from had an uninterrupted view of the whole clinic, from its front to its no longer quite so shadowy side.

CHAPTER 23

BIRMINGHAM, FEBRUARY 1980

Oh, Evie, you stupid girl. Always with your nose where it shouldn't be. Always on some pointless crusade. When will you ever learn to walk away?

It wasn't a question worth wasting any time on. Evie hadn't left Birmingham; Helen hadn't expected her to. The call from the clinic to say that her daughter was poking about where she shouldn't be hadn't come as a surprise. Which meant that Evie had to be dealt with yet again, although not here, not now; not in a way that would draw attention to the clinic.

Helen stared at the building which was her kingdom as Evie and Sebastian carried on talking to the nurse in the mistaken belief that they were hidden. Its windows shone; there wasn't a speck of dirt on the steps. It was a far cry from the neglected and run-down facility it had been when she found it. It was no wonder that her interest in running it almost thirty years ago had caused such a shock. Remembering that day still amused her.

. . .

'It's not exactly where I pictured you making your next move, Doctor Ritter. The Heights is a challenging neighbourhood to say the least. Wouldn't you prefer a more comfortable placement?'

The man from the Health Board – whose name Helen had instantly forgotten – had nicotine-stained fingers and clammy skin and was visibly exhausted. Helen knew why – she'd done her homework into his daily challenges.

Alabama, like every other state in early 1950s America, was caught in the middle of a medical boom and a medical crisis. Every scientific journal Helen picked up was bursting with new treatments and new medicines and life-changing discoveries – barely a day went by without a miracle breakthrough. But the cost of implementing the wonder cures had almost doubled and – despite there being more insurance companies offering their services than anyone could keep track of – almost half the population was unable to pay for the use of them. Or find a hospital or a doctor to treat them, given the current shortages of both. Armed with this information, Helen knew that Health Board Man would raise his eyebrows and wonder at her request to be the one selected to fill the director's vacancy at the Fountain Heights clinic. And that he was beset by too many other problems to refuse such an excellent candidate. So she smiled at him as if he was Clark Gable and made herself indispensable to another easily flattered man.

'And comfortable is where my talents would be wasted, don't you think? The clinic on 12th Street is struggling – we both know that. The same as we both know that you need a success, and that you deserve one with the long hours you work, so why don't you let me deliver it?'

Her use of *we* had already won him – his eyes were shining – but Helen always liked to belt and brace a deal.

'I will overhaul the place. I'll make it into a dedicated women's clinic which I will run more efficiently and more economically than any comparable facility in this state or any other. Don't forget that I've done this kind of thing before in Santa Fe. By the time I've finished, Birmingham will look like a health pioneer. Wouldn't that be a nice feather in your cap?'

Helen had told him what he wanted to hear. She hadn't told him how much she'd hated working with the poverty-stricken patients in Santa Fe. Or that she'd only accepted the position there because there wasn't another hospital for miles around and she needed to start accumulating the hours that were required to turn her German qualifications into acceptably American ones. Or that she was sick of paying her dues, that she had too much vision to be taking orders from other people.

And she hadn't told him why the Fountain Heights clinic mattered to her. That her one interest in the women who would seek out her services there was to keep them firmly in the place where Helen believed they belonged. To prevent yet more poverty-stricken families having yet more offspring who would suck up the resources they didn't deserve. She hadn't explained her thinking about *right and wrong people* to him. She hadn't shared her feelings about how the members of the Jewish or the black or any of the other communities who lived in the Heights and who she didn't value should be treated. Instead, she'd let her interviewer believe that she was the medical ideal: an excellent doctor with a generous heart. And she'd walked away with the job.

And now here we are, with a clinic that's even more successful than I promised it would be, however you choose to measure it.

Helen sat in her car watching Evie and Sebastian drive away with no interest in how horrified they'd be at the way she would define success. The clinic was her life, in the same way that her work for Himmler had once been her life.

In the early days – when what had mattered was earning

the community's goodwill so that nobody would ask questions – she'd moved slowly. She'd founded a place that was synonymous with trust, in an area where people had little reason to trust anyone, and The Fountain had gone from strength to strength. Now she presided over a much-envied operation, built on her reputation as a doctor who never turned even the poorest patient away. And on the donations provided by the other side of the city. The generous contributions from Birmingham's wealthier residents, who relied on Helen to deal as seamlessly with the babies their errant teenage daughters were never allowed to mother, and had the deep pockets to do it.

Good stock sent to good homes; poor stock disposed of and discouraged. One side feeding the other until the balance was properly set. It was the system designed to build a strong and thriving population which Helen had been faithfully practising since she'd signed up for her first National Socialist Party racial science class. And Fountain Heights wasn't the sole recipient of her engineering talents. Some of her best doctors – the ones Helen had carefully trained in her way of thinking – were out in other communities in other cities now. Making their mark, making a difference. The Fountain Clinic had become the centre of a hub dedicated to creating the only kind of world Helen and people like her intended to live in. And all that mattered now was protecting it.

She got out of the car and checked her watch before she slipped on a thin pair of gloves. She hadn't enjoyed that moment of fear when Evie's colleague had thrown his strange and too-knowing accusation at her. She wasn't going to give him, or Evie, the satisfaction of wrong-footing her again. She was going to do what she was good at and clean up the evidence.

The day was almost done; the night staff would be arriving soon. The little traitor of a nurse would be packing up her things, and she would be doing that alone. She was always alone; she didn't fit in. She wouldn't have been asked to join in whatever Saturday night excursions the other single nurses would be running off to.

She should never have been employed in the first place; she doesn't have the temperament.

Helen crossed the road and entered the clinic's back door, making a mental note to fire her personnel manager. The clinic's success depended on her leadership, but it also depended on the calibre of her lieutenants. There was no room, and no tolerance, for mistakes.

No one saw her enter; she met no one on the way to the nurses' changing room on the third floor. Not that she would have worried if she had. The only person she encountered was her target.

'Are you leaving, dear? Why don't I walk out with you? It would be nice to have a chat about how you're doing here.'

'No. I mean, that's kind, and if I wasn't in a hurry, I'd...'

The fumbled excuses fell away. Helen's hand was already on the girl's elbow and steering her out of the room. She didn't waste time on pleasantries. They both knew why she was there.

'What did you tell my daughter and her friend?'

To give the girl her due – which Helen always did when it was deserved – she didn't lie. Her body was shaking, but she still managed to turn and look Helen straight in the eye.

'I told her that something bad is happening to the girls here.'

'*Something bad?*' Helen didn't bother to hide her smile as she led the girl through a doorway at the end of the corridor and clicked the lock firmly into place behind them. 'Well now, isn't that a worrying allegation.'

They were standing in the oldest part of the house, in a section undergoing restoration. They were also standing at the top of a worn and twisting staircase whose banisters were more rot than wood. The nurse must have guessed what was coming but – once again to Helen's admiration – she didn't plead for forgiveness or beg.

'It should be. I told her the truth. That you treat white patients differently. That you treat everyone else like dirt. And she believed me. She knows that this place is wrong, that you are wrong. She knows that—'

But Helen was bored with heroics. One sharp push and the girl was gone, her cry silenced, her spirit broken along with her bones.

Helen slipped out of the stairwell and headed back to her car. The body would be found on Monday when the builders returned, but that wasn't a problem. Why would anyone suspect Helen's involvement? Nobody knew that she'd been on site – she'd chosen a route well out of view of the clinic's one security camera. Nobody would connect her to the nurse. Except Evie of course, but Evie wouldn't be in a position to comment on that by Monday morning.

Helen got back into the car and took off her gloves. One problem was solved; now for the next one, and the next step – locating which hotel her daughter was staying at. That would require some driving around, which might take time, but time wasn't an issue for Helen. Anything worth doing well always demanded care in the preparation, and it wasn't as if she needed to hurry. She'd seen a piece of paper pass from the nurse's hand to Evie's. She assumed that Evie and the man would stay in Birmingham and keep poking around. Nothing needed to be completed tonight. And although the task Helen had for him wouldn't be a challenge for his technical abilities and he certainly wouldn't question it, Ulrich would need a day to get the right materials together.

She pulled out onto the road. One problem solved, one to be dealt with, then their world could flow smoothly on.

The way we promised each other it would on our wedding

day. The two of us together, complete and forever and unbreakable.

That was the life they'd chosen, with space for two not three souls in it. That was the life Evie kept interfering with.

Not anymore, not with so much at stake.

She slowed down as she approached the first of a line of motels which edged the road between the city and the airport and turned into the car park. A slow cruise around that produced nothing, so Helen moved on to the next. She took no pleasure in stalking her daughter; she took no pleasure in what was coming.

Evie had been a problem since the moment she was born. Helen had wasted too many years dealing with her troublemaking, wishing she'd left the girl behind in Berlin. And too many years avoiding the truth: that a problem left unsolved starts to fester.

It was time to reach for a cure.

CHAPTER 24

BIRMINGHAM, FEBRUARY 1980

'Don't.'

Evie shivered as Sebastian's arm snaked round her waist. His skin touching hers was a story she already knew would never grow old.

'Don't get up.' His lips were feathers on the back of her neck. 'Don't open the curtains and let the world in.' Now they were drifting over her collarbone. 'Once you do that, I'll have to share you. And the last thing I want to do is share you.' And now they were moving down her body in a wave of butterfly kisses that fluttered everything else away.

I could lose myself in the magic of him.

It was a tempting thought. To live inside the bliss of his touch would be easy to do. A world with only the two of them in it would be far preferable to the impossible one waiting outside. Especially as, once again, she'd thought they would never manage to build it.

Last night hadn't started as happily as it had ended. They'd driven the short distance from the clinic to the motel locked inside their own heads. As soon as they'd arrived, Evie had gone to make the two phone calls she'd promised to make – one full of apologies to Marty and one full of pleading to Kersiah – leaving Sebastian lost in his thoughts in the lobby. They hadn't discussed how the rest of the night would progress: the words they needed to do that had been overwritten by their visit to the clinic. Evie had gone to use the phone in the manager's office, convinced that they'd stalled again. She'd come back out intending to at least lighten their surroundings, even if she couldn't manage to lighten their mood. Intending to say, 'Let me check out of here; let's find somewhere that's a little cheerier.'

The motel definitely wasn't a cheerful place. Evie had chosen it based entirely on its proximity to the airport. She'd barely looked at the decor when she checked in; she certainly hadn't registered its nicotine-stained drabness. As soon as she did, it was all too obvious that nothing about the place said 'We could shake off the day here; we could find comfort in each other', and Evie really needed somewhere to say that. She started to suggest moving to a nicer location, then Sebastian looked up and smiled at her and the comfort had been there all along.

Leaving suddenly meant another hour wasted in the car or standing at a busy reception desk. Leaving could have led to more silences; it could have turned the night into another Berlin, where the weight of broken lives had pushed them not together but apart. Evie hadn't wanted another Berlin; she hadn't wanted another wasted hour. So she'd held out her hand to him instead.

And we turned a drab little room into heaven. We can do that now wherever we go.

Believing that allowed Evie to sit up and wriggle away from his arms more definitely the second time she tried. It allowed Sebastian to say, 'I wish we didn't have to rejoin the rest of the planet,' but not, 'Don't.' They'd finally found each other, but that didn't mean they'd lost Helen. And acknowledging that they were in love, no matter how many times they'd said it during the night, didn't really wipe the rest of the world away.

The transition back to that wasn't, however, an easy one. They dressed slowly, conscious of each other. Pausing as the memory of undoing the buttons and unfastening the zips they were now closing flooded back. Trading smiles and kisses which almost reversed the process. It took the buzz of a nearby diner and the fragrant smell of crisp bacon and scrambled eggs to properly push them into the day.

'Did Marty forgive you once he'd finished delivering a lecture?'

Evie nodded. 'I wouldn't say he was happy I'm here, but he agreed that we should follow up on the nurse's lead and keep looking into Helen and the clinic. As long as I report in again to him tonight.'

'And what about Kersiah? Do you think she'll actually talk?'

Evie put down her knife and fork, although she was ravenous. Sebastian's question was a reasonable one, but she wasn't sure how definite she could be with her answer. Kersiah had suggested a time and a meeting place for that afternoon, but she hadn't exactly promised she would be there.

'I hope so. She was very shocked – she almost hung up on me, and it didn't help that I'd no idea what the nurse who gave us her number was called. But I told her what was said – about the adoption and her anger. And I told her we were concerned that the clinic was being badly managed. I couldn't think of another way to put it. She listened, but I'm not sure she fully trusted me. And she was so sad when she talked about her lost baby. To hear a young girl sound so old was heartbreaking.'

Evie stopped, aware a moment too late who she was talking to.

'I am really sorry for what Annaliese went through, for what you are both still going through. And for... for what Helen did. I can't call her my mother to you. I won't. That she still has the power to inflict all this pain sickens me. It can't carry on. Whatever she's doing here, it can't carry on.'

Whatever she's doing shivered in the air. Evie couldn't let it go.

'Do you think she's still hurting children? I mean physically hurting them? Do you think she's capable of that?'

And there it was, her darkest fear out on display. It was almost a relief when Sebastian nodded.

'I think she's capable of anything.' Evie let her breath go as he picked up her hand and cradled it in his. 'But that is going to end – I know it. Because you, my love, are capable of anything too.'

Kersiah was older than the teenager Evie had expected. She was a poised young woman in her early twenties and far less vulnerable than she'd sounded on the phone. That was the first surprise. And she hadn't come alone, which was the second. There were two slightly younger girls waiting with her in the back room of the community centre behind 5th Avenue which Kersiah had described as safe. Once first names had been shared and nobody seemed to know where to go next, Evie asked what she'd meant by that.

'Exactly what I said – there's no prying eyes here. Your mother is a powerful woman, Miss Ritter. She's not the kind of person most people would choose to cross, especially if you live on this side of town.'

Kersiah's tone was a confident one, but Evie still frowned at *powerful*. And Kersiah quickly put her right.

'I didn't choose the wrong word. I don't mean that she's powerful like a man makes himself powerful – you don't see her running for office or swaggering about on the news. She doesn't need to do that. She knows whose secrets are worth keeping. She knows how to keep people in their place.'

The bitterness in Kersiah's last statement brought a chorus of agreement from her companions. But Evie – whose neck was prickling at *secrets* – still had to ask again exactly what the girl meant.

'I mean she knows how to take hold of people's lives.'

Kersiah hesitated and turned to her friends, waiting for them to nod again before she went on.

'You're not the only one who's been asking around about your mother, Miss Ritter; I've done my share. The doctor works all across the city, not just at the clinic, finding homes for rich girls' kids in the same way she does for ours. Although I bet those girls have an easier time of it with her than we do; I bet they get sent on a long holiday the minute they start showing. And I bet they're easier to manage too. Girls like that, from *grand* families, are all about appearances. Losing your reputation is bad enough here, but for them? It's probably the only thing worse than her threats.'

The nurse had talked about threats too, specifically directed towards Kersiah. But Evie didn't want it to seem as if she was running an interrogation, so she made sure her question included the other girls.

'Have you all been threatened by Doctor Ritter?'

They managed a *yes*, but once again it was left to Kersiah to fill in the details. This time she didn't need prompting.

'Everyone who asks questions or causes a fuss at The Fountain – who doesn't do what's expected and smile and say thank you – hits some kind of trouble. Our college places disappear, or our brothers get arrested on trumped-up charges, or our fathers lose their jobs. I was training to be a teacher, but that's not happening now – after I kicked off at the clinic, the principal said I wasn't viewed as a suitable candidate to work with children anymore.' Kersiah shook her head and blew out a tight breath. 'That was a nice sting in the tail. People see that stuff happening and they don't want to ask questions. They say thank you and they don't rock the boat.'

'But you're rocking it.' Sebastian leaned forward so he was looking straight at her. 'Can I interrupt and tell you my story? Do you mind? I promise it's relevant.'

Kersiah looked surprised but she agreed. And she didn't interrupt once Sebastian began talking.

'I was adopted when I was three weeks old, although that's not what my mother wanted. I was taken forcibly away from her when she was about your age. That was almost forty years ago, and she never stopped hoping or believing she'd find me, even though the chance of that happening grew smaller every year. And she never got over the pain of losing me either. So I know how hard this is to talk about, and how brave you are for coming forward. But the main reason I'm telling you this is because it was Helen Ritter who tore our lives apart. She did the same thing to my mother in 1941 as she's done to you now.'

His words stripped Kersiah's confident mask away, revealing the heartbroken girl underneath.

'She's been doing this for forty years? She's been hurting people for that long?'

When Sebastian nodded, Kersiah burst into tears.

'What happened to you, Kersiah? What happened to all of you? Can you tell us?'

Evie slipped her arm round the nearest shoulder while Sebastian held Kersiah's hand. It took a few moments for the storm to break, but then all the girls started talking at once and the stories came tumbling. They were hard to tell and hard to hear. They were a litany of promises that had been made to be broken. Assurances that a caesarean under general anaesthetic was the only safe choice for mother and baby. That there would be plenty of time to consider whether adoption was the right route once the birth itself was done. That there would be plenty of time for having babies in the future, when they were older and more settled. Promises that had collapsed into sterilisations performed straight after delivery because of 'unforeseen circumstances' and babies who disappeared while their mothers were still in recovery. Or were stillborn and whisked away without ever being seen. Promises that had led to ruined dreams and a web of misery that spread far wider than the three girls in the room.

'None of us wanted a baby when we got pregnant; I'm not saying we did. But we wanted another chance of that in the future, and none of us were warned that option could be taken away.' Kersiah pushed Sebastian's hand away as the memories reared back. 'We didn't understand why we had to go under the knife rather than delivering our babies naturally. We didn't understand what *unforeseen circumstances* meant, and nobody explained. Everything we were told to do and everything that was done to us was wrapped up in medical jargon, in a blanket, "It's all for the best." There was no one to advise or to advocate for us. We were just dumb kids to them. The staff pretended to be kind, but it was obvious they thought we couldn't do the *right thing* and say no in the first place. And they thought we were too stupid to raise our own children too.'

Kersiah's tears gave way to a fury that sliced through the room. 'And that's the other thing. We were supposed to have time to change our minds. We were told that the babies would go to foster homes for two weeks in case we wanted them back. That was another lie. I came for my boy within days, before I should have been out of bed, but they said he'd already been adopted and I'd no right to know where he'd gone.'

Evie wished she could bottle Kersiah's fury and fling it at her mother – its heat would burn her like acid. All the testimony she'd gathered so far against Helen was damning, but this was raw. And – despite the distress that retelling their experiences was causing the girls – she needed to collect more of it.

'I know this is hard and I'm sorry for asking, but I have to be sure. They didn't tell you anything? They didn't warn you that your tubes might be tied during the operation or ask for your consent to that? They didn't tell you that you couldn't see your child if it was stillborn, or that some of the children might be placed for adoption at once?'

All three of them shook their heads as Kersiah carried on talking.

'No, nothing. That's why I was so mad; that's why I ransacked the filing cabinet. I was trying to find his name; I was trying to find out where he went.' She shook her head again as Evie started to speak. 'I didn't find any record of my boy, but I thought I'd found where they'd sent him – there was a place called The Cradle Adoption Society that appeared on a couple of the forms I managed to see. I went there too, but it was a complete waste of time.' Kersiah's sudden laugh was as bitter as her words. 'The woman who runs it wouldn't give me the time of day. She said they didn't deal with *babies like mine.*'

The anger was burning again. Evie didn't want to keep adding to the girl's pain, but she couldn't avoid the next question.

'That's horrible and so is what I have to ask you next, so I'm sorry for both. But we've been told that white girls received different treatment at the clinic. Do you know if that's true?'

As soon as Evie said it, she wished she could have at least phrased the question with more tact. Now there was a different fire flaring in Kersiah's eyes. One that held the terrible echoes of flaming crosses and 'No Coloreds' signs. Evie waited for the explosion her clumsiness and privileged position deserved.

It didn't come. Kersiah looked away from her instead and all she said was, 'This is Alabama – what do you think?'

She fell into a silence then which Evie knew meant, 'It's time that you left.' She wasn't ready to do that; she owed the girls too big a debt.

'What I think is that you deserve justice.' She left a pause for that word to sink in and for all the girls to look at her. 'If we can get the clinic shut down, that will be a start. If we can find your children, that will be the very least you're owed. And if I can hold Helen Ritter to account for the wrongs she's done to you – and for far more crimes than I can tell you about now – then maybe the healing will start.'

Evie meant every word, but the girls had heard too many false promises to put any faith in hers. There was no doubting now how Kersiah felt – her turned-away face and her shrug, which the others copied, clearly meant 'Go'. Evie and Sebastian left her holding her friends in a huddle of shared grief they had no right to witness.

'That was tough, but it gave us more insight than I'd hoped for. We have to find a phone book now and track down that adoption society. Then, first thing tomorrow morning, we can check in with social services and see what, if any, their involvement has been with The Fountain.'

Sebastian hurried straight to the car, tapping his fingers against his leg as he spoke, as if he was checking off a list. Evie didn't bother to point out that it was Sunday, that the adoption society would surely be closed. She knew what he was thinking: that it was better to have a task to do, even a pointless one, than to stand still. She needed the safety of activity too. If she gave 'Where are the babies?' another minute's space in her head, she'd start screaming.

Unfortunately locating the adoption society wasn't the simple task it should have been. They found phone booths easily enough, but the directories in the three they tried had been reduced to an empty chain and a pile of torn pages. The only alternative was to return to the motel, where Evie used her official position rather than pleading this time to get private access to the manager's office. His huffily expressed shock at her language when she found the society's address was the day's one bright moment.

'This makes sense of what Kersiah said – it's no wonder she was turned away so abruptly. It's in Vestavia Hills, which might as well be Mountain Brook – it's the same sort of affluent, country-club-loving suburb. I doubt anyone who lives there would give house room to a girl from Fountain Heights.'

Sebastian still insisted they went. And he insisted they weren't going to give up when the streets and houses turned out to be exactly as grand as Evie assumed they would be, and the adoption society's address led them to a mansion.

'There could be someone at home – it's clearly a private house as well as a business. It's worth a try.'

Evie didn't believe that. She assumed if they were going to be met with anything, it would be more lies. But she walked up to the front door with him anyway. That was opened by a maid, who shut it again with instructions that they should wait. When it reopened, they could hear music and laughter coming from inside, but the woman standing there with her hands behind her back didn't invite them in.

'How can I help you? If it's the adoption service you're after, it's closed. You do realise it's Sunday, don't you?'

Evie had been hoping for a warmth she could appeal to, but it was immediately obvious that wasn't going to be on offer. Everything about the woman was lacquered, from her expensive blow-dry to her frosted nails, and there wasn't a spare ounce of flesh on her frame. She decided therefore to cut straight to the chase and worry about the consequences later.

'I am aware of that yes, but my colleague and I are from the Justice Department and we have a couple of questions we want to ask you about adoptions in the area. Can we ask those now? Or would you prefer a more formal interview?'

Formal was a bluff – Evie had no power to insist on any sort of interview. It had to be *now* and it had to be *yes* to an immediate conversation. Any lawyer the woman decided to telephone would instruct her not to say a word, and might very well send a patrol car. Luckily, she was distracted by her guests, so she replied with a sharp, 'As long as you're quick,' which Evie was more than happy to comply with.

'Are you acquainted with Doctor Helen Ritter? Do you arrange private adoptions with her?'

The woman's face relaxed a little. 'Of course I am. Doctor Ritter is a very well-respected practitioner and a model of discretion, which is why I and many local families put our trust in her.'

Evie noted *local* and knew it meant wealthy, and moved swiftly on. 'And do you ever have difficulties with girls who regret their decision after the fact and want to reclaim their babies?'

The tight smile that answered her dripped with condescension. 'Of course not. Adoptions are closed matters; all personal information is sealed. The birth mother isn't told where the child is placed, so there can be no *reclaiming* as you put it. I would have thought the Justice Department would be well aware of that.'

Evie could hear doubt creeping in, so she jumped straight to what she guessed would be her last question. 'So you're saying there's been no problems at all? Not even with girls from The Fountain Clinic?'

The reaction to that name was immediate – the woman recoiled into the doorway.

'I assume you're referring to that dreadful girl who turned up here last year and made a fool of herself. I can assure you that was an unfortunate and highly unusual occurrence, and nothing to do with me.'

A wave of music and laughter reached the front door again, and the woman stepped further back. 'If I'm honest, I've never understood why Doctor Ritter bothers with that place, and I have as little to do with it as possible. As I told the girl, those children are hardly the kind our parents are looking for. And now, if you don't mind, I think it's time I returned to my guests. If you need anything else, you can contact my lawyer.'

'Maybe you don't take many of the babies from there, but—'

The door slammed shut.

'I think you take the white ones.'

Evie finished the sentence anyway, even though there was nobody but Sebastian to hear it. His voice was hollow when he finally spoke.

'There we have it – more proof that nothing about Helen's methods has changed. There's still two prongs to her work. She arranges adoptions for white children, preferably ones from wealthy backgrounds, and—'

'For every perfect baby that's born, there's a child who isn't the ideal, who is surplus.'

Evie stared across lawns which were so smooth they looked polished, not mown, and the money-soaked homes nestling behind them as she cut across his words. 'That's pretty much what you said, isn't it? That's how the Nazis intended to build their *better* world? Making room for the children with *value* and removing the children with none. That's how my mother operated, isn't it? When she was making her judgements, when she was choosing who would live.'

She stopped as the chasm yawned and tried to scramble back from it.

'This is crazy; this is impossible. And we're too close to it. We could have it all wrong. Maybe we're spinning out our own nightmares instead of looking for the facts, and making our monsters bigger than they could ever be. We can't do this on our own anymore. We need a clear set of eyes; we need to get Marty down here.'

Sebastian didn't argue. Evie knew without him saying it that he wanted his suspicions to be wrong as much as she did. That he wanted to believe what she was hoping for too: that, yes, the mothers had been cruelly treated but not the children. That they'd find a list of them placed in loving homes.

They drove back to the motel, where Evie called Marty, who promised to be on the first plane in the morning. And then they did what they'd been longing to do since they'd left it that morning – they went back to the sanctuary they'd built the previous night. Their world which had no room for monsters.

CHAPTER 25

BIRMINGHAM, FEBRUARY 1980

'Sebastian, wake up.'

Evie shot out of sleep as the figures on the clock face jumped straight into her eyeline.

'We forgot to set the alarm. Marty could arrive at any moment.'

Oversleeping hadn't been the plan. The plan – which had definitely existed because they'd talked it through the previous night – was to be out of bed long before Marty's early morning flight from Washington landed. Evie was going to collate her notes; Sebastian was going to call social services. They were going to be prepared for a full debriefing and ready to start work – Marty had made it clear in his call that he intended to hit the ground running.

'We have to move fast. Your mother is likely to have got the CIA on the case again. They could be closing down your contacts as we speak, and they could be cooking up reasons to throw the book at the two of you. Or the woman from the adoption society, or someone from the clinic, could start sending out alarm calls. It's a leaky boat this one. It could hurt a lot of people if it goes down.'

Marty hadn't dismissed any of Evie or Sebastian's fears as wild imaginings. He'd been doing his own research into the treatment of children in the occupied territories during the war – reaching out to his contacts and hers and operating as if he didn't need sleep. Nothing he'd learned was good.

'It was huge, Evie. Far bigger than I imagined when we first talked about priorities. There were over three hundred and fifty Polish villages that were left completely empty in 1945 because all their inhabitants had been murdered. Or maybe removed in the case of the children. That's like wiping Salt Lake City or Tallahassee off the map. And the scale keeps getting bigger with every piece of information that comes in. It was industrial.'

She'd heard his exhaustion – it had dripped through his words. He'd sounded like a man who'd gone days without sleep. And he'd sounded more horrified than she'd ever known him.

'There were orphanages emptied by the Nazis all across occupied Europe. There were five thousand children taken to new families in Germany by Lebensborn operatives in Lodz alone; there was another five thousand taken from Katowice. That's just two cities and one country, and the numbers go on and on, across eastern Europe and the Nordics and France. Hundreds of thousands of little ones spirited away and lost behind new names and languages. And most of those are behind the Iron Curtain now and unreachable, even if anyone could track their birth stories down. It was barbaric, and I doubt that we'll ever be able to do more than scratch the surface.'

But he wanted to scratch – he'd been very certain about that – and he wanted to make an example of Helen.

'Your mother was up to her neck in it. Not just in the running of the Lebensborn homes and the kidnappings, but in the selections and the killings that followed. The testimony from Ethan's grandmother linking her to the use of mobile gas vans is good – if we can also tie her to the deportation of children to the Chelmno extermination camp, then we really have a case. And I know you wanted to run the whole thing yourself...'

Her 'Not now; it's too big' had lightened his voice a little.

'Good, thank you. I hoped you'd say that, so I've already put feelers out to some of the other Polish American associations. The beautiful blond Angel of Death has struck some chords already, and I doubt we'll have any issues matching her with Helen. And as for what you've learned in Birmingham... I wouldn't discount your suspicions, no matter how awful they seem. I don't believe that anybody who held her beliefs, and pursued them so ruthlessly, would easily change them – someone that rotten stays rotten. But we have to tread carefully, Evie, we really do. We've got to keep a lid on this tinderbox.'

Marty's caution hadn't surprised Evie. His fear that, if it became public that Helen had implemented a Nazi-developed racially based system of eugenics at the clinic, riots would follow was one she shared. And that he was coming with a plan to manage the situation had been an enormous relief.

'We have to change the script and get the CIA off her side and onto ours. And the FBI and the President too if that's what it takes for someone to listen. We have to make the intelligence services aware that she's an ongoing threat – and that threat matters more than some hushed-up wartime entry programme – before this blows up in our face. It's not going to be easy, but I've had some thoughts, so I'll see you in the morning, and I'll brief you then. Hang tight and be safe until I get there.'

Evie had put the phone down feeling more confident than she'd felt for days. As much as she loved Sebastian, he was no more objective about Helen than she was. Marty was the safe pair of hands she needed. He would keep her firmly attached to her professional, not her personal, head.

Which will be great, except there's nothing professional about the state of this room.

There were clothes strewn everywhere and almost no time to get into them.

'Sebastian, please. This is not how I want to greet my boss. Get up – get a move on.'

She got him out from under the duvet, but it was too late. They barely had time to get their shirts on before there was a knock and the door flew open. And Evie remembered that they'd also been too distracted by each other the night before to fasten the lock.

'Right, okay. Well this is awkward, although I suppose the closed curtains and one room number should have given me a clue.'

'I am so sorry. We missed the alarm and...'

Evie gave up. Trying to find anything to follow *and* would simply prolong the embarrassment.

'I'd hazard a guess then that your notes aren't ready and lover boy hasn't rung social services yet? Excellent. That makes me so glad I got up at a thoroughly godless hour to get here.'

Evie was about to launch into another apology when she realised Marty was laughing. And that Sebastian wasn't half as covered in confusion as she was.

'If you turn this into a joke to entertain the office, I'll kill you. Is that understood?'

Marty bowed and threw up his hands in mock surrender. 'Heaven forbid. I'd offer to go for coffee and give you two a chance to get organised, but I got a taxicab here from the airport – the queue at the rental shop was crazy.'

Coffee suddenly sounded like a wonderful idea.

Evie grabbed her bag and tossed her keys to Marty. 'That would be so good, if you don't mind. Take my car – the licence plate's on the tag. There's a diner five minutes down the road which isn't half bad, and don't feel that you have to bring back bagels or doughnuts, or both, with you as well as the coffee, but it might help us get our thoughts straight if you did...'

Marty huffed and puffed as if the idea that he should act as an errand boy was outrageous, but his smile said the opposite.

'I'll see what I can do. But then we get sorted and out of here fast, okay? There's a CIA agent on secondment to the local law enforcement academy who I woke up very early. He's agreed to meet with us if we can be there by eleven. It's cost me a year's worth of favours to buy us that much, so I don't want to arrive late and miss him.'

They both agreed that they were his to command for the rest of the day as he pocketed the keys and left with a deadpan, 'Wouldn't that be a nice change.'

The moment Marty closed the door, Evie retreated to the bathroom to tackle her mussed-up hair. Sebastian switched on the television and almost immediately called for her to come back into the main room again.

'You have to see this news bulletin. Someone's found a body in a stairwell at the clinic and it looks like—'

But Evie didn't get to hear who the body looked like. She didn't get to ask him to turn up the volume. The explosion which ripped through the car park turned her deaf. She couldn't hear herself screaming. But she saw the windows shatter, and she saw the shards fly, and she felt the hail of broken glass.

CHAPTER 26

Someone was screaming in a wail loud enough to pierce an eardrum. It wasn't until Evie stopped to draw breath that she realised the source of the screaming was her.

She was lying on the floor, her arms curled round her head, her knees pulled tight to her chest. Her hearing had returned, but her body was jolted, her bones jangling as if they'd been dropped from a height. She blinked her eyes open; carefully stretched her fingers, her arms, her legs. Nothing was broken, but her skin felt as if it had been stung by a swarm of bees, and it was a struggle to take a deep breath. When she shook her head to clear it, tiny pieces of glass trickled round her like rain.

There was an explosion. Marty left the room and then there was an explosion.

With that one clear memory, the world roared back to life. An oily smell hit the back of her throat. The carpet turned into a cracked mirror. Other people's screams, and sirens that grew increasingly louder, burst through the holes where the windows had been. Marty was outside – she needed to check he was safe, but first...

'Sebastian. Oh dear God, Sebastian.'

She could see his legs and the lower part of his body on the far side of the room. He wasn't moving. He hadn't had the protection of the bathroom wall which had partly sheltered her.

Evie crawled across the floor towards where he was lying, sobbing his name, oblivious to the glass biting at her hands and her knees. 'Sebastian, speak to me. Don't be dead. Please don't be dead.'

He'd fallen, or flung himself, or – please God not that – he'd been thrown by the blast against the side of the bed. He was tissue-paper white and his head was bleeding. Evie groped across his body, grabbed at his wrist; cried harder when she found a strong pulse. When he moaned and opened his eyes, all she could think was, 'Thank you.'

'I'm okay, I'm okay.'

He could say it, but he couldn't sit up, and his eyes kept slipping away from her.

'Stay still. You've hit your head – you could have a concussion.'

She pressed her fingers to his lips as he struggled to ask what had happened.

'I'm not sure yet. There was some sort of an explosion which blew out the windows, and I think there's a fire in the parking lot. I can smell burning...'

And everything happened in the minutes after Marty took my car keys and went out.

'No. No. That can't be right. That can't be possible.'

But it was.

Evie pulled herself up from Sebastian's side and threw herself towards the empty window frame, her mind refusing to accept what she could now see. Thick black smoke and a fireball. A burning wreck where her hire car had once been.

She stumbled out of the motel room, telling Sebastian to wait, not to worry, that she loved him. Saying anything she could to block out the news that was waiting for her outside, that would topple her. Telling herself she was wrong, that Marty was fine.

She managed barely half a dozen steps towards the wreckage before a policeman caught hold of her arm.

'You can't go any closer. We're still trying to assess the scene. We don't know how many casualties there are, or whether there could be a second device.' He tightened his grip as Evie heard *device* and bucked hard against him. 'And you're hurt, ma'am; your hands are bleeding. You need medical help.'

But Evie didn't want medical help. She wanted Marty to come wandering around the side of the building from reception. She wanted Marty to tell her that the coffee at the motel had turned out to be drinkable after all and he hadn't needed to drive anywhere. She wanted it to be another vehicle, another person, a mistake.

'Are you sure it was a bomb?'

The policeman, who'd taken more responsibility on himself for the cause of the explosion than he was entitled to do, started to backtrack. 'I wouldn't say *sure.* That's a guess based on a witness description. Obviously there needs to be a full investigation.'

His hesitation gave Evie a glimmer of hope, and she grabbed hard at it. 'So you haven't been close to the wreckage yet? You don't have the full details? You see, my friend was meant to be in that car, the one that's on fire. He was meant to be going to the diner to get breakfast. But he mightn't have gone – that's possible, isn't it? You don't know that there was anybody in there?'

The look in the policeman's eyes was enough. His 'I'm afraid our witness saw a man get into the driver's seat seconds before it blew up' stripped her skin away. And his 'I'm very sorry' and 'It would have been instant' weren't a comfort; they weren't wanted.

Evie shook off his hand and sank down to the ground. 'I know who did it. I know who killed him.'

The policeman wasn't listening. He was calling for assistance, assuming she was in shock. It didn't matter. She would keep saying it; she would make somebody listen to her.

I know them; I know what kind of people they are.

Evie's head started to spin as she realised what her naivety had cost. She'd said those words so easily to Marty; she'd been so convinced that she was the one in control. She'd insisted that she could finish the job, that she knew what she was doing, that she was a match for them. She'd said, 'Trust me,' and Marty had.

But I didn't have a clue.

Evie wrapped her arms around her head as the truth hit her. She hadn't any real idea who her mother was. Or what Helen and her father – because if there had been a device, that had to be her scientist father, acting hand in hand with his wife the way he always did – were truly capable of. She'd dismissed the danger they posed; she'd acted as if she was immune to it. And now her head was spinning as fragments of the morning's conversation came crashing back.

Take my car... A body in a stairwell at the clinic...

The bomb had been meant for her. Marty had died, but he wasn't the target – he was the innocent bystander.

And so was the nurse. My mother killed her for talking to me – who else could that body be? And her next target was me. She wanted me dead. Both my parents wanted me dead. They'll go to any lengths to protect themselves, and they don't care who gets in the way.

Everything impossible and unimaginable was true. Evie had to force herself to breathe, not to drown. Not to crumble in the face of such... She didn't have a word. Hatred wouldn't do. That implied there may once have been love there, the flipside of the coin. Hatred implied a depth of emotion she doubted Helen had ever felt towards her.

Maybe the only word that fits what she intended for me is clearance.

She stared at the funeral pyre where the car had been, wondering if her mother was already writing the invitations and planning her wake.

Someone that rotten stays rotten.

Marty had known how deep the rot ran. Wanting to uproot it had cost him his life.

No, that's too easy. I cost him his life; I cost the nurse her life. I could have cost Sebastian his too.

The pain she'd been pushing away suddenly raged through her, as ferocious as the flames still devouring the car. Evie knew it would never leave her, that she would wear Marty's murder as a scar for the rest of her life. But she also knew she couldn't buckle; that his murder wasn't where this story ended. *It cannot happen* had happened despite every plan she'd made, so she had to do more.

All the killings, all the years of lies and cruelty and playing God stop now.

Evie got to her feet as the paramedic arrived and insisted that her cuts needed tending. She would get herself cleaned up; she would make sure that Sebastian was safe and cared for and then she would get on with the only job that mattered.

Making the police and the CIA and the FBI and anyone who could help her listen. Making everybody understand what she understood all too well: that appearances lied, that angels were evil and monsters were real.

And making her parents pay.

CHAPTER 27

BIRMINGHAM, FEBRUARY 1980

Evie tried to be heard. She made her account as simple and as damning as she could, so she could tell it quickly. It made no difference. It was as if everyone she spoke to was still standing inside the radius of the blast, unable to hear a word.

The first detective on the scene was more suited to a desk than the carnage awaiting him and was utterly out of his depth. He did little more than walk the police cordon while he waited for what he overexcitedly called 'the big guns' to arrive. When Evie – whose cuts had proved to be little worse than scratches – suggested that he might want to stall the journalists who'd swarmed to the car park, he treated her as if she had a concussion. This was his moment in the spotlight, and he was determined to milk every moment of it. He refused to accept that his grandstanding could impede a serious investigation. As far as he was concerned, a police badge far outweighed a Department of Justice identity card, and a man's authority far outweighed a woman's.

He ignored her warnings. He gave a series of television interviews that left Evie desperate to drag him away from the cameras. He took no notice of her furious, 'You've just told the prime suspects they missed their main target.' Once he heard who she worked for, he'd instantly put the blame for the attack on extremists – a catch-all word he couldn't define – who were so outside the decent bounds of society they would be quickly caught. When Evie agreed that his word choice was correct but insisted that those extremists were her very respectable parents, he suggested she might want to go back to the ambulance crew.

Evie tried again when the FBI agents appeared to take control of the case. They arrived in dark cars and wearing dark glasses and acting as if the local force should scatter at their coming, and they were of little more practical use. They did Evie the courtesy of listening to her, and Marty's, reasons for being in Birmingham; they took her parents' details. When she explained that the bombing was linked to the murder of a nurse at The Fountain Clinic, they made the note she asked them to make. She had no sense that investigating any of what she'd said mattered to them. They were also wedded to the idea of extremists, and they had their own list.

With no one in her corner, Evie was floundering. Marty hadn't told the CIA agent at the academy the reason why he wanted to meet, so the agent was reluctant to involve himself and wouldn't take her call. Even if Sebastian had been well enough to corroborate her story, he had no official standing. He was simply the boyfriend, and he was too concussed to be a reliable witness. In the end, Evie gave up what was a hopeless and frustrating fight, and persuaded one of the few policemen who she hadn't scared off to take her to the hospital where Sebastian had been admitted.

'I won't let this go. I won't let Marty down again. They have to get on board with me eventually.'

She held Sebastian's hand as he moved in and out of a sleep which the nurse had said was no longer anything to worry about. She kept on talking, although she doubted he could follow her, because she couldn't bear silence. That was too full of Marty and a grief that would ruin her.

'They'll go through their processes and get nowhere, then they'll follow up my leads. They have to. They're not stupid; they're just blind to anything outside their own thinking. But *eventually* isn't enough. *Eventually* is the chink my parents will slip through. Because that's what they'll do – I know it. They'll have heard by now that it was a man not a woman who died in the explosion. They'll know I'm still alive and still capable of identifying them and they won't wait to be caught. They'll find somewhere else to run and reinvent themselves. I can't let that happen, so I'm going to find them and make sure that it doesn't.'

Sebastian didn't react, except to hold on to her hand. Evie knew that his injuries were largely superficial – if they'd been life-threatening, she would have fought her battles with the men who were deaf to her on another day. He was, however, still very disorientated. His eyes were open, and he was looking at her, but he'd clearly got lost long before her torrent of words eased. Which, if Evie was being honest with herself, was something of a relief.

If Sebastian had been fully awake, he would have told her to wait. Until he was better, or until the FBI finally made the right connections and accepted that Evie's reading of the case was the correct one. He would have told her not to go back to Rockridge Road. Not to dig through the house for clues. Not to follow her parents wherever it was they'd gone. He would have told her to stop and let herself think about Marty and grieve for him. So it was a good thing he couldn't tell her any of that. Or point out that she was putting herself in danger. That he had to stay where he was in a hospital bed.

And she didn't.

Their car was gone; the house was silent.

Evie parked her second hire car of the trip and rang the bell once for form's sake. Then she went round to the back door and broke the lock with a well-aimed kick.

Nobody came running.

She moved through the ground floor like a hunting dog, sniffing for any trace of Helen or Alex. There was nothing in the air except the faint tang of bleach. She followed that through the connecting door from the kitchen into the garage and poked about among the tools and containers laid out in neat rows on her father's workbench. Their language was a foreign one. If the place had been used as a bomb-making factory, it was spotless and innocent now.

They can't have been gone long; the bench is still damp where it's been wiped. They can't have got that far away yet.

Her spirits buoyed a little by that realisation, Evie returned to the house and went systematically through every room. She opened cupboards and drawers and rifled through them, but there was nothing to uncover – the whole place had been stripped clean. There were no address books, no maps, no dropped banknotes that would give away her parents' destination. There were no passports either, but that offered Evie nothing beyond the likelihood of an ever-widening search.

Evie repeated the same exercise upstairs, leaving their bedroom for last. So many years had gone by since she'd been forbidden access to it, but it still remained a difficult threshold to cross. She pushed the door open half-expecting to find swastikas draped over the nightstands and a portrait of Hitler in pride of place on the wall.

The reality was a neatly kept and unremarkable bedroom. Cream walls, blue silk and velvet bed coverings; a French-style dressing table with only one perfume bottle left on the top, and a walk-in closet which had been divided in two. Like the missing passports, the only clues in the bedroom were in the gaps – the space on the closet shelf which was wide enough to hold two suitcases, the missing summer clothes. And there wasn't enough in that to build a picture of anything except a couple who'd known what they were doing when they took flight.

Evie sank down on the bed and tried not to feel strange as she did so. They'd taken the car; presumably, she assumed, because they didn't want to risk an airport where their identities would be checked. Beyond that, she didn't have a clue what they were thinking or which way to head. Her parents' lives were a mystery to her beyond their top notes; she had no idea what a bolthole would look like to them. They hadn't been a family who'd travelled far from home; holidays had always followed the same pattern. A fortnight in the winter skiing at Cloudmont, which was less than two hours' drive away. A fortnight in the summer at a country club in Georgia which Evie had never been able to tell apart from Beech Brook. They were too well known in both those places to have risked going to either of them.

The club.

The connection came to her so fast, Evie almost expected a lightbulb to start flashing over her head. Maybe the members of Beech Brook – her parents' home-from-home and the only place where they'd ever established a circle – could shed some light on their movements.

A circle of like-minded people, yes, but that's not necessarily the same thing as confidantes.

That thought almost stopped her. *Confidante* and her parents didn't fit in the same sentence – it didn't seem possible that they would have shared their plans. But they'd left no trace of themselves in the house, and the clinic was a crime scene, so Evie was out of options. The club, and the clique at their regular dinner table, was the only place left to look.

. . .

Her appearance in the candlelit room was met – exactly as Evie had expected – with a coolness from the couples sitting at the table which quickly hardened into hostility. She sat down in one of the seats her parents' absence had left empty and ignored the tutting. Every minute she wasted listening to refusals to help or to excuses was another minute in which Helen and Alex slipped further away. Evie launched into her prepared speech and didn't give the men and women staring frostily at her any minutes to waste.

'Some time tomorrow, Helen and Alex Ritter will be the lead story on every news channel. I'm not entirely sure how the FBI will frame it, but some or all of the following will come out. That they were prominent Nazis, members of Hitler's inner circle to be precise, and that my mother is guilty of war crimes, primarily committed against children. That she is wanted in connection with the murder of a young nurse whose body has been found at her clinic, and in connection with... let's call them serial abuses there. That both of them are also wanted for questioning about a car bombing which killed my boss earlier today. You may have already seen reports of that.'

She held up a hand to stop the spluttering. 'I don't want to hear how ridiculous you think any of those charges sound. These are the facts; I'm not here to debate them. What I am here to do is to get information because they've fled, and I think that one, or all, of you may have some idea where they've gone.'

She held up her hand again as the spluttering turned into outrage. 'Please don't waste my time. Don't pretend you know nothing, or you're above getting your hands dirty if they've come to you for help. I know you.'

Three little words but they instantly brought silence. Evie switched to a trick which had always worked well for her in court. She moved her gaze slowly around her audience, waiting to see who would meet it and who would flinch. Every last one of them blinked and recoiled. She smiled; it wasn't returned.

'You can't hide yourselves from me – don't make a mistake and forget that. I've been around you people since I was a child. When I say I know you, I really do.'

She leaned forward and dropped her voice but not the menace running through it. 'I know who had the strongest Klan links in the past, and who still holds that allegiance today. I know which of you helped to hide the church bombers who killed those four little girls all those years ago. I know whose daughter has been helped by my mother to deal with an awkward pregnancy. Whose generous donation in thanks for that links them too closely with The Fountain Clinic. I could give the FBI enough material on your little coven to ruin your reputations for good.'

She knows whose secrets are worth keeping. She knows how to keep people in their place.

That was Helen's skill, not Evie's. Ninety per cent of Evie's performance in the dining room was a bluff. But it was an accurate bluff, built on all the whispers and stories she'd heard as a child. Her shaken audience heard her voice, but they heard Helen's threats. They imagined a world where doors closed against them and tables were no longer available; where they weren't important or valued. They crumbled.

'That's better.' Evie waited for the sweatiest of the men to meet her eyes. 'What do you know?'

He coughed and cleared his throat more times than was necessary, but he started to talk.

'Nothing about the nonsense you're spouting. Helen telephoned me this morning. She said that she and Alex needed to go somewhere quiet and out of the public eye for a while because he was being harassed about some work he once did in the war, building rockets in Germany. I told her that was a disgrace, that she should—'

He subsided as Evie raised her eyebrows and asked him if he wanted her to call the FBI straight away.

'Fine, fine, there's no need to be hasty. She asked for my help, and I gave it to her. There was a route we used to use in the old days, when people needed to leave town in a hurry and lie low for a while – or disappear. It follows the back roads not the main highways out of the state. She knew about it like we all did, and she wanted the details, so I gave them to her.'

The old days.

Evie didn't want to dwell on those, or on the type of people who'd been helped then, although it wasn't hard to picture them. Men who'd swung baseball bats and rigged up nooses for their innocent victims. Who'd dragged terrified boys along dirt roads from chains fastened to the back of their trucks for no reason except the colour of their skin. Racists and murderers who, with the help of their privileged friends, had skipped even the little that had passed for too long as justice. History repeating itself. She had to bite down on the impulse to roar her disgust. Instead, she pulled a pad from her bag and threw it across the table.

'Write the route down – sketch every inch of it. And add all the stops – hotels or guest houses – that were recommended to the men who were sent down it. And then pass it round the table for your friends to check.'

She waited until the drawing and the accompanying notes were complete, and they'd all agreed it was accurate, before adding her last threat.

'If this turns out to be a trick or a lie, you'll be sorry. If I follow it and nobody's seen even a glimpse of them, I'll give all your names to the Justice Department and we'll turn you over. Taxes, citizenship, every friend you've made since you were children; whatever we can poke our way into.'

She paused for a second, waited until they were all looking at her and not down at the suddenly fascinating tablecloth.

'We will crawl over every inch of your lives and, I promise, they will never feel like yours again once we're done.'

Evie took the map and walked out, leaving a horrified silence behind her at the table and enough craning heads and whispers for it to be clear that at least some damage had already been done.

Her parting shot had been another bluff. She didn't have the authority to order an investigation on that scale, as their lawyers would let them know soon enough. Nobody watching her calm exit would have guessed that.

She drove away from the club and parked in a side street before she looked at the notes; she couldn't bear to be on its territory a second longer than she had to be.

The route they'd drawn was a sprawling one, punctuated by a number of overnight stops where Evie assumed the owners didn't ask many questions. She realised that she hadn't asked where most people had waited their exile out, or if anyone had actually fled the whole length of it. If they had, the journey was a long one, stretching over a thousand miles from Birmingham to the far side of Texas and the border. One of the women had added a line which continued the route into Mexico, which – with her addition of an airplane symbol and a question mark – suggested that it could carry even further on.

Evie gave herself a moment to digest that possibility. She allowed Argentina and Chile and Brazil – the countries which had become Nazi havens after the war and were easily accessed from a Mexican airport – a minute or two's space in her head. She imagined her parents following in Eichmann and Mengele's footsteps and living a comfortable life in South America, out of the reach of justice. Then she shook herself and switched that fear off again. Even if that was the intention, nothing suggested they could have got that far yet. And, yes, the route as it stood was a long one, but any place marked on it could be a stopping point, a spot to set a snare. All she had to do was think about the pursuit as a series of steps.

All we need to do to get organised is to set our priorities.

Marty was in her head. She could hear his voice and see his smile. This time she let the tears come pouring.

Marty's the one I'm doing this for.

Marty wasn't Helen's only crime; his murder was the latest in a long list. Her mother had done so many terrible things, and she deserved to be punished for all of them. Evie wouldn't stand for anything less. But Evie couldn't focus on the full breadth of those today, any more than she could focus on a thousand miles. She had to push what Helen was capable of out of her head before she made her opponent too big. Evie would never have gone into court thinking that a case was already lost, and she wouldn't set out on the road believing that beating her mother was a battle she couldn't win. There had to be justice for all Helen's victims, including the lost children and Annaliese and Sebastian and the nurse, but that was too many people to take on the journey with her.

So my priority is avenging Marty.

The police had allowed her to take her handbag from the motel room, but she couldn't go back and collect the rest of her belongings. She drove around until she found a store that was still open and bought herself a change of clothes. She left a message with the hospital for Sebastian, telling him not to worry, that she would call him with an update as soon as she could and suggesting that he might want to call Annaliese in case she saw a news report and was frightened. And then she filled up the car, bought a better map and drank three very strong cups of coffee.

Six hours, maybe seven in the first go. I can do that before I need a proper break. And they're surely going to tire faster than I do.

She spread the map out on the passenger seat and compared it to the sketch. Vicksburg, Mississippi was the first stop listed, then Greenwood in Louisiana. Four hours to reach the first, three give or take to reach the second; seven hours of driving overall. That was doable, and that was two steps which would give her a very good start.

She folded the map over so that it showed her destination, turned the radio up loud and – with a whispered, 'I'm coming after you,' that was as much for Marty as it was for herself – Evie started to drive.

CHAPTER 28

TEXAS, FEBRUARY 1980

'Law enforcement agencies are urging the public not to approach the couple, who may be dangerous. Anyone spotting them should immediately report the sighting on the helpline number below or contact their nearest precinct.'

Evie nodded to the waitress waiting to refill her coffee cup as the news bulletin played out on the small television above the counter. Nobody other than her was paying attention to it, except a man who looked up at *dangerous* and laughed. Evie couldn't blame him. The photograph the police had used was a black-tie image presumably taken at a charity ball. It made her father look like a candidate for President and her mother a shoo-in for First Lady. The *at least something is finally out there* she tried to console herself with felt very hollow.

Evie had been keeping an eye out everywhere she stopped for a news bulletin or a newspaper report which featured her parents. This first one had taken almost forty-eight hours from the bombing to appear, and it was deeply disappointing. It offered no information about the couple beyond their names and home state. Instead of the raft of possible charges which Evie had laid out at the club, all it said was that the two were wanted in connection with a suspicious death. It was hardly the stuff to stir up a manhunt.

Evie drained her coffee and decided against a third cup, although her body and her eyelids were as heavy as lead. Sticking to meandering back roads for much of the drive rather than well-lit and speedy highways – and dealing with hotel managers who were overly concerned for their other guests' privacy – had been more exhausting than she had anticipated. And even when she'd given in and made a proper stop, as she'd done the previous night, sleep hadn't come easily.

After the second nightmare woke her – a particularly vivid one which had turned her mother into a macabre Pied Piper – she'd given up trying. Which was why she was in a diner with a cleared plate before the staff were barely awake themselves. But, as tired as she was, she hadn't given up the pursuit. That was going far better than she'd expected.

Which means I can finally tell Sebastian where I am.

Evie had been regularly checking in with the hospital for updates on his condition, but she hadn't spoken to Sebastian directly: she'd wanted her first call to be positive news that couldn't lead to an argument. Now she was in a position to make that, she settled her bill, adding the coins from her change to the store she'd been steadily accumulating over the last two days, and made her way to the diner's public telephone.

The restaurant was an old-fashioned one – the phone booth at the back had a little door on it for privacy and a padded seat. Evie settled herself inside it and rang the hospital, crossing her fingers that she would get a nurse at the start of her shift and not an exhausted one at the end of it. And that Sebastian was well enough to walk to the phone.

Her luck held on both counts. His voice appeared on the line as she was feeding in another handful of coins.

'Evie, oh thank God. I've been imagining all sorts. This really wasn't the time to choose radio silence.'

Evie was so delighted to hear him sounding healthy and lucid, it took her a moment to recognise that Sebastian was also angry. And to accept that he had good reason to be. For the first time since Monday, she put herself in his shoes. She'd been the target of a bomb attack and then she'd immediately gone running after her attackers. And she hadn't told him anything beyond the couple of 'Let him know I'm fine' messages she'd left with the nurses. Shame instantly flooded through her.

'I am so sorry. I didn't want you to worry and that's exactly what I've done. I had to go after them – you understand that, don't you? I couldn't wait around for the FBI. But I didn't need to disappear and be selfish to do that. And I should have called you before now, but I've been stopping at such odd hours, there wasn't time—' She stopped herself launching into any more excuses. 'No, that's not true. I didn't make time. I was too wrapped up in my own head.'

Her honesty was rewarded. His answering 'I'm just glad you're in one piece; I couldn't bear it if anything happened to you' was far softer.

'But where are you now? Have you managed to track them down?'

Evie took Sebastian quickly through what had happened at Beech Brook and described the route she'd been following.

'And they didn't trick me, which I thought they might – it's the right one. My parents were seen in Louisiana and again in Matagorda County. They're a charming couple by all accounts, enjoying some *late-in-life travelling*. And now – if I'm right, if they're still in Texas and if they're planning to cross the border at Hidalgo – then I'm not far behind them, I'm barely an hour away.'

It was a lot of *ifs*.

Evie being correct assumed that her parents had found the driving even more tiring than she had and had made longer stops. It assumed that they were currently in a hotel and intending on making a morning crossing when there was other traffic to shelter them, rather than a night-time trip which might draw attention. It assumed that they weren't already safely in Mexico or on a plane to South America. Evie was grateful Sebastian didn't point any of those weaknesses out. That he offered her, 'That's a good result so far then,' instead. Although she wished he'd left it there.

'But you need to stop dealing with this on your own now, Evie, and speak to the FBI. They'll listen. Two agents came to the hospital yesterday and they've accepted your version of events – they're on your side.'

He cut across her 'That's good, but it doesn't change anything' before she could push him away with excuses.

'It does. Listen to me. The FBI have started their own search and they're thinking Texas too, although they're focusing on Santa Fe rather than Hidalgo. Apparently, your parents were based there when they first came to the States, so there's agents trying to establish if they still have contacts there, and monitoring the border crossings. That's a long way from where you are, I know, but there will be other agents based closer who can get to you. Or local police if they can't. You have to reach out to them directly.'

There was too much in what he'd said for Evie to respond to. Santa Fe was new information, and this wasn't the time to start asking about it. And she didn't want FBI agents or the police coming any closer – or not yet. She wanted to be the first one on the scene, the first one demanding answers. And she wanted to know why the news bulletin had said so little. Evie responded by deflecting and asking Sebastian that.

'Because that's all they could say.'

She lost her temper then, but he didn't give her a chance to launch into a tirade.

'No, Evie, I get that it's frustrating, but it's not ridiculous. Nobody has come forward yet who saw Helen enter the clinic.

They can't make a link with the bomb public because there's no evidence yet for that either – there was no security camera in the car park and no equipment found at the house. As for the rest – they're trying to play that down as far as the public is concerned, and that's the right call. Outing the two of them as Nazis won't help – not because of Paperclip; nobody cares about that right now – but because there are so many layers to this which could...'

He paused, but Evie still heard *blow up*.

Sebastian swallowed hard before he restarted. 'This is delicate stuff for the community, Evie, just like Marty said it could be. The investigations at the clinic have found something, but the FBI can't let it go public, not yet. There were other remains found not far from the nurse's body, bones that are... small. There's soil analysis underway now – and some digging. And I told the agents to speak to Kersiah and the girls, but I don't know if they've done that yet. It seems like we were right, although I wish we weren't. It seems like Helen has a lot more than war crimes to hide.'

'And a lot more to lose if that's true.'

There was a silence in which Evie couldn't shake the thought of *remains* and *small* and knew that Sebastian was stuck there too. When he finally spoke, she could hear all the fear for her safety in his voice that she'd been running away from.

'Exactly. So don't do this on your own anymore – please.' He paused, but Evie had nothing to offer him. 'They're not going to come in quietly; they might not come in at all. Don't you get that? Your mother has no conscience, no sense of guilt. She won't accept being judged; I doubt she'll let that happen. Call the FBI now, or let me call them. Go to Hidalgo if you must, but wait there. Be a witness, not the one who charges in.'

He paused again; she stayed silent again. When he continued speaking, the anger was back.

'For God's sake, Evie, will you stop acting as if you're the only one with a stake in this? If you won't speak to the FBI, could you at least wait for me? I'm being released this morning. I could get on a plane to San Antonio; I could be with you by the afternoon. Can you take a moment? Can you do that? Can you let me help you clean this mess up?'

The phone pips started demanding more money as Evie said *no* and *I can't* and *I'll be fine*. This time she pretended not to have any more coins. She hoped he heard, 'I love you.' That he'd calm down and understand that this battle with her mother was still personal. That he would forgive her, whatever the outcome.

They might not come in at all.

There wasn't a scenario in which Evie had considered that possibility. Now Sebastian had said it, she felt like a fool.

We need a big fish.

That had been Marty's main aim for the OSI, but he'd always known that the chance of landing the prize the department needed had already run past them. The big fish had decided their own fates long ago, even the ones like Göring and Himmler, who'd briefly been trapped by the Allies. Poison. Bullets. Escape. Whichever route they'd chosen in order to avoid the disgust and the punishment they deserved, none of them – with the exception of Eichmann and that hadn't been done willingly – had come in. So why would Helen and Alex stop and surrender simply because she wanted them to? Why would they give up even if the FBI arrived? Or if the border was blocked and impassable?

It is never I; it is always us. We are complete and unbreakable and everything.

Evie had heard her mother say that to her father once, on an evening when she had been what she always was to them: invisible. She'd watched Alex wrap Helen up in his arms, press his lips to her hair and smile the smile filled with delight that he kept only for his wife. That had never once been offered to his daughter. It had been an image of togetherness which needed nobody else, an image of a love which excluded the world.

And if they are arrested, that bond gets broken. They'll be separated. Wouldn't they do anything – to others or to themselves – to stop the possibility of that happening?

Evie fled from the phone booth and ran to her car. She'd acted like a character in a storybook – following a map, believing that right was on her side; thinking that her goodness and their evil entitled her to win. She hadn't considered what would come at the end of the chase, beyond a set piece. She'd pictured her parents in handcuffs, being marched away, and herself as the triumphant architect of their downfall. She hadn't prepared. She hadn't marshalled or tested her arguments. She hadn't written a winning closing speech.

And she hadn't considered what was obsessing her now: that however the last battle played out, there could be more bodies.

CHAPTER 29

TEXAS, FEBRUARY 1980

Hidalgo was as sleepy as the diner.

The shops dotted along what appeared to be the small town's main street were shuttered. The only people Evie could see were reluctant dog-walkers. The only landmark was the wide green sweep of the Rio Grande and the swathe of grey concrete snaking across it. There was a beauty to this border. It wasn't a solid barrier like the Wall in Berlin; it didn't distort the landscape. But, fluid or not, it was still an end-stop where men in uniform held the power. Its presence turned Hidalgo into a waiting room.

Evie parked the car at one of the viewpoints close to the foot of the bridge and got out. This close to the water, the air was cool and there was finally a breeze. She leaned against the bonnet and watched the traffic trickling over the river, trying to get a sense of its ebb and flow. There appeared to be more cars crossing out of Mexico than out of Texas. The three cars she watched arrive from the Mexican side were all stopped; one of them was searched. The one truck leaving Hidalgo was waved through with only the briefest check.

Poison. Bullets. Escape.

Evie had a sudden image of her parents sailing through the checkpoint. Too far ahead of the chase to be concerned by news bulletins or the police; smiling on their way to start another protected life. Escape might be the fate they had chosen, but it couldn't be as simple as that.

There was a hotel behind her, the only one she'd noticed as she drove through the town. It was a tired-looking place with battered stucco and sagging nets, but – if a guest picked the right bedroom – it was a good place from which to keep an eye on the bridge.

To keep an eye on me.

Adrenaline pumped through her. She left the car where it was and circled round the back of the hotel. And her luck – because that was all Evie had left to believe in – held. Her parents' brown Oldsmobile Cutlass was there in the parking lot. That they hadn't swapped it for something less traceable suggested they weren't concerned about being caught. Which also meant that there was every chance she might catch them off guard.

Except when is my mother ever caught off guard?

Evie stood very still and let the adrenaline go.

There was no room for error now, no room for thinking that it was enough to have right on her side. Marching into the hotel and assuming that the element of surprise gave her any kind of upper hand would be a very foolish mistake. She couldn't lose sight of who she was dealing with.

Her parents had walked away from Germany completely untouched by the lives they'd led, and the lives they'd ruined, there. They had prospered in America equally untouched by guilt and found new ways for their hatreds to flourish. They were survivors and planners, as clever as they were cruel. A few seconds of surprise would make no more impression on them than snowflakes would on a fire.

I can't just turn up and confront them like I did last time. I

*need an ally inside. I need to make someone feel important
enough to help me stop whatever they try to do.*

It hadn't been easy getting even the most basic information
about their guests from the other hotels Evie had visited, and
she didn't have time to waste now spinning a back story. She
went round to the hotel's main door, staying close to the building, and entered the gloomy reception hall, hoping that this
place might be a little more lax than the other guest houses
when it came to guarding their customers' privacy.

The boy leaning listlessly against the desk looked hopeful
enough in that regard, although – in terms of an ally – his
appearance and manner wouldn't have put him close to the top
of Evie's list. He'd either shaved badly or wasn't yet capable of
growing a proper beard, and he was far more interested in the
television set tucked into his lair than in greeting a potential
guest. But he was also – or so Evie hoped – perhaps still young
enough to jump when presented with an official-looking document. So Evie didn't greet him or introduce herself. She
dropped her Justice Department identity card onto the open
reservations book instead. To her relief, his eyes instantly
widened, and his narrow shoulders found a shape.

'Have you seen the news this morning?'

He was looking at her now rather than the badge and his
cheeks had started to turn pink. Words were clearly a stretch,
but he managed a nod.

Evie kept her tone brisk. 'Good. And did you see the
bulletin about the FBI chasing that older couple, the ones they
thought might be heading for Texas? Did they look familiar to
you at all?'

She could almost see the wheels grinding. His jaw fell open
with the speed of a cartoon.

'Excellent. I'll take that to mean that they're staying here. I
knew as soon as I saw you that you were the observant type.
And do you know where they are right now?'

He nodded again and this time answered her in a whisper that was almost as loud as Evie's normal speaking voice.

'They're in the dining room, eating breakfast. They're the only ones in there – most people come down later.'

Evie had to stop herself punching the air. Her parents weren't just planners; they were creatures of habit. Breakfast began at eight fifteen and was completed by nine, whatever the demands of the day.

Poison. Bullets. Escape. Whether it's a bunker and then a gun, or cyanide in a cell once the verdict is in, there's always a back-up plan. It's never just one or the other.

She dropped her voice and hoped the boy would copy her. 'I've got one last question, and I need you to think very carefully. Did you notice if the woman was carrying anything when they came down from their room?'

This time the boy closed his eyes and left a pause Evie thought would never end. Then he blinked and broke into a beam.

'No, she wasn't. He was carrying a newspaper, and she had one hand tucked in his arm, but she wasn't holding anything in the other.'

He was grinning as eagerly as a puppy waiting for a reward. It wasn't hard to grin back – when Evie told him she knew she'd picked the right man for the job, and his pink cheeks instantly turned scarlet, she meant it.

'You've been such a help, and I'm going to tell the police that. But now I have to ask you to really step up. I need you to do something for me that's going to sound like a crime, something I know a boy like you would never do unless it was to stop someone really bad from escaping their punishment. Is it okay? Can I do that?'

He'd agreed to the plan before she finished explaining it.

· · ·

The dining room was as weary as the rest of the hotel. Her parents were sat at a table in the centre, their linen and silk elegance turning the carpet and the curtains even shabbier. Evie watched as Alex poured coffee into her mother's cup and offered her the limp contents of the toast rack.

It doesn't matter where they are, or whether they're eating off silver or plastic. They create their own elegantly framed world.

And breaking that was how she was going to break them, but it had to be carefully done. Evie stayed where she was, a few steps inside the doorway; she didn't announce herself. Helen always waited a moment or two before she acknowledged that the *help* had come in. She would look up when she was ready and the point had been made.

When she eventually did so, Evie got her moment of surprise, or – more accurately – the seconds that she'd expected. Helen had recovered her poise before she put her cup down, but it was Alex who spoke.

'Not a waitress then. That's a shame – we could have done with warmer toast. Enlighten us, Evie, why don't you? Do you have a specific reason for being here? Have you brought law enforcements along too? If not – and I'm thinking not – if this is another of your grandstanding moments, why don't we all save time and not do it. Your mother and I have other places to be.'

He addressed her as if she was a stranger. He might as well have said, 'You are nothing to us.'

Which I'm not.

'Why did you have me?'

That wasn't the question Evie had intended to open with – or ask at all. She'd meant to avoid anything so personal: she knew from long experience that such an emotional plea took all her power away. But it was a question she'd been picking at for almost thirty years, and now – never mind pushing her out of their lives – her parents had tried to kill her. Emotional and needy or not, it was a question that had to be asked.

Alex frowned and looked at Helen; Helen sighed her sigh. The old familiar pattern. Her mother's tone made her father's sound warm.

'Oh, Evie, really? With everything you now claim to know about us, do I honestly have to spell that out?'

She waited but, when Evie made no attempt to answer, she sat back in her chair and folded her napkin. She barely bothered to make eye contact.

'Fine, have it your way then. We had you, daughter dear, because it was our duty to have a child for the Führer and to pass on our Aryan bloodline. Unfortunately, you were a girl not a boy and so you were of limited use. And then the Reich failed and you were no use at all. So there we are, the truth you're so fond of is out. But why does it matter to you? You're not the only child in the world who was born and not wanted. You really do need to stop whining.'

Evie couldn't pinpoint the exact word that did it. Perhaps it was *duty* or *bloodline* or *whining*. The exact word didn't matter. Whichever one it was, it snapped the last straining thread that linked her to her parents.

They didn't love me and thank God for that. What kind of person would I be if these miserable creatures had wanted me in their lives?

She was beyond their reach; it was a joy not to matter to them, not a burden or a curse. She drew up a chair at the table without being asked, and she ignored Helen's protest.

'And *you* really need to understand that the tide has turned. You don't hold the cards anymore; your protection is gone. The CIA will deny they know you; the FBI and the local police are on their way. Between your war records, the murders and abuses at the clinic and the bombing, there are enough charges to bury you both. And the day that happens will be a very good day.'

Neither of them responded. Instead, Helen leaned over and

whispered in Alex's ear. When he got up and left the room, Evie knew she'd guessed right. She looked across at her mother and managed not to let her knowledge show. If Helen guessed that Evie was a step ahead of her, she would surely change the rules.

'Whose idea was the bomb?'

She shook her head as Helen laughed and asked if she was wearing a wire.

'No, I'm not. I'd simply like to know which of my parents was the first one who decided to kill me.'

Helen picked up the coffee pot but, instead of refilling her own cup, she plucked a spare one from the next table and poured coffee for Evie. It was such a normal thing for a mother to do for a daughter, but they weren't a normal mother and daughter, and here all the gesture did was give away Helen's plans.

'Why would you think in terms of *one* or *first*? You were a problem to both of us, so both of us decided how to deal with you.'

Both of them had planned her death. They truly were united in everything. It wasn't pleasant to hear, but it was no longer a surprise.

'Presumably because I am the evidence?'

The look Helen gave Evie then could have been described as one of admiration, if Evie had known what that emotion looked like from her mother. Whatever the intention, she didn't react to it; she let Helen have the floor.

'Well done. Yes. Without you, what other evidence is there? You can list all the crimes you think we're guilty of for as long as you like, but the FBI won't find anything concrete to link us to them.' Helen pushed the milk jug across the table; Evie ignored it. 'Any testimony from your boyfriend – or from those girls who aren't as clever at hiding who they meet with as they think – wouldn't have stood up without you to add yours. He'd have been dismissed as harbouring a grudge, and who would really believe it was me who took him from Annaliese? The girls would have crawled back into the woodwork.' She took a sip of her own coffee and shrugged. 'I grant you the gossip and the attention wouldn't have been an enjoyable experience, but we would have ridden it out. We've ridden out far worse after all.'

Alex was back, carrying Helen's navy-blue Hermès handbag. Evie watched him hand it over, waited while Helen opened it and went in search, or so she said, of a cigarette. Waited until her mother's search became frantic.

'It isn't there. The pillbox or the capsules, or whatever you keep the poison in. They're the evidence now.' Evie nodded at her coffee cup. 'You won't be able to kill me, if that's what you were planning to try and do again. You won't be able to run for the border: the bridge has been locked down. And when the police arrive, which will be in the next moment or two – because my little friend at the desk, the one who went through your handbag upstairs, is desperate to do every step of this right for me – you won't have another way out. You won't be able to kill yourselves.'

She stopped for a moment and let what she'd done sink in.

'You thought you'd get to decide your own fate, didn't you? Well you don't. You're not Himmler, escaping your captors with a pill. There won't be some Magda and Joseph Goebbels'-style suicide pact. It's over. You're going to be dragged through the courts and jailed, or deported, or both. You're not going to escape this time; you're going to face your punishment.'

Evie paused and made sure they were looking at her, not at each other. Their faces were satisfyingly horror-struck.

'There are no prisons open to couples. If you are jailed instead of deported, you won't be sent to the same state – I'll make certain of that. You are going to be separated. After this day, you are going to be apart for the rest of your lives.'

That was her moment. That was when she should have

turned her back on them and walked out. The police had arrived; Evie could hear the sirens. The police could take over. She could walk away and ring Sebastian, and say, 'I did it – I won. Everybody is going to get justice.'

But Evie didn't do that. Evie stayed at the table instead.

Evie was listening to her mother's howl of pain and enjoying it. Evie was watching her father clutch at Helen's hands as the hope drained from his face. She was enjoying that too. For the first time in her life, Evie had stepped away from the woman she was and had become someone who could take pleasure in another person's distress. Which left her deaf and blind to the world and to consequences.

And looking the wrong way.

CHAPTER 30

WASHINGTON, JUNE 1980

'Are you all right? Do you need to sit down? Are you in pain?'

Evie shook her head as Sebastian asked the questions he'd been asking her at least once a day since Helen's attack. He tried hard not to do it, but he still had moments when he treated her like porcelain. Or when he looked at her and turned pale. Evie still had moments like that herself, when she remembered how close she'd come a second time to death.

Evie had rightly guessed that Helen's handbag would contain a pillbox not a gun, but she hadn't thought to get the boy to check for a knife inside the lining.

She would never know what had alerted her – whether it was a sixth sense or a policeman's shout, everything had happened too fast to be sure of the details. Whatever it was, it had made her turn and raise her arm, and it had kept her alive. The blade had sliced not from ear to ear as Helen had intended, but from ear to shoulder. Evie had lived, but Sebastian hadn't quite recovered from the sight of her bandaged and unconscious in a hospital bed. And Evie couldn't keep her fingers away from the scar. It was as if every hurt her mother had inflicted on her since childhood was suddenly visible.

And all of them are finally outside my body.

Which was why she was able to smile and say, 'No, I'm not in pain anymore,' every time Sebastian asked.

She'd escaped her mother's assault, but so many others hadn't, and there was a storm brewing. The FBI had done their best to contain the extent of Helen's crimes, but they couldn't keep the story quiet forever. Newspapers were sniffing. There were a lot of people in Fountain Heights who needed money and weren't afraid to shout about their suffering anymore. There were plenty in Mountain Brook ready to profit from the *horror* and the *deception* they'd now decided was the narrative of their friendship with the Ritters. Eventually the journalists would track down Evie and Sebastian and break their lives open too.

The back of the clinic had been swathed in white for weeks while the forensic teams sifted through the soil and dug up the tiny bone fragments that had been buried there. A cleaner had reported seeing Helen sitting in her car on the night the nurse was murdered. The wiped-down bench in the garage had yielded traces of residue. There was evidence and fury and a storm ready to break. But it hadn't broken yet, and neither Sebastian nor Evie would talk willingly to the papers, or anyone else, and keep Helen's story alive when it did.

Unless Kersiah and the other girls need us to speak out. Or riots and violence erupt. I'll do anything that's needed to stop that. Inflicting more damage cannot be her legacy.

That was Evie's biggest fear: that all the wounds Helen had inflicted hadn't been safely staunched. That wasn't a certainty, despite all the evidence and the ongoing investigation. The clinic was closed. The deputy director was under arrest. The search for Helen's pupils had begun in hospitals all over the country. The forces of the law were well and truly mobilised, but nobody knew if that would be enough.

Every baby's body that was found was another spark that

could light a terrible fire. And Helen had stoked that threat. She'd pleaded guilty, to the murder of the nurse and the babies and even to the bombing, in a misguided attempt to save Alex from deportation. She'd also agreed to answer questions about her activities in the war. That had made her sentencing simpler, but, by her willingness to talk, she'd robbed the community of the emotional release, and the potentially healing experience, a trial might have offered them. And she'd wrong-footed everybody charged with prosecuting her.

Nobody had expected a guilty plea. The defence attorney who recorded Helen's statement hadn't understood why she'd capitulated so easily. Her willingness to talk had taken everybody by surprise, but not Evie. Evie knew that guilty was the wrong word: Helen hadn't admitted her guilt; she'd laid out her achievements. And Evie knew why. Alex was lost to her.

Her father was in a low-security federal prison awaiting a deportation order which West Germany had agreed to with surprising speed. The crimes against humanity at Mittelbau-Dora had apparently moved up their lists, and Ulrich Reitter was a valuable addition to their investigation. His fate was sealed. There would be no last meeting for husband and wife; letters between them were forbidden. The two were as completely divided as Evie had promised they would be and, without the husband whose life was inseparable from hers, Helen had nothing. The centre of her life was gone. Announcing who she was to the world and revealing the power she'd wielded over innocent lives for almost forty years was the one victory she had left.

Or it would have been.

The judge had allowed Evie to attend Helen's arraignment. Evie had sat at the back and witnessed Helen's shock when she saw that the courtroom was closed to press and public and empty. And her fury, when she got to her feet to praise the cruel world which she'd dedicated her life to constructing, and her security detail immediately dragged her back down again.

The empty court reduced Helen to a nobody. It left her without a voice and an audience. She'd barely noticed when the judge sentenced her to life imprisonment in a high-secure facility with no hope of release. The Angel of Death had fallen to earth and become as vulnerable and helpless as the women and children she'd preyed on. Justice had been perfectly served.

And her story isn't hers anymore. It belongs to the people who hate her, who will tell it honestly. If she's remembered by history at all, it will be as one of its nightmares. And as one of the fish who got caught.

That was the real victory Evie wanted. That might balance the scales and keep Birmingham quiet. That was a fitting legacy for Marty.

Evie caught Sebastian looking at her again with his brow creased and pulled her hand back from her scar. At some point, she would have to explain that it was relief not pain that sent her fingers there. That the mark was proof that the worst days were over. That her mother had been excised, and Evie's wounds at least had closed up. But not now. This wasn't the time to be talking about Helen when he was scanning the arrivals board and hopping like a child from foot to foot.

'She's landed, look. She'll be through the gates any minute.'

Annaliese was visiting her son in Washington for the first time since their reunion in Florida. The past months hadn't been easy for her. Both her marriage and her relationship with her other children were faltering – Tony was struggling to make his wife's involvement with an SS officer fit with the woman he thought he'd married, and her son and daughter were in shock and refusing to talk. The fallout from that had impacted Annaliese's health, but her delight in rediscovering her son hadn't wavered. She told Sebastian that constantly when they spoke, much to his delight.

'I know that the timing of this isn't ideal, but are you ready to meet her?'

Evie looked up at the man she loved more than she'd ever loved anyone. Who she knew loved her back with the same intensity. Who cared enough to worry that introducing his mother – because that was what Annaliese now really was to him – into their lives when Evie had let go so completely of hers could be a challenge. Not that he needed to worry: Evie was completely in step with the life he wanted for them. When she smiled and told him that, Sebastian grinned.

'She's going to fall for you, exactly the same way that I did.'

Evie was suddenly in his arms, her feet half off the ground, much to the amusement of the people waiting with them in the arrivals hall. She'd never seen him look so boyish and carefree; it was beautiful.

'This is just the start, Evie. We're going to build our own family – you, me, my mother and maybe a child of our own, if we could, if that felt like the right thing one day. But this is us for good now – you know that, don't you? And you do want it, don't you, as much as I do? You really mean that?'

Evie reached up and pulled his face down to hers. She kissed him long enough to draw whistles.

Because a kiss was the only answer he needed.

Because she did.

A LETTER FROM CATHERINE

Dear reader,

I want to say a huge thank you for choosing to read *The German Child*. If you did enjoy it, and want to keep up to date with all my latest releases, just sign up at the following link. Your email address will never be shared, and you can unsubscribe at any time.

www.bookouture.com/catherine-hokin

This is a book that I've been wanting to write for a long time, ever since I first uncovered a mention of the Brown Sisters while I was researching my novel *The Girl in the Photo*. The history behind it, the sheer numbers involved and the fact that the population engineering policies adopted by the ministers of the Third Reich resulted in a Europe-wide and ongoing well of suffering, continues to take my breath away.

As I have described in the novel, the Lebensborn initiative was a far more dangerous entity than the 'stud farm' it was depicted as in pulp fiction and B-movies after the war, although that image still lingers. The countries occupied by Germany during the war were systematically mined for every drop of what the Nazis considered to be 'lost' Aryan blood. It is estimated that almost 200,000 children were kidnapped in Poland alone, and either sent to Germany for Aryanisation if they met the sixty-two physical characteristics they were required to meet, or were murdered if they didn't. Of that number, less than 20 per cent were reunited with their original families after the war, and thousands more, and their descendants, still have no idea that they were ever anything other than German.

From its start, Lebensborn was a programme shrouded in secrecy, and the suffering it caused far outlasted the war. So many of the accounts I've read talk about the shame when the truth is discovered, or the bullying and ostracism that went with being identified as a Lebensborn child. The stories from Norway are particularly heartbreaking.

What is also heartbreaking is that, as I've been writing this book, stories have started to emerge from Ukraine about large scale child-kidnappings by Russia. The current estimate stands at 19,000, and videos have emerged from the camps where some of them are being held showing Ukrainian children being taught the Russian national anthem and 'relearning' their history. I feel that I shouldn't be asking for a review this time (although they do help my books find readers) but instead asking for donations to UNICEF, who are desperately trying to protect more children from what President Zelensky has rightly described as genocide.

I would love to hear from you, about this book or the issues behind it, and there are lots of ways you can get in touch through social media or my website. Thank you again for taking the time to read *The German Child*.

Best wishes,

Catherine

KEEP IN TOUCH WITH CATHERINE

www.catherinehokin.com

 facebook.com/Cathokin

 instagram.com/cathokinauthor

x.com/catherineh66267

ACKNOWLEDGEMENTS

As always, so many books went into the writing of this one, but there are some specific sources I would like to acknowledge, and recommend if you want to know more about the subjects that I've covered in *The German Child*.

For Nazis in America and the attempts to bring them to justice: *The Nazis Next Door* by Eric Lichtblau and *Quiet Neighbours* by Allan Ryan, plus specific CIA and OSI reports which have been made public. What the investigators didn't know in the early 1990s and has now finally been admitted by the CIA is astonishing. For Lebensborn and Aryanisation programmes, *Hitler's Forgotten Children* by Ingrid von Oelhafen and Tim Tate, *Master Race* by Catrine Clay and Michael Leapman, *Did the Children Cry* by Richard C. Lukas, *Of Pure Blood* by Marc Hillel and Clarissa Henry, and a number of personal accounts, in particular: *Nowhere's Child* by Kari Rosvall and *Das endlose Jahr* by Gisela Heidenreich. And for the scientists, *Operation Paperclip* by Annie Jacobsen.

If anyone is interested in finding out more about the Birmingham bombings, could I recommend the superb Spike Lee film, *4 Little Girls*.

And now to the thanks which may sound familiar to anyone who's made it this far! To my editors Harriet Wade and Jayne Osborne for doing such an excellent job. To the Bookouture team, especially Sarah the marketing magician and Sally my eagle-eyed copy-editor. To all my non-writer friends who help me keep a sense of perspective in this crazy job. And to Daniel and Claire and Robert, none of whom can remember which book we're now on but who do as they're bid and keep cheering. Much love to you all.

PUBLISHING TEAM

Turning a manuscript into a book requires the efforts of many people. The publishing team at Bookouture would like to acknowledge everyone who contributed to this publication.

Audio
Alba Proko
Sinead O'Connor
Melissa Tran

Commercial
Lauren Morrissette
Jil Thielen
Imogen Allport

Data and analysis
Mark Alder
Mohamed Bussuri

Cover design
Nikki Dupin

Editorial
Jayne Osborne
Imogen Allport

Printed in Great Britain
by Amazon

40759867R00189